CHAOS WALKING
BOOK THREE

MONSTERS OF MEN

PATRICK NESS

CANDLEWICK PRESS

For Denise Johnstone-Burt

Copyright © 2010 by Patrick Ness

"Idioteque" by Thomas Edward Yorke, Philip James Selway, Edward John O'Brien, Colin Charles Greenwood, Jonathan Richard Guy Greenwood, and Paul Lanksy © Warner/Chappell Music Ltd (PRS) and Warner/Chappell Music Publishing Ltd (PRS). All rights reserved.

First U.S. paperback edition 2011

The Library of Congress has cataloged the hardcover edition as follows:

Ness, Patrick, date
Monsters of Men / Patrick Ness. — 1st U.S. ed.
p.   cm. — (Chaos walking ; bk. 3)
Summary: As a world-ending war surges to life around them, Todd and Viola face monstrous decisions, questioning all they have ever known as they try to step back from the darkness and find the best way to achieve peace.
ISBN 978-0-7636-4751-3 (hardcover)
[1. Science fiction. 2. War — Fiction. 3. Space colonies — Fiction.
4. Social problems — Fiction. 5. Telepathy — Fiction.]   I. Title. II. Series.
PZ7.N43843Mon 2010
[Fic] — dc22   2009049727

ISBN 978-0-7636-5665-2 (paperback)

13 14 15 16 17 18 BVG 10 9 8 7 6 5 4 3

Printed in Berryville, VA, U.S.A.

This book was typeset in Fairfield and Tiepolo.

Candlewick Press
99 Dover Street
Somerville, Massachusetts 02144

visit us at www.candlewick.com

Who's in the bunker?
Who's in the bunker?

Women and children first
And the children first
And the children

I laugh until my head comes off

I swallow 'til I burst

–Radiohead, "Idioteque"

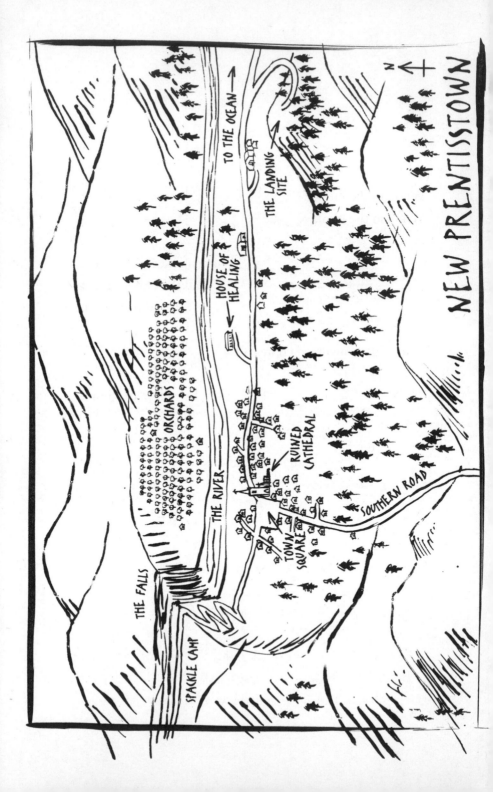

"WAR," SAYS MAYOR PRENTISS, his eyes glinting. "At last."

"Shut up," I say. "There ain't no *at last* about it. The only one who wants this is *you*."

"Nevertheless," he says, turning to me with a smile. "Here it comes."

And of course I'm already wondering if untying him so he could fight this battle was the worst mistake of my life–

But no–

No, it's gonna keep her safe. It's what I had to do to keep her safe.

And I will make him keep her safe if I have to kill him to do it.

And so with the sun setting, me and the Mayor stand on the rubble of the cathedral and look out across the town square, as the army of Spackle make their way down the zigzag hill in front of us, blowing their battlehorn with a sound that could tear you right in two–

As Mistress Coyle's army of the Answer marches into town behind us, bombing everything in its path *Boom! Boom! BOOM!–*

As the first soldiers of the Mayor's own army start arriving in quick formayshun from the south, Mr. Hammar at their front, crossing the square toward us to get new orders–

As the people of New Prentisstown run for their lives in any and every direkshun–

As the scout ship from the incoming settlers lands on a hill somewhere near Mistress Coyle, the worst possible place for 'em–

As Davy Prentiss lies dead in the rubble below us, shot by his own father, shot by the man I just set free–

And as Viola–

My Viola–

Races out on horseback into the middle of it all, her ankles broken, not even able to stand up on her own–

Yes, I think.

Here it comes.

The end of everything.

The end of it all.

"Oh, yes, Todd," says the Mayor, rubbing his hands together. "Oh, yes, indeed."

And he says the word again, says it like it's his every last wish come true.

"War."

IT BEGINS

TWO BATTLES

[TODD]

"WE HIT THE SPACKLE HEAD ON!" the Mayor shouts at the men, aiming his Noise right in the middle of everyone's heads.

Even mine.

"They'll be gathering at the bottom of the road," he says, *"but that's as far as they're going to go!"*

I put a hand on Angharrad's flank beneath me. In under two minutes, the Mayor had us up on horseback, Morpeth and Angharrad coming running from round the back of the ruins of the cathedral, and by the time we'd hopped up, stepping over the still unconshus bodies of the men who tried to help me overthrow the Mayor, there was the army taking messy shape in front of us.

Not all of it, tho, maybe less than half, the rest still stretched up along the southern road to the hill with the notch on it, the road to where the battle was *sposed* to be.

Boy colt? Angharrad's thinking and I can feel spikes

of nerves all thru her body. She's scared nearly half to death.

So am I.

"BATTALIONS READY!" the Mayor shouts and immediately Mr. Hammar and the later-arriving Mr. Tate and Mr. O'Hare and Mr. Morgan snap salutes and the soldiers start lining up in the right formayshuns, twisting thru each other in coils and getting into order so quickly it almost hurts my eyes to watch it.

"I know," the Mayor says. "It's a thing of beauty, isn't it?"

I point my rifle at him, the rifle I took from Davy. "You just remember our agreement," I say. "Yer gonna keep Viola safe and you ain't gonna control me with yer Noise. You do that and you stay alive. That's the *only* reason I let you go."

His eyes flash. "You realize that means you can't let me out of your sight," he says, "even if you have to follow me into battle. Are you ready for that, Todd?"

"I'm ready," I say, even tho I ain't but I'm trying not to think about it.

"I have a feeling you'll do well," he says.

"Shut up," I say. "I beat you once, I'll beat you again."

He grins. "Of that I have no doubt."

"THE MEN ARE READY, SIR!" Mr. Hammar shouts from his horse, saluting fiercely.

The Mayor keeps his eyes on me. "The men are ready, Todd," he says, his voice teasing. "Are you?"

"Just get on with it."

And his smile gets even wider. He turns to the men. *"Two divisions down the western road for the first attack!"* His voice snakes thru everyone's head again, like a sound you can't ignore. *"Captain Hammar's division at the front, Captain Morgan taking the rear! Captains Tate and O'Hare will round up the rest of the men and armaments yet to arrive and join the fray with the greatest dispatch."*

Armaments? I think.

"If the fight isn't already over by the time they join us—"

The men laugh at this, a loud, nervous, aggressive kind of laugh.

"Then as a united army, we will drive the Spackle back up that hill and make them regret the day they were EVER BORN!"

And the men give a roaring cheer.

"Sir!" Captain Hammar shouts. "What about the army of the Answer, sir?"

"First we beat the Spackle," says the Mayor, "then the Answer will be child's play."

He looks across his army of men and back up the hill to the Spackle army, still marching down. Then he raises his fist and gives the loudest Noise shout of all, a shout that bores right down into the very center of every man hearing it.

"TO BATTLE!"

"TO BATTLE!" the army cries back at him and sets off at a fierce pace outta the square, racing toward the zigzag hill—

The Mayor looks at me one last time, like he can barely keep from laughing at how much fun he's having. And without another word, he spurs Morpeth hard in the sides and they gallop into the square after the departing army.

The army heading off to war.

Follow? Angharrad asks, fear coming off her like sweat.

"He's right," I say. "We can't let him out of our sight. He's got to keep his word. He's got to win his war. He's got to save her."

For her, Angharrad thinks.

For her, I think back, all my feeling about her behind it.

And I think her name—

Viola.

And Angharrad leaps forward into battle.

{VIOLA}

Todd, I think, riding Acorn through the mash of people crowding across the road, each of them trying to run away from those awful horn blasts in one direction and the bombs of Mistress Coyle in the other.

BOOM! goes another one and I see a ball of flame coughed up into the sky. The screaming around us is almost unbearable. People running up the road get tangled with people running *down* the road and everyone gets in our way.

Gets in the way of us getting to the scout ship first.

The horn blasts again and there's even more screaming. "We have to go, Acorn," I say between his ears. "Whatever that sound is, the people on my ship can–"

A hand grabs my arm and nearly yanks me off the saddle.

"Give me the horse!" a man screams at me, pulling harder. *"Give it to me!"*

Acorn twists around to try to get away but there are too many people in the road crowding us–

"Let go!" I shout at the man.

"Give it to me!" he screams. *"The Spackle are coming!"*

This surprises me so much he nearly gets me off the saddle. *"The what?"*

But he's not listening and even in the dying light I can see the whites of his eyes blazing in terror–

HOLD! shouts Acorn's Noise and I grip even harder on his mane and he rears up, knocking the man away and leaping forward into the night. People scream to get out of our way and we knock more of them over as Acorn plows up the road, me holding on for dear life.

We reach a clearing and he charges on even faster.

"The *Spackle?*" I say. "What did he mean? Surely they couldn't be–"

Spackle, Acorn thinks. **Spackle army. Spackle war.**

I turn to look back as he runs, back to look at the lights coming down the distant zigzag hill.

A Spackle army.

A Spackle army is coming, too.

Todd? I think, knowing that I'm getting farther away from him and the tied-up Mayor with every hoofbeat.

The best hope is the ship. They'll be able to help us. *Somehow,* they'll be able to help me and Todd.

We stopped one war, we can stop another.

And so I think his name again, *Todd,* sending him strength. And Acorn and I race up the road toward the Answer, toward the scout ship, and I'm hoping against hope that I'm right–

[Todd]

Angharrad runs after Morpeth as the army surges down the road in front of us, brutally knocking down any citizens of New Prentisstown who happen to be in their way. There are two battalions, the first led by a screaming Mr. Hammar on horseback and a less shouty Mr. Morgan leading the second behind him. It's maybe four hundred men in all, rifles up, their faces twisted in screams and yells.

And their Noise–

Their Noise is a monstrous thing, tuned together and twisted round itself, roaring as a single voice, like a loud and angry giant pounding its way down the road.

It's making my heart beat right outta my chest.

"Stay close to me, Todd!" the Mayor shouts from Morpeth, pulling up to my side as we ride on, fast.

"You ain't gotta worry bout that," I say, gripping my rifle.

"I mean, to save your life," he says, looking over. "And don't forget your end of the bargain either. I'd hate for there to be any casualties from friendly fire."

And he winks at me.

Viola, I think right at him, sending it to him in a fist of Noise.

He flinches.

And he ain't smiling so much now.

We ride after the army thru the west end of town, down the main road, past what can only be the wreckage of the original jails the Answer burned down in their biggest attack before today. I only ever been down here once, when I ran thru it the other way with Viola in my arms, carrying her down the zigzag road when she was dying, carrying her into what I thought was safety, but all I found was the man riding by my side, the man who killed a thousand Spackle to start this war, the man who tortured Viola for informayshun he already knew, the man who murdered his own son—

"And what other kind of man would you want leading you into battle?" he says, reading my Noise. "What other kind of man is suitable for war?"

A *monster*, I think, remembering what Ben told me once. *War makes monsters of men.*

"Wrong," says the Mayor. "It's war that makes us men in the first place. Until there's war, we are only children."

Another blast of the horn comes roaring down at us, so loud it nearly takes our heads off and it puts the army off its stride for a second or two.

We look up the road to the bottom of the hill. We see Spackle torches gathering there to meet us.

"Ready to grow up, Todd?" the Mayor asks.

{ V I O L A }

BOOM!

Another explosion just up ahead of us now, sending smoking debris flying high above the trees. I'm so scared I forget the state of my ankles and I try to spur on Acorn like I've seen in vids on my ship. I curl forward from the pain. The bandages that Lee—still out there somewhere, trying to find the Answer in the wrong place, oh please be safe, *please* be safe—the bandages he wound around my feet are good but

11

the bones are still broken and for a minute the agony flashes all the way up my body, right to the throbbing burn in the band around my forearm again. I pull back my sleeve to look. The skin around the band is red and hot, the band itself still just thin steel, immovable, uncuttable, marking me as number 1391 until the day I die.

That's the price I paid.

The price I paid to find him.

"And now we've got to make it worth it," I say to Acorn, whose Noise says, **Girl colt** back to agree with me.

The air is filling with smoke and I can see fires burning up ahead. People are still running past us in all directions, though fewer and fewer as the town starts to thin out.

If Mistress Coyle and the Answer started at the Office of the Ask, marching toward the center of town from the east, then they'd already be past the hill where the communications tower used to be. Which is the most likely place where the scout ship landed. Mistress Coyle would have turned around and taken a fast cart to get there, to be the first one to talk to them, but who would she have left in charge?

Acorn presses ahead, around the road as it curves–

And *BOOM!*

There's a flash of light as another dormitory goes up in flames, reflecting the road for a shining second–

And I see them–

The Answer.

Lines of men and women, blue *A*'s written across their fronts and sometimes even painted on their faces.

And every one with guns pointed out–

In front of carts loaded with weaponry–

And though I recognize some of them (Mistress Lawson, Magnus, Mistress Nadari), it's like I don't know them at all, they look so fierce, so focused, so scared and brave and committed and for a second I pull back on Acorn's reins, too afraid to ride toward them.

The flash of the explosion dies and they're plunged into darkness again.

Forward? Acorn asks.

I take in a breath, wondering how they'll react to seeing me, wondering if they'll see me at all and not just blow me right out of the saddle in the confusion.

"We've got no choice," I finally say.

And just as he readies himself to move again–

"Viola?" I hear from out of the darkness.

[TODD]

The road outta town reaches a wide clearing bounded by the river on the right, with the massive crashing of the falls and the zigzag road down the hill direcktly in front of us. The army roars into the clearing, Captain Hammar in the lead, and even tho I've only been here once, I know there were trees here before, trees and small houses, and so the Mayor musta had his men clearing it all this time, making it ready to be a battlefield–

As if he knew this was coming–

But I can't stop to think about that cuz Mr. Hammar is shouting "HALT!" and the men are stopping in formayshun and looking across the clearing–

Cuz there they are—

The first troops of the Spackle army—

Fanning out into the open ground, a dozen, two dozen, ten dozen of 'em, surging down the hill like a river of white blood, torches held high, bows and arrows and some weird long white stick things in their hands and there are Spackle foot soldiers swarming round other Spackle riding these huge white creachers, built wide like a bullock but taller and broader and with a massive single horn shooting out from the end of their noses and the creachers are covered in heavy armor that looks like it's made from clay and I see that a lotta the Spackle soldiers are wearing it too, the clay covering their white skin—

And there's another horn blast so loud I swear my ears are starting to bleed and you can see the horn with yer own eyes now, strapped to the backs of two of the horned creachers up on the hilltop and being blown by that huge Spackle—

And oh, God—

Oh, my, God—

Their *Noise*—

It comes tumbling down the hill like a weapon on its own, cresting across the open ground like foam on a raging river, and it's coming right for us, pictures of their army cutting us down, pictures of our soldiers being ripped to pieces, pictures of ugliness and horror that you could never describe, pictures—

Pictures that our own soldiers are sending right back to 'em, pictures rising from the mass of men in front of me, pictures of heads torn from bodies, of bullets ripping Spackle apart, of slaughter, of endless endless–

"Keep your focus, Todd," the Mayor says, "or the battle will take your life. And I, for one, am more than curious as to what sort of man you're going to turn out to be."

"FORM A LINE!" we hear Mr. Hammar shouting and the soldiers immediately behind him start spreading out. "FIRST WAVE READY!" he shouts and the men stop and raise their rifles, poised to rush forward at his command as the second wave lines up behind 'em.

The Spackle have stopped too, forming an equally long line at the bottom of the hill. A horned creacher parts their line in the middle, a Spackle standing on its back behind a U-shaped white thing that looks like it's made of bone, half-again as wide as a man and mounted on a stand on the creacher's armor.

"What *is* that?" I ask the Mayor.

He grins as if to himself. "I think we're about to find out."

"MEN READY!" Mr. Hammar shouts.

"Stay back with me, Todd," the Mayor says. "Keep out of the fighting as much as you can."

"Yeah, I know," I say, heavy feeling in my Noise. "You don't like to get your hands dirty."

He catches my eye. "Oh, there are going to be plenty of dirty days ahead. Don't you worry."

And then "CHARGE!!!" Mr. Hammar screams at the top of his lungs–

And the war is on.

"Wilf!" I yell, riding over to him. He's driving an oxcart, out in front and off to the side of the first line of the Answer, still marching down the road in the smoky gloom.

"Yer *alive!*" Wilf says, hopping down off the cart and scooting over to me. "Mistress Coyle tol' us yoo were dead."

Anger fills my stomach again over what Mistress Coyle tried to do, at the bomb she intended for the Mayor and how she didn't seem to mind that it would take me with it. "She's wrong about a lot of things, Wilf."

He looks up at me and in the light of the moons, I can see the fright in his Noise, fright in the most unflappable man I've ever met on this whole planet, a man who risked his life to save both me and Todd more than once, fright in the one man around here who's never afraid. "The Spackle are comin, Viola," he says. "Ya gotta get outta here."

"I'm riding to get help, Wilf–"

Another *BOOM* rips through a building across the road from us. There's a small blast wave and Wilf has to hold on to Acorn's reins to keep standing up. *"What the hell are they doing?"* I yell.

"Mistress's orders," Wilf says. "To save the body, ya sometimes have to cut off the leg."

I cough from the smoke. "That sounds *exactly* like the kind of stupid thing she'd say. Where is she?"

"Took off when that ship done flew over. Riding fast to where it landed."

My heart jumps. "Where did it land, Wilf? Where exactly?"

16

He motions back down the road. "Yonder hill, where tower used to be."

"I *knew* it."

There's another distant blast of the horn. Every time it goes off, there's yet more screaming from the townsfolk running everywhere. I even hear some screaming from the army of the Answer.

"Ya gotta run, Viola," Wilf says again, touching my arm. "Spackle army is bad news. Ya gotta go. Ya gotta go *now*."

I fight down a flash of worry about Todd. "You've got to go, too, Wilf. Mistress Coyle's trick didn't work. The Mayor's army is already back in town." Wilf sucks in air over his teeth. "We've got the Mayor," I continue, "and Todd's trying to stop the army, but if you attack head on, you'll be slaughtered."

He looks back at the Answer, still marching down the road, faces still set, though some of them are seeing me and Wilf, seeing me alive on horseback, and surprise is starting to dawn. I hear my name more than once.

"Mistress Coyle said to keep marching," Wilf says, "keep bombing, no matter what we heard."

"Who'd she leave in charge? Mistress Lawson?" There's a silence and I look back down at Wilf. "It's you, isn't it?"

He nods slowly. "She said Ah was the best at follering orders."

"Yet another mistake she made," I say. "Wilf, you *have* to turn them round."

Wilf looks back at the Answer, still coming, still marching. "Other mistresses won't lissen to me," he says, but I can hear him thinking.

"Yes," I say, agreeing with his thought, "but everyone *else* will."

He looks back up to me. "Ah'll turn 'em round."

"I have to get to the ship," I say. "There'll be help there."

Wilf nods and points his thumb back over his shoulder. "Second big road up back yonder. Mistress Coyle's got twenty minutes on ya."

"Thank you, Wilf."

He nods again and turns back to the Answer. *"Retreat!"* he yells. *"Retreat!"*

I urge Acorn along again and we ride past Wilf and the astonished faces of Mistresses Lawson and Nadari at the front of the Answer line. "On whose authority?" Mistress Nadari snaps.

"Mine!" I hear Wilf say, strong as I've ever heard him.

I'm already passing through the Answer and pushing Acorn as fast as he'll go and so I don't see Wilf when he says, "And hers!"

But I know he's pointing at me.

[TODD]

Our front line sprints across the clearing like a wall falling down a hill–

Men running in a V shape with Mr. Hammar screaming on horseback at its tip–

The next line of men sets off a split second later so now there's two rows running at breakneck speed toward the line of Spackle, guns out but–

"Why ain't they firing?" I ask the Mayor.

He breathes out a little. "Overconfidence, I should say."

18

"What?"

"We've always fought the Spackle at close quarters, you see. It was most effective. But . . ." His eyes play over the front line of Spackle—

Which ain't moving.

"I think we may want to be back a bit farther, Todd," he says, turning Morpeth down the road before I can even say anything.

I look back to the men running—

And the Spackle line that ain't moving—

And the men getting closer—

"But why–?"

"Todd," the Mayor calls, now a good twenty yards behind me—

There's a flash of Noise thru the Spackle—

A signal of some kind—

Every Spackle on the front line raises his bow and arrow—

Or his white stick—

And the Spackle on the horned creacher takes a lighted torch in each hand—

"READY!" Mr. Hammar calls, thundering forward on his horse, heading right for the horned creacher—

The men raise their rifles—

"I really would get back if I were you," the Mayor calls to me—

I pull a little on Angharrad's reins—

But my eyes are still on the battle and the men running cross the clearing in front of me and the men behind 'em ready to do the same and more men behind *them*—

And me and the Mayor waiting at the back of the pack—

"AIM!" screams Mr. Hammar with his voice and his Noise—

I turn Angharrad and ride back to the Mayor—

"Why ain't they *firing*?" I say as I get close—

"Who?" the Mayor says, still studying the Spackle. "The men or the enemy?"

I look back—

Mr. Hammar's not fifteen yards from the horned creacher—

Ten—

"Either one," I say—

Five—

"Now, *this*," says the Mayor, "should be interesting."

And we see the Spackle on the horned creacher bring the two torches together behind the U-shaped thing—

And **WHOOMP!**

An exploding, spilling, tumbling, churning flood of fire looking for all the world like the rushing river beside it comes *whooshing* out of the U-shaped thing, *way* bigger than looks possible, expanding and growing and eating the world like a nightmare—

Coming right for Mr. Hammar—

Who pulls his horse hard to the right—

Leaping outta the way—

But too late—

The fire swoops round him—

Sticking to Mr. Hammar and his horse like a coating—

And they're burning burning burning as they try to ride away from it—

20

Riding straight for the river—

But Mr. Hammar don't make it—

He falls from the burning saddle of his burning horse—

Hitting the ground in a jerking pile of flame—

Then lying still as his horse disappears into the water—

Screaming and screaming—

I turn my eyes back to the army—

And see that the men on the front line don't got horses that'll carry 'em outta the way—

And the fire—

Thicker than normal fire—

Thicker and heavier—

Cuts thru 'em like a rockslide—

Eating the first ten men it touches—

Burning 'em up so fast you can barely hear 'em scream—

And they're the lucky ones—

Cuz the fire spreads out—

Sticking to the uniforms and the hair—

And the skin—

And my God the *skin* of the frontline soldiers off to each side—

And they fall—

And they burn—

And they scream like Mr. Hammar's horse—

And they keep on screaming—

Their Noise rocketing up and out over the Noise of everything else—

And as the blast of fire finally dissipates and Mr. Morgan is yelling "FALL BACK!" to the front lines of soldiers and as those soldiers are already turning and running but firing their rifles as they go and as the first arrows from the Spackle bows start arcing thru the air and as the other Spackle raise their white sticks and flashes come outta the ends and the men hit by the arrows in the back and in the stomach and in the face start to fall and as the men hit by the flashes from the white sticks start losing bits of their arms and their shoulders and their heads and falling to the ground dead dead dead—

And as I grip Angharrad's mane hard enough to pull out hair—

And she's so terrified she don't even complain—

All I can hear is the Mayor next to me—

Saying, "At last, Todd—"

And he turns to me and he says—

"A worthy enemy."

{ V I O L A }

Acorn and I are barely a minute away from the army of the Answer when we pass the first road and I recognize where we are. It's the road down to the house of healing where I spent my first weeks in New Prentisstown, the house of healing where Maddy and I snuck out one night.

The house of healing where we took Maddy's body to prepare it for burial after Sergeant Hammar shot her for no reason at all.

"Keep going, Acorn," I say, pushing the thought away. "The road up to the tower has to be around—"

The dusky sky suddenly lights up behind me. I turn and Acorn does, too, and though the city is far away and behind trees, we can see a huge flash of light, silent from this distance, no rumble of an explosion, just a bright, bright glow that grows and grows before dying away, lighting up the few people on the road who've reached this far out of town, and I wonder what could possibly have happened back in the city to make a light like that.

And I wonder whether Todd is in the middle of it.

[TODD]

The next blast of fire comes before anyone's ready for it—
WHOOMP!
Shooting across the open ground and catching the retreating soldiers, melting their guns, burning up their bodies, laying 'em to the ground in the worst sorta heap—

"We gotta get outta here!" I shout at the Mayor, who's watching the battle like he's hypnotized, his body still but his eyes moving this way and that, taking in everything.

"Those white sticks," he says quietly. "Obviously a ballistic of some sort but do you see how destructive they are?"

I stare at him wide-eyed. "DO SOMETHING!" I shout. "They're getting slaughtered!"

He raises one eyebrow. "What exactly do you think war is, Todd?"

"But the Spackle have got better weapons now! We won't be able to stop 'em!"

"Won't we?" he says, nodding at the battle. I look, too. The Spackle on the horned creacher readies his torches for another blast but one of the Mayor's men has risen from where he's fallen, burns all over him, and he raises his gun and fires—

23

And the Spackle on the horned creacher drops one torch and slaps a hand to his neck where the bullet hit him, then falls sideways off the creacher to the ground–

A cheer goes up from the Mayor's men as they see what's happened–

"All weapons have their weaknesses," the Mayor says.

And quick as that, they're regrouping and Mr. Morgan is riding his horse forward, leading *all* the men now, and more rifles are getting fired and tho more arrows and white flashes are coming from the Spackle and more soldiers are falling, Spackle are falling, too, their clay armor cracking and exploding, falling under the feet of other Spackle marching behind 'em–

But they keep coming–

"We're outnumbered," I say to the Mayor.

"Oh, ten to one easily," he says.

I point up the hill. "And they've got more of those fire things!"

"But not ready yet, Todd," he says and he's right, the creachers are backed up behind Spackle soldiers on the zigzag road, not ready to blast unless they want to take out half their own army.

But the Spackle line is really crashing into the line of men now and I see the Mayor do a counting moshun with his hands and then look back down the empty road behind us.

"You know, Todd," he says, taking Morpeth's reins. "I think we're going to need every man."

He turns to me.

"It's time for us to fight."

And I know with a stab in my heart that if the Mayor himself is gonna fight–

Then we're *really* in trouble.

{Viola}

"There!" I shout, pointing at what has to be the road up the hill to the tower. Acorn flies straight up the incline, bits of foamy sweat flying from his shoulders and neck. "I know," I say between his ears. "Almost there."

Girl colt, he thinks and for a second I think he might even be laughing at my sympathy. Or maybe he's just trying to comfort *me*.

The road is incredibly dark as it curves around the back of the hill. For a minute, I'm cut off from absolutely everything, all sound from the city, all light from what's happening, all Noise that might tell me what's going on. It's like Acorn and I are racing through the black beyond itself, that weird quiet of being a small ship in the hugeness of space, where your light is so feeble against the surrounding dark, you might as well not have a light at all–

And then I hear a sound coming from the top of the hill–

A sound I recognize–

Steam escaping from a vent–

"Coolant systems!" I shout to Acorn, like they're the happiest words in the whole world.

The steam sound gets louder as we near the crest of the hill and I picture it in my mind: two huge vents at the back of the scout ship, just above the engines, cooling them down after entry into the atmosphere–

The same vents that didn't open on my own scout ship when the engines caught fire.

The same vents that caused us to crash and killed my mother and father.

Acorn reaches the top of the hill and for a second, all I see is the vast empty space where the communications tower used to be, the tower Mistress Coyle blew up rather than have the Mayor use it to contact my ships first. Most of the metal wreckage has been cleared away in huge scrap heaps and when Acorn races across the open ground, at first I only see the heaps in the moons-light, three big ones, covered in the dust and dullness of the months since the tower fell–

Three groupings of metal–

And behind them a fourth–

Shaped like a huge hawk, wings outstretched–

"There!"

Acorn puts on a burst of energy and we race toward the back of the scout ship, steam and heat pouring out of the vents into the sky, and we get nearer and I see a shaft of light on the left that must be the bay door open under a wing of the ship–

"Yes," I say to myself. "They're really *here*–"

Because they really *are* here. I almost believed they'd never come and I can feel myself getting lighter and my breath start rushing faster because they're here, they're actually *here*–

I see three figures standing on the ground at the bottom of the bay doors, silhouetted against the shaft of light, their shadows turning as they hear Acorn's hoofbeats–

Just to the side, I see a cart parked in the darkness, its oxes nibbling on grass–

And we get closer–

And closer–

And the figures' faces suddenly loom up as Acorn and I enter the shaft of light, too, juddering to a stop–

And it *is*, it's exactly who I thought it would be and my heart does a skip of happiness and homesickness, and in spite of all that's happening, I feel my eyes get wet and my throat start to choke–

Because it's Bradley Tench from the *Beta* and Simone Watkin from the *Gamma* and I know they came looking for *me*, they came all this way looking for my mother and my father and *me*–

And they step back, startled at my sudden appearance, and then take a second to see past all the dirt and the grime and the longer hair–

And I'm bigger, too–

Taller–

Almost grown–

And their eyes get wider as they realize who I am–

And Simone opens her mouth–

But it's not her voice that speaks.

It's the third figure, the one whose eyes–now that I finally look at them–open even wider, and she says my name, says it with a look of shock that I have to say gives me a surprising flash of pleasure.

"*Viola!*" Mistress Coyle says.

"Yeah," I say, looking right into her eyes. "It's *Viola*."

[TODD]

I don't even think when the Mayor and Morpeth run after the soldiers into the battle. I just spur Angharrad and she trusts me and leaps right off after 'em—

I don't want to be here—

I don't want to fight anyone—

But if it keeps her safe—

(*Viola*)

Then I'll ruddy well fight—

We ride past soldiers on foot still charging forward, and the battleground at the bottom of the hill is heaving with men and Spackle and I keep on looking up the zigzag road, which is still pouring down with more and more Spackle soldiers and it feels like I'm an ant riding into an anthill and you can hardly see the ground for writhing bodies—

"This way!" calls the Mayor, peeling off to the left, away from the river. The lines of men have pushed the Spackle back against both the river and the base of the hill, holding 'em there—

NOT FOR LONG, THOUGH, says the Mayor, straight into my head.

"You don't *do* that!" I shout at him, raising my rifle.

"I need your attention and I need a good soldier!" he shouts back. "If you can't do that, then you're no good in this war and you give me far less reason to help you!"

And I think to myself, how did it turn into *his* choosing to help *me*, I had him tied up, I had him at my mercy, I *won*—

But there's no time cuz I see where he's heading—

The left flank, the one away from the river, is the weakest, it's where the men are thinnest and the Spackle have seen that and a surge of 'em is pressing forward. "ATTEND TO ME!" the Mayor shouts and the soldiers nearest us turn and follow him—

Doing it immediately, like they don't even think about it—

And they follow us toward the left flank and we cross the ground way faster than I'd like and I'm just swamped on all sides by how *loud* it all is, the men shouting, the weapons firing, the thump of bodies hitting the ground, that effing Spackle horn still blasting every two seconds, and the Noise, the Noise, the Noise, the Noise—

I'm riding into a nightmare.

I feel a *whisk* of air by my ear and turn quickly to see a soldier behind me shot in the cheek by the arrow that just missed my head—

He screams and he falls—

And then he's left behind—

MIND YOURSELF, TODD, the Mayor puts in my head. WOULDN'T WANT YOU LOST IN THE FIRST BATTLE, NOW, WOULD WE?

"Effing STOP that!" I shout, whirling round to him.

I'D RAISE MY GUN IF I WERE YOU, he thinks at me—

And I turn—

And I see—

The Spackle are on us—

{VIOLA}

"You're alive!" Mistress Coyle says and I see her face change, making one kind of astonishment into a different, lying kind of astonishment. "Thank God!"

"Don't you dare!" I yell at her. *"Don't you dare!"*

"Viola—" she starts but I'm already sliding off Acorn, grunting badly at the pain in my ankles, but I stay standing, just, and turn to Simone and Bradley. "Don't believe anything she's told you."

"Viola?" Simone says, coming forward. "Is it really you?"

"She's as responsible for this war as the Mayor. Don't do anything she—"

But I'm stopped by Bradley grabbing me in a hug so tight I can barely breathe. "Oh, my God, *Viola*," he says, deep feeling in his voice. "We'd heard nothing from your ship. We thought—"

"What *happened,* Viola?" Simone says. "Where are your parents?"

And I'm overwhelmed by seeing them, so much so I can't speak for a minute, and I pull a little away from Bradley and the light catches his face and I see him, really *see* him, see his kind brown eyes, his skin the same dark shade that Corinne's was, his short curly hair, graying at the temples, Bradley who was always my favorite on the convoy, who used to teach me arts and math, and I look over and see the familiar freckled skin of Simone, too, the red hair tied back in a ponytail, the teeny tiny scar on the rise of her chin and I think, in all that's happened, how much they disappeared to the back of my mind, how much the process of just surviving on this stupid, stupid world made me forget that I came from a place where I was loved, where people cared for me and for each other, where someone as beautiful and smart as Simone and as gentle and funny as Bradley would actually come after me, actually want what was best.

My eyes are flooding again. It's been too painful to remember. Like that life happened to a whole different person.

"My parents are dead," I finally choke out. "We crashed and they died."

"Oh, Viola–" Bradley says, his voice soft.

"And I was found by a boy," I say, getting stronger. "A brave and *brilliant* boy who saved me over and over again and now he's down there trying to stop a war that *she* started!"

"I did no such thing, my girl," Mistress Coyle says, not looking fake-astonished anymore.

"Don't you dare call me that–"

"We are fighting a tyrant down there, a tyrant who killed hundreds if not thousands, who imprisoned and banded women–"

"You *shut up*," I say, low and threatening. "You tried to *kill me* and you don't get to say anything more about *anything*."

"She *what*?" I hear Bradley say.

"You had Wilf, kind, sweet, peaceful Wilf, marching into town blowing up buildings–"

Mistress Coyle starts. "*Viola–*"

"I said, *shut up!*"

And she shuts up.

"Do you know what's happening down there now?" I say. "Do you know what you were sending the Answer into?"

She just breathes at me, her face a storm.

"The Mayor figured out your trick," I say. "He would have had a full army waiting for you by the time you reached the center of town. You would have been annihilated."

But all she says is, "Don't underestimate the fighting spirit of the Answer."

"What's the Answer?" Bradley asks.

"A terrorist organization," I say, just to see the look on Mistress Coyle's face.

It's worth it.

"You are speaking *dangerous* words, Viola Eade," Mistress Coyle says, stepping toward me.

"What are you going to do about it?" I say. "Blow me up again?"

"Whoa, whoa," Simone says, moving between us. "Whatever's going on," she says to Mistress Coyle, "you clearly haven't told us the whole story."

Mistress Coyle sighs in frustration. "I haven't lied to you about what that man did," she says and turns to me. "Have I, Viola?"

I try to outstare her, but no, he really did do terrible things. "We've already *beaten* him, though," I say. "Todd's down there right now with the Mayor tied up but he needs our help because–"

"We can sort out our differences later," Mistress Coyle says over me to Bradley and Simone. "It's what I've been try-ing to tell you. There's an army down there that needs to be stopped–"

"Two armies," I say.

Mistress Coyle turns to me, frustrated. "The Answer does *not* need to be stopped–"

"That's not what I'm talking about," I say. "There's an army of Spackle marching down the hill by the waterfall."

"An army of what?" Simone asks.

But I'm still looking at Mistress Coyle.

Because her mouth has dropped open.

And I can see fear move right across her face.

[TODD]

Here they come—

This part of the hill is all rock and steepness so the Spackle can't come straight down onto us but they're surging cross the clearing toward the weakness in the line of men and here they come—

Here they come—

Here they come—

I raise my gun—

I'm surrounded by soldiers, some pushing forward, some pushing back, knocking into Angharrad, who keeps calling **Bꝏy cꝏlt, bꝏy cꝏlt!** in her Noise—

"It's okay, girl," I lie—

Cuz here they are—

Gunfire erupts everywhere, like a flock of birds taking off—

Arrows *zing* thru the air—

The Spackle fire their sticks—

And before I can even have a thought, a soldier in front of me staggers back with a weird fizzing sound—

Grasping at his throat—

Which ain't there no more—

33

And I can't take my eyes off him as he stumbles to his knees—

And there's blood just everywhere, all over him, *real* blood, *his* blood, so much I can smell the iron tang of it—

And he's looking up at me—

Catching my eyes and holding 'em—

And his Noise—

My God his Noise—

And I'm suddenly *in* it, inside what he's thinking, and there's pictures of his family, pictures of his wife and his baby son and he's trying to hold onto 'em but his Noise is breaking into bits and his fear is pouring thru like a bright red light and he's reaching for his wife, he's reaching for his little bitty son—

And then a Spackle arrow hits him in the rib cage—

And his Noise stops—

And I'm jerked back onto the battlefield—

Back into hell—

KEEP IT TOGETHER, TODD! the Mayor puts in my head.

But I'm still looking at the dead soldier—

His dead eyes looking back up at me—

"Dammit, Todd!" the Mayor yells at me and—

I AM THE CIRCLE AND THE CIRCLE IS ME.

Thudding thru my brain like a dropped brick—

I AM THE CIRCLE AND THE CIRCLE IS ME.

In his voice and my own—

Twisted together—

Right in the center of my head—

"Eff off," I try to shout—

But my voice is weirdly quiet—

And–

And–

And I look up–

And I feel calmer–

Like the world is clearer and slower–

And a Spackle breaks thru where two soldiers have separated–

And he raises his white stick at me–

And I'm gonna have to do it–

(killer–)

(yer a killer–)

I'm gonna have to shoot him before he shoots me–

And I raise my gun–

Davy's gun that I took from him–

And I think, *Oh, please,* as I put my finger on the trigger–

Oh, please, oh, please, oh, please–

And–

Snick–

I look down in shock.

My gun ain't loaded.

{ V I O L A }

"You're lying," Mistress Coyle says, but she's already turning, as if she could see over the trees and into town. She can't, there's just the shadows of the forest against the distant glow. The steam from the vents is so loud we can barely hear ourselves talk, much less anything from the town, and if she took off after the ship the second she saw it come in for landing, she wouldn't have heard the horn at all.

35

"That's impossible," she's saying. "They agreed, they signed a truce!"

𝓢𝓹𝓪𝓬𝓴𝓵𝓮! Acorn says, behind me.

"What did you say?" Simone asks me.

"No," Mistress Coyle says. "Oh, no."

"Would someone please explain what the hell's going on?" Bradley asks.

"The Spackle are the indigenous species," I say. "Intelligent and smart–"

"Vicious in battle," Mistress Coyle interrupts.

"The only one I met was gentle and much more frightened of humans than the humans here seem to be of them–"

"You didn't fight them in a war," Mistress Coyle says.

"I also didn't enslave them."

"I will not stand here and have this conversation with a *child*–"

"It's hardly as if they're coming for no reason." I turn back to Bradley and Simone. "They're attacking because the Mayor committed a genocide of all the Spackle slaves, and if we can maybe just *talk* to them, tell them we're not like the Mayor–"

"They'll kill your precious boy," Mistress Coyle says. "Won't even think twice about it."

My breath immediately stops as panic starts to rise from what she says, but then I try to remember that she'd *like* it if I panicked. If I was afraid, I'd be easier to control.

But I won't be, because we'll stop this. We'll stop all of this.

That's what me and Todd do.

"We've *caught* the Mayor," I say, "and if the Spackle *see* that–"

"With all due respect," Mistress Coyle says to Simone, "Viola is a girl with an extremely limited knowledge of the history of this world. If the Spackle are attacking, we've got to fight back!"

"Fight back?" Bradley says, frowning. "Who do you think we *are*?"

"Todd needs our help," I say. "We can fly down there and stop this before it's too late–"

"It's already too late," Mistress Coyle interrupts. "If you could just take me up in your ship, I could show you–"

But Simone's shaking her head. "The atmosphere was thicker up top than we expected. We had to land in full coolant mode–"

"No!" I say but of course they did. Two vents open–

"What does that mean?" Mistress Coyle asks.

"It means we don't fly for at least another eight hours as the engines cool and replenish their fuel cells," Simone says.

"Eight hours?" Mistress Coyle says. She makes a fist, actually makes a fist in the air in frustration.

For once, I know how she feels.

"But we've got to help Todd!" I say. "He can't control one army and hold off another–"

"He'll have to let the President go," Mistress Coyle says.

"No," I say quickly. "No, he wouldn't do that."

Would he?

No.

Not after we fought so hard.

"War makes ugly necessity," Mistress Coyle says. "And however good your boy may be, he's one against thousands."

37

I fight down the panic again and turn to Bradley. "We have to do something!"

He looks hard over to Simone and I know they're wondering what disaster they've landed themselves in. Then Bradley snaps his fingers like he's remembered something.

"Hold on!" he says and rushes back into the scout ship.

[TODD]

I pull the trigger again–

All I get is another *snick*–

I look up–

The Spackle's raising his white stick–

(what are those things?)

(what are they that causes so much damage?)

And I'm dead–

I'm dead–

I'm–

BANG!

A gun goes off right by my head–

And the Spackle with the white stick jerks to one side, a trail of blood flying from his neck above the line of his armor–

The Mayor–

The Mayor shot him from the back of Morpeth–

And I'm staring over at him, ignoring the fighting that's going on all around us–

"You sent yer son to war with an *EMPTY GUN*?" I scream, shaking from anger and from having just about died–

"Now is not the time, Todd," the Mayor says–

And I flinch again as the *whisk* of an arrow flies right past me and I grab the reins and try to turn Angharrad to get the hell outta here and I see a soldier stumble back into Morpeth, blood rushing out from a nightmarish-looking hole in the stomach of his uniform and he raises his bloody hands to the Mayor for help—

And the Mayor snatches the soldier's rifle from him and tosses it over to me—

I catch it out of reflex, my hands instantly wet from the blood all over it—

NOW IS ALSO NOT THE TIME FOR NICETIES, the Mayor puts in my head. TURN! FIRE!

And I turn—

And I fire—

{VIOLA}

"Survey probe!" Bradley says, coming back down the ramp, carrying what looks like an oversize insect, maybe a foot and a half long, shiny metal wings spread open over a thin metal body. He holds it up to Simone as if asking her. She nods and I see that she's Mission Commander for this trip.

"*What* kind of probe?" Mistress Coyle asks.

"They scope out the landscape," Simone says. "Didn't you have them when you landed?"

Mistress Coyle snorts. "Our ships left Old World twenty-three years before yours, my girl. We practically flew here steam-powered compared to what you've got."

"What happened to yours?" Bradley says to me, setting up the probe.

"Destroyed in the crash," I say. "Along with nearly everything else. I barely even had any food left."

"Hey," Simone says, trying to say it soft and comforting. "But you made it. You're alive." She moves to put an arm around me.

"Careful," I say. "Both my ankles are broken."

Simone looks horrified. *"Viola–"*

"Look, I'll live," I say, "but I'm only alive because of Todd, okay? If he's in trouble down there, Simone, we *have* to help him–"

"Always thinking of her boy," Mistress Coyle mutters. "Making it personal at the expense of the entire world."

"It's because no one and nothing matters to you that you're willing to blow the world to pieces!"

Pieces, Acorn thinks, shifting nervously beneath me.

Simone looks at him, furrowing her forehead. "Wait a minute–"

"Ready!" Bradley says, standing back from the probe, a small control device in his hand.

"How does it know where to go?" Mistress Coyle asks.

"I've set it to fly toward the brightest source of light," Bradley says. "These are just area probes with limited altitude, but it should be enough to clear a few hills."

"Can you set it to look for a specific person?" I say.

But I stop because the night sky lights up again with the same glow I saw on my ride here. Everyone looks toward the city.

"Get the probe up!" I say. "Get it up now!"

[TODD]

I fire the gun before I can even think if I want to–

BANG!

I ain't ready for the kickback and it knocks me in my collarbone and I grab Angharrad's reins and we spin round in a full circle before I finally see–

A Spackle–

Lying on the ground in front of me–

(with a knife stuck in his–)

With a gunshot wound bleeding from a hole in his chest–

"Nice shot," the Mayor says.

"*You* did it," I say, turning to him. "I told you to stay the hell outta my head!"

"Not even to save your life, Todd?" he says, firing his gun again, and another Spackle falls.

I turn, gun raised–

They're still coming–

I aim at a Spackle raising his bow at a soldier–

I fire–

But I pull it to the side on purpose at the last second, missing altogether (shut up)–

The Spackle jumps away, tho, so it worked–

"That's not how you win wars, Todd!" the Mayor yells, firing his gun at the Spackle I missed, catching him in the chin and sending him sprawling–

"You have to choose," the Mayor says, ranging his gun round, looking for the next thing to shoot. "You said you'd kill for her. Did you mean it?"

Then there's another *whisk* sound–

And the worst squeal imaginable from Angharrad–

I turn round in the saddle–

She's been hit in the back right flank with an arrow–

BOY COLT! she yells. **BOY COLT!**

And I'm immediately reaching back to try and grab the arrow and not fall off from her leaping around at the pain of it and it snaps in two in my hand and I leave a broken bit stuck into her back leg and **BOY COLT! BOY COLT! TODD!** and I'm trying to calm her so she doesn't throw me down into the heaving mass of soldiers all round us–

And that's when it happens again–

WHOOMP!

A huge flash of light and I turn to look–

The Spackle have another fire weapon at the bottom of the hill.

The flames spill out from the top of the horned creacher and cut right thru the middle of the soldiers and men are screaming and burning and screaming and burning and soldiers are turning back and running and the line is breaking and Angharrad is bucking and bleeding and squealing and we're slammed by a wave of men retreating and she bucks again and–

And I drop my gun–

And the fire expands out and up–

And men are running–

And smoke is everywhere–

And suddenly Angharrad spins free and we're somehow in a place where no man stands, where the army is behind us and the Spackle are in front of us and I don't got my gun and I don't know where the Mayor is–

And the Spackle on the back of the horned creacher with the fire-making thing has seen us—

And he starts coming right toward us—

{VIOLA}

Bradley presses the screen on the remote device. The probe lifts lightly off the ground, straight up with almost no sound except a little *zip*. It hovers for a second, extends its wings, and then takes off for the city so fast you almost don't see it go.

"Wow," Mistress Coyle says under her breath. She looks back to Bradley. "And we'll be able to see what's happening?"

"And hear," he says, "to a limited degree."

He presses the remote again, dialing the screen with his thumb until a light flashes out the end of the remote device, projecting a three-dimensional picture that hangs in midair, lit up in bright greens because of night vision. Trees rush by, a flash of the road, a few blurs of tiny people running—

"How far is the city from here?" Bradley asks.

"Six miles, maybe?" I say.

"Then it should almost be—"

And then the probe's there, at the edge of the city, rushing over buildings burning where the Answer set them alight, rushing on over the ruins of the cathedral, rushing over crowds of townsfolk running in panic from the square—

"My God," Simone whispers, turning to me. "Viola—"

"It's still going," Mistress Coyle says, watching.

It *is* still going, flying past the town square and down the main road.

"Brightest light source—" Bradley starts to say—

43

And then we see just exactly what the brightest light source is.

[TODD]

Men burning—
Everywhere—
The screaming—
And the terrible smell of cooked meat—
I gag in my throat—
And the Spackle's riding right toward me—
He's standing on the back of a horned creacher, his feet and lower legs strapped into boot-type things on either side of the saddle, letting him stand there without needing to balance—
And he's got a burning torch in each hand and the U-shaped fire-making thing in front of him—
And I see his Noise—
I see *me* in his Noise—
I see me and Angharrad alone in the middle of an emptiness—
Her screaming and twisting with the broken arrow in her flank—
Me staring back at the Spackle—
Me without a gun—
And behind me is the weakest part of our line—
And I see the Spackle shooting the fire in his Noise and taking out me and the men behind me—
Leaving the Spackle an opening to come pouring into the city—

Their war won before it's barely even started—

I grab Angharrad's reins and try to move her but I can see the pain and fright shooting thru her Noise as she keeps calling out **Boy colt! Todd!** and it's ripping my heart as she calls it and I wheel round trying to find the Mayor, trying to find *anyone* who'll shoot the Spackle on the horned creacher—

But the Mayor ain't nowhere I can see—

Hidden by smoke and panicking men—

And no one is lifting a gun—

And the Spackle is raising his torches to fire the weapon—

And I think, *No*—

I think, *It can't end this way*—

I think, *Viola*—

I think, *Viola*—

And then I think, *"Viola"*?

Would it work on a Spackle?

And I sit up as high in the saddle as I can—

And I think about her riding away from me on Davy's horse—

I think of her broken ankles—

I think of us saying we'd never part, not even in our heads—

I think of her fingers twirling round mine—

(I don't think about what she'd say if she knew I let the Mayor go—)

I just think *Viola*—

I think **Viola**—

Right at the Spackle on the horned creacher—

I think–

VIOLA!

And the Spackle's head jerks back, and he drops both torches and falls backward over the horned creacher, slipping outta the boots and onto the ground, and the horned creacher turns from the sudden shift in weight, stumbling back into the line of advancing Spackle, knocking 'em this way and that–

And I hear a cheer behind me–

I turn to see a line of soldiers, recovering, surging forward, past me, all round me–

And the Mayor's suddenly there, too, riding beside me, and he's saying, "Excellent work, Todd. I knew you had it in you."

And Angharrad's tiring beneath me but still calling–

Bᴏy colt? Bᴏy colt? Todd?

"No time to rest," the Mayor says–

And I look up and I see the same huge wall of Spackle coming down the hill, coming to eat us alive–

{VIOLA}

"Oh, my God," says Bradley.

"Are those–?" Simone says, shocked, stepping toward the projection. "Are they on *fire*?"

Bradley presses the remote and the picture suddenly gets closer and–

They really *are* on fire–

Through great swathes of smoke, we see chaos, men running this way and that, some pressing forward, some running backward–

46

And some just burning–

Burning and burning and sometimes running for the river and sometimes falling to the ground and staying there.

And I just think, *Todd.*

"But you said there was a *truce,*" Simone says to Mistress Coyle.

"After a bloody war that killed hundreds of us and thousands of them," Mistress Coyle says.

Bradley dials again. As the camera pulls back, showing the whole road and the bottom of the hill, swarming with an impossible number of Spackle, in reddish and brown armor and holding what look like sticks or something and riding–

"What is *that?*" I say, pointing at some kind of massive tanklike animal stomping down the hill, a single thick horn curving out the end of its nose.

"Battlemores," Mistress Coyle says. "At least, that's what *we* called them. The Spackle don't have a spoken language, it's all visual, but none of this matters! If they overrun the Mayor's army, they'll just keep coming and kill the rest of us."

"And if he beats them?" Bradley asks.

"If he beats them, then his control over this planet will be absolute and that's not a place you'd ever want to live."

"And what if *you* had absolute control over this planet?" Bradley asks, surprising fire in his voice. "What kind of place would that be?"

Mistress Coyle blinks in surprise.

"Bradley–" Simone starts to say–

But I'm no longer listening to them–

I'm looking at the projection–

Because the camera's moved down the hill and south a little–

And there he is–

Right in the middle of it all–

Surrounded by soldiers–

Fighting off Spackle–

"Todd," I whisper–

And then I see a man on horseback next to him–

My stomach drops–

The *Mayor* is next to him–

Untied and set free, just like Mistress Coyle said–

Todd's let him go–

Or the Mayor's forced him to–

And Todd's at the very front of the battle–

Then smoke rises up and he disappears.

"Get the camera in closer!" I say. "Todd's down there in it!"

Mistress Coyle gives me a look as Bradley dials the controls again and the image on the projection searches through the battle, seeing bodies everywhere, living and dead, men and Spackle mixed together, until how can you tell who you're fighting, how can you safely fire any kind of weapon without killing your own side?

"We have to get him out of there!" I say. "We have to save him!"

"Eight hours," Simone says, shaking her head. "We can't–"

"No!" I shout, hobbling over to Acorn. "I've got to get to him–"

But then Mistress Coyle says to Simone, "You have some kind of weapons on this ship, yes?"

I spin round.

"You wouldn't have landed unarmed," Mistress Coyle says.

Bradley's face is as stern as I've seen it. "That is no concern of yours, madam—"

But Simone's already answering, "We have twelve point-to-point missiles—"

"*No!*" Bradley says. "That is *not* who we are. We're here to settle the planet *peacefully*—"

"—and the standard complement of hoopers," Simone finishes.

"Hoopers?" Mistress Coyle says.

"A kind of small bomb," Simone says. "Dropped in clusters, but—"

"Simone," Bradley says angrily. "We did *not* come here to fight a—"

Mistress Coyle interrupts again. "Can you fire any of them from a ship that's landed?"

[TODD]

We push forward—

Forward forward forward—

Into the line of attacking Spackle—

There's so many—

And Angharrad is whinnying beneath me in pain and fright—

I'm sorry, girl, I'm sorry—

But there's no time—

There ain't no time for nothing in war except *war*—

"Here!" the Mayor says, shoving another gun in my hand—

And we're at the front of a small rush of men—

Racing toward a bigger rush of Spackle—

And I'm pointing the gun—

And I'm pulling the trigger—

BANG!

I close my eyes at the pop and I don't see where I shot cuz there's too much smoke already in the air and there's Spackle falling and men calling out on either side and Angharrad screaming and pressing forward anyway and the Spackle armor cracking and bursting under repeated fire and more arrows and white sticks and I'm so terrified I can't even breathe and I'm just firing my gun and firing my gun, not even seeing where the bullets are going—

And the Spackle keep coming, climbing over the bodies of soldiers, and their Noises are wide open and so are the Noises of every soldier and it's like a thousand wars at once, not just the one I'm seeing but ones happening over and over again in the Noise of the men and the Spackle round me till the air and the sky and my brain and my soul are filled with war and I'm bleeding it outta my ears and spitting it outta my mouth and it's like it's the only thing I ever knew, the only thing I can ever remember, the only thing that's ever gonna happen to me—

And there's a *fizzing* sound and a burning feeling in my arm and I instinctively lean away from it but I see a Spackle with one of those white sticks pointed at me and I see the cloth from my uniform burning away in a foul-smelling steam and the skin under it feeling like it's been slapped and I realize if I'd been just one inch over I'd have probably just lost my arm and—

BANG!

A rifle shot beside me and the Mayor's there and he's shot the Spackle, shot him to the ground, saying, "That's twice now, Todd."

And he plunges back into battle.

{VIOLA}

Bradley starts to answer Mistress Coyle but Simone speaks first, "Yes, we can."

"Simone!" Bradley snaps.

"But fire them where?" Simone continues. "Into which army?"

"Into the Spackle!" Mistress Coyle shouts.

"A moment ago you wanted our help to stop this President's army!" Bradley says. "And Viola told us you tried to kill her to suit your own ends. Why exactly should we trust your opinion?"

"You *shouldn't,*" I say.

"Not even when I'm *right,* my girl?" Mistress Coyle says, pointing at the projection. "The battle is being lost!" We can see a break in the darker line of men and a pulse like a river bursting its banks as the Spackle pour through.

Todd, I think. *Get out of there.*

"We could send a point-to-point at the base of the hill," Simone says.

Bradley turns to her, shocked. "And have our first action here be killing hundreds of the local species, the local *intelligent* species that, in case you're forgetting, we're going to have to live with for the *rest of our lives*?"

"The rest of your very short lives if you don't hurry up and *do something*!" Mistress Coyle practically screams.

"We could just show them our fire power," Simone says to Bradley. "Get them to back off and then try and negotiate–"

Mistress Coyle makes a hard clucking sound. "You *can't* negotiate with them!"

"*You* did," Bradley says and turns back to Simone. "Look, we jump into the middle of a *war*? Without even knowing which side to *trust*? We just blow something up and hope the consequences aren't too terrible?"

"People are dying!" Mistress Coyle yells.

"People you were just asking us to KILL!" Bradley shouts back. "If the President committed genocide, maybe they're just after *him* and us attacking will only cause an even bigger mess!"

"That's enough!" Simone snaps, suddenly like the Mission Commander. Bradley and Mistress Coyle stop. Then Simone says, "Viola?"

They all look at me.

"You're the one who's been here," Simone says. "What do *you* think we should do?"

[TODD]

We're losing–

There ain't no two ways about it–

Me knocking down the Spackle on the horned creacher only made things better for a second–

The men keep pushing forward and firing their guns and Spackle are falling and dying everywhere–

But they keep coming down the hill—

And there's so many more of 'em than there are of us—

The only thing that's saved us so far is that they ain't been able to get another one of those fire things down to the bottom of the hill yet—

But there're more coming—

And when they get here—

I AM THE CIRCLE AND THE CIRCLE IS ME.

Thumping thru my head as the Mayor's horse bumps into Angharrad, so exhausted now she's barely lifting her nose—

"Keep in the moment!" he shouts, firing his gun past me. "Or all is lost!"

"All *is* lost!" I shout back. "We can't win this!"

"It's always darkest before the dawn, Todd."

I look at him, baffled. "No, it ain't! What kinda stupid saying is that? It's always *lightest* before the dawn!"

DOWN! he puts in my head and I duck before I even think about it and an arrow flies right thru the space where my head just was.

"That's three times," the Mayor says.

And then there's another blast of the Spackle horn, so loud you can almost *see* the sound, bending the air, twisting it, and there's a new note to it—

A note of victory—

We spin round—

The line of soldiers has broken—

Mr. Morgan has fallen under the feet of a horned creacher—

Spackle are pouring down the hill now—

Pouring onto the battlefield from all direkshuns—

Cutting thru the men who still fight—

Pouring like a wave straight at me and the Mayor—

"Ready yourself!" shouts the Mayor—

"We have to retreat!" I shout back. "We have to get outta here!"

And I try to turn Angharrad's reins—

But I look behind us—

The Spackle have come round the back of the men—

We're surrounded—

"Ready!" the Mayor shouts into the Noise of the soldiers around him—

Viola, I think—

There's too many of 'em, I think—

Oh, help, I think—

"FIGHT TO THE LAST MAN!" screams the Mayor.

{ V I O L A }

"*Her?!*" Mistress Coyle says. "She's just a *girl*—"

"A girl we *trust*," Simone says. "A girl trained to be a settler just as much as her parents were."

My face flushes a little at this but only partly out of embarrassment. Because it's *true*. I did train for this. And I've been through more than enough in this place for my opinion to count—

I look back at the projection, back at the battle, which seems to be getting even worse, and I try to *think*. It looks awful as anything down there, but the Spackle aren't attacking for no reason. And their target could just be the Mayor and we did beat him before but—

"Your Todd's down there," Mistress Coyle says. "He's going to be killed if you don't do something."

"Don't you think I know that?" I say. Because that's the thing, the thing that overrides everything. I turn to Bradley and Simone. "I'm sorry, but we *have* to save him. We *have to*. Me and him were *this close* to saving the whole planet until they screwed it all up–"

"But would saving him be at the cost of something *greater*?" Bradley says, kindly, but very serious, trying to make me see. "Think hard now. What you do first anywhere is remembered *forever*. It sets the whole future."

"I'm not inclined to trust this woman, Viola," says Simone and Mistress Coyle glowers. "But that doesn't mean she's not right about this. If you say it's right, Viola, we'll intervene."

"If you say it's right, Viola," Bradley says, echoing Simone with a little snap, "we start our new life here as conquerors and you'll be setting up brand-new wars for generations to come."

"Oh, for goodness' sake!" Mistress Coyle shouts in frustration. "The power is *here*, Viola! Here is where we can change *everything*! Not even for me, my girl, for *Todd*, for *you*! Right here, right now, what you decide can *end* all of this!"

"Or," Bradley says, "you can start something even worse."

They're all looking at me. I look back to the projection. The Spackle are throughout the men now and more and more are coming–

And Todd's down there in it–

"If you do nothing," Mistress Coyle says, "your boy dies."

Todd, I think–

Would I start a new war just to save you?

Would I?

"Viola?" Simone says again. "What's the right thing to do?"

[TODD]

I fire my gun but there's so many Spackle and men mixed together I have to aim high to make sure I don't hit none of my own side and cuz of that I don't hit no Spackle neither and one is suddenly in front of me raising a white stick to Angharrad's head and I swing the barrel of the gun round and hit the Spackle hard behind his too-high ear and he falls and another one is already right there and he's grabbing my arm and I'm thinking **VIOLA** right into his face and he stumbles back and there's a *rip* at my opposite sleeve and an arrow's flown right thru it and just misses going into the soft spot underneath my jaw and I'm pulling Angharrad's reins to turn her cuz there ain't no way outta this alive and we gotta *run* and a soldier gets hit with a blast from a white stick right next to us and a spray of blood covers my face and I turn away not seeing where I'm going and I'm pulling Angharrad with me and all I can think, all I can think in the middle of so much Noise, all I can think as I hear men die and Spackle die and see them die in Noise even with my eyes shut, all I can think is—

Is this what war is?

Is this what men want so much?

Is this sposed to make them *men*?

Death coming at you with a roar and a scream so fast you can't do nothing about it—

And then I hear the Mayor's voice—

"FIGHT!" he's shouting—

In his voice and his Noise—

"FIGHT!"

And I wipe away the blood and open my eyes and it's plain as anything that fighting is all that's ever gonna happen in the world till we die and I see the Mayor on Morpeth and both he and his horse are bloodied and he's fighting so hard I can actually hear his Noise and it's still cold as stone but it's saying TO THE END, TO THE END—

And he catches my eye—

And I realize it really is the end—

We've lost—

There's too many of 'em—

We've lost—

And I grab Angharrad's mane with both my hands and I hold it tight and I think *Viola*—

And then—

BOOM!

The entire bottom section of the hill the Spackle are coming down explodes in a roar of fire and dirt and flesh—

Rising up and over everything, pelting us with stones and soil and bits of Spackle—

And Angharrad's yelling and we're both falling sideways to the ground and there's men and Spackle screaming all round us and running this way and that way and my leg is pinned under Angharrad, who's trying to work her way back up to standing, but I see the Mayor ride past–

And I can hear him *laughing*–

"What the hell was that?" I scream at him.

"A GIFT!" he screams back as he rides thru the dirt and the smoke and he's yelling to the men, "ATTACK! ATTACK NOW!"

{Viola}

We snap our attention back to the projection. "What was that?" I say.

There was a sudden *boom* but all the probe is showing is a solid block of smoke. Bradley dials the screen of the remote and the probe rises again, but smoke is covering everything.

"Is it recording?" Simone says. "Can you rewind?"

Bradley dials some more and suddenly the picture is going back on itself, back down into the cloud, the smoke rapidly gathering together and–

"There," Bradley stops it and runs it forward again in slow motion.

The battle is as chaotic and terrible as it was, the men being overwhelmed by the Spackle army and then–

BOOM!

There's an explosion at the base of the hill, a sudden violent eruption sending dirt and rock and the bodies of Spackle and their battlemores flying up and out, spinning into the cloud of smoke that rapidly covers everything–

Bradley rewinds again and we watch it once more, a small flash and then a whole section of the hill is picked up and thrown into the air and right there on the screen we see Spackle die–

Die and die and die–

Dozens of them–

And I remember the one on the riverbank–

I remember his *fear*–

"Is this you?" Simone says to Mistress Coyle. "Has your army reached the fighting?"

"We don't have *missiles*," Mistress Coyle says, not taking her eyes off the projection. "If we did, I wouldn't be asking you to fire yours."

"Then where did it come from?" Simone says. Bradley's fiddled with the controls and the picture is bigger and clearer and on the slowest setting you can see something flying into the base of the hill, see even more slowly the earth flying up, the Spackle bodies being torn, not caring what lives they had, who they loved, what their names are or were–

Just bodies flying apart–

Lives ending–

We did this to them, we *made* them attack, we enslaved and killed them, or at least the Mayor did–

And here we are killing them all over again–

Simone and Mistress Coyle are arguing but I'm really not hearing them–

Because I also know this.

When Simone asked me what to do–

I was going to say fire the missile.

I was.

I was going to cause this damage myself. I was going to say, yes, do it, fire it–

Kill all these Spackle, these Spackle with their *real* reason to attack someone who deserves it more than anyone on this planet–

If it would save Todd, it wouldn't have mattered, I was going to do it–

I would have killed hundreds, *thousands* to save him.

I would have started an even bigger war for Todd.

And that realization is so huge I have to reach out a hand to Acorn to steady myself.

Then I hear Mistress Coyle's voice rise over Simone's. "It can only mean that he's been building artillery himself!"

[TODD]

In the smoke and the screaming, Angharrad rocks her way back up to her feet, her Noise not saying nothing now, not saying it in a way that makes me really scared for her, but she's up again and I'm looking back and I'm seeing it, I'm seeing where the blast came from–

The other army units. Led by Mr. Tate and Mr. O'Hare, back from collecting the rest of the soldiers, back from collecting the armaments the Mayor was talking about.

Armaments that I for one didn't know he had.

"Secret weapons only work if they're secret," he says, riding back up to me.

He's smiling wide now.

Cuz here comes a surge of new soldiers from the city road, hundreds of 'em, fresh and screaming and ready to fight–

And already the Spackle are turning–

Already the Spackle are looking back up the hill, trying to see if there's any way over where the ground exploded–

And there's another flash and a whistling sound over our heads and–

BOOM!

I flinch and Angharrad screams as another hole is blasted into the hill and more dirt and smoke and Spackle bodies and horned creacher parts go flying into the air.

The Mayor don't flinch at all, just looks happy as the new soldiers flood round us, as the Spackle army collapses into chaos and turns and tries to run–

And is cut down by our new arrivals–

And I'm breathing heavy–

And I'm watching the tide turn–

And I gotta say–

I gotta say–

(shut up)

I feel a rush as I see it–

(shut up)

I feel relief and I feel joy and I feel my blood pumping as I see the Spackle fall–

(shut up shut up *shut up*)

"You weren't worried there, were you, Todd?" the Mayor asks.

I look back at him, dirt and blood drying on my face, the bodies of men and Spackle around us everywhere, a new bright flood of Noise filling the air even tho I didn't think it could ever get any louder—

"Come!" he says to me. "See what it's like to be on the winning side."

And he rides off after the new soldiers.

I ride after him, gun up, but not shooting, just watching and feeling—

Feeling the thrill of it—

Cuz that's it—

That's the nasty, nasty secret of war—

When yer winning—

When yer winning, it's effing *thrilling*—

The Spackle are running back up the hill, climbing over the rubble and running—

Running away from *us*—

And I raise my gun—

And I aim it at the back of a running Spackle—

And my finger's on the trigger—

And it's ready to pull—

And the Spackle stumbles over the body of another Spackle, but it ain't just one body, it's two, it's three—

And then the smoke is clearing and I'm seeing more, I'm seeing bodies everywhere, men and Spackle and horned creachers—

And I'm back in the monastery, back where the Spackle bodies were piled up—

And it don't feel so thrilling no more—

"CHASE THEM UP THE HILL!" the Mayor shouts to his soldiers. "MAKE THEM SORRY THEY WERE EVER BORN!"

{Viola}

"It's finishing," I say. "The battle's ending."

Bradley let the projection play normally again, and we all saw the arrival of the rest of the army.

Saw the second explosion.

Saw the Spackle turn and try to run back up on themselves, over the wreckage of the bottom of the hill, chaos sending some of them falling into the river, into the road below, into the battle where they didn't live for long.

The amount of death is making me feel physically sick, throbbing along with my ankles, and I have to lean against Acorn as everyone else argues.

"If he can do *that*," Mistress Coyle says, "then he's even more dangerous to you than I've been saying. Is *that* who you want in charge of the world you're about to join?"

"I don't know," Bradley says. "Are you the only alternative?"

"Bradley," Simone says, "she's got a point."

"She *does*?"

"We can't make a new settlement in the middle of a war," Simone continues. "And this is our last stop. There's nowhere else for the ships to go. We have to find a way to make it work *here*, and if we're in danger–"

"We could land somewhere else on the planet," Bradley says.

Mistress Coyle takes a sharp breath. "You wouldn't."

"There's no law that says we *have* to join up with the previous settlement," Bradley says to her. "We never had any communication from you, so we were already landing on the assumption you hadn't made it. We could just leave you to your war. Find our own place to start life new."

"*Abandon* them?" Simone says, sounding shocked herself.

"You'd end up fighting the Spackle anyway," Mistress Coyle says, "without anyone experienced to help you."

"Whereas here we'd end up fighting both Spackle *and* men," Bradley says. "And probably *you*, eventually."

"Bradley–" Simone says.

"No," I say, loud enough for them to hear me.

Because I'm still watching the projection, watching men and Spackle die–

And I'm still thinking of Todd, of all the death *I* would have caused for him–

It makes me dizzy.

And I don't ever want to be in that position again.

"No weapons," I say. "No bombing anyone. The Spackle are retreating. We beat the Mayor before and if we have to do it again, we will. Same thing for a truce with the Spackle."

I look at Mistress Coyle's face, hardening at my words. "No more death," I say. "Not by my choice, not even for an army that deserves it, Spackle or human. We'll find a peaceful solution."

"Well said," Bradley says strongly. And he looks at me with a face I remember well, a face full of kindness and love and a pride so fierce it stings.

And I have to look away because I know how close I came to having them fire the missile.

"Well, then, if you're all so sure," Mistress Coyle says, her voice cold as the bottom of a river. "I've got lives to save."

And before anyone can stop her, she's gone, running to her cart and driving off into the night.

[TODD]

"CUT THEM DOWN!" the Mayor's yelling. "SEND THEM RUNNING!"

It don't matter what he yells, tho. He could be screaming types of fruit and the soldiers would still be surging up the lower part of the zigzag road, climbing over where it's been blown away, hacking and shooting at the Spackle scrambling up it before 'em.

Mr. O'Hare is at the front of the new group of men, leading the charge, but the Mayor's stopped Mr. Tate and called him over to where we're waiting on the open ground at the bottom.

I hop off Angharrad to get a closer look at the arrow wound. It don't seem that bad but she still ain't saying nothing in her Noise, not even plain horse sounds, just silence, which I don't know what it means but I'm sure it ain't good.

"Girl?" I say, trying to rub calm hands over her side. "We'll get you stitched up, okay? We'll get you all healed up like new, all right? Girl?"

But she hangs her head down toward the ground, foam coming up round her lips and in the sweat on her sides.

"Sorry for the delay, sir," Mr. Tate's saying to the Mayor behind me. "We'll have to work on their mobility."

I glance over to where the artillery sits: four big cannons on the backs of steel carts pulled by tired-looking oxes. The metal of the cannons is black and thick and like it wants to knock your skull clean off. Weapons, secret weapons, built away from the city somewhere, the men doing it kept separate so their Noise wouldn't be heard, building weapons meant to be used on the Answer, ready to blow 'em to bits with no problem whatsoever and now used to do the same to the Spackle.

Ugly brute weapons that only make him stronger.

"I leave improvements in your capable hands, Captain," the Mayor says. "Right now, find Captain O'Hare, tell him to draw back to the base of the hill."

"Draw back?" says Mr. Tate, surprised.

"The Spackle are on the run," the Mayor says, nodding at the zigzag road, almost clear of Spackle now as they disappear over the top of the hill into the upper valley. "But who knows how many thousands are waiting on the road above? They'll regroup and replan and we shall do the same here and be ready for them."

"Yes, sir," Mr. Tate says and takes off on his horse.

I lean into Angharrad, pressing my face against her side, closing my eyes but still seeing everything in my Noise, the men, the Spackle, the fighting, the fire, the death, the death, the death—

"You did well, Todd," the Mayor says, riding up close behind me. "Very well indeed."

"It was—" I say but I stop.

Cuz how was it?

"I'm proud of you," he says.

I turn to him, my face a picture.

He laughs at my expresshun. "I *am*," he says. "You didn't

buckle under extreme pressure. You kept your head. You kept your steed even though she was injured. And most importantly, Todd, you kept your word."

I look into his eyes, those black eyes the color of river rock.

"These are the actions of a man, Todd, truly they are."

And his voice feels true, his words feel true.

But then they always do, don't they?

"I don't feel nothing," I say. "Nothing but hate for you."

He just smiles at me.

"It may not seem like it, Todd," he says, "but you will look back on this as the day you finally became a man." His eyes flash. "The day you were transformed."

{ V I O L A }

"It does seem to be ending down there," Bradley says, looking at the projection.

A separation is opening up on the zigzag road. The Mayor's men are pulling back and the Spackle are retreating, leaving an empty hill between them. We can see all of the Mayor's army now, see the big cannons he's somehow gotten, see his soldiers starting to gather themselves in some order at the bottom of the hill, regrouping to prepare to fight again, no doubt.

And then I see Todd.

I say his name out loud and Bradley zooms in to where I'm pointing. My heart rushes as I see how he leans into Angharrad, and he's alive, he's alive, he's alive–

"That your friend?" Simone asks.

"Yeah," I say. "That's Todd, he's–"

I stop because we see the Mayor riding over.

Riding over to talk to Todd, like it was just a normal day.

"Wouldn't that be the tyrant, though?" Simone asks.

I sigh. "It's complicated."

"Yeah," Bradley says. "I'm getting that impression."

"No," I say firmly. "If you ever doubt anything here, if you ever not know what to think or who to trust, you trust Todd, okay? You remember that."

"Okay," Bradley says, smiling at me, "we'll remember."

"But there remains the bigger asking," Simone says. "What do we do now?"

"We were expecting dead settlements and hopefully you and your parents in the middle of it all," Bradley says. "Instead we got a dictator, a revolutionary, and an invading army of natives."

"How big is the Spackle army?" I say, turning back to the projection. "Can you fly up?"

"Not much higher," he says, but he dials some more and the probe moves up the zigzag hill, cresting the top of it and–

"Oh, my God," I say, hearing Simone take in a breath.

Reflected in the light of both moons and of the campfires they're burning and the torches they're holding–

A whole nation of Spackle stretches back down the river road above the falls in the upper valley, far, far bigger than the Mayor's army, enough to overwhelm them in a flood, enough to never, ever be beaten.

Thousands of them.

Tens of thousands.

"Superior numbers," Bradley says, "versus superior fire power. A recipe for unending slaughter."

"Mistress Coyle said there was a truce," I say. "If there was one before, there can be another."

"What about the competing armies?" Simone asks.

"Competing generals, really," I say. "If we can sort those two out, then it'll be easier."

"And maybe we should start," Bradley says to me, "by meeting your Todd."

He dials the remote again until the view zooms back in to the men on horses, on Todd next to Angharrad.

And then Todd looks up, right at the probe, right into the projection–

Right into me.

We see the Mayor notice and look up, too.

"They've remembered we're here," Simone says. She starts back up the ramp into the scout ship. "I'll get something for your ankles, Viola, then I'll contact the convoy. Though I don't even know where to begin explaining. . . ."

She disappears into the ship. Bradley comes over to me again. He reaches over and gently squeezes my shoulder. "I'm so sorry about your parents, Viola. More than I can say."

I blink away fresh wet from my eyes, not just at the memory of my mom and dad dying in our crash, but at Bradley's kindness–

And then I remember, almost with a gasp, that it was Bradley who gave me the gift that proved so useful, the box that made the fire, the box that made a light against the darkness, the box that eventually blew up a whole bridge to save me and Todd.

"It flickers," I say.

"What's that?" he says, looking up.

"Way back on the convoy," I say, "you asked me to tell you what the night sky looks like by firelight, because I'd be the first one to know. It flickers."

He smiles, remembering. He breathes in deep through his nose. "So this is what fresh air smells like," he says, because of course it's the first time he's ever breathed it. He spent his whole life on a ship, too. "It's different from what I expected." He looks back at me. "Stronger."

"Lots of things are different from what we expected."

He squeezes my shoulder again. "We're here now, Viola," he says. "You're not alone anymore."

I swallow and look back at the projection. "I wasn't alone."

Bradley sighs again, looking with me. It flickers, he says.

"We'll have to build a fire so you can see for yourself," I say.

"See what?"

"That it flickers."

He looks at me puzzled for a minute. "What you said earlier?"

"No," I say. "Just now, you said–"

What's she talking about? he says.

But he doesn't say it.

And my stomach turns in a knot.

No.

Oh, no.

"Did you hear that?" he says, looking even more puzzled and turning around. "It sounded like my voice. . . ."

But how could it be my—? he thinks and then stops.

He looks back at me.

And *Viola?* he says.

But he says it in his Noise.

He says it in his brand-new Noise.

[TODD]

I hold the bandage to the wound on Angharrad's flank and let the medicine enter her bloodstream. She still don't say nothing, but I keep my hands on her, keep saying her name.

Horses can't be alone and I need to tell her I'm part of her herd.

"Come back to me, Angharrad," I whisper into her ears. "Come on, girl."

I look over to the Mayor, talking to his men, and I try to think how the hell it came to this.

We had him *beat*. We did. Beaten and tied up and we'd *won*.

But now.

Now he's just walking round again like he owns the place, like he's completely in charge of the whole goddam world again, like what I did to him and how I beat him is of no concern at all.

But I *did* beat him. And I will again.

I untied a monster to save Viola.

And now I've somehow gotta keep hold of the leash.

"The eye in the sky is still there," he says to me, walking

over and looking up to the dot of light the Mayor's pretty sure is a probe of some kind. We first saw it hovering over us an hour ago when the Mayor was giving orders to his captains, telling 'em to build a camp down here at the bottom of the hill, to send out spies to see what we're up against and send out other troops to find out what's happened to the army of the Answer.

But so far no one's been sent to the scout ship.

"They can see us already," the Mayor says, still looking up. "When they want to meet, they can just come to me, now, can't they?"

He looks round us slowly, at the men sorting themselves out for what's left of the night.

"Just listen to the voices," he says in a strange whisper.

The air is still filled with the Noise of the men but the look in the Mayor's eyes makes me wonder if he's talking bout something else.

"What voices?" I ask.

He blinks, like he's surprised I'm still here. He smiles again and reaches out a hand to rest on Angharrad's mane.

"Don't touch her," I say and I stare at him till he takes his hand away.

"I know how you feel, Todd," he says gently.

"No, you don't."

"I do," he insists. "I remember my first battle in the very first Spackle War. You think you're going to die now. You think this is the worst thing you've ever seen and how can you live now you've seen it? How can *anyone* live after seeing it?"

"Get outta my head," I say.

"I'm only talking, Todd. That's all I'm doing."

I don't answer him. I just keep whispering to Angharrad. "I'm here, girl."

"But you'll be fine," the Mayor says. "So will your horse. You'll both be stronger. You'll be better for it."

I look at him. "How can anyone be better after that? How can anyone be more of a *man* after that?"

He leans down close to me. "Because it was exciting, too, wasn't it?"

I don't say nothing to that.

(cuz it was–)

(for a minute there–)

But then I remember the soldier dying, the one reaching for his baby son in his Noise, the one who won't never see him again–

"You felt the excitement when we chased them up the hill," the Mayor's saying. "I saw it. It blazed through your Noise like a fire. Every man in the army felt the same thing, Todd. You're never more alive than in battle."

"Never more dead after," I say.

"Ah, philosophy," he smiles. "I didn't know you had it in you."

I turn away from him, back to Angharrad.

And then I hear it.

I AM THE CIRCLE AND THE CIRCLE IS ME.

I look back at him and I slap **VIOLA** at him.

He flinches but he don't lose his smile. "Exactly, Todd," he says. "I said it before. Control your Noise and you control yourself. Control yourself–"

"And you control the world," I finish. "Yeah, I heard you

73

the first time. I only wanna control myself, thank you. I ain't got no interest in the rest of the world."

"Everyone says that. Until they get their first taste of power." He looks up again at the probe. "I wonder if Viola's friends would be able to tell us what sort of numbers we're actually up against."

"*Too* many, that's how many," I say. "It's probably the whole Spackle world up there. You can't kill 'em all."

"Cannons against arrows, my boy," he says, looking back at me. "Even with their nifty new fire weapon and whatever those white sticks are, they don't have cannons. They don't"–he nods to the eastern horizon where the scout ship landed–"have flying ships. I'd call us just about even."

"All the more reason to end it now," I say.

"All the more reason to keep fighting," he says back. "There's only room on this planet for one side to be dominant, Todd."

"Not if we–"

"No," he says more strongly. "You set me free for one reason. To make this planet safe for your Viola."

I don't say nothing to that.

"And I've agreed to your condition and now you will let me do what needs to be done. You will let me make this planet safe for her and for the rest of us. And you will let me do this for you, because you cannot do it for yourself."

And I remember how the soldiers followed his every command, throwing themselves into battle and dying, just cuz he told 'em to.

And he's right, I don't know that I'd ever be able to do that.

I need him. I hate that I do, but I do.

I turn away from him again. I close my eyes and press my forehead against Angharrad.

I am the Circle and the Circle is me, I think.

If I can control my Noise, I can control myself.

And if I can control myself—

Maybe I can control him.

"Maybe you can," he says. "I've always said you had power."

I look at him.

He's still smiling.

"Now," he says. "Settle your horse down for the night and get some rest."

He sniffs in some air, it's starting to feel cold now that we're not thinking about dying every second, and he looks up the hill to the glow of Spackle campfires coming over the hilltop.

"We've won the first skirmish, Todd," he says. "But the war has only just begun."

And a Third

THE LAND WAITS. I WAIT WITH THEM.

And I *burn* with the waiting.

Because we had our enemy beaten. At the foot of their own hill, on the outskirts of their own city, we had the army of men surrounded and at our mercy. They were broken and confused and ready to be conquered—

The battle was nearly won. We had them *beaten*.

But then the ground erupted beneath our feet and our bodies were thrown into the air.

And we retreated. We pulled back, stumbling up the hill over broken rock and damaged road to reach the hilltop to treat our wounds and mourn our dead.

But we were close to victory. We were so close I could taste it.

I still *can* taste it, as I look out onto the valley below, where the men from the Clearing make their camp, tend to their own wounds, and bury their dead while leaving ours in carelessly thrown piles.

I remember other piles of bodies, in another place.

And I burn again at the memory.

Then I see something from where I sit on the edge of the hilltop, beside where the river crashes into the valley below. I see a light, hovering in the night air.

Watching us. Watching the Land.

I get to my feet to go and find the Sky.

I walk down the river road, deeper into our camp, the night's full blackness held back by campfires. Wet spray from the rushing river throws up mist, and the light from the fires gives everything a low glow. The Land watches me as I weave through them, their faces friendly, if weary from the battle, their voices open.

The Sky? I show with my voice as I walk. *Which way to the Sky?*

In answer, they show me the way among the campfires and secreted bivouacs, the feeding crèches and the paddocks for the battlemores—

Battlemore, I hear whispered just out of sight, whispered with no small shock and even disgust, as the word is not a word in the language of the Land, it is a word from the language of the enemy, of the Clearing, and so I make my voice even louder to cover it and I show *The Sky?*

The Land keeps showing me the way.

But behind their helpfulness, do I hear their doubts?

For who am I, after all?

Am I hero? Am I savior?

Or am I broken? Am I danger?

Am I beginning or end?

Am I truly of the Land?

If I am honest, I do not know the answers either.

And so they show me the way to the Sky as I move through them up the road and I feel like a leaf floating on the river, above it, on it.

But perhaps not of it.

And then they begin to send ahead news of my coming.

The Return approaches, they show, one to the other. *The Return approaches.*

For that is their name for me. The Return.

But I have another name, too.

I have had to learn what the Land calls things, pulling words from their wordless language, from the great single voice of the Land, so that I can understand them. The Land is what they call themselves, have always called themselves, for are they not the very Land of this world? With the Sky watching over them?

Men do not call them the Land. They invented a name based on a mistaken first attempt at communication and were never curious enough to fix it. Maybe that was where all the problems began.

"The Clearing" is the Land's name for men, the parasites who came from nowhere and sought to make this world a nowhere of their own, killing the Land in huge numbers until a truce forced a separation, the Land and the Clearing forever apart.

Except, that is, for the Land that was left behind. The Land that remained as slaves to the Clearing as a concession to peace. The Land that ceased being called the Land, the Land that ceased *being* the Land, forced even to take on the language of the Clearing. The Land that was left behind was a great shame for the Land, a shame that came to be called the Burden.

Until that Burden was erased by the Clearing in a single afternoon of killing.

And then there is me, the Return. So called not only because I am the single survivor returned from the Burden, but because my return has caused *the Land* to return here to this hilltop, after the years of truce, poised and ready above the Clearing, with better weapons, with better numbers, with a better Sky.

All brought here by the Return. By me.

But no longer attacking.

The Return approaches, shows the Sky when I find him, his back to me. He is addressing the Pathways, who sit in a semicircle in front of him. He shows them messages to take throughout the Land, messages that pass by so quickly I have difficulty reading them.

The Return will relearn the language of the Land, shows the Sky, finishing with the Pathways and coming over to me. *In time.*

They understand my words, I show back, looking out at the Land who watch me as I speak to the Sky. *They use them themselves when they speak of me.*

The words of the Clearing are in the memory of the Land, the Sky shows, taking me by the arm and walking me away. *The Land never forgets.*

You forgot about **us**, I show him, heat behind my words that I cannot suppress. *We waited for you. We waited for you until our deaths.*

The Land is here now, he shows.

The Land has retreated, I show, with greater heat. *The Land sits on a hilltop when it could be destroying the Clearing now, right now, this very night. We outnumber them. Even with their new weapons, we—*

You are young, he shows to me. *You have seen much,* **too** *much, but you are not even fully grown. You have never lived among the Land. The heart of the Land weeps that it was too late to save the Burden—*

I interrupt him, a rudeness unheard of in the Land: *You did not even* **know—**

But the Land rejoices that the Return was saved, he continues as if I had shown nothing. *The Land rejoices that it can avenge the memory of the Burden.*

No one is avenging **anything!**

And my memories spill into my voice, and it is only here, now, when the pain of them grows too great, when I am unable to speak the language of the Burden, it is only *now* that I speak the true language of the Land, wordless and felt and pouring out of me all at once. I am unable to stop from showing them my loss, from showing how the

Clearing treated us like animals, how they regarded their voices and ours as curses, as something to be *cured,* and I cannot stop from showing the Land my memories of the Burden dying at the hands of the Clearing, of the bullets and the blades and the silent screaming, of the field of bodies piled high—

Of the one in particular I lost.

The Sky shows me comfort in his voice, as do all of the Land around us, until I find I am swimming in a river of voices reaching out and touching mine to soothe it and calm it, and I have never felt so much a part of the Land, I have never felt so at home, so comforted, so at one with the single joined voice of the Land—

And I blink as I realize that this only happens when I feel so much pain I forget myself.

But that will pass, shows the Sky. *You will grow and heal. You will find it easier to be among the Land—*

I will find it easier, I show, *when the Clearing are gone from here forever.*

You speak the language of the Burden, he shows. *Which is also the language of the Clearing, of the men we fight, and though we welcome you as a brother returned to the Land, the first thing you must learn—even as I tell it to you in language you will understand—is that there is no I and there is no **you.** There is only the Land.*

I show nothing to him in response.

You sought the Sky? he finally asks.

I look up again into his eyes, small for the Land—though nothing like the hideous smallness of the eyes of the

82

Clearing, small, mean eyes that hide and hide and hide—but the eyes of the Sky are still big enough to reflect the moons, the firelight, me looking into them.

And I know that he waits for me.

For I have lived my life among the Clearing and I have learned much from them.

Including how to hide my thoughts behind other thoughts, how to conceal what I feel and think. How to layer my voice so it is harder to read.

Alone among the Land, I am not fully joined to the Land's single voice.

Not yet.

I make him wait for a moment more, then I open my voice to show him the light I saw hovering, what I suspect it to be. He understands in an instant.

A smaller version of what flew over the Land as it marched here, he shows.

Yes, I show and I remember. Lights in the sky, one of their machines flying down the road, so high above it was almost nothing but a sound.

Then the Land shall make an answer, he shows, and he takes my arm again to lead me back to the hill's edge.

As the Sky watches the light hovering out from the hill-top, I look down upon the Clearing as they settle in for the night. I look among their too-small faces on bodies stocky and short in unhealthy shades of pink and sand.

The Sky knows what I am looking for.

You seek him, he shows. *You seek the Knife.*

83

I saw him in battle. But I was too far back.

For the Return's own safety, the Sky shows.

He is **mine**—

But I stop.

Because I see him.

In the middle of the camp, he is leaning into his pack animal, his *horse*, in their language, talking to it, no doubt with great feeling, with great anguish at what he has seen.

No doubt with great care and emotion and kindness.

And this, perversely, is why the Return hates the Knife, shows the Sky.

He is worse than the others, I show. *He is worst of all of them.*

Because—

Because he **knew** *he was doing wrong. He felt the* **pain** *of his actions*—

But he did not amend them, shows the Sky.

The rest are worth as much as their pack animals, I show, *but worst is the one who knows better and does* **nothing**.

The Knife set the Return free, the Sky offers.

He should have killed me. He killed one of the Land before with the knife in his voice that he cannot put down. But he was too cowardly to even do the Return that favor.

If he had killed you as you wished, shows the Sky in a way that pulls my eyes toward his, *then the Land would not be here.*

Yes, I show. *Here where we do nothing. Here where we wait and watch instead of* **fight**.

Waiting and watching is part of fighting. The Clearing has grown stronger in the time of truce. Their men are fiercer, as are their weapons.

But the Land is fierce, too, I show. *Is it not?*

The Sky holds my gaze for a long moment, and then he turns and speaks in the voice of the Land, starting a message that is passed from one to another until it reaches one of the Land who I now see has prepared a bow with a burning arrow. She takes aim and lets the arrow fly into the night, sailing out from the hilltop.

The entire Land watches it fly, either with their own eyes or through the voices of others, until it hits the hovering light, which spirals and spins and crashes into the river below.

Today was a battle, the Sky shows to me, as a small outcry rises from the Clearing's camp. *But a war is made of many battles.*

Then he reaches across and takes my arm, the one on which I keep the sleeve of lichen growing heavily, the one that hurts, the one that will not heal. I pull away from him but he reaches again and this time I let his long white fingers lift it gently from the wrist, let him brush away the sleeve.

And we will not forget why we are here, the Sky shows.

And this spreads, in the language of the Burden, the language that the Land fears for its shame; it spreads among them until I can hear them all, feel them all.

Feel all of the Land saying, *We will not forget.*

As they all see my arm through the eyes of the Sky.

85

As they see the metal band, with writing on it in the language of the Clearing.

As they see the permanent mark upon me, the true name that sets me apart from them forever.

1017.

SECOND
CHANCES

THE CALM

THE URGENCY OF Bradley's Noise is awful.

Loud It's so loud
Simone and Viola staring at me like I'm dying
am I dying?
Landing in the middle of a war
55 days to the convoy
Is there somewhere else to go?
55 days until proper medicine arrives
55 days to wait to die
Am I dying?

"You're not *dying*," I say from the bed where Simone is injecting bone-mending into my ankles. "Bradley–"

"No," he says, holding up his hands to stop me. "I feel . . ."

NakednakedNaked "I can't tell you how naked this makes me feel."

Simone's turned the sleeping quarters of the scout ship into a makeshift house of healing. I'm on one bed and Bradley's in the other, his eyes wide open, his hands mostly to his ears, his Noise getting louder and louder–

"You're sure he's going to be all right?" Simone whispers close to me as she finishes the injections and starts bandaging my ankles. I can hear the strain in her voice.

"All I know," I whisper back, "is that men here got used to it eventually and that–"

"There was a cure," she interrupts. "Which this Mayor person burned every last bit of."

"Yes," I say, "but at least that means one is possible."

Quit whispering about me, Bradley's Noise says.

"Sorry," I say.

"For what?" he says, looking over, and then he realizes. "Could you both possibly leave me be for a while, please?"

And his Noise says, For Chrissakes get the hell out of here and give me some peace!

"Just let me finish up with Viola," Simone says, voice still shaky and trying not to look at him. She ties the last bandage around my left ankle.

"Could you grab another one?" I ask her quietly.

"What for?"

"I'll tell you outside. I don't want to upset him anymore."

She looks at me suspiciously for a second but then grabs another bandage out of a drawer and we make our way to the door, Bradley's Noise filling the little room from wall to wall.

"I still don't understand it," Simone says as we go. "I'm hearing it with my ears, but I'm hearing it inside my head, too. Words"–she looks at Bradley, her eyes growing wide–"and pictures."

She's right. Pictures are starting to come from him, pictures that could be in your head or hanging in the air in front of you–

90

Pictures of us standing here watching him, pictures of himself on the bed–

Then pictures of what we saw in the probe projection, of what happened when a flaming Spackle arrow hit it and the signal gave out–

And then pictures of the scout ship coming down from orbit, pictures of this planet far below as they flew in, a vast bluish green ocean next to miles of forest, not even thinking to look for a Spackle army blending into the riverbank as the ship circled over New Prentisstown–

And then other pictures–

Pictures of Simone–

Pictures of Simone and Bradley–

"Bradley!" Simone says, shocked and taking a step back.

"Please!" he shouts. "Just leave me alone! This is *unbearable!"*

I'm shocked, too, because the pictures of Bradley and Simone are really clear and the more Bradley tries to cover them, the clearer they get, so I take Simone's elbow and pull her away, hitting a panel to close the door behind us, which only muffles his Noise in the way it might muffle a loud voice.

We head outside. **Girl colt?** Acorn says, coming over from where he's been munching grass.

"And the animals, too," Simone says as I rub Acorn's nose. "What kind of place *is* this?"

"It's information," I say, remembering Ben describing how New World was for the first settlers, telling me and Todd that night in the cemetery which seems so impossibly long ago now. "Information, all the time, never stopping, whether you want it to or not."

"He seems so frightened," she says, her voice breaking on the word. "And those *things* he was thinking—" She turns away and I'm too embarrassed to ask if Bradley's pictures were things he was remembering or things he wished for.

"He's still the same Bradley," I say. "You've got to remember that. What would it be like if everyone could hear all the things you didn't want to say out loud?"

She sighs, looking up to the two moons, high in the sky. "There are over two thousand male settlers on the convoy, Viola. Two thousand. What's going to happen when we wake them all up?"

"They'll get used to it," I say. "Men do."

Simone snorts through the thickness in her voice. "Do women?"

"Well, that's sort of a complicated issue around here."

She shakes her head again, then notices she's still holding the bandage. "What did you need this for?"

I bite my lip for a second. "Now, don't freak out."

I slowly pull back my sleeve and show her the band on my arm. The redness of the skin around it is even worse than it was before, and you can see my number shining in the moons-light. 1391.

"Oh, *Viola*," Simone says, her voice dangerously quiet. "Did that man do this to you?"

"Not to me," I say. "To most of the other women, though." I cough a little. "I did this to myself."

"To *yourself*?"

"For a good reason. Look, I'll explain later, but I could really use a bandage on it right now."

She waits for a moment, then keeps her eyes on mine as

she wraps the bandage gently around my arm. The coolness from the medicine feels immediately better. "Sweetheart?" she asks, so much fierce tenderness in her voice it's hard to look at her. "Are you *really* okay?"

I try a barely-there smile to shake off some of her worry. "I've got a lot to tell you."

"I think you do," she says, tying off the bandage. "And maybe you should start."

I shake my head. "I can't. I've got to get to Todd."

Her forehead furrows. "What . . . you mean *now*?" She stands up straighter. "You can't wander down into the middle of a war!"

"It's calmed down. We saw it."

"We saw two huge armies camped at the front line and then our probe was shot out of the sky! There's no *way* you're going down there."

"It's where Todd is," I say. "It's where I *have* to go."

"You aren't. As Mission Commander, I forbid it and that's the end of it."

I blink. "You *forbid* it?"

And I feel a really surprising anger start to rise from my belly.

Simone sees the look on my face and softens her own expression. "Viola, what you've obviously survived for the past five months is beyond amazing, but *we're* here now. I love you far too much to allow you to put yourself in that kind of danger. You can't go. No way."

"If we want peace, we can't let the war get any bigger."

"And how are you and one boy going to stop *that*?"

And then the anger *really* starts to rise, and I try to

remember that she doesn't know. She doesn't know what I've been through, what me and Todd have done. She doesn't know I'm about a million miles past people forbidding me to do stuff.

I reach over for Acorn's reins and he kneels down.

"Viola, *no*," Simone says, stomping over–

Submit! Acorn yells, startled.

Simone takes a frightened step back. I swing my sore but mending leg over Acorn's saddle.

"No one is the boss of me anymore, Simone," I say quietly, trying to stay calm but surprised at how strong I feel. "If my parents had lived, it might be different. But they didn't."

She looks like she wants to come over, but she's seriously wary of Acorn now. "Just because your parents aren't here doesn't mean there aren't still people who care for you, who *can* care for you."

"Please," I say. "You have to trust me."

She looks at me in a kind of sad frustration. "It's too early for you to have grown up this much."

"Yeah, well," I say, "sometimes you don't have a choice." Acorn stands up, ready to go. "I'll be back as soon as I can."

"Viola–"

"I *have* to get to Todd. That's all there is to it. And now that the fighting's stopped, I'll have to find Mistress Coyle, too, before she can start blowing things up again."

"You shouldn't go alone at least," she says. "I'll come with you–"

"Bradley needs you more than I do," I say. "Whatever you might not want to find out, he needs you."

"*Viola–*"

"It's not as if I *want* to go riding into a war zone," I say, a little softer, trying to apologize now that I realize how scared I am. I look up at the scout ship. "Maybe you could send another probe to follow me?"

Simone looks thoughtful for a moment, then she says, "I've got a better idea."

[TODD]

"We've rounded up blankets from the houses nearby," Mr. O'Hare says to the Mayor. "Food, too. We'll be getting some to you as soon as possible."

"Thank you, Captain," says the Mayor. "Make sure you bring enough for Todd as well."

Mr. O'Hare looks up sharply. "Everything's pretty scarce, sir—"

"Food for Todd," the Mayor says, more firmly. "And a blanket. It's getting colder."

Mr. O'Hare takes in a breath that don't sound too happy. "Yes, *sir*."

"For my horse, too," I say.

Mr. O'Hare scowls at me.

"For his horse, too, Captain," the Mayor says.

Mr. O'Hare nods and storms off.

The Mayor's men have cleared a little area for us at the edge of the camp the army's made. There's a fire and space to sit around it and a coupla tents being put up for him and his officers to sleep in. I sit a bit away from him, but close enough to keep watch. I have Angharrad here with me, her head still down, her Noise still silent. I keep petting her and stroking her, but she's not saying nothing, nothing at all.

So far there ain't been much to say to the Mayor neither. It's been one report after another, Mr. Tate and Mr. O'Hare updating him on this and that. And plain soldiers, too, who keep coming up all shy-like to congratulate him on his victory, seeming to forget he's the one who caused all this trouble in the first place.

I lean my face into Angharrad. "What do I do now, girl?" I whisper.

Cuz what *do* I do now? I set the Mayor free and he won the first battle, keeping the world safe for Viola, just like I made him promise.

But he's got an army that'll do anything he says, that'll *die* for him. What does it matter if I can beat him if there's all these men who wouldn't even let me try?

"Mr. President?" Mr. Tate comes up now, carrying one of the Spackle's white sticks. "First report on the new weapons."

"Do tell, Captain," the Mayor says, looking very interested.

"They seem to be a sort of acid rifle," Mr. Tate says. "There's a chamber with what looks to be a mixture of two substances, probably botanic." He moves his hand up the white stick to a hole that's been cut into it. "Then a kind of ratchet aerates a dose and mixes it with a third substance that's instantly permeated through a gel via a small incendiary"—Mr. Tate points to the end of the stick—"and fired out here, vaporizing yet somehow holding cohesion until it hits its target, at which point—"

"At which point it's a burning acid corrosive enough to

96

take your arm off," the Mayor finishes. "Impressive work in a short space of time, Captain."

"I encouraged our chemists to work quickly, sir," Mr. Tate says with a grin I don't like.

"What the hell did all that mean?" I ask the Mayor as Mr. Tate leaves.

"Didn't you finish your chemistry in school?"

"You closed the school and burned all the books."

"Ah, so I did." He looks to the hilltop, to the glow we can see up above it in the spray from the waterfall, the glow from the campfires of the Spackle army. "They used to be just hunters and collectors, Todd, with some limited wild farming. Not exactly scientists."

"Which means what?"

"Which means," he says, "that our enemy has spent the thirteen years since the last war listening to us, learning from us, no doubt, on this planet of information." He taps his chin. "I wonder *how* they learn. If they're all part of some larger single voice."

"If you hadn't killed all the ones in town," I say, "you coulda *asked*."

He ignores me. "All of which adds up to the fact that our enemy gets more formidable by the moment."

I frown. "You sound almost happy."

Captain O'Hare comes back over to us, his hands full and his face sour. "Blankets and food, sir," he says. The Mayor nods toward me, forcing Mr. O'Hare to hand them over to me himself. He does and then storms away again, tho like Mr. Tate, you can't hear his Noise to see what's making him so mad.

I spread the blanket over Angharrad, but she still ain't saying nothing. Her wound is healing already, so it ain't that. She just stands there, head down, staring at the ground, not eating, not drinking, not responding to nothing I do.

"You could tie her up with the other horses, Todd," the Mayor says. "She'd at least be warmer that way."

"She needs me," I say. "I gotta stick by her."

He nods. "Your loyalty is admirable. A fine quality I've always noticed in you."

"Seeing as you don't got none at all?"

In reply, all he does is smile that smile again, that one that makes you want to knock his head right off. "You should eat and sleep while you can, Todd. You never know when the battle will need you."

"A battle you started," I say. "We wouldn't even be here if you hadn't—"

"Here we go again," he says, his voice sharper. "It's time you stopped whining about what might have been and start thinking about what *is*."

And this makes me a little mad—

And so I look at him—

And I think about what is—

I think about him falling in the ruins of the cathedral after I blasted him with Viola's name. I think about him shooting his own son without even pausing for thought—

"Todd—"

I think about him watching Viola struggle under the water in the Office of the Ask as he tortured her. I think about my ma talking about him in her journal when Viola read it to me and what he did to the women of old Prentisstown—

"That isn't true, Todd," he says. "That's not what happened–"

I think about the two men who raised me, who *loved* me, and how Cillian died on our farm to buy me time to escape and how Davy shot Ben on the roadside for doing exactly the same thing. I think about Manchee, my brilliant bloody dog, dying after saving me, too–

"Those were nothing to do with me–"

I think about the fall of Farbranch. I think about the people there being shot while the Mayor watched. I think about–

I AM THE CIRCLE AND THE CIRCLE IS ME.

He sends it, hard, straight into the middle of my head.

"Stop that!" I yell, flinching back.

"You give too much away, Todd Hewitt," he snaps, finally almost angry. "How do you ever expect to lead men if you broadcast every last sentiment?"

"I don't expect to lead men," I spit back.

"You were going to lead this army when you had me tied up, and if that day comes again, you'll need to keep your own counsel, now won't you? Have you kept up your practice with what I taught you?"

"I don't want nothing you could teach me."

"Oh, but you do." He steps closer. "I'll say it to you as often as it takes you to believe it: there's power in you, Todd Hewitt, power that could rule this planet."

"Power that could rule *you*."

He smiles again, but it's white hot. "Do you know how I keep my Noise from being heard, Todd?" he says, his voice all twisty and low. "Do you know how I keep everyone from hearing every last secret I've got?"

"No—"

He leans forward. "With as little effort as possible."

And I'm saying, "Get back!" but—

There it is again, right in my head, I AM THE CIRCLE AND THE CIRCLE IS ME—

But this time it's different—

There's a lightness—

A breath-stealing feeling—

A weightlessness to it that makes my stomach rise—

"I give you a gift," he says, his voice floating thru my head like a cloud on fire. "The same gift I've given to my captains. Use it. Use it to defeat me. I *dare* you."

I look into his eyes, into the blackness of them, the blackness that swallows me whole—

I AM THE CIRCLE AND THE CIRCLE IS ME.

And that's all I can hear in the whole world.

{VIOLA}

The town is eerily quiet as Acorn and I walk through it, some of it even silent, the people of New Prentisstown having fled into the cold night somewhere. I can't imagine how terrified they must be, not knowing what's happening or what might be waiting for them.

I look behind me as we ride through the empty square in front of the ruins of the cathedral. Hanging up there in the sky, above the still-standing bell tower, is another probe, keeping its distance from Spackle arrows but tracking me, watching me go.

But that's not all I've got.

Acorn and I make our way out of the square and down the road that leads to the battlefield, closer and closer to the army. Close enough so I can see them waiting there. They watch me as I ride up, soldiers sitting on their sleeping bags, huddled around fires. Their faces are tired and almost shocked, looking at me like I could be a ghost coming out of the darkness.

"Oh, Acorn," I whisper nervously. "I don't really have a plan here."

One of the soldiers stands as I approach, pointing his rifle at me. "Stop right there," he says. He's young, dirty-haired, with a fresh wound on his face, stitched badly by firelight.

"I want to see the Mayor," I say, trying to keep my voice steady.

"The who?"

"Who is it?" another soldier asks, standing up, too, also young, maybe even as young as Todd.

"One of them terrorists," the first one says. "Come here to set off a bomb."

"I'm not a terrorist," I say, glancing over their heads, trying to find Todd out there, trying to hear his Noise in the rising ROAR –

"Off the horse," the first soldier says. "Now."

"My name is Viola Eade," I say, Acorn shifting beneath me. "The Mayor, your *President*, knows me."

"I don't care what yer name is," says the first one. "Off the horse."

Girl colt, Acorn warns–

"I said, *off the horse!*"

I hear the cocking of a rifle, and I start yelling, *"Todd!"*

"I'm not warning you again!" says the soldier and other soldiers are standing now–

"TODD!" I shout again–

The second soldier grabs Acorn's reins and others are pressing forward. **Submit!** Acorn snarls, teeth bared, but the soldier just hits him in the head with his rifle–

"TODD!"

And hands are grabbing at me and Acorn's whinnying **Submit, submit!** but the soldiers are pulling me off the saddle and I'm holding on as hard as I can–

"Let her go," a voice says, cutting through all of the shouting, even though it doesn't sound raised at all.

The soldiers let me go at once, and I right myself on Acorn's saddle.

"Welcome, Viola," the Mayor says as a space opens between us.

"Where's Todd?" I say. "What have you done with him?"

And then I hear his voice–

"Viola?"

–a step behind the Mayor and pushing past him, shoving him hard in the shoulder as he forces his way toward me, his eyes wide and dazed, but here he comes–

"Viola," he says, reaching up to me, and he's smiling and I'm reaching for him, too–

But for a second, just a quick second, there's something weird about his Noise, something light, something vanishing–

For a second, I can barely hear it–

And then his feelings wash over it and he's Todd again and he grips me hard and says, "Viola."

"And then Simone said, *I've got a better idea,*" Viola says and opens the flap on the new bag she's carrying. She reaches in and takes out two flat metal things. They're small as skimming stones, curved and shiny, shaped perfectly to fit in yer palm. "Comms," she says. "You and I can talk to each other no matter where we are."

She reaches over and puts one in my hand—

—and I feel her fingers there for a second and I feel the relief all over again, the relief of seeing her, the relief of having her *here,* right here in front of me, even in the way her silence pulls at me still, even in the way she's still looking at me a bit funny—

It's my Noise she's looking at, I know it is.

I am the Circle and the Circle is me. He put it into my head, light and disappearing. Said it was a "teknique," something I could practice to make it so I could be just as silent as him and his captains.

And for a minute there, for a minute there I think I was—

"Comm one," she says into her comm and suddenly the metal on mine turns into a palm-sized screen filled with Viola's smiling face.

It's like I'm holding her right in my hand.

She shows me her comm with a little laugh and there's my own face, looking surprised.

"The signal's relayed through the probe," she says, pointing back toward the city, where a dot of light is hovering far down the road. "Simone's keeping it back so this one doesn't get shot down."

"Smart move," says the Mayor from where he's been standing nearby. "May I see one of those?"

"Nope," Viola says, not even looking at him. "If you do *this*," she says to me, pressing her comm at the edge, "you can talk to the scout ship, too. Simone?"

"I'm here," says a woman, popping up next to Viola on the screen in my hand. *"Are you okay down there? There was a minute where—"*

"I'm okay," says Viola. "I'm with Todd. This is him, by the way."

"Nice to meet you, Todd," says the woman.

"Uh," I say. "Hi?"

"I'll be back as soon as I can," Viola says to the woman.

"I'll be watching. And Todd?"

"Yeah?" I say, looking at the woman's little face.

"You take care of Viola, you hear?"

"Don't you worry," I say.

Viola presses her comm again and the faces disappear. She takes a long breath and gives me a tired smile. "So I leave you for five minutes and you go off and fight a *war*?" she says and she's saying it to be kinda funny but I wonder—

I wonder if seeing all that death is why she looks a little different to me. More *real*, more *there*, like it's just the most incredible thing in the world that we're both still *alive* and I feel my chest get all funny and tight and I think, *Here she is, right here, my Viola, she came for me, she's* here—

And I find myself thinking how I want to take her hand again and never let it go, to feel the skin of it, the warmth of it, hold it tight against my own hand and—

"Your Noise is funny," she says, looking at me strange again. "It's blurry. I can feel the feelings there"–and she looks away and my face goes red for no reason at all–"but it's hard to read clearly."

I'm about to tell her about the Mayor, about how I sorta blanked out for a minute but when I opened my eyes again, my Noise *was* lighter, *was* quieter–

I'm about to tell her this–

But she lowers her voice and leans in close. "Is it like with your horse?" she asks, cuz she saw how quiet Angharrad was when she rode up, Acorn not even able to get a herd-greeting out of her. "Is it because of what you saw?"

And that's enough to make the battle come rushing back to the front of my thoughts, rushing back in all its horror, and even if my Noise is blurry she must be able to tell cuz she takes my hand and it's just care and calm and I suddenly feel like I want to curl up into it for the rest of my life and just cry there forever and my eyes get wet and she sees and she breathes, *"Todd,"* with all her kindness and I have to look away from her again and somehow we both end up looking over at the Mayor, standing across the campfire, watching everything we do.

I hear her sigh. "Why'd you let him *go,* Todd?" she whispers.

"I didn't have no choice," I whisper back. "The Spackle were coming and the army was only gonna follow *him* into war."

"But it's probably him the Spackle want in the first place. They're only attacking because of the genocide."

"Yeah, well, I'm not all that sure about that," I say and

for the first time I let myself really think about 1017 again, about me breaking his arm once in anger, about pulling him from the pile of Spackle bodies, about how no matter what I did, good or bad, he still wanted me dead.

I look back at her. "What do we do now, Viola?"

"We stop the war is what we do," she says. "Mistress Coyle says there was a truce, so we try to get one again. Maybe Bradley and Simone can talk to the Spackle. Tell them we're not all like this."

"But what if they attack again before you can?" We look over to the Mayor again, who nods at us. "We're gonna need him to stop 'em from killing us in the meantime."

Viola frowns. "So he gets away with his crimes again. Because we need him."

"He's the one with the army," I say. "They follow *him*. Not me."

"And he follows you?"

I sigh. "That's the plan. He's kept his word so far."

"So far," she says quietly. Then she yawns and rubs her eyes with the heels of her hands. "I can't remember the last time I slept."

I look down at my own hand, no longer holding hers and remember what she said to Simone. "So yer going back?"

"I have to," she says. "I've got to find Mistress Coyle so she can't make it any worse."

I sigh again. "Okay. Remember what I said, tho. I ain't leaving you. Not even in my head."

And then she does take my hand again and she don't say nothing but she don't have to cuz I know, I *know* her and she knows me and we sit there for a little while more but then there's nothing for it and she has to go. She gets stiffly to her feet. Acorn gives one last nuzzle to Angharrad, then comes back over to pick Viola up.

"I'll tell you how I'm doing," she says, holding up the comm. "Tell you where I am. I'll be back as soon as I can."

"Viola?" the Mayor says, stepping over from the campfire as she climbs on Acorn's saddle.

Viola rolls her eyes. *"What?"*

"I was wondering, please," he says, like he was just asking to borrow an egg, "if you could kindly tell the people on your ship that I will happily meet them at their earliest convenience."

"Yeah, I'll be sure to do that," she says. "And in return, let me say this." She points back at the probe, still hanging there in the distant sky. "We're watching you. You lay a hand on Todd, and there are weapons on that ship that will blow you to smithereens just because I tell them to."

And I swear the Mayor's smile just gets bigger.

Viola gives me a last, long look, but then she's on her way, back thru the city, back to find wherever Mistress Coyle might be hiding.

"She's quite a girl," the Mayor says, stepping up beside me.

"Yer not allowed to talk about her," I say. "Not never."

He lets that slide by. "It's almost dawn," he says. "You should get some rest. It's been a big day."

"One I don't wanna repeat."

"I'm afraid there's nothing we can do about that."

"Yes, there is," I say, feeling better now that Viola's said there might be a way outta this. "We're gonna make a truce

107

with the Spackle again. You just need to hold 'em back till we do."

"Is that so?" he says, sounding amused.

"Yes," I say, a little harder.

"That's not quite how it works, Todd. They won't be interested in talking to you if they think they're in a position of strength. Why would they want peace if they're certain they can annihilate us?"

"But–"

"Don't worry, Todd. I know this war. I know how to *win* this war. You show your enemy you can beat him and then you can have any kind of peace you want."

I start to say something back but I'm finally too tired to argue. I can't remember the last time I slept neither.

"You know something, Todd?" the Mayor says to me. "I could swear your Noise is a bit quieter."

And–

I AM THE CIRCLE AND THE CIRCLE IS ME.

He sends into my head again, with that same lightness, that same floating feeling–

That same feeling that makes my Noise disappear–

The feeling I didn't tell Viola about–

(cuz it makes the screaming of the war disappear, too, makes it so I don't gotta see all the dying over and over–)

(and is there something else there, too?)

(a low *hum* behind the lightness–)

"You stay outta my head," I say. "I told you if you tried to control me, I'd–"

"I'm not in your head, Todd," he says. "That's the beauty of it. It's all you. Practice it. It's a gift."

"I don't want no gift from you."

"I'm sure that's the case entirely," he says, still smiling.

"Mr. President?" It's Mr. Tate interrupting again.

"Ah, yes, Captain," the Mayor says. "Are the first spy reports in?"

"Not yet," Mr. Tate says. "We expect them just after dawn."

"When they'll tell us there's limited movement to the north above the river, which is too wide for Spackle troops to cross, and to the south along the ridge of hills, which is too remote for the Spackle to use effectively." The Mayor looks back up to the hill. "No, they'll attack us from there. Of that I have no doubt."

"That's not why I've come, sir," Mr. Tate says, and he holds up an armful of folded cloth. "It took a while to find in the wreckage of the cathedral, but it's surprisingly unsullied."

"Excellent, Captain," the Mayor says, taking the cloth from him, real pleasure in his voice. "Most excellent indeed."

"What is it?" I ask.

With a snap of his hands, the Mayor unfurls the cloth and holds it up. It's a smart-looking jacket and matching trousers.

"My general's uniform," he says.

Mr. Tate and me and all the soldiers nearby at their campfires watch as he takes off his blood- and dust-stained regular jacket and puts on a perfectly fitted dark blue one with a gold stripe running down each sleeve. He smoothes it with his palms and looks back up at me, that amused twinkle still in his eye.

"Let the battle for peace commence."

{ V I O L A }

Acorn and I go back up the road and across through the square, the distant sky getting a pink tinge as dawn approaches.

I watched Todd as I left until I could no longer see him. I'm worried about him, worried about his Noise. Even when I left, it still had the strange blurriness to it, where it was hard to see details but was still just *vivid* with feelings–

(–even *those* feelings, the ones that were there for a minute before he got embarrassed, the physical feelings, the ones without words, the ones concentrated right on my skin, of how he wanted to touch it more, those feelings that made me want to–)

–and I wonder again if he's in the same shock as Angharrad, if what he saw in battle was so bad, it somehow made him unable to even *see* it, even in his Noise, and my heart just breaks at the thought of it–

Another reason for no more war.

I pull the coat Simone gave me tighter. It's cold and I'm shivering, but I can also feel myself sweating, which I know from my healer training means I have a fever. I pull up my left sleeve and look underneath the bandage. The skin around the band is still angry and red.

And now there are red streaks from it reaching down to my wrist.

Streaks that I know mean infection. Bad infection.

Infection that's not being knocked back by the bandage.

I pull the sleeve back down and try not to think about it. Try not to think that I didn't tell Todd how bad it was either.

Because I've still got to find Mistress Coyle.

"Well," I say to Acorn, "she's always talking about the ocean. I wonder if it's really as far away as she-"

I jump as the comm beeps suddenly in my pocket.

"Todd?" I say, answering it immediately.

But it's Simone.

"You'd better come straight back here," she says.

"Why?" I say, alarmed. "What's happened?"

"I've found your Answer."

Before

THE SUN IS ABOUT TO RISE as I take some food from the cookfires. Members of the Land watch as I collect a pan and fill it with stew. Their voices are open—they could hardly be closed and still be members of the Land—so I can hear them discussing me, their thoughts spreading one to the other, forming one opinion, then a contrary one and back again, all so fast I can barely follow it.

And then they come to a decision. One of the Land rises to her feet to offer me a large bone spoon so that I do not merely have to drink the stew from the bowl, and behind her I can hear the Land's voices, their *voice,* offering it to me in friendship.

I reach out to take it.

Thank you, I say, in the language of the Burden—

And there it is again, the slight discomfort at the language I speak, the distaste at something so alien, so *individual,* so representative of something shameful. It is quickly bundled away and argued against in the swirling voice, but it was definitely there for an instant.

I do not take the spoon. I hear their voices calling after me in apology as I walk away, but I do not turn around. Instead, I walk to a path I have found and start my way up the rocky hill by the side of the road.

The Land has mostly made its camp along the flat of the road, but I see others on the hillside as I climb, others from areas where the Land lives in mountains and who are more comfortable on the steepness. Likewise down below, there are those from where the Land lives near rivers who sleep in quickly made boats.

But then, the Land is all one, is it not? The Land has no *others,* it has no *they* or *those.*

There is only one Land.

And I am the one who stands outside it.

I reach a point where the hill becomes so steep I have to pull myself up. I see an outcropping where I can sit and look at the Land below me, much as the Land can look over the lip of the hill and see the Clearing.

A place where I can be alone.

I should not be alone.

My one in particular should be here with me, eating our meals together as the dawn slowly brightens, fighting off sleep, waiting for the next phase of the war side by side.

But my one in particular is not here.

Because my one in particular was killed by the Clearing as the Burden were first rounded up from back gardens and basements, from locked rooms and servant's quarters. My one in particular and I were kept in a garden shed, and when the shed door was opened that night, my one in particular fought. Fought for me. Fought to keep them from taking me.

And was brought down by a heavy blade.

I was dragged away making the inadequate clicking sound the Clearing left us with after forcing us to take its "cure," a sound that said *nothing* of what it was like to be torn from my one in particular and thrown into a gathered band of the Burden, who had to hold me down to keep me from running back to the shed.

To keep me from being cut down myself.

I hated the Burden for that. Hated them for not letting me die there and then, when my grief was not quite enough to kill me on its own. Hated them for the way they—

For the way *we* accepted our fates, the way we went where we were told, ate what we were told, slept where we were told. In all that time, we fought back once, only once. Against the Knife and the other one with him, the loud one who was bigger but seemed younger. We fought when the Knife's friend strapped a band around one of our necks for pure, cruel fun.

For a moment, in silence, the Burden understood each other again. For a moment we were truly one again, connected.

Not alone.

And we fought.

And some of us died.

And we did not fight again.

Not when a group of the Clearing returned with rifles and blades. Not when they lined us up and began to kill us. Shooting us, hacking at us, making that high stuttering sound they call *laughing*. Killing the old and the young, mothers and babies, fathers and sons. If we tried to resist, we were killed. If we did not resist, we were killed. If we tried to run, we were killed. If we did not run, we were killed.

One after the other after the other after the other.

With no way to share our fear. No way to coordinate and try to protect ourselves. No way to be comforted as we died.

And so we died alone. Every one of us.

Everyone but one.

Everyone but 1017.

Before the killing began, they looked at our bands until they found me, and they dragged me to a wall and made me watch. Watch as the clicks of the Burden grew fewer and fewer, as the grass grew stickier with our blood, as at last I was the only Burden left alive on this entire world.

And then they clubbed me on the head and I awoke in a pile of bodies with faces that I recognized, hands that had touched mine in comfort, mouths that had shared their food, eyes that had tried to share their terror.

I woke up, alone among the dead, and they pressed on me, suffocated me.

And then the Knife was there.

Is here now—

Is pulling me from the bodies of the Burden—

116

And we tumble to the ground and I fall away from him—

We stare at each other, our breaths making clouds in the cold—

His voice is open wide with pain and horror at what he sees—

The pain and horror he always feels—

The pain and horror that always threatens to topple him over—

But never does.

"Yer *alive*," he says, and he is so *relieved*, so *happy*, to see me in the middle of all that death where I am alone and alone and alone forever, he is so happy that I vow to kill him—

And then he asks me about his own one in particular—

Asking if, among all the killing of my own kind, I have seen one of *his*—

And my vow becomes unbreakable—

I show him I will kill him—

In the weakness of my returning voice, I show him I will kill him—

And I will—

I will do it now, I will do it *right now*—

You are safe, says a voice—

I am on my feet, my fists swinging in panic.

They are caught easily by the Sky in his larger hands, and as I pull back from the shock of the dream, I nearly topple off the outcropping. He has to catch me again, but his hand grabs the band and I cry out as he pulls me upright, his voice instantly surrounding the pain in mine, wrapping it away, lessening it, holding it until the fire in my arm calms down.

It remains so painful? the Sky asks gently in the language of the Burden.

I am breathing heavily, from the surprise of being woken, from the surprise of finding the Sky near me, from the surprise of the pain. *It does,* is all I can show for the moment.

I am sorry we have been unable to heal it, he shows. *The Land will redouble its efforts.*

The Land's efforts are better used elsewhere, I show. *It is a poison of the Clearing, meant for their animals. It is probably only within their power to cure.*

The Land learns much in the ways of the Clearing, the Sky shows. *We hear their voice even when they do not hear ours. And we learn.* His voice rises with real feeling. *We will save the Return.*

I do not need saving, I show.

You do not **want** *saving, which is a different matter. One which will also occupy the Land.*

The pain in my arm is easing and I rub my face, trying to wake myself up.

I did not mean to sleep, I show. *I wish never to sleep until the Clearing are gone from here.*

And only then will your dreams know peace? the Sky shows, bemused.

You do not understand, I show. *You cannot.*

Again, I feel the warmth of him encircling my voice. *The Return is incorrect. The Sky can share the past in the Return's voice, that is the nature of the voice of the Land, that all experience is as one, that nothing is forgotten, that all things are—*

It is not the same as being there, I interrupt, conscious again of the rudeness. *A memory is not the thing remembered.*

He pauses again, but the warmth remains. *Perhaps not,* he finally shows.

What is it that you want? I show, a bit too loud, feeling shamed by his kindness.

He places a hand on my shoulder and we look out to the Land stretched beneath us down the road, on the right to the very tip of the hill that looks out over the Clearing, on the left back as far as can be seen, past a bend in the river and farther beyond that, I know.

The Land rests, shows the Sky. *The Land waits. Waits for the Return.*

I show nothing.

You are one of the Land, he shows. *However separate you feel now. But that is not all the Land waits for this day.*

I look over to him. *Is there a change? Will we be attacking?*

Not yet, he shows, *but there are a number of ways to fight a war.*

And then he opens his voice and shows me what is seen in the eyes of others in the Land—

Of others in the light of the newly rising sun as it reaches the deeper valley—
And I see.
I see what is to come.
And I feel my own small flicker of warmth.

THE STORM

"CAN YOU THINK of a safer place, my girl?" Mistress Coyle says.

After Simone's call, Acorn and I rode fast straight back to the hilltop.

Where the Answer now makes camp.

The cold sun is rising on an open area filled with carts and people and the first makings of campfires. They've already organized a mess tent where Mistress Nadari and Mistress Lawson are busy coordinating supplies and rationing food, blue A's still written across the front of their clothes and on a few scattered faces throughout the crowd. Magnus and other people I recognize are starting to set up tents, and I wave over at Wilf, who's taking charge of the Answer's animals. His wife, Jane, is with him, and she waves back so vigorously it looks like she might hurt herself.

"Your friends may not want to get involved in a war," Mistress Coyle says, eating her breakfast on the back of the cart where she's made her bed, parked near the bay doors of the scout ship. "But if the Mayor or the Spackle decide to attack, I'd imagine they'd be willing to protect themselves."

"You've got some nerve," I say angrily, still up on Acorn.

"Yes, I do have some nerve," she says, taking another bite of porridge, "because some nerve is exactly what's going to keep my people alive."

"Until you decide to sacrifice them again."

Her eyes flare at that. "You think you know me. You call me bad and evil and a tyrant and yes, I've made tough decisions, but they were decisions with only one aim, Viola. Getting rid of that man and returning to the Haven we had before. *Not* slaughter for its own sake. *Not* the sacrifice of good people for no reason. But, as it turns out, the same goal as you, my girl. *Peace.*"

"You've got a pretty warlike way of going about it."

"I've got an *adult* way of going about it," she says. "A way that isn't nice or pretty, but that gets the job done." She looks at someone behind me. "Morning."

"Morning," Simone says, coming down the ramp from the scout ship.

"How is he?" I ask her.

"Talking to the convoy," she says, "seeing if they have any medical advice." She crosses her arms. "None so far."

"I don't have any cure left," Mistress Coyle says, "but there are natural remedies that can help take the edge off."

"You stay away from him," I say.

"I am a *healer*, Viola," she says, "whether you like it or not. I'd even like to heal *you*, as I can see from a glance that you're feverish."

122

Simone looks at me, concerned. "She's right, Viola. You don't look well."

"This woman is never going to touch me," I say. "Ever again."

Mistress Coyle sighs heavily. "Not even to let me make amends, my girl? Not even as a first peaceful gesture between us?"

I look at her, wondering about her, remembering how well she healed, how hard she fought for Corinne's life, how she managed through sheer willpower to turn a band of healers and stragglers into an army that might have toppled the Mayor, just like she said, had the Spackle not come.

But I remember the bombs, too.

I remember the last bomb.

"You tried to kill me."

"I tried to kill *him*," she says. "There is a difference."

"Got room for more up here?" says a voice behind us.

We all turn. It's a dust-covered man with a ragged uniform and a sly look in his eyes. A look I recognize.

"Ivan?" I say.

"I woke up at the cathedral and there was a war a-going on," he says.

I see other men behind him, heading for the food tent, the men who tried to help me and Todd overthrow the Mayor, the ones knocked unconscious in the Mayor's Noise attack, Ivan the last to fall.

I'm not actually sure I'm pleased to see him.

"Todd always said you went where the power was," I say.

His eyes flash. "It's what's kept me alive."

"You're very welcome here," Mistress Coyle says, like she's

in charge. Ivan nods and heads off to feed himself. I look back at her, and I can see her smiling at what I'd said about power.

Because he came to her, didn't he?

[TODD]

"It's the smart thing to do," the Mayor says. "It's what I would do in her place. Try to get our new residents on her side."

Viola called me first thing and told me all about the Answer showing up on the hilltop. I found myself seeing if I could hide it from the Mayor, trying to keep my Noise light, trying to do it without any effort at all.

He still heard me.

"There ain't no *sides*," I say. "There can't be no more. It's all of us against the Spackle now."

The Mayor just makes an *mmm* sound with his throat.

"Mr. President?" It's Mr. O'Hare with another report. The Mayor reads it, his gaze hungry.

Cuz nothing's happened yet. I think he expected a new battle at first light but the cold sun rose and nothing happened and now it's closer to midday and still nothing. Like all that fighting yesterday never happened.

(except it did–)

(except it's *still* happening in my head–)

(*I am the Circle and the Circle is me,* I think, light as I can–)

"Not particularly illuminating," the Mayor says to Mr. O'Hare.

"There's reports of possible movement to the south–"

The Mayor shoves the papers back at Mr. O'Hare,

cutting him off. "Do you know, Todd, if they chose to come at us with full numbers, there'd be nothing we could do? Our weapons would eventually run out of ammunition, our men would eventually die, and there would still be more than enough of them left to wipe us out." He clicks his teeth together in thought. "So why aren't they coming?" He turns to Mr. O'Hare. "Tell the men to go in closer."

Mr. O'Hare looks surprised. "But, sir—"

"We need to know," the Mayor says.

Mr. O'Hare stares at him for a second, then says, "Yes, sir," before leaving, but you can tell he's unhappy about it.

"Maybe the Spackle don't think the way you do," I say. "Maybe their goal ain't just war."

He laughs. "Forgive me, Todd, but you do not know our enemy."

"Maybe you don't neither. Not as much as you think."

He stops laughing. "I beat them before," he says. "I will beat them again, even if they're better, even if they're smarter." He brushes some dust off his general's trousers. "They will attack, mark my words, and when they do, I will beat them."

"And then we'll make peace," I say firmly.

"Yes, Todd," he says. "Whatever you say."

"Sir?" It's Mr. Tate this time.

"What is it?" the Mayor says, turning to him.

But Mr. Tate ain't looking at us. He's looking *past* us, across the army, where the **ROAR** of the men is changing as they see it, too.

The Mayor and I turn to look.

And for a second, I truly don't believe my eyes.

{ VIOLA }

"I really think Mistress Coyle should have a look at this, Viola," Mistress Lawson says, her worried hands rebandaging my arm.

"You're doing fine on your own," I say.

We're back in the little makeshift healing room on the scout ship. As the morning went on, I really did start to feel unwell and sought out Mistress Lawson, who nearly fell over herself with concern when she saw me. Barely pausing to get permission from Simone, she dragged me aboard and set about reading the instructions for every new tool they landed with.

"These are the strongest antibiotics I found," she says, finishing the new bandage. It feels cool as the medicine sinks in, though the red streaks are now stretching in both directions from the band. "All we can do now is wait."

"Thank you," I say, but she barely hears me as she goes back to inventorying the scout ship's medical supplies. She was always the kindest of the mistresses, tiny and round and in charge of healing the children of Haven, always the one who wanted more than anything to stop other people from suffering.

I leave her to it and head back down the ramp from the bay doors onto the hilltop, where the Answer's camp is already looking almost permanent with the hawklike shadow of the scout ship watching over them. There are rows of orderly tents and fires, supply areas and meeting places. In barely the space of a morning, it looks almost like the camp they had back at the mine when I first joined up with them.

Some of them were happy to greet me when I walked through it, but some wouldn't speak to me at all, unsure of my place in all this.

I'm not too sure of my place in it either.

I had Mistress Lawson treat me because I'm going back down to see Todd, though I'm so tired right now, I'm not sure I won't fall asleep in the saddle. I've already talked to him twice this morning. His voice on the comm is tinny and distant, and his Noise is muffled, overwhelmed on the tiny comm speakers by the Noise of the army around him.

But seeing his face helps.

"Are these all friends of yours, then?" Bradley says, coming down the ramp behind me.

"Hey!" I say, walking right into his hug. "How are you feeling?"

Loud, his Noise says and he gives a little smile, but it actually is a bit calmer today, less panicky.

"You *will* get used to it," I say. "I promise."

"As much as I might not want to."

He brushes a strand of hair away from my eyes. **So grown up,** his Noise is saying. **And looks so pale.** And he shows a picture of me from last year, learning a math segment in the classes he taught. I look so small, so *clean,* that I have to laugh.

"Simone's been speaking with the convoy," he says. "They agree with the peaceful approach. We try to meet with these Spackle and offer humanitarian help to the people here, but the last thing we want to do is get involved in a war that has nothing to do with us." His hand squeezes my shoulder. "You were right to want to keep us out of it, Viola."

127

"I just wish I knew what to do now," I say, turning away from his praise, remembering how close I came to choosing the other way. "I've been trying to get Mistress Coyle to talk to me about how the first truce worked but–

I stop because we both see someone running across the hilltop, looking this way and that, searching each face, then seeing the ship, seeing *me* and running even faster–

"Who's that?" Bradley asks, but I'm already pulling away from him–

Because it's–

"LEE!" I shout and start running toward him–

Viola, his Noise is saying, **Viola, Viola, Viola,** and he reaches me and spins me around in a breath-squeezing embrace that makes my arm ache. "Thank God!"

"Are you okay?" I'm saying as he lets me go. "Where'd you–?"

"The river!" he says, his breath heaving. "What's happening to the river?"

He looks over to Bradley and back to me. His Noise gets louder; so does his voice. *"Haven't you seen the river?"*

[TODD]

"But *how?*" I say, staring up at the falls–

Staring as they get quieter and quieter–

Staring as they start to disappear altogether–

The Spackle are turning off the river.

"Very clever," the Mayor is saying to himself. "Very clever indeed."

"What is?" I nearly shout at him. "What are they *doing?*"

Every man in the army is watching it now, ROARing loud about it like you wouldn't believe, watching as the falls trickle back just exactly like someone turning down a tap, with the river below shrinking, too, miles of mud popping up where riverbank used to be.

"No word from our spies, Captain O'Hare?" the Mayor says in a voice that ain't happy.

"None, sir," Mr. O'Hare says. "If there's a dam, it's back quite a ways."

"Then we need to find out exactly, *don't* we?"

"Now, sir?"

The Mayor turns to him, fury-eyed. Mr. O'Hare just salutes and leaves quickly.

"What's going *on*?" I say.

"They want a siege, Todd," the Mayor says. "Instead of a battle, they take away our water and wait until we're so weak they can walk right over us." His voice sounds almost angry. "This isn't what they were supposed to do, Todd. And we will *not* let them get away with it. Captain Tate!"

"Yes, sir," says Mr. Tate, who's been waiting and watching with us.

"Get the men in battle formations."

Mr. Tate looks surprised. "Sir?"

"Is there a problem with your orders, Captain?"

"The uphill battle, sir. You said yourself–"

"That was before the enemy declined to play by the rules." His words start filling the air, twirling around and slipping into the heads of the soldiers around the edge of our camp–

"Every man will do his duty," the Mayor says. "Every man

will fight until the battle is won. They won't be expecting us to come at them so hard and surprise will win us the day. Is that clear?"

Mr. Tate says, "Yes, sir," and heads off into the army, shouting orders, while the soldiers nearest us are already gearing up and making lines.

"Prepare yourself, Todd," the Mayor says, watching him go. "This is the day we settle it."

{VIOLA}

"How?" Simone says. "How did they do it?"

"Can you send the probe back upriver?" Mistress Coyle asks.

"They'd just shoot it down again," Bradley says, dialing some more on the probe's remote panel. We're gathered around the three-dimensional projection, Bradley aiming it under the shadow cast by the wing of the ship. Me, Simone, Bradley, and Lee, with Mistress Coyle and more and more people from the Answer crowding in as word spreads.

"There," Bradley says, and the projection gets even bigger.

There are gasps in the crowd. The river's almost completely dry. There's almost no waterfall at all. The picture rises a bit, but all we can see is the river drying up above the falls as well, the Spackle army a white- and clay-colored mass on the road to the side.

"Are there other sources of water?" Simone asks.

"A few," Mistress Coyle says, "streams and ponds here and there, but . . ."

"We're in trouble," Simone says. "Aren't we?"

Lee turns to her, perplexed. "You think our trouble is just starting *now*?"

"I told you not to underestimate them," Mistress Coyle says to Bradley.

"No," Bradley replies, "*you* told us to bomb them into oblivion, without even trying for peace first."

"And you're saying I was wrong?"

Bradley dials on the remote screen again, and the probe rises higher in the sky, showing even more of the Spackle army stretching down the road in their thousands. There are further gasps behind us as the Answer sees for the first time how big the Spackle army is.

"We couldn't kill them all," Bradley says. "We'd only be guaranteeing our own doom."

"What's the Mayor doing?" I ask, my voice tight.

Bradley changes the projection angle again, and we see the army sorting itself into lines.

"No," Mistress Coyle whispers. "He can't be."

"Can't be what?" I say. "Can't be *what*?"

"Attacking," she answers. "It'd be suicide."

My comm beeps and I answer it immediately. "Todd?"

"*Viola?*" he says, his worried face in my hand.

"What's going on?" I say. "Are you all right?"

"*The river, Viola, the river's—*"

"We can see it. We're watching it right—"

"*The falls!*" he says. "*They're in the falls!*"

131

[TODD]

There's a line of lights in the shadows under the disappearing falls, stretching down the path Viola and I once took when we were running from Aaron, a watery, slippery stone path under the crashing wall of water that led to an abandoned church stretched across a ledge. The inside wall was marked with a white circle and two smaller circles orbiting it, this planet and its two moons, and you can see it glowing there, too, above the line of lights gathered across the rocky face of what's now just a wet cliff.

"Can you see 'em?" I say to Viola thru the comm.

"Hold on," she says.

"Do you still have those binos, Todd?" the Mayor says.

I'd forgotten I'd taken them back from him. I run over to where Angharrad's still standing silently next to my stuff.

"Don't you worry," I say to her, digging thru my bag. "I'll keep you safe."

I find the binos and don't even go back to the Mayor before I put 'em up to my eyes. I hit some buttons and zoom in—

"We see them now, Todd," Viola says from the comm in my other hand. *"It's a bunch of Spackle on that ledge we ran down—"*

"I know," I say. "I see 'em, too."

"What do you see, Todd?" the Mayor says, coming over to me.

"What are they holding?" Viola asks.

"A kind of bow," I say, "but those don't look like—"

"Todd!" she says and I look up above the binos—

132

One speck of light is leaving the line from the falls, flying out from under the church symbol in a slow arc down the riverbed–

"What is it?" says the Mayor. "It's too big for an arrow."

I look back thru the binos, trying to find the light, coming closer by the second–

There it is–

It looks like it's wavering, flickering in and out–

We all turn as it flies down the river, as it takes a rounded path over the last trickles of water–

"Todd?" Viola says.

"What *is* it, Todd?" the Mayor growls at me.

And I see thru the binos–

As its path curves in the air–

And starts heading back toward the army–

Back toward us–

That it ain't flickering after all–

It's *spinning*–

And that the light ain't just light–

It's *fire*–

"We need to get back," I say, keeping the binos to my eyes. "We need to get back into the city."

"It's heading right for you, Todd!" Viola's screaming–

The Mayor can't help it no more and tries to yank the binos from my hand–

"Hey!" I yell–

And I punch him in the side of his face–

He staggers back, more surprised than hurt–

And it's the screaming that makes us turn round–

The spinning fire has reached the army–

The crowd of soldiers is trying to part, trying to get away as it flies toward 'em–

Flies toward *us*–

Flies toward *me*–

But there's too many soldiers, too many people in the way–

And the spinning fire comes blazing thru 'em–

Right at head height–

And the first soldiers it hits are blasted nearly in two–

And it ain't *stopping*–

It ain't *effing stopping*–

The spinning don't even drop speed–

It rips thru the soldiers like matches being struck–

Destroying the men directly in its way–

And engulfing the men on either side in a sticky, white fire–

And it's *still* flying–

Still as fast as it was–

Coming right toward me–

Right toward me and the Mayor–

And there ain't nowhere to run–

"Viola!" I yell–

{ V I O L A }

"Todd!" I yell into the comm as we watch the fire curve through the air and slam into a group of soldiers–

Through a group of soldiers–

Screams start rising in the air behind us from people seeing the projection–

The fire slices through the army as easy as someone drawing a line with a pen, curving as it goes, tearing the soldiers to pieces, sending them flying, coating everything it even comes close to in fire—

"Todd!" I shout into the comm. *"Get out of there!"*

But I can't see his face anymore, just the fire cutting a path in the projection, killing everything in the way, and then—

Then it *rises*—

"What the hell?" Lee says next to me—

It rises up above the army, out of the crowd, out of the men it was killing—

"It's still curving," Bradley says.

"What *is* it?" Simone asks Mistress Coyle.

"I've never seen it before," Mistress Coyle answers, her eyes not leaving the projection. "The Spackle obviously haven't been idle."

"Todd?" I say into my comm.

But he doesn't answer.

Bradley draws a square with his thumb on the remote and a box appears in the projection, surrounding the fiery thing and enlarging it out to one side of the main picture. He dials some more and the image slows down. The fire burns on a spinning bladed S, so bright and ferocious it's hard to even look at it—

"It's going back to the falls!" Lee says, pointing back to the main projection, where the fiery thing has risen up out of the army, still curving, still flying viciously fast. We watch as it lifts higher in the air, completing one long circle, rising up the zigzag hill, heading toward the ledge under the now-dry falls, still spinning and burning. We can see the Spackle there now, dozens of them holding more burning blades at the end of their bows. They don't flinch as the flying one heads right toward them, and we see a Spackle with an empty bow, the one who fired the first shot–

We watch as he flips his bow up, revealing a curved hook at the bottom end, and with perfect timing he snatches the flying S right out of the air, turning it with a practiced motion, and immediately it's reset, ready to fire again, tall as the body of the Spackle itself.

In the reflected light of the fire, we see that the Spackle's hands, arms, and body are covered in a thick, flexible clay, protecting him from the burning.

"Todd?" I say, into the comm. "Are you there? You need to run, Todd! You need to *run*–"

And in the larger view, we can see all the Spackle raising their bows–

"Todd!" I yell. *"Answer me!"*

And as one–

They all fire–

[TODD]

"VIOLA!" I scream–

But I don't got the comm no more, the binos neither–

They were knocked outta my hands by a wall of running soldiers, pushing and shoving and screaming–

And burning–

The spinning fire ripped a curve thru the men right in front of me, killing 'em so fast they barely knew what happened and setting 'em alight in two or three rows on either side–

And just as it was about to take off my own head–

It lifted–

Up into the air–

Curving round–

And flying back to the ledge where it came from–

I whirl round now to see where I can run–

And then, over the shouting of the soldiers–

I hear Angharrad screaming–

And I'm pushing back and hitting out and shoving men aside to get to my horse–

"Angharrad!" I yell. "ANGHARRAD!"

And I can't see her–

But I hear her screaming in terror–

I push forward even harder–

And I feel a hand on my collar–

"No, Todd!" the Mayor shouts, pulling me back–

"I've got to get to her!" I shout back and yank away from him–

"We have to run!" he yells–

And this is so completely something the Mayor would never say I spin round to look at him–

But his eyes are on the falls–

And I look, too–

And–

And–

Holy God–

An expanding arc of fire is racing out from the ledge–

The Spackle have fired every single bow–

Dozens of 'em–

Dozens of 'em that'll reduce the army to nothing but ash and bodies–

"Come on!" the Mayor's yelling, grabbing me again. *"To the city!"*

But I see a break in the men—

I see Angharrad rearing up in fright—

Her eyes wide open at the hands grabbing her—

And I lunge toward her—

Away from the Mayor—

Soldiers filling the space twixt us—

"I'm here, girl!" I yell, pressing forward—

But she's just screaming and screaming—

I reach her and I knock back a soldier trying to climb into her saddle—

And the spinning fires are getting closer and closer—

Curving both ways, this time—

Coming from either side—

And the men are running in every direkshun, up the road to the town, into where the river's trickling away, even back to the zigzag hill—

And I say, "You have to *run*, girl!"

And the spinning fires reach us—

{ V I O L A }

"Todd!" I scream again and I see the fires zooming in over the river and some coming round the other way, curving along the hills of the valley—

Coming at the army from both sides—

"Where is he?" I yell. "Can you see him?"

"I can't see anything in this mess," Bradley says.

"We have to do something!" I say.

Mistress Coyle catches my eye. She's searching my face, searching it hard–

"Todd?" I say into the comm. "Answer me, *please*!"

"They've reached the army!" Lee yells.

And we all look back at the projection–

Where the spinning fires are slashing through the fleeing army in all directions–

They're going to reach Todd–

They're going to kill him–

They're going to kill every man down there–

"We have to stop this!" I say.

"Viola," Bradley says, a warning in his voice.

"Stop it how?" Simone says, and I can see her considering it again.

"Yes, Viola," Mistress Coyle says, staring right into my eyes. "Stop it how?"

I look back in the projection, back at the army burning and dying–

"They'll kill your boy," Mistress Coyle says, like she's reading my mind. "No two ways about it this time."

And she can see my face–

See me thinking it–

Thinking it again–

Thinking about all that death.

"No," I whisper. "We can't–"

Can we?

[TODD]

WHOOSH!

One spinning fire flies right by us on our left and I see the head taken off a soldier trying to duck–

I pull on Angharrad's reins but she rears up again in panic, her eyes wide and white, her Noise just a high-pitched scream I can barely stand–

And another fire *WHOOSHES* across the path in front of us, spilling flames everywhere, and Angharrad's so terrified she lifts me off my feet by the reins and we fall back into a crowd of soldiers–

"THIS WAY!" I hear yelled behind us.

The Mayor, screaming, as a spinning fire makes a wall of flames outta the soldiers just behind me and Angharrad–

And when he yells it, it's like I feel a *pull* in my feet, almost turning me round to face him–

But I force myself back to Angharrad–

"Come *on*, girl!" I yell, trying to get her moving, any way, *anyhow–*

"TODD! LEAVE HER!"

I turn and I see the Mayor, somehow back up on Morpeth, leaping twixt men and racing out from under a spinning fire as it rises back into the sky–

"TO THE CITY!" he shouts at the soldiers–

Planting it in their Noises–

Planting it in mine–

Throbbing thru it with a low *hum–*

And I knock him back again in my head–

But the soldiers near him are running even faster–

I look up and see the spinning fires still cutting thru the sky like swooping birds–

But they're heading back to the ledge–

There are burning men everywhere but the army that's still alive is also noticing that the fires are going back–

That we've got a few seconds before they come again–

And the men are reaching the city now, the first ones heading up the road, running where the Mayor's yelling–

"TODD! YOU'VE GOT TO RUN!"

But Angharrad's still screaming, still pulling away from me, still flailing in terror–

And my heart's ripping in two–

"COME ON, GIRL!"

"TODD!" shouts the Mayor–

But I ain't leaving Angharrad–

"I AIN'T LEAVING HER!" I shout back at him–

Dammit, I *ain't*–

I left Manchee–

I left him behind–

And I ain't doing it again–

"*TODD!*"

And I look back–

And he's away from me, peeling back to the city–

With the rest of the men–

And me and Angharrad are being left alone in the emptying camp–

"We are *not* firing a missile," Bradley says, his Noise roaring. "That decision has already been made."

"You have *missiles*?" Lee says. "Why the hell aren't you using them?"

"Because we want to make peace with this species!" Bradley shouts. "If we fire, the consequences would be disastrous!"

"They're disastrous right *now*," Mistress Coyle says.

"Disastrous to an army *you* wanted us to fight," Bradley says. "Disastrous for the army that brought on the attack!"

"Bradley–" Simone says.

He spins round to her, his Noise filled with incredibly rude words. "We have nearly five thousand people that are our responsibility. You really want them to wake up to find we've thrown them into an unwinnable war?"

"You're already *in* the war!" Lee says.

"No, we're *not*!" Bradley says even louder. "And *because* we're not, we might just be able to get the rest of you *out* of it!"

"All you have to do is show them they've got more than just cannons to worry about," Mistress Coyle says, strangely, to *me*, rather than Bradley or Simone. "We negotiated peace with them the first time, my girl, because we were in a position of strength. That's how wars work; that's how *truces* work. We show them we've got more power than they imagine and they're more willing to make peace."

"And then they come back in five years' time when *they've* gotten stronger and kill every human here," Bradley says.

142

"Five years' time where we can build bridges with them and make sure a new war isn't necessary," Mistress Coyle says back.

"Which you obviously did a *fantastic* job of last time!"

"What are you waiting for? Fire the missile!" Ivan calls from the crowd and more voices join around him, too.

"Todd," I whisper to myself and I look back at the projection–

The burning fires are flying back to the falls again, being caught and reloaded–

And then I *see* him–

"He's alone!" I yell. "They're *leaving him behind!*"

The army is fleeing down the road to the city, pushing against each other in crowds past Todd and into the first trees–

"He's trying to save his horse!" Lee says.

I click on the comm again and again. "Dammit, Todd! *Answer me!*"

"My girl!" Mistress Coyle snaps to get my attention. "We are here at the crucial moment again. You and your friends are getting a second chance to make your decision."

Bradley's Noise makes an angry sound and he turns to Simone for help, but Simone's eyes just flick to the crowd around us, the crowd demanding that we fire. "I don't see how we have any choice," she says. "If we do nothing, those people will die."

"And if we do something, those people will *also* die," Bradley says, his surprise flashing everywhere. "And so will we and so will everyone arriving on the ships. This is not our fight!"

"It will be one day," Simone says. "We'd be demonstrating strength. That might make them willing to negotiate with us *now*."

"Simone!" Bradley says and his Noise says something *really* rude. "The convoy wants us to pursue peaceful–"

"The convoy aren't seeing what we're seeing," Simone says.

"They're firing again!" I say–

Another arc of spinning fire is launching from the ledge under the falls–

And I think to myself, *What would Todd want?*

He'd want me safe, first of everything–

Todd would want a world that was safe for me–

He would; I know he would–

Even if he wasn't in it–

But he's still down there in the middle of the battle–

Still down there alone with the fire coming at him–

And the fact I can't get out of my head, peace or not, is what I also know to be true–

True but not right–

True but so dangerous–

Which is that if they kill him–

If they *hurt* him–

Then there won't be enough weapons on this ship for all the Spackle who'll have to pay.

I look over to Simone, who reads my face easily.

"I'm getting a missile ready," she says.

"Come on, girl, *please*," I say–

There's bodies around us everywhere, burning in heaps, some of 'em still screaming–

"Come *on!*" I shout–

But she's resisting me, flinging her head this way and that, pulling away from the fire and smoke, from the bodies, from the few soldiers still running past us–

And then she falls–

Back and down, onto her side–

Dragging me to the ground with her–

I land near her head–

"Angharrad," I call, right into her ears. *"PLEASE, get up!"*

And there's a twist to her neck–

A twist to her ears–

And her eye spins to me–

Spins right at me for the first time–

And–

Boy colt?

Quivery and small–

Tiny and quiet and frightened as anything–

But it's there–

"I'm right *here,* girl!"

Boy colt?

And my heart's leaping with hope–

"Come on, girl! Get up, get up, get up, get up–"

And I'm leaning back on my knees, pulling on the reins–

"Please please please please please–"

145

And she's lifting her head—

And her eyes go back to the falls—

Boy colt! she shouts—

And I look back—

Another arc of spinning fires is coming right at us—

"Come on!"

She rocks up to her feet, unsteady on the ground, stumbling away from a burning body near us—

Boy colt! she's still screaming—

"Come on, girl!" I say and try to get to her side—

Get on her saddle—

But here come the fires—

Like swooping burning eagles—

One sails right over the top of her—

Right over where my head woulda been if I'd been on her back—

And suddenly she's dashing forward in terror—

I hang onto her reins and run after her—

Stumbling along the ground—

Half running, half pulled—

As spinning fires come flying in from all direkshuns around us—

Like the whole *sky* is ablaze—

And my hands are twisted in the reins—

And Angharrad is screaming, **Boy colt!**

And I'm falling—

The reins are pulling away—

Boy colt!

"Angharrad!"

And then I hear **SUBMIT!**

Yelled in a different horse voice–

And as I fall to the ground, I hear another set of hooves, another horse–

The Mayor, riding Morpeth–

Swinging a cloth round Angharrad's head–

Covering her eyes, blinding her from the rain of fire storming down around us–

And then he reaches down and grabs me hard by the arm–

Lifting me up and into the air–

And throwing me outta the way of a spinning fire that burns the ground where I had just fallen–

"COME ON!" he yells–

And I scrabble over to Angharrad, grabbing her reins to guide her–

And the Mayor is riding a circle round us–

Dodging the fires in the sky–

Watching me–

Watching to see me get safe–

He came back to save me–

He came back to save *me*–

"BACK TO THE CITY, TODD!" he yells. "THEIR RANGE IS LIMITED! THEY CAN'T REACH–"

And he disappears as a spinning fire slams right into the broad chest of Morpeth–

{ Viola }

"Think what you're doing," Bradley says, his Noise roaring **Stupid, selfish bitch** behind Simone in the cockpit seat. "Sorry," he says immediately through clenched teeth. "But we don't need to do this!"

We're crammed in here, Bradley and Mistress Coyle stepping into each other's space behind me and Lee.

"I've got telemetry," Simone says. A small panel opens, exposing a square, blue button. You can't just press on a screen to fire a weapon. It has to be physical. You have to mean it. "Target locking," Simone says.

"The field is clearing!" Bradley says, pointing at the viewscreen above the cockpit. "It doesn't even look like the fires can reach any *farther*!"

Simone doesn't respond but her fingers hesitate above the blue button–

"Your boy is still down there, my girl," Mistress Coyle says, still talking right to me, as if I was in charge of this whole thing–

But it's true, he *is* still down there, trying to pull Angharrad to her feet, somehow we can still see him, in the middle of the twisting smoke and fire, small and alone and not answering my comm–

"I know what you're thinking, Viola," Bradley says, trying to keep his voice calm even as his Noise rages. "But it's one life against thousands."

"Enough talking!" Lee yells. "Fire the goddam thing!"

But on the viewscreen, I see that the battlefield *is* emptying, clearing out except for Todd and a few other stragglers and I think, if he can make it, if he can just *make it out*, then maybe it's true, maybe the Mayor will realize how outmatched he is against weapons that powerful, because who'd want to fight this? Who could?

But Todd has to make it–

He *has* to–

And his horse is running now, pulling him along–

And the fires are whooshing in–

No, *no*–

Simone's fingers are still hesitating above the button–

"*Todd,*" I say out loud–

"Viola," Bradley says strongly, getting my attention–

I turn to him–

"I know how much he must mean to you," he says, "but we can't, there are so many more lives at stake–"

"Bradley–" I say–

"Not for one person," he says. "You can't make war personal–"

"LOOK!" Mistress Coyle shouts–

And I turn back to the viewscreen–

And I see–

A spinning fire slam right into the front of a running horse–

"NO!" I scream. *"NO!"*

And the screen erupts in a blast of flame–

And crying out at the top of my lungs, I lunge past Simone and I slam my fist down onto the blue button–

[TODD]

Morpeth don't even have time to scream–

His knees buckle as the bolt of fire cuts right thru him–

I jump away from the blast, pulling Angharrad's reins again, dragging her from the impact as the fire roars right over the top of us–

She comes easier now that at least her eyes are dark, her Noise trying to find the ground to run on–

And the bolt of fire flies on, flames pouring out everywhere–

But another batch of fire separates from it–

Tumbling out to one side and hitting the ground-

The Mayor, rolling furiously toward me–

I grab the blanket off Angharrad and fling it down on top of him, smothering the flames on his general's uniform–

He rolls a few more times in the dirt and I jump around, patting down spots of fire on him–

I'm dimly aware that the fires are returning to the ledge again–

That we have another few seconds to get moving–

The Mayor stumbles up, still smoking, face black with soot, hair singed some, but mostly unharmed–

Not so Morpeth, whose body is barely recognizable in the burning heap–

"They're going to pay for that," the Mayor says, his voice rough from the smoke–

"Come on!" I shout. "We can make it if we run!"

"This isn't how it was supposed to go, Todd," he says angrily, as we head up the road. "They can't come as far as the city, though, and I think they've got vertical limitations, too, which must be why they didn't fire them from the hilltop–"

"Just shut up and *run!*" I say, huffing Angharrad along, thinking that we ain't gonna make it by the time the next fires come–

"I'm telling you this because you shouldn't think we're

beaten!" the Mayor yells. "This isn't a victory for them. It's merely a setback! We'll still go after them. We'll still–"

And then there's a sudden *shriek* in the air above us, whipping by like a bullet and–

BOOM!

–the whole hillside explodes outward like a volcano of dust and fire and the blast wave knocks me and the Mayor and Angharrad down to the ground and a hail of pebbles splatters down on top of us, big boulders landing nearby that could smash us flat–

"*What?!*" the Mayor says, looking back up–

The dry falls is collapsing into the emptied pool below, taking all the spinning-fire Spackle with it, dust and smoke heaving into the sky as the zigzag road is obliterated, too, the whole front section of the hill tumbling down on itself, leaving a jagged wreck along the top–

"Was that yer men?" I shout, my ears ringing from the boom. "Was that the artillery?"

"We didn't have time!" he shouts back, his eyes reading the destruckshun. "And we don't have anything like that kind of power."

The first billows of smoke start to clear a little, showing a big, gaping funnel where the lip of the hill was, jagged rocks everywhere, a scar ripped right outta the hillside–

And *Viola*, I think–

"Indeed," says the Mayor, realizing it, too, a sudden, ugly pleasure in his voice.

And standing up in front of a field of dead soldiers, a field covered with the burned remains of men I saw walking and talking not ten minutes before, men who fought and died for him, in a battle he started—

In front of all of this—

The Mayor says, "Your friends have joined the war."

And he smiles.

Weapons of War

THE BLAST HITS US ALL.

The hill that overlooks the valley is torn from the earth.
The archers of the Land are killed instantly, as are all the
Land near the edge of the hill when it exploded, the Sky
and I only saved by a matter of body lengths.

And the blast keeps on occurring, echoing through
the voice of the Land, stretching back down the river,
amplifying over and over until it seems to be continually
happening, the shock of it roaring through us again and
again and again, leaving the Land dazed as one, wondering
what the sheer size of the explosion means.

Wondering what will come next.

Wondering if it will be big enough to kill us all.

The Sky stopped the river shortly after the sun rose. He
sent a message through the Pathways to the Land who were

building the dam far upriver, telling them to raise their final walls, drop their final stones, turn the river back onto itself. The river began to subside, slowly at first, then faster and faster until the arcs of color thrown up by the spray of the waterfall disappeared and the vast width of the river became a muddy plain. As the sound of rushing water vanished, we could hear the voices of the Clearing raised in bafflement and fear at the bottom of the hill.

And then came the hour of the archers, and our eyes went with them. They had slipped beneath the falls under cover of darkness, waiting until the sun rose and the water stopped.

And then they raised their weapons and fired.

Every part of the Land watched as it happened, seeing through the eyes of the archers as the burning blades tore through the Clearing, as the Clearing ran and screamed and died. We watched as one as our victory unfolded, watched as they were powerless to retaliate—

And then came the sudden tearing in the air, the *whoosh* of something moving so fast it was sensed more than seen, a final, thudding flash that filled the mind and soul and voice of every member of the Land, signaling that our apparent victory would come at a cost, that the Clearing had bigger weapons than we thought, that now they would use them to destroy us all—

But further explosions do not come.

* * *

The vessel that flew over us, I show to the Sky when the Land begins to stumble to its feet again. He helps me up from where the blast knocked us back, neither of us hurt more than small cuts but the ground around us littered with bodies of the Land.

The vessel, the Sky agrees.

We go right to work, fearing a second blast every moment. He sends out commands to the Land for immediate regrouping, and I help him move the wounded to healing crèches, a new camp already organizing itself farther up the dry riverbed even in the early moments after the blast because that is what the Sky has ordered, a place for the voice of the Land to gather itself together again, to become one again.

But not *too* far up the riverbed. The Sky wants the Clearing still in physical sight, even though the hill is so destroyed now there is no longer space for an army to march down it, unless it were to climb down single file.

There are other ways, he shows to me, and already I can hear the messages being passed from him to the Pathways, messages that rearrange where the body of the Land rests, messages that tell it to start moving along roads that the Clearing is unaware of.

It is strange, he shows, hours later, when we finally stop to eat and a second blast has still not come. *To fire once, but not again.*

Maybe they only had the one weapon, I show. *Or they know that such weapons are useless against the*

155

force of a backed-up river. *If they destroy us, we will release it and destroy them.*

Mutually assured destruction, the Sky says, words that catch oddly in his voice, like foreign things. His voice turns in on itself for a long moment, searching deep within the voice of the Land, looking for answers.

Then he stands. *The Sky must leave the Return for now.*

Leave? I show. *But there is work to do—*

There are things the Sky must first do alone. He looks down on my bewilderment. *Meet me by my steed at dusk.*

Your steed? I show, but he is already walking away.

As the afternoon dwindles away, I do as the Sky asks and walk back up the dry riverbed, past the cookfires and healing crèches, past the Land's soldiers, recovering after the blast, tending to their weapons, readying themselves for the next attack, and mourning the body of the Land that died.

But the Land must also keep living, and as I get far enough upriver from the blast site, I pass members of the Land regurgitating the materials used to build new bivouacs, with several huts already reaching their way into the still smoky evening. I walk by the Land tending to flocks of whitebirds and scriven, part of our living larder. I walk by the bivouacs of grain and the fish stores, replenished now from the emptied river. I walk past the Land digging new latrine holes and even through a group of young ones singing the songs that will teach them how to sort out the history of the Land from all the voices, how to turn and twist and weave the mass of sound into one single voice that will tell them who they are, always and forever.

A song whose language I still struggle to speak, even when the Land talks to me at the pace they would to one of those children.

I walk through the singing until I find myself at the paddock of the battlemores.

Battlemores.

They were always creatures of legend to me, seen only in the voices of the Burden as I grew, in dreams and tales and histories of the war that left us with the Clearing. I half believed they were fantasies, exaggerated monsters that either did not exist at all or would be grave disappointments in the flesh.

I was wrong. They are magnificent. Huge and white, except when covered in clay battle armor. Even without it, their hides are thick and formed into hard plates. They are nearly as wide as I am tall, with a broad back that can easily be stood upon, the Land using the traditional foot saddles to stay upright.

The Sky's steed is biggest of all. The horn that thrusts up from its nose is longer than my entire body. It also has a rare secondary horn as well, one that only grows on the leader of the herd.

Return, it shows as I approach the paddock fence. The only word of the Burden it knows, taught it by the Sky, no doubt. *Return,* it shows, and it is gentle, welcoming. I reach out and place a hand in the space between its horns, rubbing gently with my fingers. It closes its eyes with pleasure.

That is a weakness of the Sky's steed, shows the Sky, coming up behind me. *No, do not stop.*

Is there news? I show, taking my hand away. *Have you made a decision?*

He sighs at my impatience. *The Clearing's weapons are stronger than ours,* he shows. *If there are more, the Land will die in waves.*

They have already killed thousands these years past. They will kill thousands more even if we do nothing.

We will continue with our original plan, the Sky shows. *We have shown our new strength and driven them back. We control the river, which deprives them of water and lets them know we can drown them at any moment should we release it all at once. And now, we will see how they respond.*

I stand up straighter, my voice rising. *"See how they respond'? What possible good can—?"*

I stop, as a thought comes, a thought that stops all other thoughts.

*You do not mean—*I show, stepping forward. *You **cannot** mean that you will see if they offer a peaceful solution—*

He shifts his stance. *The Sky has never shown that.*

*You **promised** they would be destroyed!* I show. *Does the slaughter of the Burden mean **nothing** to you?*

158

Calm yourself, he shows and for the first time, his voice is commanding me. *I will take your counsel and experience, but I will do what is best for the Land.*

What was best once before was leaving the Burden behind! As slaves!

We were a different Land then, he shows, *under a different Sky and with different skills and weapons. We are better now. Stronger. We have learned much.*

*And yet you would **still** make peace—*

I have not shown that either, young friend. His voice is growing calmer, more soothing. *But there are more vessels coming, are there not?*

I blink at him.

You have told us this. You heard it yourself in the voice of the Knife. There is a convoy of vessels coming with more weapons like the one fired today. These things must be taken into account for the long-term life of the Land.

I do not respond. I keep my voice to myself.

And so, for now, we will move the body of the Land into an advantageous position and we will wait. The Sky walks to his steed and scratches its nose. *They will soon find they cannot live without water. They will make their move, and even if it involves another weapon like today's, we will be ready for it.* He turns to me. *And the Return will not be disappointed.*

As dusk turns to night, we return to the Sky's own campfire. And as the Land and the Sky turn toward sleep, as the

Clearing makes no move below us to attack again, I layer my voice to obscure it like I learned from a lifetime with the Clearing, and within it, I examine two things.

Mutually assured destruction, showed the Sky.

Convoy, showed the Sky.

Words in the language of the Burden, words in the language of the Clearing.

But a phrase I do not know. A word I have never used.

Words that are not from the long memory of the Land.

They are *new* words. I could almost smell the freshness on them.

As the night pulls in and the siege of the Clearing begins, that is what I keep hidden in my voice.

The Sky left me today, to be alone, as the Sky occasionally does. It is a need of the Sky, of any Sky.

But he returned with new words.

So where did he hear them?

DOWN IN THE VALLEY

{VIOLA}

"I THOUGHT YOU WERE HIT," I say, putting my head in my hands. "I saw one of those things hitting a horse and a rider and I thought it was you." I look back up at him, tired and shivery. "I thought they'd killed you, Todd."

He opens his arms and I press into him and he holds on to me, just holds on to me while I cry. We're sitting next to a fire the Mayor's built in the square, where the army's making its new camp, the less than half of it that's left after the attack of the spinning fires.

The attack that stopped after I fired a missile.

I came racing down on Acorn immediately after the blast, riding through the square, shouting Todd's name until I found him. And there he was, his Noise still shocked and even more blurry from another battle, but alive.

Alive.

Something I changed the whole world to make sure of.

"I'd have done the same," Todd says into my head.

"No, you don't understand." I pull away a little bit. "If they'd hurt you, if they'd *killed* you . . ." I swallow hard. "I'd have killed every last one of them."

"I'd do the same, Viola," he says again. "Without even thinking twice."

I wipe my nose with my sleeve. "I know, Todd," I say. "But does that make us dangerous?"

Even through the blur, his Noise gets a confused feeling to it. "How do you mean?"

"Bradley keeps saying war can't be personal," I say. "But I dragged them into this war because of *you*."

"They'd have had to do something eventually, if they're half as nice as you say–"

My voice rises. "But I gave them no choice–"

"Stop it." And he pulls me to him again.

"Everything all right?" the Mayor says, coming over to us.

"Go away," Todd says.

"At least allow me to say thank you to Viola–"

"I said–"

"She saved our lives, Todd," he says, standing a bit too close. "With one simple action, she changed everything. I can't tell you how much I appreciate that."

And in Todd's arms, I go really still.

"Leave us alone," I hear Todd say. "Now."

There's a pause and then the Mayor says, "Very well, Todd. I'll be over here if you need me."

I look up at Todd as the Mayor leaves. *"If you need me?"*

Todd shrugs. "He coulda just let me die. It woulda made things easier for him if I wasn't hanging around. But he didn't. He saved me."

"He'll have a reason," I say. "And not a good one."

Todd doesn't answer, just takes a long look at the Mayor, who's talking to his men but watching us, too.

"Your Noise is still hard to read," I say. "Even more than before."

Todd's eyes don't quite meet mine. "It was the battle," he says. "All that screaming–"

And I hear something, deep in his Noise, something about a circle–

"But are *you* okay?" he asks. "You don't look good, Viola."

And now I'm the one who turns away, and I realize I'm unconsciously pulling my sleeve down. "Lack of sleep," I say.

But it's a weird moment, like there's something not quite truthful hanging in the air for both of us.

I reach into my bag. "Take this," I say, handing him my comm. "To replace yours. I'll get a new one when I get back."

He looks surprised. "Yer going *back*?"

"I have to. It's full-out war now and it's my fault. *I'm* the one who fired that missile. *I* have to make it right–"

And I get upset again because I keep seeing it in my mind. Todd safe in the viewscreen, not dead after all, and the army getting out of range of the spinning fires.

The attack was over.

And I fired anyway.

And dragged Simone and Bradley and the whole convoy into war, one that might now be ten times worse.

"I'd have done the same, Viola," Todd says, one more time.

And I know he's saying nothing but the truth.

But as he hugs me again before I leave, I can't help but think it over and over.

If this is what Todd and I would do for each other, does that make us right?

Or does it make us dangerous?

[TODD]

The days that follow are kinda scarily quiet.

A night and a day and another night pass after the spinning fire attack and nothing happens. Nothing from the Spackle up the hill, even tho we can still see their campfires glowing in the night. Nothing from the scout ship neither. Viola's told them all about what kinda man the Mayor is. They'll wait till he comes to them, I guess, and send whatever messages thru me. The Mayor don't seem in no hurry. Why should he? He got what he wanted without even having to ask.

In the meantime, he's placed a heavy guard around New Prentisstown's one big water tank on a side street just off the square. He's also had soldiers start to gather up the town's food and put it into an old stable next to the tank to make a foodstore. All under his control, of course, and at the edge of his new camp.

Also in the square.

I'd have thought he'd take over nearby houses, but he said he preferred a tent and a fire, saying it felt more like proper war out in the open with the army's Noise ROARing its way around him. He even took one of Mr. Tate's uniforms and had it fixed for himself so he was a spiffy new general again.

But he also had a tent set up for me across from him

and the captains. Like I was one of his important men. Like I was worth the life he came back to save. He even put in a cot for me to sleep on, to *finally* sleep on after being awake thru two straight days of battle. It seemed almost embarrassing to sleep, and practically impossible to do in the middle of a war. But I was so tired I slept anyway.

And dreamed of her.

Dreamed of when she came looking for me after the blast and how I held her when she got upset and how her hair stank a little and her clothes were sweaty and how she somehow felt both hot and cold, but it was her, it was *her* in my arms—

"Viola," I say, waking up again, my breath clouding in the cold.

I breathe heavy for a second or two, then get up and outta my tent. I head straight over to Angharrad and press my face against her warm horsey side.

"Morning," I hear.

I look up. The young soldier who's been bringing Angharrad fodder since we set up camp has arrived with her early feed.

"Morning," I say back.

He's not quite looking at me, older than me but shy of me anyway. He puts a feedbag on Angharrad and another on Juliet's Joy, Mr. Morgan's horse who the Mayor took now that Morpeth's gone, a bossy mare who snarls at everything that passes by.

Submit! she says to the soldier.

"Submit yerself," I hear him mumble. I chuckle cuz that's what I say to her, too.

I stroke Angharrad's flank, retying her blanket so she'll be warm enough. **Boy colt**, she says. **Boy colt**.

She still ain't right. She barely raises her head no more and I ain't even tried to ride her since we got back into the city. But she's talking again at least. And her Noise has stopped screaming.

Screaming about war.

I close my eyes.

(*I am the Circle and the Circle is me,* I think, light as a feather–)

(cuz you can silence yer Noise for yerself, too–)

(silence the screaming, silence the dying–)

(silence all that you saw that you don't wanna see again–)

(and that *hum* still in the background, felt rather than heard–)

"You think something's gonna happen soon?" the soldier asks.

I open my eyes. "If nothing ain't happening," I say, "nobody ain't dying."

He nods and looks away. "James," he says, and thru his Noise I can see he's telling me his name with a kinda hopeful friendliness, from someone whose friends are all dead.

"Todd," I say.

He catches my eye for a second and then looks behind me and dashes away to whatever his next job is.

Cuz the Mayor's coming outta his tent.

"Good morning, Todd," he says, stretching his arms.

"What's good about it?"

He just smiles his stupid smile. "I know waiting is

difficult. Especially under the threat of a river that would drown us."

"Why don't we just leave then?" I say. "Viola told me once there were old settlements at the ocean, we could regroup there and—"

"Because this is *my* city, Todd," he says, pouring himself a cup of coffee from the fire. "And leaving it would mean they win. It's how this game is played. They won't release the river because we'll fire more missiles. And so everyone will find another way to fight the war."

"They ain't yer missiles."

"But they're Viola's," he says, grinning at me. "And we've seen what she'll do to protect you."

"Mr. President?" It's Mr. Tate, coming off night patrol and walking over to the campfire with an old man I ain't seen before. "A representative is requesting an audience."

"A representative?" the Mayor says, looking fake impressed.

"Yes, sir," says the old man, holding his hat in his hands and not knowing exactly where to look. "From the town."

Me and the Mayor automatically look at the buildings that surround the square and the streets that spoke off around it. The town's been deserted since the first Spackle attack. But look now. Down the main road past the ruins of the cathedral, there's a line of people in the distance, older, mostly, but one or two younger women, one of 'em holding a kid.

"We don't really know what's happening," says the old man. "We heard the explosions from the battle and we ran—"

"War is what's happening," the Mayor says. "The defining

event for all of our futures is what's happening."

"Well, yes," says the old man. "But then the river dried up–"

"And now you're wondering if the town might be the safest place after all," asks the Mayor. "What might your name be, representative?"

"Shaw," says the old man.

"Well, Mr. Shaw," says the Mayor, "these are desperate hours, where your town and your army need you."

Mr. Shaw's eyes dart nervously from me to Mr. Tate to the Mayor. "We're certainly ready to support our brave men in battle," he says, twisting the hat in his hands.

The Mayor nods, almost in encouragement. "But there's no electricity, is there? Not since the town was abandoned. No heat. No way to cook food."

"No, sir," Mr. Shaw says.

The Mayor's silent for a second. "I'll tell you what, Mr. Shaw," he says. "I'll have some of my men restart the power station, see if we can't get the lights on in at least part of the city."

Mr. Shaw looks astonished. I know how he feels. "*Thank you, Mr. President,*" he says. "I only meant to ask if it was okay to–"

"No, no," says the Mayor. "Why are we fighting this war if not for you? Now when that's accomplished, I wonder if I may count on your help and the help of the other towns-folk to provide vital supplies to the front line? I'm talking food, mainly, but help rationing water, too. We're all in this together, Mr. Shaw, and an army is as nothing without support behind it."

"Uh, of course, Mr. President." Mr. Shaw is so surprised he can barely get his words out. "Thank you."

"Captain Tate?" the Mayor says. "Will you send a team of engineers to accompany Mr. Shaw and see if we can keep the people we're protecting from freezing to death?"

I look at the Mayor in amazement as Mr. Tate leads Mr. Shaw away.

"How can you give 'em heating when all we've got is campfires?" I ask. "How can you spare the men?"

"Because, Todd," he says. "There's more than one battle being fought here." He looks down the road as Mr. Shaw returns to the other townsfolk with the good news. "And I intend to win them all."

{VIOLA}

"Right," Mistress Lawson says, bandaging my arm again. "We know the band is meant to grow into the skin of the animal wearing it and bind it permanently, and that if we take it off, the chemicals in it will prevent us from being able to stop the bleeding. But if you leave the band alone, it's also supposed to heal and that's *not* what's happening to you."

I'm on the bed in the healing room of the scout ship, a place where I've spent way more time than I'd like since getting back from seeing Todd. Mistress Lawson's remedies are keeping the infection from getting worse, but that's all they're doing. I'm still feverish, and the band on my arm still burns, burns enough to keep me coming back to this bed.

As if it hadn't been a hard enough couple of days as it was.

My welcome back to the hilltop surprised me. It was getting dark when I rode in, but lights from the campfires let people from the Answer see me coming.

And they cheered.

People I know like Magnus and Mistress Nadari and Ivan came over to pat Acorn's flanks and say things like, "That'll show 'em!" and "Well done!" They thought firing the mis-s-ile was the best possible choice we could have made. Even Simone told me to try not to worry.

Lee did, too.

"They'll just keep coming if we don't show them we can fight back," he said that night, sitting next to me on a tree stump as we ate our dinner.

I looked over at him, his shaggy blond hair touching the collar of his coat, his big blue eyes reflected in the moons-light, the softness of the skin at the base of his neck–

Anyway.

"They might keep coming *worse* now, though," I said, a bit too loud.

"You had to do it. You had to do it for your Todd."

And in his Noise, I could see that he wanted to put his arm around me.

But he didn't.

Bradley, on the other hand, wouldn't even speak to me. He didn't have to. Selfish girl and the lives of thousands and let a child drag us into war and all kinds of even ruder things in his Noise lashed at me every time I got near him.

"I'm just angry," he said. "I'm sorry you have to hear it."

But he didn't say he was sorry for thinking it and then he

spent the entire next day briefing the convoy on what happened. And avoiding me.

I was in bed more of that day than I wanted to be anyway, so much that I wasn't able to talk to Mistress Coyle at all. Simone went out to try and catch her and ended up spending the day helping her arrange search parties for sources of water, sorting out inventories of food, and setting up a place for that many people to use the toilet, which involved a set of chemical incinerators from the scout ship that were supposed to be used for the first settlers.

That's Mistress Coyle for you. Taking whatever advantage she can get.

And then that night the fever got worse yet again, and so here I am *still* this morning, when there's so much work to be done, so much I have to do to try and set the world right.

"You shouldn't be wasting all this time on me, Mistress Lawson," I say. "I *chose* to have this band put on. I knew it was a risk and if–"

"If it's happening to you," she says, "what about all the women out there still hiding who didn't have a choice?"

I blink. "You don't think–?"

VIOLA, I hear, out in the corridor. Viola MISSILE Viola SIMONE stupid Noise–

Bradley pokes his head into the room. "I think you'd better come out here," he says. "Both of you."

I sit up in the bed, feeling so dizzy I have to wait before I stand. By the time I'm able to get up, Bradley's already leading Mistress Lawson out of the room.

"They started coming up the hill about an hour ago," he's saying to her. "Twos and threes at first, but now . . ."

173

"Who did?" I ask, following them outside and down the ramp, joining Lee, Simone, and Mistress Coyle at the bottom. I look out across the hilltop.

Which now has three times as many people as it did yesterday. Ragged-looking groups of all ages, some still wearing the nightclothes they were in when the Spackle first attacked.

"Do any of them need medical attention?" Mistress Lawson asks, not waiting for a reply before she heads off toward the largest batch of newcomers.

"Why are they coming *here*?" I ask.

"I've been talking to some of them," Lee says. "People don't know whether it's safer to have the scout ship protect them or stay in town and have the army do it." He looks over at Mistress Coyle. "When they heard the Answer was here, that made up some of their minds."

"Which way?" I say, frowning.

"There's got to be five hundred people here," Simone says. "We don't have anything like that kind of supply of food or water."

"The Answer does in the short term," Mistress Coyle says, "but you can bet there'll be more coming." She turns to Bradley and Simone. "I'm going to need your help."

As if you'd have to ask, Bradley's Noise rattles. "The convoy agrees that our primary mission is humanitarian," he says. He looks over at me and Simone, and his Noise rattles some more.

Mistress Coyle nods. "We should probably have a talk about the best way to do that. I'll get the mistresses together and—"

174

"And we'll include it with a talk about how to sign a new truce with the Spackle," I say.

"That's a thorny issue, my girl. You can't just wander in and ask for peace."

"And you can't just sit back and wait for more war either." I can tell from Bradley's Noise that he's listening to me. "We have to find a way to make this world work together."

"Ideals, my girl," she says. "Always easier to believe in than live."

"But if you don't at least *try* to live them," Bradley says, "then there's no point in living at all."

Mistress Coyle looks at him slyly. "Which is another ideal in itself."

"Excuse me," a woman says, approaching the ship. She looks nervously over all of us before settling her eyes on Mistress Coyle. "You're the healer, aren't you?"

"I am," Mistress Coyle replies.

"She's *a* healer," I say. "One of many."

"Can you help me?" the woman says.

And she pulls up her sleeve to reveal a band so infected it's clear even to me that she's already lost her arm.

[TODD]

"They kept coming through the night," Viola says to me thru the comm. *"There's three times as many here now."*

"Same here," I say.

It's just before dawn, the day after Mr. Shaw spoke to the Mayor, the day after townsfolk started showing up on Viola's hill, too, and more keep popping up everywhere. Tho it's mostly men in town and mostly women up on the hill. Not all, but mostly.

"So the Mayor gets what he wants," Viola sighs, and even on the small screen I can see how pale she still looks. *"Men and women separated."*

"You all right?" I ask.

"I'm okay," she says a bit too quick. *"I'll call you later, Todd. Busy day ahead."*

We hang up and I come outta my tent and find the Mayor already waiting for me with two cups of coffee. He holds one out. After a second, I take it. We both stand there drinking, trying to get some warmth inside of us as the sky gets pinker. Even at this hour, there are some lights on where the Mayor's men got power running into some of the bigger buildings so the townsfolk could gather in warmth.

The Mayor's eyes are on the Spackle hilltop, like always, still in the dark half of the sky, still hiding an unseen army behind itself. And I realize that just right now, just for these few minutes while the Mayor's army sleeps, you can hear something besides their sleeping ROAR, something faint and in the distance.

The Spackle got a ROAR, too.

"Their voice," the Mayor says. "And I really do think it's one big voice, evolved to fit this world perfectly, connecting them all." He sips his coffee. "You can hear it sometimes on quiet nights. All those individuals, speaking as one. Like the voice of this whole world, right inside your head."

He keeps staring at the hill in a kinda spooky way, so I ask, "Yer spies ain't heard 'em planning nothing?"

176

He takes another drink but don't answer me.

"They can't get close, can they?" I say. "Else they'll hear *our* plans."

"That's the nub of it, Todd."

"Mr. O'Hare and Mr. Tate don't got Noise."

"I'm already down two captains," he says. "I can't spare any more."

"Well, you didn't really burn all the cure, did you? Just give it to yer spies."

He don't say nothing.

"You didn't," I say, then I realize. "You *did*."

He still don't say nothing.

"*Why?*" I ask, looking round at the soldiers nearby. The **ROAR** is already getting louder now as they wake. "The Spackle can sure hear *us*. You coulda had an advantage–"

"I have other advantages," he says. "Besides, there may be another among us soon who could be most useful in regard to spying."

I frown. "I ain't never gonna work for you," I say. "Not never."

"You already *have* worked for me, dear boy," he says. "For several months, if I remember correctly."

I can feel my temper rising *right* up but I stop cuz James has come over with the morning feedbag for Angharrad. "I'll take it," I say, setting down my coffee. He hands me the bag and I loop it gently round Angharrad's head.

Boy colt? she asks.

"It's okay," I say into her ears, stroking 'em with my fingers. "Eat, girl." It takes another minute but then I start seeing her jaws work as she takes the first bites. "Attagirl," I say.

James is still there, staring at me blankly, his hands still up from when he gave me the bag. "Thanks, James," I say.

He still stands there, staring, not blinking, hands still up.

"I said, *thanks*."

And then I hear it.

It's hard to catch in the ROAR of everyone else's Noise, even James's, which is thinking about how he used to live upriver with his pa and his brother and how he joined the army when it marched past cuz it was either that or die fighting and now here he is, in a war with the Spackle, but he's happy now, happy to be fighting, happy to be serving the President–

"Aren't you, soldier?" says the Mayor, taking another sip of his coffee.

"I am," James says, still not blinking. "Very happy."

Cuz underneath it all lies the little vibrating *buzz* of the Mayor's Noise, seeping into James's, twining round it like a snake, pushing it into a shape that ain't too disagreeable to James but still ain't quite his own.

"You may go," the Mayor says.

"Thank you, sir," James blinks, dropping his hands. He gives me a funny little smile and then walks back into the thick of the camp.

"You can't," I say to the Mayor. "Not all of 'em. You said you just started being able to control people. That's what you *said*."

He don't answer, just turns back up to the hill.

I stare at him, figuring it out some more. "But yer getting stronger," I say. "And if they're cured–"

"The cure turned out to mask everything," he says. "It made them, shall we say, harder to reach. You need a lever to work a man. And Noise turns out to be a very good one."

I look round us again. "But you don't *have* to," I say. "They're already following you."

"Well, yes, Todd, but that doesn't mean they're not open to suggestion. It can't have escaped your attention how quickly they follow my orders in battle."

"Yer working up to controlling a whole army," I say. "A whole *world*."

"You make it sound so sinister." He smiles that smile. "I'd only ever use it for the good of us all."

And then there's a sound behind us, fast footsteps. It's Mr. O'Hare, outta breath, his face blazing.

"They've attacked our spies," he pants at the Mayor. "Only one man each returned from north and south. Obviously left so they could tell us what happened. The Spackle slaughtered the rest."

The Mayor grimaces and turns back to the hilltop. "So," he says, "that's how they're playing the game."

"What's that sposed to mean?" I say.

"Attacks from the northern road and the southern hills," he says. "The first steps toward the inevitable."

"The inevitable what?"

He raises his eyebrows. "They're surrounding us, of course."

{ V I O L A }

Girl colt, Acorn greets me as I give him an apple I stole

179

from the food tent. He stables in an area at the tree line where Wilf's taken all the Answer's animals.

"He giving you any trouble, Wilf?" I ask.

"Nah, ma'am," Wilf says, attaching feedbags to a pair of oxes next to Acorn. **Wilf,** they say, while they eat. **Wilf, Wilf.**

Wilf, Acorn says, nudging in my pockets for another apple.

"Where's Jane?" I ask, looking around.

"Helpin hand out food with the mistresses," Wilf says.

"That sounds like Jane," I say. "Listen, have you seen Simone? I need to talk to her."

"She's off huntin with Magnus. Ah heard Mistress Coyle suggestin it to her."

Ever since the townsfolk started showing up, food has been our most pressing issue. Mistress Lawson, as usual, is in charge of inventory and has set up regular food chains to feed the people who are arriving, but the Answer's food stocks aren't going to last forever. Magnus has been leading hunting parties to supplement it.

Mistress Coyle, meanwhile, has been deep in the medical tents, working on women with infected arms. There's been a huge variation in how bad they are. Some of the women are so sick they're barely able to stand; for others it's nothing more than a bad rash. It does seem to affect every woman somehow, though. Todd says the Mayor's giving medical help to the few women down there, too, all concerned now about the bands *he* put there, saying he'll do whatever it takes to help them, not having intended this at all.

It's enough to make me feel even sicker.

"I must have been in the healing room when she left," I say, feeling the burning in my arm, wondering if my fever's back *again*. "I guess it'll have to be Bradley then."

I head off back to the scout ship, but I hear Wilf say, "Good luck" as I go.

I listen out for Bradley's Noise, still louder than any other man here, until I find his feet sticking out of a section on the front of the ship, a panel laying on the ground and tools everywhere.

Engine, he's thinking. **Engine** and **war** and **missile** and **food shortage** and **Simone won't even look at me** and **Someone there?**

"Someone there?" he asks, scooting his way out.

"Only me," I say as he emerges.

Viola, he thinks. "Something I can help you with?" he says, way shorter than I'd like.

I tell him what Todd told me about the Spackle and the Mayor's spies, about the Spackle maybe being on the move.

"I'll see what I can do to make the probes more effective," he sighs. He looks out at the camp that now completely surrounds the scout ship, out to all sides of the clearing, with other makeshift tents up beyond the line of trees, too. "We have to protect them now," he says. "It's our duty, now that we've upped the stakes."

"I'm sorry, Bradley," I say. "I couldn't have done any other thing."

He looks up sharply. "Yes, you could have." He pulls himself to his feet and says it again, more firmly. "*Yes*, you *could* have. Choices may be unbelievably hard but they're never impossible."

"What if it'd been Simone down there instead of Todd?" I say.

And Simone is all over his Noise, his deep feelings for her, feelings I don't think are returned. "You're right," he says. "I don't know. I hope I'd make the right choice, but, Viola, it *is* a choice. To say you have no choice is to release yourself from responsibility and that's not how a person with integrity acts." A child, his Noise says, A CHILD, and his voice softens. "And I do believe you're a person with integrity."

"You do?" I say.

"Of course I do," he says. "What's important is taking responsibility for it. Learning from it. Using it to make things better."

And I remember Todd saying, *It's not how we fall. It's how we get back up again.*

"I know," I say. "I'm trying to make things right."

"I believe you," he says. "I'm trying, too. You fired the missile, but we made it possible for you to do it." And I hear Simone in his Noise again, with some spikes of difficulty around it. "You tell Todd to tell the Mayor we'll only help with things that *save* lives, that we're working for peace and nothing else."

"I already have."

And I must look so sincere about it, he smiles. It's so much what I've been waiting for that I feel a little leap in my chest. Because his Noise is smiling, too. A little bit.

We see Mistress Coyle coming out of a healing tent, blood on her smock.

"Unfortunately," Bradley says, "I think the road to peace lies through her."

"Yeah, but she's always acting so busy. Too busy to talk."

"Maybe you should get busy, too, then," he says. "If you're feeling up to it."

"It doesn't matter if I'm not feeling up to it. It's something I have to do." I look back over to where Wilf is working the animals. "I think I know just who to ask, too."

[TODD]

My dearest son, I read. *My dearest son.*

The words my ma uses at the top of every page of her journal, words written to me just before and after I was born, saying everything that happened to her and my pa. I'm inside my tent, trying to read 'em.

My dearest son.

But they're pretty much the only words I can make out in the whole stupid thing. I run my fingers down the page and then the next one over, too, looking at the scrawl of words stretching everywhere.

My ma, talking and talking.

And I can't hear her.

I reckernize my name here and there. And Cillian's. And Ben's. And my heart starts to hurt a bit. I wanna hear my ma talking about Ben, Ben who raised me, Ben who I lost, *twice.* I wanna hear his voice again.

But I can't–

(stupid effing idiot)

And then **Food?** I hear.

I put down the journal and poke my head outta the tent. Angharrad's looking at me. **Food, Todd?**

183

I'm immediately up, immediately over to her, immediately agreeing.

Cuz it's the first time she's said my name since—

"Of course, girl," I say. "I'll get you some right now."

She nudges her nose against my chest, almost playful, and my eyes go wet with relief. "I'll be right back," I say. I look round but don't see James nowhere. I head over past the campfire, where the Mayor's frowning over yet more reports with Mr. Tate.

He didn't have many men to spare but after the attacks on the spies this morning, he said he didn't have no choice about sending small squadrons of men to the north and south with orders to press on till they heard the Spackle ROAR, then to camp there, far enough away so the Spackle knew we weren't just gonna let 'em march into town and steamroll over us. They'll tell us when the invasion is coming, at least, even if they won't be able to stop it.

I head out into the army, glancing cross the square to where you can just see the top point of the water tank peeking up over the food store, buildings I never bothered noticing till they turned into life or death.

I see James coming away from 'em, into the square.

"Hey, James," I greet him. "Angharrad needs some more feed."

"More?" He looks surprised. "She's already been fed today."

"Yeah, but she's still only coming outta the shock of the battle and all that. Besides," I say, scratching my ear, "for the first time, she's actually asking."

He gives a knowing smile. "You gotta watch out for that,

184

Todd. Horses know where to take their advantage. You start feeding her every time she asks, she's gonna start asking all the time."

"Yeah, but–"

"You need to show her who's boss. Tell her she's had her feed today and that she'll get some in the morning like she's sposed to."

He's still smiling, his Noise is still friendly, but I'm finding my own self getting a bit annoyed. "Show me where it is and I'll get some myself."

He frowns a little. "Todd–"

"She *needs* it," I say, my voice rising. "She's recovering from a wound–"

"So am I." He lifts up the hem of his shirt. There's a burn all the way cross his belly. "And *I* only ate once today."

And I can see what he's saying and I can see how friendly he means to be by it but there's **Boy colt?** running thru my Noise and I remember how she cried out when she was hit and then the silence that followed and the few words I've been able to get from her since but still barely nothing compared with how she used to be and if she wants to eat then I'm damned if I'm not gonna feed her and this annoying little pigpiss needs to *get it for me* cuz I am the Circle and the Circle is me–

"I'll get it for you," he says–

And he's looking at me–

And he ain't blinking–

And I can feel something twisting, some winding curling invisible cord in the air–

185

And it's twixt my Noise and his Noise—

And there's a little *buzz*—

"I'll go get it right now," he says, not blinking. "I'll just bring it on over."

And he turns and starts walking back to the food store.

I can feel the *buzz* still bouncing thru my Noise, hard to follow, hard to pin down, like a shadow that's just left the spot wherever I turn to look—

But it don't matter—

I wanted him to do it, I *wanted* it to happen—

And it did.

I controlled him. Just like the Mayor.

I watch him go, still walking to the food store, like it was his own idea.

My hands are shaking.

Bloody hell.

{ V I O L A }

"You're the one here who knows the most about the truce," I say. "You were a leader of New Prentisstown then and there's no way—"

"I was a leader of *Haven,* my girl," Mistress Coyle says, not looking up from where we're handing out food to a long queue of townspeople. "I have nothing at all to do with *New Prentisstown.*"

"Here ya go!" Jane practically shouts next to us, putting the small rations of vegetables and dried meat into whatever containers people have brought with them. The queue stretches right across the hilltop, where there's barely a handkerchief of free space to be seen. It's practically become its own frightened and hungry town.

"But you said you knew about the truce," I say.

"Of course I know about the truce," Mistress Coyle says. "I helped negotiate it."

"Well, then you could do it *again*. Tell me at least how you started."

"A bit too much *talking*?" Jane says, leaning over toward us, concern on her face. "Not enough handing out the food?"

"Sorry," I say.

"Only, the mistresses get mad when you talk too much," Jane says. She turns to the next person in line, a mother holding the hand of her young daughter. "I get in trouble all the *time*."

Mistress Coyle sighs and lowers her voice. "We started by beating the Spackle so badly they *had* to negotiate, my girl. That's how these things work."

"But–"

"Viola"–she turns to me–"do you remember the fear you felt run through the people when they heard the Spackle were attacking?"

"Well, yes, but–"

"It's because we came *so close* to being wiped out last time. That's not something you ever forget."

"All the more reason to stop it from happening again," I say. "We've shown the Spackle how much power we have–"

"Matched by the power they have to release the river and destroy the town," she says. "Making the rest of us easy pickings for an invasion. It's a stalemate."

187

"But we can't just sit here and wait for another battle. That's giving the Spackle *more* advantage; that's giving the *Mayor* more advantage–"

"That's not what's happening, my girl."

And her voice has a funny note to it.

"What do you mean by that?" I say.

I hear a little moan beside me. Jane has stopped handing out food, distress all over her face. "Yer gonna get in *trouble*," she whispers loudly to me.

"I'm sorry, Jane, but I'm sure it's okay if I talk to Mistress Coyle."

"She's the one who gets *maddest*."

"Yes, Viola," Mistress Coyle says. "I *am* the one who gets maddest."

I pull my lips tight. "What did you mean?" I say, under my breath for Jane's sake. "What's happening with the Mayor?"

"You just wait," Mistress Coyle says. "You just wait and see."

"Wait and see while people die?"

"People aren't dying." She gestures to the line, the line of hungry faces looking back at us, mostly women, but some men, too, and children, all haggard and dirtier than I expect they're used to being, but Mistress Coyle's right: they're not dying. "On the contrary," she says, "people are living, surviving together, depending on each other. Which is exactly what the Mayor needs."

I narrow my eyes. "What are you saying?"

"Look around you," she says. "Here's half the human planet right here, the half that isn't down there with him."

"And?"

188

"And he's not going to *leave* us here, is he?" She shakes her head. "He needs us to have complete victory. Not just the weapons on your ship, but the rest of us to rule afterward and no doubt the convoy, too. That's how he thinks. He's been down there waiting for us to come to him, but you watch. There will come a day, there will come a day *soon* when he comes to us, my girl."

She smiles and goes back to handing out food.

"And when he does," she says. "I'll be waiting."

[TODD]

By the middle of the night, I've had enough tossing and turning and I go out to the campfire to warm up. I can't sleep after the weird thing with James.

I controlled him.

For a minute there, I did.

I ain't got no idea how.

(but it felt—)

(it felt powerful—)

(it felt *good*—)

(shut up)

"Can't sleep, Todd?"

I make an annoyed sound. I hold my hands out to the fire and I can see him watching me across it.

"Can't you just leave me alone for once?" I say.

He laughs a single time. "And miss out on what my son got?"

My Noise squawks outta sheer surprise. "Don't you talk to me about Davy," I say. "Don't you even *dare*."

189

He holds up his hands in a make-peace kinda way. "I only meant the way you redeemed him."

I'm still raging but the word catches me. "Redeemed?"

"You changed him, Todd Hewitt," he says, "as much as anyone could. He was a wastrel, and you nearly made him a man."

"We'll never know," I growl. "Cuz you killed him."

"That's how war goes. You have to make impossible decisions."

"You didn't have to make that one."

He looks into my eyes. "Maybe I didn't," he says. "But *if* I didn't, it's you who's showing that to me." He smiles. "You're rubbing off on me, Todd."

I frown hard. "Ain't nothing on this earth can redeem *you*."

And it's just then that all the lights in the city go off.

From where we're standing we can see 'em in a cluster cross the square, keeping the townsfolk feeling safe–

And in an instant they go black.

And then we hear gunfire from a different direkshun–

Just one gun, lonely on its own somehow–

Bang and then *bang* again–

And the Mayor's already grabbing his rifle and I'm right behind him, cuz it's coming from behind the power stay-shun, off a side road near the empty riverbed and some soldiers are already running toward it, too, with Mr. O'Hare, and it gets darker as we all race away from the army camp, darker with no more sounds of anything happening–

And then we get there.

There were just two guards on the power stayshun,

no more than engineers really, cuz who's gonna attack the power stayshun when the whole army's twixt it and the Spackle–

But there are two Spackle bodies on the ground outside the door. They're lying next to one of the guards, his body in three big, separate pieces, blown apart by the acid rifle things. Inside, the power stayshun is a wreck, equipment melting from the acid, which is just as good at destroying things as it is people.

We find the second guard a hundred yards away, halfway cross the dry riverbed, obviously firing at Spackle as they ran.

The top half of his head is missing.

The Mayor ain't happy at all. "This isn't how we're meant to fight," he says, his voice low and sizzling. "Slinking around like cave rats. Nighttime raids rather than open battle."

"I'll get reports from the squadrons we sent out, sir," says Mr. O'Hare, "see where the breach was."

"You do that, Captain," the Mayor says, "but I doubt they'll tell you anything other than that they saw no movement at all."

"They wanted our attenshun somewhere else," I say. "Looking out rather than in. That's why they killed the spies."

He looks at me slowly, carefully. "Exactly right, Todd," he says. Then he turns back to look at the town, darker now, with townsfolk out in their bedclothes, lined up to see what's happened.

"So be it," I hear the Mayor whisper to himself. "If that's the war they want, then that's the war we'll give them."

The Embrace of the Land

THE LAND HAS LOST a part of itself, the Sky
shows, opening his eyes. *But the job is done.*

I feel the hollowness that echoes through the Land at
the loss of those who led the smaller attack on the heart
of the Clearing, those who went knowing they probably
would not return, but that by their actions, the voice of the
Land might sing on.

I would give my own voice, I show to the Sky as the
campfire warms us in the cold night, *if it would mean
the end of the Clearing.*

*But what a loss the silencing of the Return would
be,* he shows, reaching out his voice to mine. *Not when
you traveled so far to join us.*

Traveled so far, I think.

For I did travel far.

***

After the Knife pulled me from the bodies of the Burden, after I showed him my vow to kill him, after we heard the approach of horses on the road and he begged me to run—

I ran.

The town was in burning turmoil at the time, the confusion and smoke letting me pass through the southern end of it unseen. Then I hid myself until nightfall, when I made my way up the crooked road out of town. Sticking to the underbrush, I crept up, zig by zag, until there was no cover left and I had to stand and run, fully exposed for the last stretch, expecting every moment a bullet to the back of my head from the valley below—

An end which I craved but also feared—

But I made it to the top and over.

And I ran.

I ran toward a rumor, a legend that lived in the voice of the Burden. We were of the Land, but some of us had never seen it, some of the young like me, born into the war that left the Burden behind when the Land made a promise never to return. And so the Land, like their battlemores, was shadows and fables, stories and whispers, dreams of the day they would return to free us.

Some of us gave up that hope. Some of us never had it, never forgiving the Land for leaving us there in the first place.

Some like my one in particular who, though only older than me by a matter of moons and likewise never having seen the Land, would gently show to me that I should let go any hope of rescue, of any life other than one we might carve out ourselves among the voices of the Clearing, telling me this on the nights I was afraid, telling me that our day would come, it would, but that it would be our day and not the day of a Land that had clearly forgotten us.

And then my one in particular was taken.

And so was the rest of the Burden.

Leaving only me to seize the chance.

So what choice did I have but to run towards the rumor?

I did not sleep. I ran through forests and plains, up hills and down, across streams and rivers. I ran through settlements of the Clearing, burned and abandoned, scars on the world left wherever the Clearing touched it. The sun rose and set and still I did not sleep, did not stop moving, even when my feet were covered in blisters and blood.

But I saw no one. No one from the Clearing, no one from the Land.

No one.

I began to think I was not just the last of the Burden but the last of the Land as well, that the Clearing had achieved their goal and had wiped the Land from the face of the world.

That I was alone.

And on the morning I thought this, a morning where I stood on a riverbank, where I looked around yet again and saw only myself, only 1017 with the permanent mark burning into his arm—

I wept.

I crumpled to the ground and I wept.

And that was when I was found.

✳ ✳ ✳

195

They came out of the trees across the road. Four of them, then six, then ten. I heard their voices first but my own voice was only just beginning to come back, just beginning to tell me who I was again after the Clearing had taken it away. I thought it was myself calling to me. I thought it was my own self calling me to my death.

I would have willingly gone.

But then I saw them. They were taller than the Burden ever grew, broader, too, and they carried spears and I knew that here were warriors, here were soldiers who would help me take revenge on the Clearing, who would right all wrongs done to the Burden.

But then they sent greetings I found difficult to understand but that seemed to say their weapons were merely fishing spears and themselves simple fishers.

Fishers.

Not warriors at all. Not out hunting for the Clearing. Not coming for vengeance on the death of the Burden. They were fishers, come to the river because they had heard that the Clearing had abandoned this stretch.

And then I told them who I was. I spoke to them in the language of the Burden.

There was great shock, an astonished recoil I could feel, but more than that, too—

There was distaste at how shrill my voice was and at the language I spoke.

There was dread and shame at what I represented, what I meant.

And there was the briefest of pauses before they crossed the final stretch of road toward me, before they came forward with their assistance and help. And they *did* come forward, they did help me to my feet and asked me for my story, which I told in the language of the Burden, and they listened to me with concern, listened to me with horror and outrage, listened while also making plans for where to take me and what would happen next and reassuring me all along that I was one of them, that I had returned to them now, that I was safe.

That I was not alone.

But before they did all of that, there was shock, there was distaste, there was dread, there was shame.

Here at last was the Land. And it was afraid to touch me.

They took me to an encampment, deep to the south, through thick woods and over a ridge of hills. Hundreds of them lived there in bulbous secreted bivouacs, so many and so loud and curious that I nearly turned and fled.

I did not look like them, being shorter, slighter, my skin a different shade of white, the lichen I grew for my clothing a different type. I barely recognized any of their food or their shared songs or the communal way they slept. Distant memories from the voices of the Burden tried to reassure me, but I felt different, I *was* different.

Different most of all in language. Theirs was almost unspoken, shared among them so quickly I could almost never follow it, as if they were just different parts of a single mind.

Which of course they were. They were a mind called the Land.

This was not how the Burden spoke. Forced to interact with the Clearing, forced to obey them, we adopted their language, but more than just that, we adopted their ability to disguise their voice, to keep it separate, private. Which is fine if there are others to reach out to when privacy is no longer wanted.

But there was no more Burden to reach out to.

And I did not know how to reach out to the Land.

While I rested and fed and was healed of all of my injuries save the red pain of the 1017 band, a message was passed through the voice of the Land until it reached a Pathway, where it went straight to the Sky faster than it would have otherwise.

Within days, he arrived in the encampment, high on his battlemore, a hundred soldiers with him and more on the way.

The Sky is here to see the Return, he showed, giving me my name in an instant and ensuring my difference before he had even seen me in the flesh.

And then he laid his eyes on me, and they were the eyes of a warrior, of a general and leader.

They were the eyes of the Sky.

And they looked at me as if they recognized me.

We went inside a bivouac secreted especially for our meeting, its curving walls reaching to a point far above our heads. I told the Sky the story as I knew it, every last detail, from being born into the Burden to the slaughter of us all, save one.

And while I spoke, his voice surrounded me in a sad song of weeping and sorrow, which was taken up by all of the Land in the encampment outside and for all I know every part of the Land this world over, and I was held in it, the Land placing me at the center of their voices, their one voice, and for a moment, for a brief moment—

I no longer felt alone.

We will avenge you, the Sky showed me.

And that was even better.

And the Sky keeps his word, he shows to me now.

He does, I show. *Thank you.*

This is only a beginning, he shows. *There is more to come, more that will be pleasing to the Return.*

Including a chance to meet the Knife in battle?

He looks at me for a moment. *All things in their due course.*

As I watch him stand, a part of me still wonders if he is leaving the possibility open for a peaceful solution, one that would avoid the outright slaughter of the Clearing, but his voice refuses to answer my doubts and for a moment I am ashamed to have thought them, especially after an attack that has taken part of the Land.

The Return has also wondered if I have a second source of information, the Sky shows.

I look up sharply.

You notice much, the Sky shows. *But so does the Sky.*

Where? I show. *How does the rest of the Land not know of it? How does the Clearing—*

The Sky asks now for the Return's trust, he shows and there is discomfort in his voice. But there is also a warning. *And it must be your unbreakable bond. You must promise to trust the Sky, no matter what you might see or hear. You must trust that there is a larger plan that might not be apparent to you. A larger purpose that involves the Return.*

But I can hear his deeper voice, too.

I have lifelong experience with the voices of the Clearing, voices that hide, voices that twist themselves in knots while the truth is always more naked than they think, and I have far more practice at uncovering concealment than the rest of the Land.

And in the depths of his voice, I see not only that the Sky, like the Return, can conceal with his voice, but I can also see part of what he is concealing—

You must trust me, he says again, showing me his plans for the days to come—

But he will not show me the source of his information.

Because he knows how betrayed I will feel when he finally does.

CLOSING IN

[TODD]

THERE'S BLOOD EVERYWHERE.

Across the grass in the front yard, on the small path leading up to the house, all over the floor inside, way more blood than you'd think coulda come outta actual people.

"Todd?" the Mayor says. "Are you all right?"

"No," I say, staring at all the blood. "What kinda person would be all right?"

I am the Circle and the Circle is me, I think.

The Spackle attacks keep coming. Every day since the first one on the power stayshun, eight days in a row, no letup. They attack and kill the soldiers who are out trying to drill wells to get us much-needed water. They attack and kill sentries at night at random points on the edge of town. They even burned down a whole street of houses. No one died, but they set another street alight while the Mayor's men were trying to put out the first one.

And all this time, there still ain't no reports from the

squadrons to the north and south, both of 'em just sitting there twiddling their thumbs, no sound of Spackle passing 'em to make it into town or on the way back from another successful attack. Nothing from Viola's probes neither, like everywhere you look, they're somewhere else.

And now they've done something new.

Parties of townsfolk, usually accompanied by a soldier or two, have been going thru the outlying houses one by one, scrounging whatever food they can find for the storehouse.

This party got met by Spackle.

In broad daylight.

"They're testing us, Todd," the Mayor says, frowning, as we stand at the doorway of the house, some way east of the cathedral ruins. "This is all leading up to something. You mark my words."

The bodies of thirteen Spackle are strewn about the house and the yard. On our side, there's a dead soldier in the front room and I can see the remains of two dead townsfolk, both older men, thru the door of the pantry, and a woman and a boy who died hiding in the bathtub. A second soldier lies in the yard, being worked on by a doctor, but he ain't got one of his legs no more and there's no way he's long for this world.

The Mayor walks over to him and kneels down. "What did you see, Private?" he asks, his voice low and almost tender in a way I know myself. "Tell me what happened."

The private's breath is all in gasps and his eyes are wide and his Noise is a thing you just can't bear looking at, filled with Spackle coming at him, filled with soldiers and townsfolk dying, filled most of all with how he ain't got one of his legs no more and how there ain't no going back from that, not never ever ever–

"Calm yourself," says the Mayor.

And I hear the low *buzz*. Twisting into the private's Noise, trying to settle him down, trying to get him to focus.

"They just kept coming," the private says, still pretty much gasping twixt each word but at least he's talking. "We'd fire. And they'd fall. And here'd come another one."

"But surely you must have had warning, Private," the Mayor says. "Surely you heard them."

"Everywhere," the private gasps, arching his head back at some new invisible pain.

"Everywhere?" the Mayor says, voice still calm but the *buzz* getting louder. "What do you mean?"

"*Everywhere,*" the soldier says, his throat really grabbing for air now, like he's talking against his will. Which he probably is. "They came. From everywhere. Too fast. Running for us. Full speed. Firing their sticks. My leg. My LEG!"

"Private," the Mayor says again, working harder on the *buzz*–

"They just kept coming! They just kept–"

And then he's gone, his Noise fading fast before stopping altogether. He dies, right there in front of us.

(I am the Circle–)

The Mayor stands up, his face all annoyed. He takes a long last look at the scene, at the bodies, at the attacks he don't seem able to predict or stop. He's got men around him, waiting for him to give 'em orders, men who look increasingly nervous as the days go on and there ain't a battle in front of 'em they can fight.

203

"Come, Todd!" the Mayor finally snaps and off he stomps to where our horses are tied and I'm running after him before I even stop to think that he's got no right to command me.

{VIOLA}

"You sure you ain't got nothing?" Todd asks over the comm. He's riding Angharrad behind the Mayor, away from an attack on a house outside of town, the eighth in a row, and I can see the worry and weariness on his face even in the little screen.

"They're hard to track," I say, lying on the bed in the healing room *again*, my fever up *again*, so consistently I haven't even been able to visit Todd. "Sometimes we see little glimpses of them, but nothing useful, nothing we can follow." I lower my voice. "Plus Simone and Bradley are keeping the probes closer to the hilltop now. The townsfolk are sort of demanding it."

And they are. It's so crowded up here now there's almost no room to move. Very poor-looking tents, made of everything from blankets to rubbish bags, stretch all the way down to the main road by the empty riverbed. Plus, things are growing scarce. There are streams near here, and Wilf brings up vats of water twice a day so our water supply problems are less than what Todd says they're facing in the city. But we've only got the food the Answer was keeping for itself, supply for two hundred that's now got to feed fifteen hundred. Lee and Magnus keep leading hunting parties, but it's nothing compared to the stored food in New Prentisstown, guarded heavily by soldiers.

They've got enough food but not enough water.

We've got enough water but not enough food.

But neither the Mayor nor Mistress Coyle would even consider leaving the places where they're strongest.

Worse, rumor spreads almost instantly in a group of people this close together, and after the attacks began on the town, people started thinking the Spackle would attack us next, that they were already surrounding the hilltop, ready to close in and kill us all. They weren't, there's been no sign of them near us, but the townsfolk keep asking what we're doing to keep them safe, saying it's our responsibility to protect everyone on the hill first, before the town below.

Some of them have even started sitting in a sort of half circle near the bay doors of the scout ship, not saying anything, just watching what we do and reporting it back along the hilltop.

Ivan's usually sitting right up front. He's even started calling Bradley "The Humanitarian."

And he doesn't mean it in a nice way.

"*I know what you mean,*" Todd says. "*The feeling ain't any better down here.*"

"I'll let you know if anything happens."

"*Likewise.*"

"Any news?" Mistress Coyle says, coming into the healing room as Todd hangs up.

"You shouldn't be listening to people's private conversations."

"There's nothing on this planet that's private, my girl. That's the whole problem." She gives me a lookover as I lie on the bed. "How's your arm?"

My arm hurts. The antibiotics have stopped working, and

the red streaking is spreading again. Mistress Lawson left me here with a new combination bandage, but even I could see she was worried.

"Never you mind," I say. "Mistress Lawson's doing a great job."

Mistress Coyle looks at her feet. "You know, I've had some success on the infections with a set of timed—"

"I'm sure Mistress Lawson will do that when she's ready," I interrupt. "Did you want something?"

She lets out a long sigh, as if I've disappointed her.

This is how the past eight days have all gone, too. Mistress Coyle refusing to do anything other than what Mistress Coyle wants to do. She keeps herself so busy with the running of the camp—sorting out food, treating the women, spending an awful lot of time with Simone—that there never seems to be a chance to talk about peace. When I do pin her down on the rare occasions I'm not stuck in this stupid bed, she says she's waiting, that peace can only come at the right moment, that the Spackle will make their move and the Mayor will make his and then and only then can we move in and make peace.

But somehow, it always sounds like peace for some of us and not necessarily everybody else.

"I wanted to talk to you, my girl," she says, looking me in the eye, maybe seeing if I'll look away.

I don't. "I want to talk to you, too."

"Then let me go first, my girl," she says.

And then she says something I never expected in a million years.

"Fires, sir," Mr. O'Hare says, not a minute after I hang up with Viola.

"I am not in fact blind, Captain," the Mayor says, "but thank you once again for pointing out the obvious."

We've stopped on the road back into town from the bloody house cuz there are fires on the horizon. Some of the abandoned farmhouses on the north hill of the valley are burning.

At least I hope they're abandoned.

Mr. O'Hare's caught up to us with a group of about twenty soldiers, who look as tired as I feel. I watch 'em, reading their Noise. They're all ages, old and young, but all old in the eyes now. Hardly any of this group wanted to be soldiers but were forced into it by the Mayor, forced from families, from farms and shops and schools.

And then they started seeing death every day.

I am the Circle and the Circle is me, I think again.

I do it all the time now, reaching for the silence, making the thoughts and memories go away, and most of the time it works on the outside, too. People can't hear my Noise, I can *hear* 'em not hearing me, just like Mr. Tate and Mr. O'Hare, and I gotta think that's part of the reason the Mayor showed me, thinking to make me one of his men.

Like that's ever gonna happen.

I ain't told Viola bout it, tho. I don't know why.

Maybe cuz I ain't *seen* her, which is something I've *hated* about the past eight days. She's stayed up on the hilltop to keep tabs on Mistress Coyle but every time I call she's in

207

that bed and looking paler and weaker and I *know* she's sick and getting sicker and she ain't telling me about it, probably so I don't worry, which only makes me worry *more* cuz if something's wrong with her, if something *happens* to her–

I am the Circle and the Circle is me.

And everything calms down a bit.

I ain't told her. I don't want her to worry. I got it under control.

Boy colt? Angharrad asks nervously under me.

"It's okay, girl," I say. "We'll be home soon." I wouldn't have taken her out if I'd known how bad the scene at the house was gonna be. She only let me back up on her two days ago and she still starts at the slightest snap of a twig.

"I can send men up to fight the fires," Mr. O'Hare says.

"There'd be no point," the Mayor says. "Let them burn."

Submit! Juliet's Joy screeches underneath him at no one in particular.

"I've *got* to get a new horse," the Mayor mutters.

And then he lifts his head in a way that makes me notice.

"What?" I say.

But he's looking round, first to the path back to the bloody house, then to the road into town. Nothing's changed.

Except the look on the Mayor's face.

"What?" I say again.

"Can you not hear–?"

He stops again.

And then I do hear it–

Noise—

Noise that ain't human—

Coming from all sides—

Everywhere, like the soldier said—

"They wouldn't," the Mayor says, his face pinching with anger. "They wouldn't *dare.*"

But I can hear it clearly now—

We're surrounded, as quickly as that.

Spackle are coming straight for us.

{Viola}

What Mistress Coyle says to me is, "I never apologized to you for the bomb at the cathedral."

I don't say anything back.

I'm too astonished.

"It wasn't an attempt to murder you," she says. "Nor did I think your life was worth less than anyone else's."

I swallow hard. "Get out," I say and I'm surprised at myself. It must be the fever talking. "Right *now.*"

"I was hoping the President would look through your bag," she says. "He'd take out the bomb and that would be the end of our problems. But I also thought it would only come into play if you were captured. And if you were captured, you were already likely dead."

"That wasn't your decision to make."

"It was, my girl."

"If you'd asked me, I might have even said—"

"You'd do nothing that might harm your boy." She waits for me to contradict her. I don't. "Leaders must sometimes make monstrous decisions," she says, "and my monstrous decision was that if your life was likely to be lost on an errand *you* insisted on taking, then I would at least take the chance, however slim, to make your death worth it."

I can feel how red my face is getting and I begin to shake from both fever and pure hot anger. "That's only *one* way it could have worked out. There are a whole bunch of other things that could have happened, all of which end up with me and Lee blown to bits."

"Then you would have been a martyr for the cause," Mistress Coyle says, "and we would have fought in your name." She looks at me hard. "You'd be surprised at how powerful a martyr can be."

"Those are words a terrorist would use—"

"*Nevertheless*, Viola, I wanted to say to you that you were right."

"I've had just about enough—"

"Let me finish," she says. "It was a mistake, the bomb. Though I may have had good reasons in my desperation to get to him, that's still not enough to take such a heavy risk with a life that isn't my own."

"Damn right—"

"And for that, I'm sorry."

There's a silence now as she says the actual words, a heavy silence which lasts, and then lasts some more, and then she makes to leave.

"What do you want here?" I say, stopping her. "Do you really want peace or do you just want to beat the Mayor?"

She arches an eyebrow at me. "Surely one is required for the other."

"But what if trying for both means you don't get either?"

"It has to be a peace worth living for, Viola," she says. "If it just goes back to the way it was before, then what's the point? Why have any of us died?"

"There's a convoy of almost five thousand people on the way. It won't be at *all* like it was before."

"I know that, my girl–"

"And think what a powerful position you could be in if you're the one who helps us make a new truce? Who helps make the world peaceful for them?"

She looks thoughtful for a moment, then she runs her hand up the side of the door frame as a way of not looking at me. "I told you once how impressed I was with you. Do you remember that?"

I swallow, because that memory involves Maddy, who was shot while helping me to be *impressive*. "I do."

"I still am. Even more than before." She's still not looking at me. "I was never a girl here, you know. I was already grown when we landed, and I tried to help found the fishing village with some others." She purses her lips. "And we failed. The fish ate more of *us* than we ate of them."

"You could try again," I say. "With the new settlers. You said the ocean wasn't all that far, two days' ride–"

"One day, really," she says. "A couple hours on a fast horse. I told you two days because I didn't want you following me there."

I frown. "Yet *another* lie–"

"But I was wrong about that, too, my girl. You would have come if it had taken a month. That's how impressed I am with you. How you've survived, how you've kept yourself in a position to make a real impact, how you're singlehandedly trying to win your peace."

"Then *help* me," I say.

She taps the door frame with the flat of her hand once or twice, as if still thinking.

"I'm just wondering, my girl," she finally says. "Wondering if you're ready."

"Ready for what?"

But then she turns and leaves without another word.

"Ready for *what*?" I call after her, and then I swing myself out of bed, getting my feet to the floor and standing up–

And immediately falling right onto the other bed out of sheer dizziness.

I take a few deep breaths to make the world stop spinning–

Then I stand back up and set out after her.

[TODD]

The soldiers raise their rifles and start looking all round but the Spackle ROAR seems to be coming from everywhere, closing in fast from all direkshuns–

The Mayor's got his own rifle up. I got mine, too, one hand on Angharrad to steady her, but there's nothing to see, not yet–

And then a soldier down the road from us falls to the ground, screaming and grabbing at his chest–

"There!" shouts the Mayor–

As suddenly a whole platoon of Spackle, *dozens* of 'em,

212

come blazing outta the woods down the road, shooting their white sticks at the soldiers, who start falling even as they're firing back–

And the Mayor's riding past me, shooting his gun and ducking under an arrow coming at him–

Boy colt! Angharrad is screaming and I'm wanting to ride her away, to get her outta this–

And there are Spackle falling everywhere under the firing of the rifles–

But as soon as one falls, there's another right behind him–

FALL BACK! I hear in my Noise–

The Mayor, sending it out–

FALL BACK TO ME!

Not even yelling it, not even buzzing, just there, right in yer head–

And I see it–

Not believing it for a second–

All the soldiers left alive, about twelve now, move all together–

FALL BACK TO ME!

Like a herd of sheep moving from the bark of a dog–

EVERY MAN!

They move, still firing their guns, but coming backward toward the Mayor, too, their feet even walking in the same rhythm, all those different men suddenly looking like the same man, like *one* man, climbing over the bodies of other soldiers like they ain't even there–

TO ME!

TO ME!

And even *I* can feel my hands turning Angharrad's reins to line up behind the Mayor–

Moving with the rest of 'em–

Boy colt!?

I curse myself and turn her away from the main fight–

But the soldiers are still coming, even as one and then another of 'em falls, here they come, now in two short rows, firing in unison–

And Spackle are dying in the gunfire, dropping to the ground–

And the men move back–

And Mr. O'Hare's come up next to me on his own horse, firing, too, in exact timing with the rest of 'em and I see a Spackle coming outta the woods nearest us, raising a white stick right at Mr. O'Hare and–

GET DOWN! I think–

Think but don't say–

And there's a *buzz* from me to him, fast as anything–

And he gets down and the Spackle fires right over the top of him–

Mr. O'Hare rises again and shoots the Spackle, then he turns back to me–

But instead of saying thanks, his eyes are full of white fury–

And then suddenly there's silence–

The Spackle are gone. Not even so you can see 'em running away, just *gone,* and the attack's over and there are dead soldiers and dead Spackle and the whole thing took less than a minute–

And here are two rows of surviving soldiers standing in perfectly straight lines, rifles all held up exactly the same, all looking to the spot where the Spackle first came from, all waiting to shoot again–

All waiting for their next order from the Mayor.

I see his face, burning with concentrayshun and a fierceness it's hard to even look at.

And I know what it means.

It means his control's getting better.

Getting quicker and stronger and sharper.

(*But so's mine*, I think, *so's mine*)

"Indeed," the Mayor says. "Indeed it is, Todd."

And it takes me a second to realize that even tho my Noise was silent, he still heard me–

"Let's get back to town, Todd," he says, smiling for the first time in ages. "I think maybe it's time I tried something new."

{VIOLA}

"That's terrific, Wilf," I hear Bradley say as I exit the scout ship, looking all around for Mistress Coyle. Wilf is moving a cart with huge vats of fresh water into place near the ship, ready for distribution.

"Tain't nothin," Wilf says to Bradley. "Just doin what needs doin."

"Glad someone is," I hear behind me. It's Lee, returning early from the day's hunting party.

"Did you see which way Mistress Coyle went?" I ask him.

"Hello to you, too," he laughs. He holds up the forest hens he's carrying. "I'm saving the fattest one for us. Simone and the Humanitarian can have the small one."

"Don't call him that," I say, frowning.

Lee looks over at Bradley, who's heading back into the ship. The half circle of people who sit by the bay doors and watch–bigger today–just mutter to each other, and in the Noise of the few men there, Ivan included, I hear it again, The Humanitarian.

"He's trying to save us," I say to them. "He's trying to make it so all of the people coming can live here in peace. *With* the Spackle."

"Yeah," Ivan calls over. "And while he's doing it, he doesn't seem to notice that his weapons'd bring peace a hell of a lot faster than *humanitarian* efforts."

"His humanitarian efforts could guarantee you a long life, Ivan," I say. "And you should mind your own goddam business."

"I do believe survival *is* our business," Ivan says loudly, and there's a woman next to him agreeing, a smug smile on her dirty face, and even though she looks ashen from the same fever I've got and wears the same band I wear, I still want to smack her and smack her and smack her so she never looks at me that way again.

But Lee's already taking my arm and leading me away, around the scout ship to the far side by the engines, still off, still cool, but the one place on the hill where no one's going to make a tent.

"Stupid, small-minded people–" I'm ranting.

"I'm sorry, Viola," Lee says, "but I kind of agree with them."

216

"Lee–"

"President Prentiss killed my mother and sister," he says. "Anything we could do to help stop the Spackle *and* him is fine by me."

"You're as bad as Mistress Coyle," I say. "And *she* tried to kill *you*."

"I'm just saying, if we've got the weapons, we could show more strength–"

"And guarantee slaughter for years to come!"

He smirks a little, infuriatingly. "You sound like Bradley. He's the only one around here who talks like that."

"Yes, because a hilltopfull of frightened and hungry people are really going to offer a *rational–*"

And then I stop because Lee's just looking at me. Looking at my *nose*. I can tell, because I can see myself in his Noise, see me shouting and getting angry, see my nose wrinkling like it must do when I'm mad, see the warmth of his feelings around that wrinkle–

And in a flash, there's a picture of him and me in his Noise, holding each other tight, no clothes anywhere, and I'm seeing the blond hairs on his chest that I've never seen in real life, the downy, soft, surprisingly thick hair that trails all the way down to his belly button and below and–

"Oh, crap," he says, stepping back.

"Lee?" I say, but he's already turning and walking away fast, his Noise flooding with bright yellow embarrassment and he's saying, loud, "I'm going back to the hunting party," and walking away even faster–

And as I head off again in search of Mistress Coyle, I realize my skin feels incredibly hot, like I'm blushing all over–

BQY COlt? Angharrad says to me all the way back into town after the Spackle attack, going faster than I'm even asking her to. **BQY COlt?**

"Almost there, girl," I say.

I ride into camp just behind the Mayor, who's still practically *glowing* from how he controlled the men on the road just now. He slides off Juliet's Joy, handing her to James, who's waiting for us. I ride over to him, too, jumping off Angharrad's saddle.

"I need some feed for her," I say quickly. "Some water, too."

"I've got feed all ready," he says, as I guide her over to my tent. "But we're rationing water so—"

"No," I say, unbuckling the saddle from her as fast as I can. "You don't unnerstand. She needs water now. We've just—"

"Is she bossing you around again?" James says.

And I turn to him, eyes wide open. He's smiling back at me, not getting what we've just been thru at all, thinking that I'm being pushed around by my horse and not that I know how to take care of her, that she *needs* me—

"She's a beauty," he says, pulling a tangle outta Angharrad's mane. "But you're still the boss."

And I can see him thinking, thinking about his farm, thinking about the horses he and his pa used to have, three of 'em, all tan-colored with white noses, thinking about how they were taken by the army but how he ain't seen 'em since, which probably means they died in battle—

A thought which makes Angharrad say B**Q**y c**Q**lt? again all worriedlike–

And that makes me even angrier–

"No," I say to James. "Get some extra water for her now."

And barely even aware that I'm doing it, I'm staring at him hard, pushing with my Noise, reaching out and grabbing his–

Taking hold of it–

Taking hold of *him*–

And I am the Circle and the Circle is me–

"What are you doing, Todd?" he says, swatting away at the front of his face like he's batting back a fly.

"Water," I say. *"Now."*

And I can feel the *buzz* coming, feel it flailing about in the air–

I'm sweating now, even in the cold–

And I can see him sweating, too–

Sweating and looking confused–

He furrows his brow. "Todd?"

And he says it in such a sad way, a way that sounds, I don't know, *betrayed,* like I reached inside him and messed him about, that I almost stop right there. I almost stop concentrating; I almost stop reaching out to him–

But only almost.

"I'll get her plenty of water," he says, his eyes dazed. "I'll get some right now."

And off he goes, back toward the water tank.

I take a second to catch my breath.

I did it.

219

I did it again.

And it felt *good*.

It felt *powerful*.

"Oh, help," I whisper under my breath, and I'm shaking so hard I have to sit down.

{Viola}

I find Mistress Coyle in a small group of women near the healing tents, her back to me.

"Hey!" I call, stomping over. My voice is *very* loud after what just happened with Lee, but I'm also feeling fainter than seems plausible and I wonder if I'm about to fall flat on my face.

Mistress Coyle turns and I see three women with her: Mistress Nadari and Mistress Braithwaite, neither of whom have even bothered to say a word to me since the Answer came to the hilltop, but I'm not looking at them.

I'm looking at Simone.

"You should be in bed, my girl," Mistress Coyle says.

I glare at her. "You don't just ask if I'm ready for something then *walk off.*"

Mistress Coyle looks at the others, including Simone, who nods. "Very well, my girl. If you're that committed to knowing."

I'm still breathing heavy and realizing from her tone that I'm probably not going to like this at all when she holds out her hand in a way that asks if she can take my arm. I don't let her, but I go with her as she walks away from the healing tents, the other two mistresses and Simone walking behind us like bodyguards.

"We've been working on a theory," Mistress Coyle says.

"We?" I say, looking again at Simone, who still says nothing.

"One that makes more sense as the days go by, I'm afraid," Mistress Coyle says.

"Can you get to the point, please?" I say. "It's been a long day and I don't feel good."

She nods, once. "All right then, my girl." She stops and faces me. "We're starting to think that there may be no cure for the bands."

I put my hand up to my arm without thinking. "What?"

"We've had them for *decades*," she says. "We had them on Old World, for heaven's sake, and of course there've been instances of cruelty or pranks when humans have been banded. But we couldn't find a single other case, not even Simone in your very extensive database, of this sort of infection."

"But how–?"

And then I stop. Because I realize what she's hinting at.

"You think the Mayor put something extra on them."

"It'd be a way for him to harm a huge number of women without anyone knowing the real agenda."

"But we would have heard," I say. "With all the Noise of the men, there'd have been rumors–"

"Think about it, my girl," Mistress Coyle says. "Think about his history. Think about the extermination of the women in old Prentisstown."

"He says it was suicide," I say, knowing how weak it sounds.

"We've found chemicals even I can't identify, Viola," Simone says. "There's real danger here. Real implications."

221

I get a sick feeling in my stomach at the way she says *implications*. "Since when have you been listening to the mistresses so closely?"

"Since I found out you and all the banded women might be in real danger from that man," she says.

"You be careful," I say. "She's got a way of getting people to do what she wants." I look at Mistress Coyle. "A way of getting people to sit in half circles of judgment on the rest of us."

"My girl," Mistress Coyle says, *"I did not–"*

"What do you want with *me*?" I ask. "What do you want me to do about it?"

Mistress Coyle sighs angrily. "We want to know if your Todd knows anything, if there's something he's not telling us."

I'm already shaking my head. "He would have told me. The second he saw it on my arm."

"But can he find out, my girl?" Her voice is taut. "Would he help us find out?"

And it takes a moment to sink in. But when it does–

"Oh, *now* I get it."

"Get what?" Mistress Coyle says.

"You want a spy." My voice gets stronger as I get madder. "It's the same old tricks, isn't it? The same old Mistress Coyle, looking for every edge to give yourself more power."

"No, my girl," Mistress Coyle says. "We've found chemicals–"

"You're up to something," I say. "All this time, refusing to tell me how you made the first truce, waiting for the Mayor to *make his move*, and now you're trying to use Todd like you used–"

"It's fatal, my girl," she says. "The infection is *fatal*."

[TODD]

"The shame disappears, Todd," the Mayor says, appearing behind me in that way he does as I watch James make his way thru the army camp to get Angharrad's extra water.

"You did this to me," I say, still trembling. "You put it in my head and *made* me—"

"I did no such thing," he says. "I merely showed you the path. You walked down it all by yourself."

I don't say nothing. Cuz I know it's true.

(but that *hum* I hear—)

(that *hum* I pretend ain't there—)

"I'm not controlling you, Todd," he says. "That was part of our agreement, which I'm keeping to. All that's happened is you've found the power I've repeatedly said was in you. It's desire, you see. You *wanted* it to happen. That's the secret to it all."

"No, it ain't," I say. "Everyone's got desire, but they don't go round being able to control folks."

"That's because the desire of most *folks* is to be told what to do." He looks back across the square, covered in tents and soldiers and townsfolk all huddled together. "People say they want freedom, but what they really want is freedom from worry. If I take care of their problems, they don't mind being told what to do."

"*Some* people," I say. "Not everyone."

"No," he says. "Not you. Which paradoxically makes you all the better at controlling others. There are two kinds of people in this world, Todd. Them." He gestures at the army. "And us."

223

"Don't you include me in no *us*."

But he just grins again. "Are you sure about that? I believe the Spackle are connected by their Noise, all bound up in one voice. What makes you think that men aren't? What connects me and you, Todd, is that we know how to use that voice."

"I ain't gonna be like you," I say. "I ain't *never* gonna be like you."

"No," he says, his eyes flashing. "I think you'll be *better*."

And then there's a sudden pulse of light–

Brighter than any electric light we've got anywhere–

Blazing cross the square–

As near the army as you can get without being in the middle of it–

"The water tank," the Mayor says, already moving. "They've attacked the water tank!"

{ V I O L A }

"Fatal?" I say.

"Four women so far," Mistress Coyle says. "Another seven that won't last the week. We're keeping it quiet because we don't want a panic."

"That's only ten or so out of a thousand," I say. "Ones who were weak and ill anyway–"

"Are you willing to risk that belief on your own life? On the life of every banded woman here? Even amputating their *arms* didn't work, Viola. Does that seem like a normal infection to you?"

"If you're asking me if I believe you'd lie to get me to do

exactly what you want, then what do you *think* my answer's going to be?"

Mistress Coyle takes a slow deep breath, like she's trying to keep her temper. "I'm the best healer here, my girl," she says, her voice fierce with feeling, "and I could not stop those women from dying." Her eyes fall to the bandages on my arm. "I might not be able to stop it for anyone with a band."

I put my hand lightly to my arm again and feel the throb of it.

"Viola," Simone says quietly, "the women are really sick."

But no, I'm thinking. *No–*

"You don't understand," I say, shaking my head. "This is how she works. She turns a small truth into a bigger lie to get you to do what she wants–"

"*Viola*," Mistress Coyle says–

"No," I say, louder, because I'm thinking more. "I can't risk you being right, can I? If it's a lie, it's a clever one, because if I'm wrong, we all die, so yeah, okay, I'll see what I can find out from Todd."

"*Thank* you," Mistress Coyle says hotly.

"But," I say, "I will *not* ask him to spy for you and you *will* do something for me in return."

Mistress Coyle's eyes light all over my face, seeing how much I mean it.

"Do what?" she finally says.

"You'll quit putting me off and tell me, step by step, every-thing you did to make peace with the Spackle," I say. "And then you'll help me start the process up again. No more delays, no more waiting. We'll start tomorrow."

I can see her brain working, crafting whatever advantage

she can get out of this. "I'll tell you what—"

"No deals," I say. "You do everything I ask or you get nothing."

There's only the smallest of pauses this time. "Agreed."

And there's a shout from the scout ship. Bradley's running down the ramp, his Noise roaring. "Something's happening in the town!"

[TODD]

We run toward the water tank, the soldiers in front of us parting to make way, even if their backs are turned—

And I can hear the Mayor working in their heads, telling 'em to move, telling 'em to get outta his way—

And as we get there, we can see it—

The water tank is teetering—

One leg has been nearly blown off, maybe even by one of those spinning fire things shot from close range, cuz sticky, white flames are spreading over the wood of the tank almost like liquid itself—

And there are Spackle everywhere—

Rifles are firing in all direkshuns and the Spackle are firing their white sticks and men are falling and Spackle are falling but that ain't the worst problem—

"THE FIRE!" the Mayor screams, hitting it inside the head of everyone standing round him. "GET THAT FIRE OUT!"

And the men start to move—

But then something goes wrong, something goes *really* wrong—

226

Soldiers on the front line start dropping their rifles to get buckets of water–

Soldiers who were in midfire, soldiers who were right next to Spackle–

They just turn and leave like they're suddenly blinded to the battle they were just fighting–

But the *Spackle* ain't blinded and men start dying in bigger numbers, not even looking at who's killing 'em–

WAIT! I hear the Mayor think. KEEP FIGHTING!

But there's some kind of catch in it now, and some soldiers who dropped their guns pick 'em up again but others just stand there sorta frozen, not knowing which to do–

And then they fall to the ground, too, hit by Spackle weapons–

And I see the Mayor's face, see it nearly splitting with concentrayshun, trying to get some men to do one thing, other men to do another, and it's all adding up to no one doing nothing and more men are dying and the water tank is gonna *fall*–

"Mr. President?!" Mr. O'Hare yells, storming in with his rifle and almost immediately struck dumb by the Mayor's messed-up control–

And the Spackle see that the army's confused, that we're not doing what we should be doing, that only some soldiers are firing, but others are just standing there and we're letting the fire spread to the food store–

And I can *feel* it in the Spackle Noise, even if I don't know the words: they're smelling a victory bigger than they thought possible, maybe the *final* victory–

And all the while, I ain't frozen–

I don't know why but I'm the only one who don't seem to be stuck under the Mayor's control–

Maybe he ain't in my head after all–

But I can't stop to think about what that means–

And I grab my rifle by the barrel and swing it hard right into the Mayor's ear–

He calls out and stumbles sideways–

The soldiers nearby yell, too, as if someone punched 'em–

The Mayor sinks to one knee, hand on his head, blood spilling twixt his fingers, a *whine* in the air coming from his Noise–

But I'm already turning to Mr. O'Hare and yelling, "Get a line of men firing, now, now, NOW!"

And I'm feeling the *buzz* a bit but I don't know if it's my words working or if he sees what needs to be done but he's already leaping and shouting to the soldiers nearest him to line up, to get their effing rifles in the air, to FIRE–

And as the gunshots start ripping thru the air again and as the Spackle start falling again and moving back, tripping over themselves in the sudden change, I see Mr. Tate running up to us and I don't even let him open his mouth–

"Put that fire OUT!" I yell.

And he looks at the Mayor, still kneeling, still bleeding, and then he gives me a nod, and starts yelling at another group of soldiers to get buckets, to save our water and food–

And the world is taking off all round us, screaming and yelling and tearing itself to pieces and there's a line of soldiers now pressing forward, pushing the Spackle back from the water tank–

And I'm standing over the Mayor, who's kneeling there, holding his head, the blood seeping out all thicklike and I ain't kneeling down next to him, I ain't seeing if he's all right, I ain't doing nothing to help him.

But I find I ain't leaving him neither.

"You hit me, Todd," I hear him say, his voice as thick as his blood.

"You needed to be hit, you idiot! You were gonna get everyone killed!"

He looks up at that, his hand still to his head. "I was," he says. "You were right to stop me."

"No effing kidding."

"But you did it, Todd," the Mayor says, breathing heavy. "For a minute there, when the moment called for it. You were a leader of men."

And then the water tank collapses.

{VIOLA}

"There's been a big attack," Bradley says as we run toward him.

"How big?" I say, reaching immediately for my comm.

"There was a bright flash on one of the probes and then–"

He stops because we hear another sound.

Screaming at the edge of the forest.

"What *now*?" Simone says.

Voices rise at the line of trees, and we see people standing up from their campfires and more screams–

And Lee–

Lee–

Stumbling out of the crowd–

Covered in blood–

Holding his hands to his face–

"LEE!"

And I'm running as fast as I can, though the fever's slowing me down and I can't catch my breath and Bradley and Mistress Coyle are running past me, and they're grabbing Lee and laying him down on the ground, Mistress Coyle having to forcibly pull his hands away from his bloody face–

And another voice screams in the crowd–

As we see–

Lee's eyes–

They're gone–

Just *gone*–

Burned away in a slash of blood–

Burned away as if by acid–

"Lee!" I say, kneeling down beside him. "Lee, can you hear me?"

"Viola?" he says, reaching out with his bloody hands. "I can't see you! I can't see!"

"I'm here!" I grab his hands, holding them tight. "I'm *here*!"

"What happened, Lee?" Bradley says, low and calm. "Where's the rest of the hunting party?"

"They're dead," Lee says. "Oh, God, they're dead. Magnus is *dead*."

And we know what he's going to say next, know because we can see it in his Noise–

"The Spackle," Lee says. "The Spackle are coming."

[TODD]

The legs of the tank give way and the huge metal container of water comes tumbling down, almost too slow to be real–

It smashes to the ground, crushing at least one soldier underneath it–

And every drop of water we had to drink comes rushing out in a solid wall–

Heading right for us–

The Mayor's still wobbly on his feet, still woozy–

"RUN!" I shout, sending it out in my Noise while grabbing a handful of the Mayor's precious uniform and dragging him away–

The wall of water slams up the street and into the square after us, knocking over soldiers and Spackle, sweeping up tents and beds in one great big soup–

And it's putting out the fire in the food store, but it's putting it out with the last of our water–

And I'm dragging the Mayor nearly on his heels, getting us outta the way, thru soldiers I'm shouting at to "MOVE!" as we near–

And they do move–

And we make it up the front steps of a house–

And the water rushes past us, sloshing up after us to our knees, but rushing by and getting lower every second, sinking into the ground–

Taking our future with it.

And then almost as fast as it came, it's gone, leaving a sopping square covered in mess and bodies of all sorts–

And I just catch my breath for a second and look out on the chaos, the Mayor recovering beside me–

And then I see–

Oh, no–

There, on the ground, pushed to the side by the water–

No–

James.

James, lying faceup, staring up at the sky above–

A hole through his throat.

I'm faintly aware of dropping my rifle, of running over to him, splashing thru the water and falling to my knees beside him.

James, who I controlled. James, who I sent over this way for no good reason other than my *desire*–

James, who I sent right to his death.

Oh, no.

Oh, please, no.

"Well, that's a damn shame," the Mayor says behind me, sounding true, sounding almost *kind*. "I'm very sorry about your friend. But you did save *me*, Todd. Twice. Once from my own foolishness and once from a wall of water."

I don't say nothing. I ain't taking my eyes off James's face, still innocent, still nice and open and friendly, even when there ain't no sound coming outta him at all.

The battle's leaving us now. Mr. O'Hare's guns are blazing on distant streets. But what good will it do?

They got the water tank.

They've killed us.

I barely hear the Mayor sigh. "I think it's time I met these settler friends of yours, Todd," he says. "And I think it's finally time I had a nice long talk with Mistress Coyle."

I use my fingertips to close James's eyes, remembering when I did it for Davy Prentiss, feeling the same hollowness in my Noise, and I can't even think *I'm sorry* cuz it don't feel like nearly enough, not like nearly enough at all, no matter if I said it for the rest of my life.

"The Spackle have turned terrorist, Todd," the Mayor says, tho I ain't much listening. "And maybe it takes a terrorist to fight a terrorist."

And then we both hear it. Over the chaos in the square, there's another *ROAR*, a whole different kind of roar in a world that seems to be *made* outta roaring.

We look east, up over the ruins of the cathedral, past the rickety brick bell tower, still standing, still looking like it shouldn't.

In the distance, the scout ship has taken to the air.

On the Brink

I AM SUBMERGED in the voice of the Land.

I am attacking the Clearing, feeling the weapons fire in my hands, seeing their soldiers die with my eyes, hearing the roars and screams of battle in my ears. I am up on the hilltop, on the rugged lip of it overlooking the valley below, but I am there in the battle as well, living it through the voices of those fighting, those giving up their lives for the Land.

And I watch as the water tank falls, though the Land close enough to see it fall die rapidly under the hand of the Clearing, each death a terrible tear at the voice of the Land, a sudden absence that pulls and pains—

But is necessary—

Necessary in small numbers only, the Sky shows to me, watching, too. *Necessary to save the entire body of the Land.*

And necessary to finish this war before the **convoy**

arrives, I show back, hitting the strange word that I did not teach him.

There is time, the Sky shows, his concentration still on the city below, still on the voices that reach us from there, fewer now, more on the run.

There is? I ask, surprised, wondering how he knows for sure—

But I set my concerns aside, because the Sky's voice opens to remind me of what is still to come tonight, now that the first goal of toppling the water tank is achieved.

One way or another, tonight is where the war will change.

Their water was the first step.

All-out invasion is the second.

The Land has not been idle these past days. The Land's parties have attacked the Clearing unpredictably, from different directions at different times, hitting them hard in surprising and isolated spots. The Land are far more at one with the ground and the trees than the Clearing and can disguise themselves more easily, and the Clearing's floating lights dare not get too close or the Land will shoot them down.

The Clearing could fire their larger weapons down the river, of course, hitting even the Sky himself, though they cannot know that he watches them from so near.

But if they did fire, the river would come to drown them.

And there may be another reason. For why would the

Clearing have such a powerful weapon and not use it? Why would they allow themselves to be attacked again and again, in increasing severity, and not answer back?

Unless, as we originally barely dared to hope, they had no more weapons to fire.

I wish I was down there, I show, as we continue to watch through the voice of the Land. *I wish I was firing a rifle. Firing it into the Knife.*

You do not, the Sky shows, his voice low and thoughtful. *They will be desperate now. We have progressed this far because they have not made a coordinated response.*

And you want them to, I show.

The Sky wants the Clearing to show itself.

We can attack now, I show, my excitement growing. *They are in chaos. If we acted now—*

We will wait, the Sky shows, *until we hear the voices from the far hilltop.*

The far hilltop. Our distant voices, the parts of the Land that go out to gather information, have shown us how the Clearing has divided itself into two camps. One in the city below, another on a hilltop in the distance. We have left the hilltop alone so far because they seem to be those of the Clearing that have fled the battle, those that are not inter-ested in fighting. But we also know that the vessel landed there, and that the larger weapon was more than likely fired from there, too.

We have been unable to get close enough to see if they have more weapons.

But tonight we find out for certain.

The Land is ready, I show, barely able to contain my excitement. *The Land is ready to attack.*

Yes, shows the Sky. *The Land is ready.*

And in his voice, I see them.

The massed bodies of the Land to the north of the city and the south of it, too, gathered there slowly these past days, along paths the Clearing is unaware of, kept just distant enough for the Clearing to be unable to hear them.

And in the Sky's voice I see another massed body, hidden, but ready and waiting near the far hilltop.

Right now, this moment, the Land is ready to march in full force on the Clearing.

And slaughter them all.

We will wait for news from the far hilltop, the Sky shows again, more firmly this time. *Patience. The warrior who strikes too early is a warrior lost.*

And if the voices show what we want them to show?

He looks at me, a glint in his eye, a glint that expands into his voice, that grows to the size of the world around me, showing what is to come, showing what will happen, showing all that I want to be true.

If, he shows, *the voices from the hilltop find that the Clearing have indeed spent all of their big weapons—*

Then the war ends tonight, I show. *With victory.*

He presses a hand on my shoulder, wrapping me in his

voice, warming me with it, pulling me into the voice of the entire Land.

If and only if, he shows.

If and only if, I show back.

And in a low voice, maybe even one that only I can hear, the Sky shows, *Does the Return now trust the Sky?*

I do, I show without hesitation. *I am sorry if I doubted you.*

And I get a feeling in my stomach, a tingling feeling of prophecy and future, a feeling that it must happen tonight, that it *will* happen, that all I want for the fate of the Clearing is here and now, in front of me, in front of all of us, that the Burden will be avenged, that my one in particular will be avenged, that I will be avenged—

And then a sudden roaring splits the night in two.

What is it? I show, but I can feel the Sky's voice searching, too, reaching out into the night, looking with his eyes as well, searching for the sound, feeling the rising terror that it is another weapon, that we were mistaken, that—

There, he shows.

In the distance, far away and small, on the far hilltop—

Their vessel is rising into the air.

We watch as it lumbers up into the night, like a river swan in the first heavy beats of its wings—

Can we not see closer? the Sky shows, sending it out far and wide. *Is there not a voice closer?*

The vessel, little more than a light in the distance, begins a slow circle over the far hilltop, tilting as it turns, and we see small flashes from its underside, dropping into the forest below, flashes that grow suddenly brighter in the trees, accompanied seconds later by booming sounds rolling across the valley towards us.

And here come the voices from the hilltop—

The Sky cries out, and we are suddenly under the flashes dropping from the ship, under the great booming explosions ripping through the trees, flashes everywhere from every side, impossible to run from, exploding the whole world, the Land's eyes seeing the flashes and feeling the pain and then snuffing out like a doused fire—

And I hear the Sky send forth the immediate command to pull back.

No! I shout.

The Sky looks at me sharply. *You would have them slaughtered?*

*They are **willing** to die. And now is our chance—*

The Sky strikes me across the face with the back of his hand.

I stagger back, astonished, feeling the pain ring through my entire head.

You said you trusted the Sky, did you not? he shows, the anger in his voice gripping me so hard it hurts.

You hit me.

DID YOU NOT? His voice knocks all thought out of my head.

240

I stare back at him, my own anger rising. But, *Yes,* I show.

Then you will trust me now. He turns to the Pathways, waiting in an arc behind him. *Bring the Land back from the far hilltop. The Land to the north and the south will await my instructions.*

The Pathways immediately set out to deliver the Sky's orders directly to the Land that waits for them.

Orders given in the language of the Burden so I am sure to understand them.

Orders for retreat.

Not attack.

The Sky will not look at me, keeping his back turned, but once again, I am a better reader of him than any of the Land here, maybe better than the Land is supposed to read its Sky.

You expected this, I show. *You expected more weapons.*

He still does not look at me, but a change in his voice shows me I am right. *The Sky did not lie to the Return,* he shows. *If there had been no further weapons, we would be overrunning them this very moment.*

But you knew there **would** *be weapons. You let me believe—*

You believed what you hoped to be true, the Sky shows. *Nothing I could have said would have taken that from you.*

My voice still rings with the pain from his slap.

I am sorry I struck you, he says.

And in his apology, I see it. For the briefest of seconds, I see it.

Like the sun through the clouds, a flash of unmistakable light.

I see his essentially peaceful nature.

You wish to make peace with them, I show. *You wish to make a truce.*

His voice hardens. *Have I not shown the opposite to be true?*

You are keeping the possibility open.

*No wise leader would do anything else. And you **will** learn that. You **must**.*

I blink, baffled. *Why?*

But he just looks back across the valley, back to the far hilltop where the vessel still flies.

We have awakened the beast, he shows. *We shall see how angry it gets.*

SPEAKING WITH THE ENEMY

{VIOLA}

MY COMM BEEPS and I know it's Todd calling, but I'm in the healing room on the scout ship, holding Lee's head in my lap and that's taken over all my thinking right now.

"Hold him steady, Viola," Mistress Coyle says, bracing herself as the scout ship lists again.

"One more pass and then we'll land," Simone says over the ship's comm system.

We can hear the low *boom*s through the floor where Simone is dropping the hoopers, small packets of bombs linked together magnetically that spread out as they fall, blanketing the forest below in fire and explosions.

One more time, we're bombing the Spackle.

After Lee told us they were coming, I helped carry him inside the scout ship where Mistress Coyle and Mistress Lawson immediately started working on him. Outside, even through the doors of the ship, we could hear the shouting of the people on the hilltop. Hear their terror, but also their anger. I could just imagine that half circle of watchers, led by Ivan, demanding to know what Simone and Bradley were going to do about it, now that we'd been attacked directly.

"They could be *ANYWHERE!*" I heard Ivan shout.

And so as Mistress Coyle sedated Lee and Mistress Lawson washed the seemingly endless blood from his destroyed eye sockets, we heard Simone and Bradley stomp aboard, arguing between themselves. Simone went to the cockpit, and Bradley came into the healing room and said, "We're taking off."

"I'm operating here," Mistress Coyle said, not looking up.

Bradley opened a panel and took out a small device. "Gyroscopic scalpel," he said. "It'll keep steady in your hand even if this ship flips over."

"So *that's* what that was," Mistress Lawson said.

"Is there trouble outside?" I asked.

Bradley just frowned, his Noise full of images of people getting into his face, calling him the Humanitarian.

Some of them spitting on him.

"*Bradley,*" I said.

"Just hold on," he said, and he stayed with us rather than join Simone in the cockpit.

Mistresses Coyle and Lawson kept on working furiously. I'd forgotten what an incredible thing it was to see Mistress Coyle heal. Ferocious and concentrated, all her attention bent on saving Lee, even as we felt the engines burn into life, felt the ship rise slowly in the air, tilting as it circled the hilltop, felt the first of the bombs explode far beneath us.

And still Mistress Coyle worked.

Now Simone is completing her last pass, and I can feel

the heat in Bradley's Noise about what we'll find on the hilltop when we open the doors.

"That bad?" Mistress Coyle says, carefully tying the last stitch.

"They weren't even interested in recovering the bodies of the people who were killed," Bradley says. "They just wanted force and they wanted it *right now*."

Mistress Coyle moves to a basin in the wall and starts washing her hands. "They'll be satisfied. You've done your duty."

"This is our duty now, is it?" Bradley says. "Bombing an enemy we've never met?"

"You took a step into this war," Mistress Coyle says, "and now you can't just step out of it. Not if lives are at stake."

"Which, of course, is exactly what you wanted."

"Bradley," I say, my comm beeping again, but I'm not ready to let go of Lee just yet. "They attacked *us*."

"After we attacked them," Bradley says. "After they attacked us, after we attacked them, and so on and so on until we're all dead."

I look back down at Lee's face, what I can see of it under the bandages, the bottom of his nose just poking out, his mouth open and breathing heavy, his blond hair in my hands, sticky with blood. I can feel him underneath my fingertips, the injured warmth of his skin, the weight of his unconscious body.

He's never going to be the same again, never ever, which makes my throat choke and my chest hurt.

This is what war does. Right here, in my hands. This is war.

In my pocket, my comm beeps one more time.

"Neutral ground?" says the Mayor, his eyebrows rising. "Now where might that be, I wonder?"

"Mistress Coyle's old house of healing," I say. "That's what Viola said. Mistress Coyle and the people from the scout ship will meet you there at dawn."

"Not exactly *neutral,* is it?" the Mayor says. "Clever, though."

He looks thoughtful for a second, glancing back down to the reports on his lap from Mr. Tate and Mr. O'Hare about how bad things are.

They're pretty bad.

The square is a wreck. Half the tents were washed away by the water from the tank. Fortunately, mine was far enough back and Angharrad was safe, too, but the rest is a soggy mess. One wall of the food store collapsed cuz of the water, and the Mayor's got men over there now, picking thru the leavings, seeing just how soon the end's gonna come.

"They've really done a number on us, Todd," the Mayor says, frowning at the papers. "With one action, they've cut our water stores by ninety-five percent. At the most reduced rations, that's just four days, with almost six weeks to go until the ships arrive."

"What about food?"

"We've had a bit of luck there," he says, holding out a report to me. "See for yourself."

I stare at the papers in his hand. I can see the squiggles of Mr. Tate's and Mr. O'Hare's handwriting skittering in blips and blobs across the page like the black microrats we used

248

to get in the barn back at the farm, twisting and turning so fast when you lifted up a board it was hard to see a single one of 'em. I look at the pages and I wonder how the hell anyone can read anything when letters look like such different things in different places and are somehow still the *same* thing–

"I'm sorry, Todd," the Mayor says, lowering the papers. "I forgot."

I turn back to Angharrad, not believing the Mayor forgets *nothing*.

"You know," he says, and his voice ain't unkind. "I could teach you how to read."

And there are the words, the words that make me burn even hotter, with embarrassment and shame and an anger that makes me wanna tear someone's head right off–

"It may be easier than you think," he says. "I've been working on ways to use Noise to learn and–

"What, in return for saving yer life?" I say, loud. "Don't like being in my debt, is that it?"

"I think we may be even on that score, Todd. Besides, it's nothing to be ashamed of–"

"Just shut up, okay?"

He looks at me for a long moment. "Okay," he finally says, gently. "I didn't mean to upset you. Tell Viola I'll meet them as they wish." He stands. "And furthermore, that I'll come accompanied only by yourself."

{ V I O L A }

"That sounds suspicious," I say into the comm.

249

"*I know,*" Todd says. "*I thought he'd try to argue, but he agreed to everything.*"

"Mistress Coyle said all along he'd come to her. I guess she was right."

"*Why don't I feel too great that she is?*"

I laugh a little, which sets me coughing.

"*You okay?*" Todd asks.

"Yeah, yeah," I say quickly. "It's Lee I'm worried about."

"*How's he doing?*"

"Stable but still bad. Mistress Lawson only brings him out of sedation to feed him."

"*Jeez,*" Todd says. "*Tell him I said hey.*" I see him look over to his right. "*Yeah, just a damn minute!*" He looks back at me. "*I gotta go. The Mayor wants to talk about tomorrow.*"

"I'm sure Mistress Coyle will, too," I say. "I'll see you in the morning."

He smiles shyly. "*It'll be good to see you. In person, I mean. It's been too long. Way too long.*"

I say good-bye and we click off.

Lee's in the bed next to me, sound asleep. Mistress Lawson sits in the corner, checking his condition on the ship's monitors every five minutes. She's also checking on me, trying out Mistress Coyle's timed treatments for the infection in my arm, which now seems to be moving into my lungs.

Fatal, Mistress Coyle said the infection was.

Fatal.

If she was telling the truth, *if* she wasn't exaggerating to force me to help her.

And that's why I think I haven't told Todd how sick I am.

Because if he got upset about it, which he would, I'd have to start thinking it might all be true–

Mistress Coyle comes in. "How are you feeling, my girl?"

"Better," I lie.

She nods and moves over to check on Lee. "Have you heard back from them?"

"The Mayor's agreed to everything," I say, coughing again. "And he's going to come on his own. Just him and Todd."

Mistress Coyle laughs in an unamused way. "The arrogance of the man. So certain we won't harm him he's making a show of it."

"I said we'd do the same. Just you, me, Simone, and Bradley. We'll lock up the ship and ride down there."

"An excellent plan, my girl," she says, checking the monitors. "With some armed women from the Answer just out of sight, of course."

I frown. "So we're not even going to start out with good intentions?"

"When will you ever learn?" she says. "Good intentions mean nothing if they're not backed up with strength."

"That's the way to endless war."

"Maybe," she says. "But it's also the only path to peace."

"I don't believe that," I say.

"And you keep on not believing it," she says. "Who knows? You might just win the day." She makes to leave. "Until tomorrow, my girl."

And in her voice I can tell how much she's looking forward to it.

The day the Mayor comes to her.

[TODD]

The Mayor and I ride down the road toward the house of healing in the cold darkness before dawn, passing the trees and buildings I used to see every day when I rode to the monastery with Davy.

It's the first time I've ridden here without him.

Boy colt, Angharrad thinks and I see Acorn in her Noise, Acorn that Davy always rode and tried to call Deadfall, Acorn who Viola now rides and who'll probably be there today, too.

But Davy won't. Davy won't never be nowhere again.

"You're thinking about my son," the Mayor says.

"You shut up about him," I say, almost by reflex. And then I say, "How can you still read me? No one else can."

"I'm hardly just anyone else, Todd."

You can say that again, I think, to see if he hears it.

"But you're quite right," he says, pulling Juliet's Joy by the reins. "You've done exceptionally well. You've picked it up far faster than any of my captains did. Who knows what you'll ultimately be capable of?"

And he gives me a grin that's almost *proud.*

The sun ain't yet risen down at the end of the road in the direkshun we're headed, just a vague pinkness in the sky. The Mayor insisted we get there first, insisted we be the ones waiting for 'em when they showed up.

Me and him and the company of men following us.

We reach the two barns that mark the turning to the house of healing and head down it toward the empty river. The sky is still mostly dark as we come round a bend and see it.

It ain't what we expected. Instead of a house of healing where we could go inside and have our meeting, it's just
a charred wooden frame, its roof missing and burnt debris
strewn across the front lawn. At first I think the Spackle
musta burned it down, but then I remember the Answer blew
up everything as it marched on the town, even its own buildings. It musta helped that the Mayor had turned it into a jail
and not a place where you'd ever really want to be healed
anymore.

The other thing that ain't expected is that they're
already here, waiting for us on the drive. Viola's on Acorn,
off to one side of an ox-pulled cart with a dark-skinned
man and a solid-looking woman who can only be Mistress
Coyle. The Mayor wasn't the only one who wanted to get
here first.

I feel him bristle beside me but he hides it fast as we
stop, facing them. "Good morning," he says. "Viola, I know,
and of course the famous Mistress Coyle, but I don't
believe I have the pleasure of the gentleman's acquaint-
ance."

"We've got armed women in the trees," Viola says before
she even says hello.

"Viola!" says Mistress Coyle.

"We've got fifty men down the road," I say. "He says we're
sposed to say it's for proteckshun against the Spackle."

Viola nods at Mistress Coyle. "She just said we were
supposed to lie."

"Which would be difficult," the Mayor says, "because I
can see them clearly in the gentleman's Noise, to whom,
I repeat, I have not been introduced."

253

"Bradley Tench," the man says.

"President David Prentiss," the Mayor says. "At your service."

"And you can only be Todd," Mistress Coyle says.

"And you can only be the one who tried to kill me and Viola," I say, holding her gaze.

She just smiles back. "I don't think I'm the only person here this morning guilty of that."

She's smaller than I expected. Or maybe I'm just bigger. After all Viola said she's done, leading armies, blowing up half the city, putting herself in place to be the next leader of the town, I expected a giant. She's stocky, sure, like a lotta people on this planet; it's how you look if you have to work for a living. But then there's her eyes and they look at you and don't brook no arguments, don't look like they ever doubt themselves, even when they should. Maybe they're the eyes of a giant after all.

I ride Angharrad over to Acorn so I can properly greet Viola, already feeling that warm rush I get whenever I see her but also seeing how sick she's looking, how pale and—

She's looking back at me, puzzled, her head tilted.

And I realize she's trying to read me.

And she can't.

{ V I O L A }

I stare at Todd. Looking at him and looking at him.

And not hearing him.

At all.

I thought it was just horrors from the war, traumatizing

him, shocking him into blurriness, but this is different. This is nearly silence.

This is like the Mayor.

"Viola?" he whispers.

"I understood there was to be a fourth member of your party?" the Mayor asks.

"Simone decided to stay with the ship," Bradley says, and even though I'm not taking my eyes off Todd, I can hear his Noise is full of Ivan and the others, who threatened outright violence if we left them unable to protect themselves. Simone finally had to agree to stay behind. Bradley's the one who should have, of course, his Noise blaring out every second, but the hilltop folk, led by Ivan, weren't going to stand being protected by the Humanitarian.

"Most unfortunate," the Mayor says. "The townsfolk are obviously hungering for strong leadership."

"That's one way of looking at it," Bradley says.

"And so here we are," the Mayor says. "At a meeting that will set the course for this world."

"Here we are," Mistress Coyle agrees, "so let's get started, shall we?"

And then she speaks and her words are enough to even make me stop looking at Todd.

"You are a criminal and a murderer," she says to the Mayor, her voice calm as a stone. "You committed a genocide of the Spackle that brought this war on us. You imprisoned, enslaved, and then permanently marked every woman you could get your hands on. You have proven powerless to stop the Spackle attacks, which have cost you half your army, and it can only be a matter of time before they rise up against your leadership and decide instead to rally around the superior fire power of the scout ship, at the very least to survive the remaining weeks until the convoy of settlers arrives."

She smiles through this whole speech, despite how Bradley and I are looking at her, how *Todd* is looking at her–

But then I see the Mayor's smiling, too.

"So, why, exactly," Mistress Coyle says, "shouldn't we just sit back and let you self-destruct?"

[TODD]

"You," the Mayor says back to Mistress Coyle, after a long, silent minute, "are a criminal and a terrorist. Rather than work with me to make New Prentisstown a welcoming paradise for the incoming settlers, you instead tried to blow it up, deciding you would rather see it destroyed than let it be something you didn't choose yourself. You killed soldiers and innocent townsfolk, including an attempt on the life of young Viola here, seeking only to overthrow me so you could set yourself up as unchallenged ruler of some new Coyleville." He nods at Bradley. "The scout ship crew are clearly only supporting you reluctantly, after you no doubt manipulated Viola into firing that missile. And how many weapons do they have after all? Enough to defeat a hundred thousand, a *million* Spackle, who will come in wave after wave until all of us are dead? You, Mistress, have as much to answer for as I do."

And he and Mistress Coyle are still smiling at each other.

Bradley sighs loudly. "Well, gosh, *that* was fun. Can we

now please get on with the reasons why we're here?"

"And what might those exact reasons be?" the Mayor asks him, sounding like he's talking to a child.

"How about the avoidance of complete annihilation?" Bradley says. "How about creating a planet that has room enough for everyone, including the two of you? The convoy's now forty days away, so how about a peaceful world for them to land in? Each of us has power. Mistress Coyle has a dedicated group behind her, though smaller and less well equipped than your army. Our position is more easily defended than yours, but it lacks room to support a population that grows more restive by the day. Meanwhile, you're subject to attacks you can't combat–"

"Yes," the Mayor interrupts, "the military wisdom of combining our forces is obvious–"

"That's not what I'm talking about," Bradley says, and his voice gets hotter, his Noise, too, rawer and more awkward than anyone I've ever heard, but buzzing with a sense of how right he is, how *sure* he is that he's doing the right thing, and how much muscle he's got to back it up.

I'm finding I kinda like him.

"I'm not talking about *military combinations* at all," he says. "I'm saying that *I've* got the missiles, *I've* got the bombs, and *I* say right now that I will happily leave you to your little conflict if you don't agree with *me* that what we're going to discuss here is a way to combine our strength to *end* this war, not *win* it."

And for the slightest of seconds, the Mayor ain't smiling.

"It should be easy," Viola says, coughing. "We have water, you have food. We exchange what we have for what we need. We show the Spackle we're united, that we aren't going anywhere, and that we want peace."

But all I'm seeing as she says it is how much she's shivering in the cold.

"Agreed," Mistress Coyle says, sounding pleased with how things have gone so far. "Then as a first point of negotiation, perhaps the President would be so kind as to tell us how to reverse the effects of the bands, which, as I'm sure was his intention all along, are now killing every woman who wears one."

{VIOLA}

"WHAT?" Todd shouts.

"I have no idea what she's talking about," the Mayor says quickly but Todd's face is already a storm.

"It's only a theory," I say. "They haven't proved anything."

"And you're feeling just fine, are you?" Mistress Coyle says.

"No, but I'm not *dying*."

"That's because you're young and strong," Mistress Coyle says. "Not every woman is so lucky."

"The bands are from a regular cattle stock you had in Haven," the Mayor says. "If you're saying I modified them to kill the women who were banded, then you are sorely mistaken and I take *great* offense–"

"Don't you get high and mighty with *me*," Mistress Coyle says. "You killed every woman in old Prentisstown–"

"The women of old Prentisstown committed suicide," the Mayor says, "because they were losing a war *they* started."

258

"*What?*" Todd says again, whirling around to look at the Mayor, and I realize this is the first time he's heard the Mayor's version of events.

"I'm sorry, Todd," the Mayor says. "But I did tell you what you knew was untrue—"

"Ben told us what happened!" Todd yells. "Don't you try to worm yer way out of it now! I ain't forgot nothing about what kinda man you are and if you hurt Viola—"

"*I did not hurt Viola,*" the Mayor says strongly. "I haven't intentionally hurt *any* woman. You'll remember I only started the bands *after* Mistress Coyle's terrorist attacks began, *after* she started killing innocent townsfolk, *after* we needed to keep track of those who were attacking us. If anyone's to blame for the necessity of ID bracelets—"

"*ID bracelets?*" Mistress Coyle shouts.

"—then point the finger at her. If I'd wanted to kill the women, which *I did not*, I could have done so in the first moment the army entered the town, but that is not what I wanted then and that is not what I want *now!*"

"Nevertheless," Mistress Coyle says, "I'm the best healer on this planet, and I'm unable to heal the infection. Does that seem likely to you?"

"Fine," the Mayor says, staring at her hard. "Our first agreement then. You have full and open access to all the information I have on the bands and on how we're treating the women in town who are affected, though they are, I must say, not in anywhere near as perilous a state as you've suggested."

I look at Todd, but he obviously doesn't know how true any of this is. I can hear a little bit of his Noise now, mostly worry and some feeling about me, but still nothing clear, still nothing like he used to have.

It's almost like the Todd I know isn't here at all.

[TODD]

"Are you sure yer okay?" I ask Viola, riding up close to her, ignoring the others as they keep on talking. "Are you *sure*?"

"There's nothing to worry about," she says and I can tell she's lying to make me feel better, which of course only makes me feel worse.

"Viola, if something's wrong with you, if something *happened*—"

"It's Mistress Coyle trying to scare me into helping, that's all—"

But I look into her eyes and I can tell that's not the whole truth and I feel my stomach falling away cuz if something ever did happen to her, if I *lost* her, if she—

I am the Circle and the Circle is me, I think.

And it goes, it falls away, it quiets down, and I realize I've closed my eyes and when I open 'em, Viola's staring back at me, horrified.

"What did you just do?" she asks. "The little bit of your Noise I could hear just disappeared."

"It's something I can do now," I say, looking away. "Make myself quiet."

Her forehead furrows with surprise. "You *want* it to be this way?"

"It's a good thing, Viola," I say, my face burning a little. "I can finally keep a secret or two."

But she's shaking her head. "I thought you'd seen something so bad it made your Noise go quiet. I didn't think you were doing it on purpose."

I swallow. "I *did* see things that bad. This makes it *stop*."

"But where did you learn? *He's* the one who knows how to do that, isn't he?"

"Don't worry," I say. "I got it under control."

"Todd—"

"It's just a tool. You chant these words and that focuses you and you put that together with desire and—"

"That sounds like *him* talking." She lowers her voice. "He thinks you're special, Todd. He always has. He could be tempting you into something you don't want, something dangerous."

"Don't you think I *know* how much I can't trust him?" I say, a little sharp. "He can't control me, Viola. I'm strong enough to fight him off—"

"Can *you* control people?" she asks, sharp right back. "If you can be silent, isn't that the next step?"

And there's the image in my head again, the image of James, lying dead in the square, and for a second I can't shake it and my shame rushes up again like I'm gonna vomit and I am the Circle and the Circle is me—

"No, I can't do that yet," I say. "It's bad anyway. I wouldn't want to."

She pushes Acorn up to me so our faces are close.

"You can't redeem him, Todd," she says, a little softer but I flinch a bit at the word *redeem*. "You *can't*. Because he doesn't want it."

"I know," I say, still not quite looking at her. "I know that."

For a second we both just watch Mistress Coyle and Mayor Prentiss fighting.

"You have more than that!" Mistress Coyle's saying. "We can see the size of your storehouse from the probes—"

"Can your probes see *inside* the storehouse, Mistress? Because that technology would amaze even me—"

Viola coughs into her hand. "Are you really okay, Todd?"

In reply, I ask, "Are you really in no danger from the band?"

And neither of us answer.

And the morning just feels colder.

{ V I O L A }

The talks go on for hours, all through the morning until the sun gets high in the sky. Todd doesn't say much and every time I try to join in, my coughing gets the better of me. It's just Bradley and the Mayor and Mistress Coyle arguing and arguing and arguing.

A lot of things get decided, though. In addition to the exchange of medical information, transports will start twice a day, water going one way, food going the other, the Mayor providing additional vehicles along with the Answer's carts, as well as soldiers for protection to make the exchange. It would make *way* more sense for us all to gather together in one place, but the Mayor refuses to leave the city and Mistress Coyle won't leave the hilltop so we're stuck dragging water six miles one way and food six miles the other.

It's a start, I guess.

Bradley and Simone will make flying patrols over the city

and our hilltop every day, in hopes of keeping the Spackle back by threat alone. And in the final agreement of a very long day, Mistress Coyle will provide the expertise of some of the Answer's best women to help the Mayor fight the Spackle's sneak attacks on the city.

"But only as a defense," I insist. "You both have to make overtures of peace to them. Otherwise, none of this will do any good."

"You can't just stop fighting and call it peace, my girl," Mistress Coyle says. "The war goes on even as you're negotiating with the enemy."

And she's looking at the Mayor as she says it.

"Quite so," says the Mayor, looking right back at her. "That's how it was done before."

"And how you'll do it this time?" Bradley says. "We have your word?"

"As a bargain for peace," says the Mayor, "it's not a bad one." He smiles that smile. "And when peace is achieved, who knows where we'll all be standing?"

"Particularly if you've managed to make yourself peacemaker just before the convoy lands?" Mistress Coyle says. "Think how impressed they'll be."

"And how impressed they'll be with you, Mistress, for skillfully bringing me to the bargaining table."

"If they're gonna be impressed with anybody," Todd says, "it'll be Viola here."

"Or Todd," Bradley jumps in, before I can say it. "They're the ones who actually made this happen. But frankly, if either of you wants a role in the future, you'd better start acting like it right now, because as of this moment as far as any objective observer can see, the President is a mass murderer and Mistress Coyle is a terrorist."

"I'm a general," the Mayor says.

"And I'm fighting for freedom," says Mistress Coyle.

Bradley gives a rueful smile. "I think we're finally finished here," he says. "We've agreed what starts today and what happens tomorrow. If we can keep that up for forty more days, then there just might be a future for this planet after all."

[TODD]

Mistress Coyle takes up the reins and snaps them on the oxes, who say **Wilf?** in response. "You coming?" Mistress Coyle calls over to Viola.

"You go on for a second," Viola says. "I want to talk to Todd."

Mistress Coyle looks like she expected as much. "Good to finally meet you, Todd," she says, giving me a long look as the cart pulls away.

The Mayor nods his good-byes to them and says, "Whenever you're ready, Todd," pulling Juliet's Joy slowly down the road to leave me alone with Viola.

"Do you think this is going to work?" she says, coughing hard into her fist.

"Six weeks till the ships get here," I say. "Not even. Call it five and a half."

"Five and a half weeks and it all changes again."

"Five and a half weeks and we can be together."

But she don't say nothing to that.

264

"Are you sure you know what you're doing with him, Todd?" she says.

"He's different round me, Viola. Not as whacked-out crazy evil like he used to be. I think I can keep him in line just enough so he don't kill us all."

"Don't let him get into your head," she says, serious as I've ever heard her. "That's where he does the most damage."

"He ain't in my head," I say. "And I can take care of myself. So you take care of *yer*self." I try to smile. I don't succeed. "You stay alive, Viola Eade. You get better. If Mistress Coyle is able heal you, you do whatever you can to *make* her."

"I'm not dying," she says. "I'd tell you if I was."

We're quiet for a second, then she says, "You're the thing that matters to me, Todd. Out of this whole planet, you're the only thing that matters."

I swallow, hard. "You, too."

And we both know we mean it, but as we part and she rides off one way and I ride off another, I bet we're each wondering if the other lied about important things.

"Well, well," says the Mayor as I catch up to him on the road back into town. "What did you make of that, Todd?"

"If the infeckshun from the band takes Viola," I say, "you'll beg me to kill you after what I'll do to you."

"I believe you," he says, as we ride along, the **ROAR** of the city rising up to greet us, "and that's why *you* have to believe I'd never do it."

And I swear he says it like it could be true.

"You gotta keep yer word about these agreements, too," I say. "We're aiming for peace now. For real."

"You think I want war for war's sake, Todd," he says. "But I don't. I want *victory*. And sometimes victory means peace, doesn't it? The convoy might not like everything I've done but I have a feeling they'll listen to a man who won peace against overwhelming odds."

Odds you made yerself, I think.

But I don't say.

Cuz again, he sounds like he's telling the truth.

Maybe I *am* rubbing off on him.

"And now," he says. "Let's go see if we can make a peaceful world."

Pathways' End

I SMOOTH THE FRESHLY GROWN LICHEN over the band on my arm, touching it gently as another day ends and I sit, alone, on my outcropping. The pain from the band is still there, still my everyday reminder of who I am, of where I have come from.

Even though it will not heal, I no longer take the Land's medicines for it.

It is illogical, but I have lately come to believe that the pain will only stop when the Clearing are gone from here.

Or perhaps only then will the Return allow himself to be healed, the Sky shows, climbing up beside me. *Come,* he shows. *It is time.*

Time for what?

He sighs at my hostile tone. *Time to show you why we will win this battle.*

***

Seven nights have passed since the Clearing's vessel bombed the Land and the Sky pulled back our invasion. Seven nights when we have done nothing but watch as our distant voices reported that the two groups of the Clearing were in contact again, as they started exchanging supplies to help one another, as the vessel on the far hilltop rose once more to fly over the entire valley, high over the armies of everyone, and again every day since.

Seven nights when the Sky let the Clearing grow stronger.

Seven nights while he waited for peace.

What the Return does not know, he shows as we make our way through the Land, *is that the Sky rules alone.*

I watch the faces of the Land as we pass, connecting their voices to each other to form the one voice, the easy link I still find so difficult to do. *Yes,* I show, *I knew that.*

He stops. *No, you did not. You do not.*

And he opens his voice, showing me what he means, showing me that being called "the Sky" is the same exile as being called "the Return," and more, not an exile he chose, that he was just another member of the Land before they selected him as Sky.

And that he was separated from the voice to become so.

I see how happy he was before, happy in his connection to those closest to him, his family, his hunting companions, his one in particular, with whom he planned to add to the voice of the Land, but then I see him pulled away from her, from all of them, separated, elevated, and I see how young he was, barely older—

Than the Return is now, he shows. He looms over me, his armor baked hard in the sun, his headpiece weighing heavily on his broad neck and shoulders, but held high by those same muscles. *The Land looks deep inside itself to find the new Sky and there is no refusal for the one chosen. The past life is over and must be left behind, for the Land needs its Sky to watch over it and the Sky can have no other than the Land.*

And there he is in his voice, assuming the garments of the role as he took the name "the Sky" and moved apart from those he ruled.

You rule alone, I show, feeling the weight of it.

But I was not always alone, he shows. *Nor was the Return.*

His voice reaches out to me suddenly, and before I am even aware of it—

I am back with—

—my one in particular in the shed where we live, locked in at night by our master from the Clearing, the master whose lawn we keep tidy, her flowers blooming, her vegetables growing. I have never known those who parented me, having been given to our master before I had any memories, and I have only ever really known my one in particular, not much older than me, but who shows me how to do our job well enough so that the beatings are infrequent, who shows me now how to start a cook fire, striking the

flint shards together to make our only source
of warmth—

—my one in particular letting me stay silent
when we take our master's vegetables to market
and meet other members of the Burden whose
voices reach forward in friendly greetings
that push me into myself in embarrassment, my
one in particular drawing their attention and
letting me be shy as long as I need to—

—my one in particular curled against my stomach,
coughing with illness from an infection, filled
with the fever that is the worst sign of sickness
in the Burden, one that will have us dragged
off to Clearing veterinarians and never seen
again. I press my body into my one in particular,
begging the mud, the rocks, the shed, begging
them all please to let the temperature fall,
please, let it fall—

—my one in particular and I on a summer's night
after a young lifetime together, washing ourselves in the bucket of water our master provides
once a week, washing ourselves, washing each
other, and making the surprising discovery that
another kind of closeness is possible—

—my one in particular silently with me after our
voices are stolen by the Clearing, after we are

cut off from each other and placed on sepa-
rate shores, as if calling across a chasm too far
to hear, my one in particular slowly, gently,
through clicks and gestures, trying to make me
understand—

—my one in particular rising when the shed
door is opened and the Clearing are there with
their guns and their blades, my one in partic-
ular standing before me again, protecting me
for the final time—

The Sky lets me go as I call out, the horror alive again in
my voice, alive like it is happening just now, all over again—
You miss him, the Sky shows. *You loved him.*
They killed my one in particular, I show, burning
and dying and burning again. *They took him from me.*
This is why I recognized you the first day I saw
you, the Sky shows. *We are the same, the Sky and the*
Return. The Sky speaks for the Land, and the Return
speaks for the Burden. And to do this, we both have
to be alone.
I am still breathing heavy. *Why do you make me*
remember this now?
Because it is important that you understand who the
Sky is, he shows. *Because it is important to **remember**.*
I raise my head. *Why?*
But all he shows is, *Follow me.*

* * *

271

We carry on through the camp until we reach a small, unremarkable path through some trees. A short way along it are two Pathway guards, who bow their heads out of respect for the Sky and let us pass. The path leads up at a sharp, sudden angle, into overgrowth that hides us almost immediately. We climb up and up, to what must be the highest point of this upper valley, along a path wide enough only for one of us at a time.

It is a necessary difficulty that the Land must sometimes keep secrets from itself, the Sky shows as we walk. *It is the only way to make hope possible.*

Is that why they make the Sky? I show back, following him up a staircase of rocks. *To bear the weight of what needs to be done?*

Yes. That is precisely why. And another way in which we are alike. He glances back at me. *The secrets we have learned to keep.*

We reach a curtain of ivy hanging from the branches above. The Sky uses his long arm to pull it back and reveal the opening beyond.

A circle of Pathways stands in a clearing. The Pathways are members of the Land with especially open voices, chosen while young to be the Sky's fastest messengers throughout the vast body of the Land, speeding the voice along. But these are all facing inward, concentrating their voices toward one another, each creating a link in the closed circle.

The Pathways' End, the Sky shows to me. *They live their entire lives here, their voices trained from birth to this one purpose. Once inside, a secret may be*

taken *from a voice and kept safely here until needed*
again. It is where the Sky leaves thoughts that are too
dangerous to be widely known.

He turns to me. *And other things besides.*

He raises his voice towards the Pathways' End, and the
circle shifts slightly, creating an opening.

And I see what is inside.

In the center of the circle is a stone bed.

And on the stone bed lies a man.

A man of the Clearing, unconscious.

And dreaming.

Your Source, I show quietly as we step into the circle
and it closes around us again.

A soldier, the Sky shows. *Found by the side of the*
road, dead from his wounds, we thought. But then
came his voice, unguarded and open at the very, very
edge of silence. We stopped it from disappearing
completely.

Stopped it? I show, staring at the man, his voice
covered over by the voices of the Pathways, removing it
from the larger voice so its secrets never leave this circle.

Any voice that can be heard can be healed, the Sky
shows, *even if it is far away from the body. And he*
was very far away indeed. We treated his wounds and
began calling to his voice, bringing it back to himself.

Bringing him back to life, I show.

Yes. And all the while his voice told us things,

things that have given us great advantage over the Clearing, things that became even more valuable after the Return came back to the Land.

I glance up. *You were already thinking of an attack on the Clearing before I returned?*

It is a duty of the Sky to prepare for any potential threat to the Land.

I look back down at the Source. *And this is why you said we will win.*

The Source's voice tells us the leader of the Clearing is a man who forms no real alliances. That he will only rule alone no matter what temporary measures he takes with the far hilltop. That he will, if pressed, betray the other side without hesitation. This is their weakness, and one the Land can exploit. Our attacks begin again at daybreak. We shall see how their alliance stands up to pressure.

I glare at him. *But you would still make peace with them. I see that in you.*

If that would save the Land, yes, the Sky would. And so would the Return.

He is not asking me. He is telling me I would do it.

But that is why I bring you here, he shows, directing my voice back to the man. *If peace comes, if that is how matters are settled, then I will give you the Source entire. To do with as you will.*

I look up to him, puzzled. **Give** *him to me?*

He is nearly healed, the Sky shows. *We keep him asleep to hear his unguarded voice, but we could wake him at any time.*

I turn back to the man. *But why would that give me vengeance? Why would—?*

The Sky makes a gesture toward the Pathways' End, causing their voices to make room for the voice of the man—

So that I can hear it.

His voice—

I walk right up to the stone tablet and lean down toward the man's worn face, covered in the hair that scars the faces of half of the Clearing. I see the Land's healing pastes on his chest, the ragged clothes he wears.

And all the time I hear him.

Mayor Prentiss, he says.

And *weapons.*

And *sheep.*

And *Prentisstown.*

And *early one morning.*

And then he says—

He says—

Todd.

I whirl round to the Sky. *But this is—*

Yes, shows the Sky.

I have seen him in the Knife's voice—

Yes, shows the Sky again.

This man is called **Ben,** I show, my voice opening wide with amazement. *He is worth almost as much to the Knife as his one in particular.*

And if peace is our outcome, shows the Sky, *then in*

payment for all that the Clearing has made you suffer,
he is yours.

I turn back to the man.

Back to Ben.

He is mine, I think. If there is peace, he is mine.

Mine to kill.

THE PEACE PROCESS

[TODD]

WE HEAR 'EM COMING thru the trees, distant but rising fast.

"Wait for it," whispers the Mayor.

"They're gonna come right at us," I say.

The first misty rays of dawn shine off his face as he turns to me. "That's the risk of being bait, Todd."

Boy colt? Angharrad says nervously below me.

"It's all right, girl," I say, tho I ain't at all sure it is.

Submit! thinks Juliet's Joy next to us.

"Shut up," the Mayor and I say at the same time.

The Mayor grins at me.

For a second, I grin back.

The past week has been almost good, compared to what went before. The food and water exchanges have gone how they're sposed to, no funny business by either the Mayor or Mistress Coyle, and it's like a rule of life that yer automatically happier when you don't gotta worry about something to drink. Things have settled down in the camps, with the town almost seeming like a town again and Viola saying the hilltop's gotten calmer, too, almost normal. She even says she's been feeling better tho I can't really tell if it's true over the comm cuz she's also found reasons every day for us not to see each other and I can't help but worry. I can't help but think–

(*I am the Circle and the Circle is me*)

But I've been busy, too, with the Mayor. Who's gone all *friendly*. He's taken to visiting the soldiers round the camp, asking bout their families and their old homes and what they hope for after the war and with the new settlers and on and on. Doing it to the townsfolk, too.

And he's also been giving me all kindsa good stuff, like having a grumbling Mr. O'Hare make my tent way more comfortable, with a softer cot and loads more blankets against the cold. He always makes sure Angharrad has more than her share of feed and water. And he tells me every day what his doctors are doing to try and cure the bands, to make sure Viola ain't in any danger.

It's been weird.

But good.

Tho all this good stuff has only really been possible cuz there ain't been no Spackle attacks for the whole week. Not that that's stopped us from planning for 'em. Using the probes, Bradley and Simone picked out a coupla different ways the Spackle might sneak into town and the Mayor set about making those ways good targets. And with the help of our new allies who ain't got Noise and can't be heard slinking round the woods at night, they prepared things.

And right now, it's looking like the preparayshun was a good idea.

We're facing down a small road that cuts thru the woods south of town and we can hear Spackle coming, right from where we thought they would.

And they're getting louder.

"There's nothing to worry about," the Mayor says to me, glancing up thru the trees to the probe hanging in the sky behind us. "It's all going according to plan."

The Spackle Noise goes up a notch, louder and steadier, too fast to be able to read anything in it.

Todd, Angharrad says, getting more nervous. **Todd!**

"Calm your horse, Todd," the Mayor says.

"We're okay, girl," I say, rubbing her flank. But I also pull her reins to the side so we're a bit more behind the well-digging equipment me and the Mayor are pretending to guard.

I bring my comm up. "Can you see anything on the probe?"

"Nothing clear," Viola says back. *"Some movement, but it's so blurry it could be the wind blowing."*

"It ain't the wind."

"I know," she says, coughing into her hand. *"Hold tight."*

The Spackle Noise gets even louder—

And louder still—

"It's happening, Todd," the Mayor says. "Here they come."

"We're ready," the comm says but it ain't Viola. It's Mistress Coyle.

And then the Spackle are pouring outta the shadows like a flash flood—

Onto the path and running right at us—

Their weapons up and ready–

"Hold," the Mayor says to me, aiming his rifle–

They keep surging onto the path–

Twenty, thirty, forty of 'em–

And me and the Mayor on our own–

"Hold," he says again–

Their Noise is filling the air–

And they keep coming–

Keep coming till they've gotta be in weapons' range–

And there's a *fizz* as one of the white sticks is fired–

"Viola!" I shout–

"Now!" I hear Mistress Coyle thru the comm–

BOOM!

The trees on either side of the road blow into a million burning splinters, ripping thru the Spackle, sending the Mayor and me reeling and I'm struggling hard to keep Angharrad from bolting or throwing me off–

By the time I spin back round, the smoke's already clearing and we can see fallen trees and burning trunks–

And no sign of any Spackle–

Just bodies on the road–

Lots of bodies.

"What the hell was that?!" I shout into the comm. "That was *way* bigger than you said it would be!"

"An error in the mixture, no doubt," Mistress Coyle says. *"I'll have a word with Mistress Braithwaite."*

But I can see her smiling in the screen.

280

"A little overenthusiastic, perhaps," the Mayor says, riding over to me, smiling big, too, "but the peace process has begun!"

Then we hear another sound behind us. The group of soldiers who laid in wait down the road in case something went wrong and we needed help. They're marching up to us now, fast and happy–

And they're *cheering*.

The Mayor rides among 'em in triumph, like he expected it all along.

{VIOLA}

"That was slaughter," Bradley says angrily. "How exactly does that constitute an overture to peace?"

"We overcooked the mixture," Mistress Coyle shrugs. "It was only our first try. Lesson learned for next time."

"Next time–" Bradley starts to say, but she's already on her way out of the cockpit where we were watching everything happen on the main screen. Simone's outside with the remote projector, displaying the whole thing in three dimensions to the hilltop crowds.

There was a big cheer when the explosion happened. There's an even bigger one when Mistress Coyle steps outside.

"She did it on purpose," Bradley says.

"Of course she did," I say. "That's what she does. Offer her an apple and she'll take the tree."

I stand up from my chair–

And sit right back down again because my head is spinning so fast.

"You all right?" Bradley says, his Noise full of concern.

"Same as usual," I say. Though it isn't, actually. Mistress Coyle's timed treatments have worked okay, but my fever came back with a vengeance this morning and hasn't left. Six more women have died, too, all older and unwell, but there are a lot of us getting sicker. Sometimes, you can tell who has a band and who hasn't just by looking at their faces.

"She hasn't found anything in the information the Mayor provided?" Bradley asks.

I shake my head, starting to cough. "If he's provided every-thing."

"Thirty-three days until the convoy arrives with a full medical bay," Bradley says. "Can you hold on?"

I nod, but only because I'm coughing too much to talk.

The past week has gone unnervingly smoothly. Wilf rides down the road with tanks of water and rides back with cartloads of food, no problems at all. The Mayor's even sent soldiers to protect him and engineers to improve the water collection. He's also accepted Mistresses Nadari and Lawson to help inventory the food and supervise the distribution.

Mistress Coyle, meanwhile, looks happier than I've ever seen her. She's even started talking about how to make the truce. Apparently, this involves a lot of blowing things up. Mistress Braithwaite, who did my soldiering training what seems like a lifetime ago, plants bombs in the trees, hoping to show the Spackle we can outwit them and also hoping to capture one who isn't killed in the blast. Then we'll send it back saying we'll keep blowing things up if they don't talk to us about peace.

Mistress Coyle swears this is how it worked last time.

My comm beeps, Todd calling with final word after the attack.

"None survived, did they?" I ask, coughing some more.

"No," he says, looking concerned. "Viola, are you-?"

"I'm fine. It's just coughing." I try to swallow it away.

I've only seen him over the comm the past week since our big meeting by the old house of healing. I haven't gone down there and he hasn't come up here. Too much to do, I tell myself.

I also tell myself it's not because a Todd without Noise makes me feel really–

Makes it seem like–

"We'll try again tomorrow," I say. "And again and again until it works."

"Yeah," Todd says. "The sooner we can get those truce talks started, the sooner this is all over. The sooner we can start making you well."

"The sooner you can be away from him," I say, realizing too late that I've said it out loud. Stupid fever.

Todd frowns. "I'm fine, Viola, I swear. He's being nicer than ever."

"Nice?" I say. "When was he ever nice?"

"Viola–"

"Thirty-three days," I say. "That's all we have to get through. Just thirty-three more days."

But I have to say, it feels like forever.

[TODD]

The Spackle attacks keep coming. And we keep stopping 'em.

Submit! we hear Juliet's Joy shouting down the road. **SUBMIT!**

And we hear the Mayor laughing.

Heavy hoofbeats come pounding outta the darkness, the Mayor's teeth shining in the moons-light. You can even see the gleam of the gold threads on the sleeve of his uniform.

"Now, NOW!" he's calling.

With a disgusted cluck of her tongue, Mistress Braithwaite presses a button on a remote device and the road behind the Mayor erupts in gales of flame, instantly burning the Spackle who were in pursuit, Spackle who thought they'd found a random soldier away from what seemed to be the obvious trap we'd laid down another path.

But that trap wasn't a trap. The random soldier was.

This is the fifth attack we've stopped in five days, each one getting cleverer with us getting cleverer in return, with fake traps and fake *fake* traps and different paths of attack and so on.

It feels pretty good actually, like we're finally really *doing* something, like we're finally–

(winning–)

(winning the war–)

(it's ruddy thrilling–)

(shut up)

(but it is–)

Juliet's Joy comes heaving to a stop next to Angharrad, and we all watch as the flames gather up into a cloud rising thru the trees and dissipating against the cold night sky.

"Forward!" the Mayor shouts, the *buzz* of it rocketing thru the Noise of the soldiers gathered behind us and they

284

surge past in formayshun, racing down the road after any Spackle who might still be alive.

But from the size of the flames, it don't look like there'll be any left this time neither. The Mayor's smile disappears as he sees just how much destruckshun there is down the road.

"And yet again," he says, turning to Mistress Braithwaite, "your detonation is mysteriously too big to leave any survivors."

"Would you rather they killed you?" she asks in a way that says that'd be fine by her.

"You just don't want us to get the Spackle first," I say. "You want to get one for Mistress Coyle."

You could pretty much eat dinner off the glare she gives me. "I'll thank you not to talk to your elders that way, boy."

Which makes the Mayor laugh out loud.

"I'll talk to you any way I damn well please, *Mistress*," I say. "I know yer leader and there ain't no pretending she's not up to something."

Mistress Braithwaite looks back at the Mayor, not changing her expresshun. "Charming," she says.

"Yet accurate," says the Mayor, "as usual."

I feel my Noise go a little pink at the unexpected praise.

"Please report to your Mistress the usual success," the Mayor says down to Mistress Braithwaite, "and the usual failure."

Mistress Braithwaite heads off back to town with Mistress Nadari, scowling at us as they go.

"I'd do the same if I were her, Todd," the Mayor says as

285

the soldiers start to return from the fire, no living Spackle found, again. "Keep my opponent from getting an advantage."

"We're sposed to be working *together*," I say. "We're sposed to be working toward peace."

He don't seem too worried about it, tho. Just look at the soldiers marching past us now, laughing and joking amongst themselves at what they see as another victory after so many defeats. And there'll be still more to congratulate him when we get back to the square.

Viola tells me Mistress Coyle's getting the same hero treatment up by the scout ship.

They're fighting a war over who can be more peaceful.

"I think maybe you're right, Todd," the Mayor says.

"Right how?" I ask.

"That we should be working together." He turns to me, that smile on his face. "I think maybe it's time we tried a different approach."

{VIOLA}

"What's happening now?" Lee says, scratching underneath his bandage.

"Stop that," I say, slapping his hand playfully, though the movement causes a terrible pain in my arm.

We're in the healing room of the scout ship, the view-screens on the walls showing the probes dotted around the valley. After yesterday's too-fiery attack by Mistress Braithwaite, the Mayor surprised us all by suggesting that Simone lead the next mission. Mistress Coyle agreed, and Simone set to

286

work, planning the whole thing with the absolute focus on capturing a Spackle and sending it back with a message of peace.

Which seems strange after we've killed so many of them to do it, but it's been obvious since the beginning that wars make no sense. You kill people to tell them you want to stop killing them.

Monsters of men, I think. *And women.*

So today, Simone's set up an even bigger diversionary tactic, positioning the probes in broad daylight to make it look like we expect the Spackle to come down one particular path from the south, where Mistress Braithwaite has planted decoy bombs, set to go off early like we made a mistake, all the while leaving another path open from the north, a path where armed women from the Answer, led by Simone, wait in hiding to capture a Spackle, hoping their lack of Noise will surprise them.

"You're not telling me anything," Lee says, scratching the bandage again.

"Wouldn't it be easier for Bradley to sit here with you?" I say. "You could see what happens through him."

"I'd rather have you," he says.

And I see myself in his Noise, nothing too private or anything, just a better-looking version of me, cleaned and washed and fit, instead of feverish and too thin and grimy in a way that doesn't ever seem to wash off.

He hasn't talked about his blindness except to make jokes about it, and when there's someone else with Noise around, he can still see through that, saying it's almost as good as having eyes. But I'm with him a lot when he's alone, as we both seem to live in this stupid healing room these days, and I can see it in him, see how most of his life disappeared all at once, that suddenly all he sees are memories and other people's versions of the world.

And how he can't even cry about it because the burns are so bad.

"When you sit there quietly," he says. "I know you're reading me."

"Sorry," I say, looking away and coughing some more. "I'm just worried. This *has* to work."

"You gotta stop thinking you're responsible," he says. "You were protecting Todd, that's all. If it had taken starting a war to save my mom and sister, I wouldn't have hesitated."

"But you can't make war personal," I say, "or you'll never make the right decisions."

"And if you didn't make personal decisions, you wouldn't be a *person*. All war is personal somehow, isn't it? For somebody? Except it's usually hate."

"Lee–"

"I'm just saying how lucky he is to have someone love him so much they'd take on the whole world." His Noise is uncomfortable, wondering what I'm looking like, how I'm responding. "That's all I'm saying."

"He'd do it for me," I say quietly.

I'd do it for you, too, Lee's Noise says.

And I know he would.

But those people who die because we do it, don't they have people who'd kill for them?

So who's right?

I put my head in my hands. It feels really heavy. Every

day, Mistress Coyle tries new approaches to the infection, and every day I feel better for a while but then it comes back a little bit worse.

Fatal, I think.

And still *weeks* until the convoy gets here, if they can help at all–

There's a sudden crackle over the comm system of the ship that makes us jump. *"They've done it,"* Bradley's voice says, sounding surprised.

I look up. "Done what?"

"They've got one," Bradley says. *"To the north."*

"But," I say, looking from screen to screen, "it's too early. There wasn't–"

"It wasn't Simone." Bradley's voice is as confused as I am. *"It was Prentiss. He captured a Spackle before we even set the plan in motion."*

[TODD]

"Mistress Coyle's gonna be *fuming,*" I say, as the Mayor keeps shaking hands with soldiers who come up to congratulate him.

"I find myself strangely calm about that prospect, Todd," he says, taking in his victory.

Cuz it turns out there was still that squadron of soldiers to the north, wasn't there? Twiddling their thumbs, being laughed at by Spackle who snuck by 'em on a regular basis to attack the town.

Mistress Coyle forgot about 'em. So did Bradley and Simone. So did *I.*

The Mayor didn't.

He watched tonight's big plan being made over the comm by Simone and agreed on the time and place where Mistress Braithwaite could plant her decoy bombs. And then when the Spackle figured out that one part of the valley on the northern road was vulnerable to attack cuz we were busy pretending we weren't watching the south, just like we wanted 'em to think, they sent forward a small group sneaking past our soldiers like usual, like they've done a dozen times before—

Except this time, they didn't find us so agreeable.

The Mayor moved his men to exactly the right place and they surged round in a flanking movement, cutting off the Spackle's route and mowing most of 'em down with gunfire before anyone knew what was going on.

All but two of the Spackle were killed and those two got marched thru town not twenty minutes later to a **ROAR** from the watching army. Mr. Tate and Mr. O'Hare took 'em to the horse stables behind the cathedral to wait while the Mayor finishes getting the congratulayshuns of all of New Prentisstown. I take the long, slow walk thru the crowds with him, handshakes and cheering and backslapping everywhere.

"You coulda *told* me," I say, raising my voice above the clamor.

"You're right, Todd," he says, stopping to look at me for a minute as the people keep swarming round us. "I should have. I apologize. Next time, I will."

And to my surprise, it sounds like he means it.

We keep on thru the crowds and eventually we make it round to the stables.

Where a couple of really angry mistresses wait.

"I demand you let us in there!" Mistress Nadari says and Mistress Lawson beside her harrumphs in agreement.

"Safety first, ladies," the Mayor smiles at them. "We have no idea how dangerous a captured Spackle might be."

"Now," Mistress Nadari says.

But the Mayor's still smiling.

And he's followed by a whole city of smiling soldiers.

"I'll just make sure the situation is safe before I do that, shall I?" he says, stepping to one side of the mistresses, who are then held back by a line of soldiers as the Mayor goes inside. I follow him in.

And my stomach grabs itself into a tight fist.

Cuz inside are the two Spackle, tied to chairs, their arms bound behind 'em in a way I know only too well.

(but neither one is 1017 and I don't know if I'm relieved or upset–)

One of 'em's got red blood all over his naked white skin, the lichen he was wearing torn off and thrown to the ground. His head's up, tho, his eyes wide open, and I'm damned if his Noise don't show all kinds of pictures of us paying for what we've done–

But the Spackle next to him–

The Spackle next to him don't look too much like a Spackle no more.

I'm ready to start yelling but, *"What the hell is this?"* the Mayor shouts first, surprising me.

Surprising the men, too.

"Askings, sir," Mr. O'Hare says, his hands and fists bloody. "We've learned quite a lot in a very short time." He gestures at the broken-looking Spackle. "Before this one unfortunately succumbed to injuries sustained during–"

There's a *whoosh*ing sound I ain't heard in a while, a slap, a punch, a bullet of Noise from the Mayor, and Mr. O'Hare's head snaps back and he falls to the floor, quivering like he's in spasm.

"We're meant to be after *peace* here!" the Mayor shouts at the other men, who look back in sheeplike astonishment. "I did *not* authorize torture."

Mr. Tate clears his throat. "This one has proven tougher under interrogation," he says, pointing at the one still alive. "He's a very hardy specimen."

"Lucky for you, Captain," the Mayor says, his voice still hot.

"I'll let the mistresses in," I say. "They can treat him."

"No, you won't," the Mayor says, "because we're letting him go."

"What?"

"What?" says Mr. Tate.

The Mayor walks behind the Spackle. "We were to capture a Spackle and let him go back with the news that we want peace." He takes out his knife. "And so that is what we will do."

"Mr. President–"

"Open the back door, please," the Mayor says.

Mr. Tate pulls up. "The *back* door?"

"With dispatch, Captain."

Mr. Tate goes and opens the back door of the stables, the one that leads away from the square–

Away from the mistresses.

"Hey!" I say. "You can't do that. You made an agreement—"

"Which I'm keeping, Todd." He leans down so his mouth is next to the Spackle's ear. "I assume the voice can speak our language?"

And I think, *The voice?*

But already there's a low flurry of Noise back and forth from the Mayor to the Spackle, something deep and black and hard flowing twixt 'em so fast no one in the room can follow it.

"What are you saying?" I say, stepping forward. "What are you telling him?"

The Mayor looks back up at me. "I'm telling him how desperately we want peace, Todd." He cocks his head. "Don't you trust me?"

I swallow.

I swallow again.

I know the Mayor wants peace to get the credit for it.

I know he's been better since I saved him after the water tank.

I also know he ain't redeemed.

I know he ain't redeemable.

(ain't he?)

But he's been *acting* like it.

"You're more than welcome to tell him, too," he says.

He keeps his eyes on me and makes a flick of his knife. The Spackle lurches forward in surprise, his arms suddenly free. He looks round for a minute, wondering what's coming, till his eyes fall on mine—

And in an instant, I try to make my Noise heavy, try to make it loud, and it *hurts*, like a muscle I ain't used in too long, but I try to hit him hard with everything that's true about what we *really* want, whatever the Mayor mighta said, that me and Viola, we *do* want peace, that we want this all to be over and–

The Spackle stops me with a hiss–

I see myself in his Noise–

And I hear–

Recognishun?

And words–

Words in my language–

I hear–

The Knife.

"The Knife?" I say.

But the Spackle just hisses again and breaks for the door, running away and away and away–

Taking who knows what message back to his people.

{VIOLA}

"The *nerve* of it," Mistress Coyle says through clenched teeth. "And how the army was *frothing* around him. Just like the worst days of when he ran the town."

"I wish I could have at least had the chance to speak to the Spackle," Simone says, back after an angry cart ride through town with the other mistresses. "Tell them all humans aren't alike."

"Todd said he was able to get across what we really wanted," I say, coughing badly. "So we have to hope that's the message that gets through."

"If it does get through," Mistress Coyle says, "Prentiss will claim all the credit for it."

"This isn't about who scores the most points," Bradley says.

"Is it not?" Mistress Coyle says. "Do you really want that man in a position of strength when the convoy arrives? Is that the settlement you're after?"

"You say that as if we have the authority to relieve someone of duty," Bradley says, "as if we can just waltz in here and impose our will."

"Well, why can't you?" Lee says. "He's a murderer. He murdered my sister and my mother."

Bradley makes to respond but Simone, weathering the shocked thunder of Bradley's Noise, says, "I tend to agree. If his actions are endangering the lives of everyone–"

"We're *here*," Bradley interrupts, "to establish a settlement for almost five thousand people who deserve not to wake up in the middle of a *war*."

Mistress Coyle just heaves a heavy sigh like she wasn't listening. "Better go out and start explaining to the people why it wasn't *us*," she says, heading out of the little healing room, "and if that Ivan says anything, I'll smack his hick face."

Bradley looks over to Simone, his Noise full of askings and disagreements, full of things he needs to know from her, pictures of her popping out all over, pictures of how much he wishes he could touch her–

"Would you stop that, please?" Simone says, looking away.

"Sorry," he says, backing up a step, then another, then leaving the room without saying anything more.

"Simone–" I say.

"I just can't get used to it," she says. "I know I should. I know I'm going to *have* to, but it's just . . ."

"It can be a good thing," I say, thinking about Todd. "That kind of closeness."

(but I can't hear him anymore–)

(and he doesn't feel close at all–)

I cough again, bringing up ugly green stuff from my lungs.

"You look exhausted, Viola," Simone says. "Any objections to a mild sedative to help you rest?"

I shake my head. She goes to a drawer and takes out a small patch, sticking it gently under my jaw. "Give him a chance," I say as the medicine starts to take hold. "He's a good man."

"I know," she says as my eyelids start to droop. "I know."

I slip into blackness, the blackness of sedation, feeling nothing at all for a long while, relishing the emptiness of it, just blackness like the black beyond–

But that ends–

And I still sleep–

And I dream–

I dream of Todd–

Just there, out of reach–

And I can't hear him–

I can't hear his Noise–

I can't hear what he's thinking.

He stares at me like an empty vessel–

Like a statue with no one inside–

Like he's dead–

Like oh God no–

He's dead–

He's *dead*–

"Viola," I hear. I open my eyes. Lee's reaching over to wake me, his Noise full of concern, but something else, too–

"What's happened?" I say, feeling the fever sweat pouring off me, how soaked through my clothes and sheets are–

(Todd, slipping away from me–)

I see Bradley standing at the foot of my bed. "She's done something," he says. "Mistress Coyle's gone and done something."

[TODD]

It's a small sound and I shouldn't be able to hear it, not thru the sleeping Noise of most of the camp.

But it's a sound I reckernize.

A *whine.*

In the air.

Boy colt? Angharrad says nervously as I leave my tent and head into the dusk that gets colder with every passing day.

"It's a tracer," I say to her, to anyone, shivering a little, looking round for the sound, seeing the men from the army who are still awake start to look for it, too, till there's a surge in their Noise as they see it arcing up in the air in a wobbly kinda way from the dry riverbed near the bottom of the falls. It's heading north, north to where some of the Spackle army are most likely hiding in the hills–

"What the hell do they think they're doing?" The Mayor's suddenly by my side, eyes fixed on the tracer. He turns to

Mr. O'Hare, who's come bleary-eyed outta his own tent. "Find Mistress Braithwaite. Now."

Mr. O'Hare goes running off half-dressed.

"A tracer is too slow to do any real damage," the Mayor says. "This must be a diversion." His eyes drift to the damaged zigzag hill. "Would you please call Viola, Todd?"

I go to my tent to get the comm and as I'm coming out we hear the distant *BOOM* of the tracer hitting some trees to the north somewhere. But the Mayor's right, *oxes* could outrun a tracer so it's only serving one purpose.

Diverting the attenshun of the Spackle.

But from where?

The Mayor's still looking at the rough edges of the hill where the Spackle came from, a hill an army can't march down no more–

Or up–

But one person could–

One person could climb up over the rubble–

One person without Noise–

The Mayor's eyes go wider and I know he's thinking it, too.

And that's when it happens–

BOOM!

From the very tiptop of the zigzag hill.

{ V I O L A }

"How did she do this?" Bradley says as we watch the tracer arc through the sky on the viewscreens in the healing room,

Lee watching it through Bradley's Noise. "How did she arrange this without us knowing?"

My comm beeps. I answer immediately. "Todd?"

But it's not Todd.

"I'd point a probe at the hilltop right now if I were you," Mistress Coyle says, smiling back at me from the screen.

"Where's Todd?" I cough. "How did you get a comm?"

A sound in Bradley's Noise makes me look. I see him remembering Simone in the spares cabinet, fiddling with two more comms, but telling him she was just doing an inventory. "She wouldn't," he says. "Not without telling me."

"We should look at the hilltop," I say.

He presses a screen for control access, then steers a probe over to the hilltop, flipping it to night vision so everything turns green and black. "What are we meant to see?"

I'm getting an idea. "Check for body heat."

He presses the screen again and–

"There," I say.

We see a lone figure, human, slinking down the hill, sticking to the underbrush, but moving quickly enough that it's clear it may not matter much if they're seen.

"That can only be a mistress," I say. "They'd have heard a man doing that."

Bradley dials the probe up a bit so we can see the lip of the hill, too. Spackle are standing along the ragged ridge, looking north to the forest where the tracer hit.

Not looking down to the mistress fleeing beneath them.

And then the screen is filled with a single flash, the heat sensors overloading, and a second later we hear the *boom* come roaring through the speakers on the probe.

299

Which is when we also hear the huge cheer from outside the ship.

"They're *watching*?" Lee says.

I see Simone in Bradley's Noise again, along with a number of rude words. I pick my comm back up. "What did you do?"

But Mistress Coyle is no longer there.

Bradley dials the screen for a comm to broadcast outside the ship. His Noise is really rumbling, getting louder and more decisive by the second.

"Bradley," I say. "What are you–?"

"Clear the immediate area," he says into the comm and I can hear it booming around the hilltop outside. "The scout ship is taking off."

[TODD]

"That bitch," I hear the Mayor say, reading the soldiers around him. The square's in chaos. No one knows what's happened. I keep trying to call Viola but the signal ain't getting thru.

"Usually when a man calls a woman a bitch," a voice calls over from a cart pulling up near us at the edge of camp, "it's because she's doing something right."

Mistress Coyle smiles back at us, looking like the dog who found the slop bucket.

"We've already sent a message of *peace*," the Mayor thunders at her. "How *dare* you–?"

"Don't you talk to me about *daring*," she thunders right back. "All I've done is show the Spackle that those of us

300

without Noise can attack anytime, even in their own backyard."

The Mayor breathes heavy for a second, then his voice becomes scarily silky. "Are you riding into town all alone, Mistress?"

"Not alone, no," she says, pointing at the probe that hovers above the camp. "I have friends in high places."

Then we hear a familiar distant *booming* on the far hilltop to the east. The scout ship's rising slowly into the air and Mistress Coyle's a beat too late hiding the surprise on her face.

"Were *all* of your friends in on your little plan, Mistress?" the Mayor says, sounding happy again.

My comm beeps and this time Viola's face pops up. "Viola—"

"Hold on," she says. *"We're on our way."*

She clicks off and I hear a sudden new uproar from the army around us. Mr. O'Hare is coming into the square from the main road, pushing Mistress Braithwaite before him in a way she ain't taking kindly to at all. At the same time, Mr. Tate's coming back round the food store with Mistresses Nadari and Lawson and he's holding a backpack out at arm's length.

"You tell your men to get their hands off those women," Mistress Coyle orders. "Immediately."

"They're just swept up in the spirit of things, I assure you," the Mayor says. "We're all allies here, after all."

"Caught her right at the bottom of the hill," Mr. O'Hare's shouting as he gets closer. "Red-handed."

"And these two were hiding explosives in their quarters,"

Mr. Tate says, handing the bag to the Mayor as he reaches us.

"Explosives we used to help *you,* idiot," Mistress Coyle spits at him.

"It's coming in for landing," I say, putting a hand up to my eyes to shelter 'em from the wind as the scout ship starts its descent. The only place it's got to land is on the square and that's full of soldiers, already scrambling to get outta the way. There don't seem to be too much heat or nothing coming off it but it's still ruddy huge. I turn round to get my face away from the rush of air as it makes contact with the ground–

And when I do, I glance back up to the zigzag hill.

Where there are lights gathering–

The door of the scout ship drops open before it's even fully landed and Viola's there immediately, using the opening to hold herself up, and she looks sick, sicker than ever, sicker than I even *feared,* weak and thin and barely standing and not even using the arm that has the band on it and I shouldn't have left her, I shouldn't have left her up there alone, it's been too long, and I'm running past the Mayor, who's reaching out to stop me but I dodge him–

And I'm reaching Viola–

And her eyes are meeting mine–

And she's saying–

Saying as I get to her–

"They're coming, Todd. They're coming down the hill."

The Voiceless

THIS IS NOT WHAT IT SEEMS, shows the Sky as we watch the strangely feeble projectile rise slowly in the air, heading toward the north edge of the valley, where the Land is already easily getting out of the way of where it might fall.

Be watchful, the Sky shows to the Land. *All eyes be watchful.*

The Clearing began to show strength. On the very morning we started attacking them again, they suddenly knew where we were coming from. We all watched that first attack through the eyes of the Land performing it, watched to see how the Clearing had regrouped itself in its new unity, to see where its strengths lay.

And those voices were cut off in a flash of fire and splinters.

There can only be one explanation, the Sky showed in the hours that followed.

The Clearing without voices, I showed.

And the Sky and I returned to the Pathways' End.

The Pathways' End binds the voices of those who enter it.

The knowledge of who the Source was, that he was the Knife's father in all but fact, that he was the one the Knife missed in his voice when he thought no one was listening, that this man had been within my reach the entire time, a way to strike back at the heart of the Knife—

These feelings blazed in me, so bright and forward it would have been impossible to hide them from the Land. But the Sky ordered the Pathways' End to speak as one, encircling our voices, ensuring that what we thought on this subject remained along this Pathway only. It would leave our voices like any other, but it would never enter the voice of the Land. It would come straight back here to Pathways' End.

We understood the voiceless were oppressed of late, showed the Sky as we stood on either side of the Source on the night of the Clearing's first fight back, *but now they have joined the battle.*

They are dangerous, I showed, thinking of my old master, who would wait behind us in silence and beat us without warning. *The voiced Clearing mistrusted them, even while living among them.*

The Sky held out a flat hand over the chest of the Source. *And so now we must know.*

His voice reached out, surrounding the Source's voice.

And the Source, in his endless sleep, began to speak.

We were silent as we left Pathways' End that night, silent as we climbed back down the hill and into the camp on the hilltop overlooking the Clearing.

That was not what I expected, the Sky finally showed.

No? I showed. *He said they were dangerous fighters, that they helped bring the Land to its knees in the last big war.*

He also said they were peacemakers, the Sky showed, stroking his chin. *That they were betrayed by the voiced Clearing into their own deaths.* He looked at me. *I do not know what to make of it.*

Make of it that the Clearing are more dangerous to us than ever, I showed. *Make of it that **now** is the time to end them once and for all, that we should release the river and erase them from this place as if they never were.*

And the Clearing that is on its way? the Sky asked. *And the Clearing that will certainly arrive after that? Because where there have been two, there will be more.*

Then we can show them what will happen to them if they do not reckon with the Land.

And they will use their superior weapons to kill us from the air, where we cannot reach them. The Sky looked back over the Clearing. *The problem remains unsolved.*

And so we sent out more raids each day, more tests to these new strengths.

We were fooled and beaten back each time.

And then today, the Land was captured by the Clearing.

And was returned. With two different messages.

Emptiness.

That was what the Land who returned to us showed, the one who had been tortured by them, forced to watch another be killed next to him, and then sent back by the leader of the Clearing with a message of exactly what he wanted.

A message of emptiness, of silence, of the silencing of all voices.

He showed you this? asked the Sky, watching him closely.

The one showed us the message once more.

Showed us the utter void, the complete *silence* of it.

*But is it what he **wants**?* the Sky showed. *Or was he showing us **himself**?* He turned to me. *You said they regard their voices as a curse, as something that must be "cured." Perhaps this is all he really wants.*

He wants our annihilation, I showed. *That is what it means. We must attack them. We must **beat** them before they get too strong—*

You are purposely forgetting the other message.

I scowled. The other message, the one delivered by the Knife, who had also obviously begun to take the voice "cure" and hide himself like the coward he is. The Sky asked the Land who returned to show us the Knife's message once more and there it was—

His horror at how the Land had been treated, an old horror, a useless horror I knew all too well, and how he, and others, too, including the ones from the vessel and the Knife's one in particular, how they did not want war at all, that above all else they wanted a world where all were welcome, where all could live.

A peaceful world.

The Knife does not speak for them, I showed. *He cannot—*

But I could see the idea of it churning in the voice of the Sky.

He left then, telling me to stay back when I went to follow him.

I seethed for hours, knowing he could only have gone to the Pathways' End to consider how to betray us into peace. When he finally returned in the cold darkness, his voice still churned.

Well? I showed angrily. *What do we do now?*

And then came the *whining* sound in the air, from the strangely slow rocket.

All eyes be watchful, the Sky shows again, and we watch as the rocket makes an arc and curves back toward the ground. We watch the air above the valley, too, for a bigger

307

missile or a return of the flying vessel, watch the roads that lead from the valley, watch for armies on the march, wait, watch, and wonder if this is an accident or a signal or a misguided attack.

We watch everywhere except the hill at our feet.

The explosion is a shock to every sense, jarring the eyes and ears and mouths and noses and skin of every portion of the Land, because part of us dies in it, torn to pieces as the lip of the hill erupts once more, members of the Land dying with their voices wide open, sending the actualities of their death to us all, so we all die with them, are all injured with them, are all covered in the same smoke, the same showers of dirt and stone, showers that knock down both me and—

The Sky, I hear—

The Sky? starting to pulse through my body, *The Sky?* a pulse carrying itself through the entire Land, because for a moment, for the briefest moment—

The Sky's voice is stilled.

The Sky? The Sky?

And my heart surges and my own voice rises to join the others and I stagger to my feet and fight through the smoke, fight through the panic, calling, *The Sky! The Sky!*

Until—

The Sky is here, he shows.

I reach for the rocks that cover him, and other hands come, too, digging him from the rubble, blood showing on his face and hands, but his armor has saved him, and he

stands, smoke and dust twirling around him—
  Bring me a messenger, he shows.

The Sky sends a messenger to the Clearing.

  Not me, though I begged.

  He sends the one who was captured and returned. We all watch through him as the Pathways follow him down the rocky face of the hill, stopping at intervals along the way so that the voice of the Land can reach into the Clearing like a tongue, speaking through the one chosen.

  We watch through his eyes as he walks into the Clearing, watch the faces of the Clearing as they step back, opening up a path, not grabbing him, not cheering over him as they did last time, and in their voices, he can hear the order given by their leader to let him come to them untouched.

  *We should release the river **now**,* I show.

  But the Sky's voice pushes mine back.

  And so the Land walks through their streets, leaving the last Pathway behind him, making the final steps across their central square himself, toward their leader, a man called *Prentiss* in the language of the Burden, standing there waiting to receive us as if he was the Clearing's Sky.

  But there are others, too. Three of the Clearing without voices, including the Knife's one in particular, whose face the Knife thought of so regularly I know it almost as well as my own. The Knife is by her side, silent as before but even now his useless worry is obvious.

  "Greetings," says a voice—

  A voice not the leader's.

It is one of the voiceless. Through the clicks they make with their mouths, she has stepped in front of the Clearing's leader, her hand out, reaching for our messenger. But her arm is grabbed by the leader of the Clearing, and for a moment there is a struggle between them.

And then the Knife steps forward, steps past them.

Steps up to the messenger.

The leader and the voiceless one watch him, each held back by the other.

And the Knife says with his mouth, "Peace. We want peace. No matter what these two tell you, peace is what we want."

And I feel the Sky beside me, feel his voice take in what the Knife has said, how he says it, and then I feel him reach out even further through the messenger, out into the Clearing itself, reaching deep into the Knife's silent voice.

The Knife gasps.

And the Sky listens.

The Land does not hear what the Sky hears.

What are you doing? I show.

But the Sky is already sending a response through the Pathways—

Sending the voice of the Land speaking as one down the hill and along the road and across the square and into the voice of the messenger—

So quickly the Sky can only have been planning it all along—

A single word—

A word that makes my voice rise in uncontainable rage—

Peace, the Sky shows the Clearing. *Peace.*
The Sky offers them peace.

I storm away from the Sky, from all of the Land, walking,
then running up the hillside to my private outcropping—
   But there is no getting away from the Land, is there?
The Land is the world and the only way to leave it is to
leave the world altogether.
   I look at the band on my arm, at the thing that makes
me forever separate, and I make my vow.
   Killing the Knife's Ben won't be enough, though I will
do it and make the Knife know that I did—
   But I will do more.
   I will block this peace. I will block it if it kills me to
do so.
   The Burden will be revenged.
   I will be revenged.
   And there will be no peace.

THE ENVOY

THE DELEGATION

"IT'S OBVIOUS," THE MAYOR SAYS. *"I* will be the one who goes."

"Over my dead body," Mistress Coyle snaps.

The Mayor smirks. "I can accept that as a condition."

We've all crammed into a little room on the scout ship. Me, the Mayor, Mistress Coyle, Simone and Bradley, with Lee, his face covered in scary-looking bandages, on one bed and Viola, looking awful, on another. This is where we're having the most important talk in the human history of New World. In a little room that smells like sickness and sweat.

Peace, the Spackle said to us, *Peace* coming thru loud and clear, like a beacon, like a demand, like an answer to what we've been asking.

Peace.

But there was something else there, too, something digging round in my head for a minute, like when the Mayor does it but faster, sleeker, and it weren't like it was coming from the Spackle in front of us neither, it was like there was some kinda mind behind his, reaching *thru* him and reading me, reading my truth, no matter if I was quiet–

Like there was just one voice in the whole world and it was talking only to me–

And it heard that I meant it.

And then the Spackle said, *Tomorrow morning. On the hilltop. Send two.* He looked round to all of us in turn, stopping on the Mayor for a second, who stared back at him hard, and then he turned and left without even seeing if we agreed.

That's when the arguing started.

"You know full well, *David,*" Mistress Coyle says, "that one of the scout ship people has to go. Which means there's only room for one of us–"

"And it won't be you," says the Mayor.

"Maybe it's a trap," Lee says, his Noise rumbling. "In which case, I vote for the President."

"Maybe Todd should go," Bradley says. "He's the one they spoke to."

"No," the Mayor says. "Todd stays."

I spin round. "*You* don't get a say in what I do."

"If you're not here, Todd," the Mayor says, "what's to stop our good mistresses from planting a bomb in my tent?"

"What a splendid idea," Mistress Coyle smiles.

"Enough bickering," Simone says. "Mistress Coyle and I would make a perfectly good–"

"I'll go," Viola says, in a quiet voice that stops all of us.

We all look at her. "No way," I start to say, but she's already shaking her head.

"They only want two of us," she says from the bed, coughing heavy. "And we all know that can't be the Mayor or Mistress Coyle."

The Mayor sighs. "Why do you two still *insist* on calling me—?"

"And it can't be you either, Todd," she says. "Someone has to keep him and her from killing us all."

"But yer sick—" I say.

"I'm the one who fired the missile into the hillside," she says, quiet. "I've got to fix it."

I swallow. But I can see on her face how much she means it.

"I can actually agree with that," Mistress Coyle says. "Viola will be a good symbol of the future we're fighting for. And Simone can go with her to lead the talks."

Simone stands up a little straighter but Viola says, "No," coughing some more. "Bradley."

Bradley's Noise sparks with surprise. Simone's would, too, if she had any. "The choice isn't yours, Viola," she says. "I'm Mission Commander here and I'm the one—"

"They'll read him," Viola says.

"*Exactly.*"

"If we send two people without Noise," she says, "how's that going to look? They'll read Bradley and they'll see peace, *for real*. Todd can stay here with the Mayor. Simone and Mistress Coyle can keep the scout ship in the air above the talks at all times to keep us safe, and me and Bradley will go up that hill."

She coughs again. "And now you all need to leave so I can rest up for tomorrow morning."

317

There's a silence as we all think about this idea.

I hate it.

But even I can see the sense of it.

"Well," Bradley says. "I suppose that settles that."

"All right then," the Mayor says. "Let's find a place to have a few words about terms, shall we?"

"Yes," Mistress Coyle says, "let's do that."

They all start filing out, the Mayor taking one last look round before he leaves. "A mighty fine ship," he says as he disappears out the door. Lee goes, too, using Bradley's Noise. Viola starts to say he can stay but I think he's leaving us alone on purpose.

"You sure about this?" I ask her when they're all gone. "You don't know what could be up there."

"I don't like it much either," she says, "but it's how it has to be."

And she says it a bit hard and she's looking at me and not saying nothing.

"What?" I say. "What's wrong?"

She starts shaking her head.

"*What?*" I say.

"Your Noise, Todd," she says. "I hate it. I'm sorry. I *hate* it."

{ V I O L A }

He looks back at me, puzzled.

But he doesn't *sound* puzzled. He doesn't sound like *anything*.

"It's a *good* thing that I'm quiet, Viola," he says. "It's gonna help us, help *me*, cuz if I can . . ."

He trails off because he's still seeing the look on my face.

I have to turn away from him.

"I'm still me," he says quietly. "I'm still Todd."

But he isn't. He isn't the same Todd whose thoughts spilled out all over the place in a big, colorful mess, the one who couldn't tell a lie if his life depended on it, who *didn't* tell a lie when his life *did* depend on it, the Todd that saved my life more than once, in more than one way, *that* Todd who I could hear every uncomfortable thought of, who I could count on, who I knew–

Who I–

"I ain't changed," he says. "I'm just more like you, more like all the men you grew up knowing, more like *Bradley* used to be."

I keep looking away from him, hoping he can't see how weary I feel, how my arm throbs with every breath, how bad the fever is gouging me out. "I'm really tired, Todd," I say. "It's only tomorrow morning. I have to rest."

"Viola–"

"You need to be out there with them anyway," I say. "Make sure the Mayor and Mistress Coyle don't set themselves up as interim leaders."

He stares at me. "I don't know what *interim* means."

And that's close enough to the Todd I know that I smile, a little. "I'll be fine. I just need some sleep."

He still stares. "Are you dying, Viola?"

"What?" I say. "No. No, I'm not–"

"Are you dying and yer just not telling me?" His eyes are boring into me now, filled with concern.

But I still can't hear him.

"I'm not getting better," I say, "but that doesn't mean I'm going to die anytime soon. Mistress Coyle's bound to find something, and if she can't, the convoy has all kinds of more advanced medical stuff than the scout ship has. I can hang on 'til then."

He's still staring. "Cuz I couldn't stand it if–" His voice is thick. "I just couldn't take that, Viola. I just *couldn't*."

And then there it is–

His Noise, still way too quiet, but there, burning away underneath him, burning away with how he's feeling and how true it is and how worried he is for me and I can hear it, just faintly but I can hear it–

And then I hear, I am the Circle–

And he goes quiet again, quiet as a stone.

"I'm not dying," I say, looking away from him.

Todd just stands there for a second. "I'll be right outside," he finally says. "You call if you need anything. You call *me* and I'll get it for you."

"I will," I say.

He nods, his lips held tight. He nods again.

Then he goes.

I sit there quietly for a while, listening to the ROAR of the army in the square outside and the raised voices of the Mayor and Mistress Coyle and Simone and Bradley and Lee still arguing.

But I don't hear Todd.

[TODD]

Bradley sighs loudly, after what seems like hours spent

320

bickering round the campfire, shivering against the freezingist part of the night. "So it's agreed then?" he says. "We offer an immediate ceasefire on both sides, with a line drawn under all past actions. After that, the issue of the river and then we start laying the groundwork for how we can all live together."

"Agreed," the Mayor says. He don't even look tired.

"Yes, fine," Mistress Coyle says, grunting with stiffness as she stands. "It's getting on toward morning. We need to get back."

"Get *back*?" I say.

"The people on the hilltop need to know what's going on, Todd," she says. "Plus, I'll need to get Wilf to bring Viola's horse down here because she's certainly not going to be able to *walk* up that hill. Not with that fever."

I look back to the scout ship, hoping Viola's at least sleeping inside, hoping she actually does feel better when she wakes.

Wondering if she lied about dying.

"How is she really?" I say to Mistress Coyle, getting up after her. "How sick is she?"

Mistress Coyle looks at me for a long, long moment. "She's not well, Todd," she says, very serious. "I just hope everyone's doing everything they can to help her."

And she leaves me standing there. I look back at the Mayor, who's watching Mistress Coyle walk away from me. He comes over. "You're worried about Viola," he says, not asking it. "I agree she's looked better."

"If something happens to her cuz of that band," I say, my voice low and strong. "I swear to God I'll—"

He holds up a hand to stop me. "I know, Todd, even more than you think." And again, his voice sounds as true as anything. "I'll have my doctors redouble their efforts. Don't worry. I'm not going to let anything happen to her."

"Me neither," Bradley says, overhearing us. "She's a fighter, Todd, and if she thinks she's strong enough to go up that hill tomorrow, we have to believe her. And I'll be there to make sure nothing happens, believe you me." And I hear in his Noise that he means every word. He sighs. "Though I guess that means I'm going to need a horse, too." Even though I don't know how to ride one, his Noise adds, a bit worried.

"I'll ask Angharrad to take you," I say, looking over to where she's munching on some hay. "She can watch over both of you."

He smiles. "You know, Viola once told us that if we were ever in doubt about what's happening here, that we could count on you above all things."

I feel my face get hot. "Yeah," I say, "well."

He gives my shoulder a hard, friendly pat. "We'll fly back down here at dawn," he says. "And who knows? Maybe peace by the end of the day." He winks. "And then maybe you can show me how you keep so quiet."

He, Lee, Simone, and Mistress Coyle make their way back to the scout ship, Mistress Coyle leaving her oxcart behind for Wilf to pick up. Bradley makes an announcement on a speaker for everyone to move back. The soldiers do, the engines start to grind, and up it rises on a cushion of air.

I hear the Mayor's voice before the ship's even halfway

back to the hill.

"Gentlemen!" he shouts, his voice twisting and turning hard into the men nearby and echoing thru to every man in the square.

"I report to you, *VICTORY!*" he shouts.

And when the cheering starts, it goes on for a long, long time.

{VIOLA}

I wake as the ship bumps back down on the hilltop and the bay doors open.

I hear Mistress Coyle shout to the waiting crowd, "We are VICTORIOUS!"

And hear the huge cheer even through the thick metal walls of the ship.

"That can't be good," Lee says, back in the next bed, his Noise imagining Mistress Coyle, arms thrust into the air, people picking her up on their shoulders and carrying her for a victory lap.

"That's probably not too far off," I say, laughing a little. Which sets me on a long chain of coughing.

The door opens and Bradley and Simone enter.

"You're missing the rally," Bradley says sarcastically.

"She's allowed her moment," Simone says. "She's an impressive women in a lot of ways."

I make to answer but the coughing comes again, so strong that Bradley takes out a medicine pad and puts it on my throat. The cooling of it feels better immediately, and I take a few slow breaths to get the fumes into my lungs.

"What's the plan, then?" I say. "How much time do we have?"

"A couple hours," Bradley says. "We'll fly back down to the city, and Simone will set up the projections for both down there and up here, so everyone can see what's going on. Then she'll keep the ship in the air for however long our meeting lasts."

"I'll be looking out for you," Simone says. "Both of you."

"Good to hear," Bradley says, quietly but warmly, then he says to me, "Wilf's bringing Acorn down for you to ride up, and Todd's giving me his horse."

I smile. "Is he really?"

Bradley smiles back. "A show of faith, I'm guessing?"

"It means he expects you to come back."

We hear two sets of footsteps coming up the ramp outside, and continuing cheers, too, though not as many as before. And the voices that approach are arguing.

"I don't find this acceptable, Mistress," Ivan is saying as Mistress Coyle comes in the door before him.

"And what makes you think your idea of *acceptable* is in any way relevant?" she snaps back, that fierceness in her voice that would cow most people.

Not Ivan, though, not quite. "I speak for the people."

"*I* speak for the people, Ivan," she says. "Not you."

Ivan glances over at me and Bradley. "You're a-sending a little girl and the Humanitarian to meet with an enemy big enough to annihilate us," he says. "I can't say as that would be the overwhelming choice of the people, Mistress."

"Sometimes the people don't know what's best for them, *Ivan*," she says. "Sometimes the people have to be convinced of things that are necessary. That's what leadership is. Not shouting your head off in support of their every whim."

"I hope you're right, Mistress," he says. "For your own sake."

A last look at all of us and he leaves.

"Everything all right out there?" Simone says.

"Fine, fine," Mistress Coyle says, her mind clearly somewhere else.

"They've started cheering again," Lee says.

And we all hear it.

But it's not for Mistress Coyle.

[TODD]

Boy colt, Angharrad says, nuzzling me. And then she says, **Boy colt yes.**

"It's for her, really," I say. "If something happens, I want him able to get her outta there even if he's gotta carry her, okay?"

Boy colt, she says, pressing against me again.

"But are you sure, girl? Are you *sure* yer okay? Cuz I ain't gonna send you nowhere if yer not—"

Todd, she says. **For Todd.**

And I get a thickness in my throat and I have to swallow a coupla times before I can say, "Thank you, girl," trying not to think what happened the last time I asked an animal to be brave for me.

"You're a remarkable young man, you know that?" I hear from behind me.

I sigh. There he is again. "I'm just talking to my horse," I say.

"No, Todd," the Mayor says, coming over from his tent. "There are some things I've been meaning to say to you, and I'd like you to allow me to say them before the world changes."

"The world changes all the time," I say, hitching up Angharrad's reins. "At least it does for me."

"Listen to me, Todd," he says, real seriouslike. "I want to tell you how much I've grown to respect you. Respect how you've fought by my side, yes, how you've been *right there* through every challenge and danger, but also how you've stood up to me when no one else would dare, how *you've* really won this peace, while all around you the world was losing its head."

He puts a hand on Angharrad, rubbing her flank gently. She shifts a little but lets him.

So I let him, too.

"I think you're the one the settlers are going to want to talk to, Todd," he says. "Forget me, forget Mistress Coyle; it's *you* who they're going to see as the leader here."

"Yeah, well," I say. "Let's wait till we get peace first before we start handing out credit, okay?"

He breathes out a cloud of cold air thru his nose. "I want to give you something, Todd."

"I don't want nothing from you," I say.

But he's already holding out a piece of paper in his hand.

"Take it," he says.

I wait for a second but then I take it. It's got a line of words written across it, dense and black and unknowable.

"Read it," he says.

I suddenly get *real* mad. "You looking to get hit?"

"Please," he says and it sounds so gentle and genuine that, even angry, I actually drop my glance back down to the paper. It's still just words, written in what I think is the Mayor's hand, a dark thicket in a line, like a horizon you can't get nowhere near.

"Look at the words," he says. "Tell me what they say."

The paper flickers in the firelight. None of the words is too long and I reckernize at least two of 'em as my name—

Even a dummy like me knows that much—

And the first word is—

My name is Todd Hewitt and I am a man of New Prentisstown.

I blink.

That's what it says, right across the page, every word burning clear like the sun.

My name is Todd Hewitt and I am a man of New Prentisstown.

I look back up. The Mayor's face is all hard concentrayshun, looking deep into me, no *buzz* of control, just a faint *hum*.

(that same *hum*, that one I hear when I think *I am the Circle*—)

"What does it say?" he asks.

I look down—

And I read it—

I read it out loud.

"My name is Todd Hewitt and I am a man of New Prentisstown."

He lets out a long breath and the *hum* dies away. "And now?"

I look at the words again. They're still on the page but they're slipping from me, slipping from their meanings—

But not all the way.

My name is Todd Hewitt and I am a man of New Prentisstown.

That's what it says.

That's what it *still* says.

"My name is Todd Hewitt," I read, saying it more slowly cuz I'm still trying to *see* it, "and I am a man of New Prentisstown."

"That you certainly are," says the Mayor.

I look up to him. "That ain't real reading, tho. That's just you putting words in my head."

"No," he says. "I've been thinking about how the Spackle learn, how they must pass on information. They have no written language, but if they're connected to each other at all times, they don't need it. They just exchange their knowledge directly. They carry who they are and what they know in their Noise and share it in a single voice of themselves. Maybe even a single voice of this world."

I look up at that. A single voice. The Spackle who came to the square. The *one* voice that seemed to be the whole world talking. Talking to *me*.

"I didn't give you words, Todd," the Mayor says. "I gave you my *knowledge* of reading, and you were able to *take* it from me, in the same way I shared my knowledge of how to stay silent. I think that was the opening of a larger connection than even I imagined, a connection like the Spackle have. It's a blunt and inelegant process right now, but it could be refined. Just think of what we could do if we mastered it, Todd, how much knowledge we could share, and how easily."

I look at the paper again. "My name is Todd Hewitt," I read quietly, still seeing most of the words.

"If you let me," he says, his voice open and honest-sounding, "I believe I could give you enough knowledge to have you reading your mother's journal by the time the settlers arrive."

I think about that. My ma's book. Still cut thru with Aaron's knife stab, still hidden away, read only once in the voice of Viola . . .

I don't trust him, not never, he *ain't* redeemable–

But I'm seeing him a bit different, sceing him as a man, not a monster.

Cuz if we *are* connected somehow, connected in a single voice–

(that *hum*–)

Maybe it's a two-way thing.

Maybe he's showing me how to do stuff–

And maybe I'm making him better in return.

We hear a distant *booming,* the familiar one of the scout ship taking to the air. In the eastern sky, the ship and the sun are both starting their rise.

"We'll have to return to this discussion, Todd," the Mayor says. "It's time to go make peace."

{ V I O L A }

"A big day, my girl," Mistress Coyle says to me where we're all gathered in the healing room as Simone flies toward the town. "For you and for all of us."

"I know how big it is," I say quietly. Bradley's watching the screens to monitor our progress. Lee's stayed back on the hilltop to listen out for how things go with Ivan throughout the day.

I hear Mistress Coyle laugh to herself. "What?" I ask.

"Oh," she says, "just the irony that I'm putting all my hopes into the girl who hates me most of all."

"I don't *hate* you," I say, realizing that, despite all that's happened, it's true.

"Maybe not, my girl," she says, "but you certainly don't trust me."

I don't say anything to that.

"Make a peace, Viola," she says, more seriously. "Make a *good* peace. Make it so well that everyone knows it was *you* who did it, and not that man. I know you don't want a world where I'm in charge, but we can't let him be in charge of it either." She looks over at me. "That has to be the goal, no matter what."

I feel the nerves in my stomach. "I'll do what I can," I say.

She shakes her head slowly. "You're lucky, you know. So young. So many chances ahead of you. You could turn out to be a better version of me. A version of me who's never forced to be so ruthless."

I don't know what to say to that. "Mistress Coyle–"

"Don't worry, my girl," she says, standing as the ship comes in for a landing. "You don't have to be my friend." Her eyes get a little fire in them. "You just have to be his enemy."

And we feel the small *bump* of the landing.

It's time.

I get myself up out of bed and to the bay doors. The first thing I see when they open onto the square is Todd at the front of a sea of soldiers, standing there with Angharrad on one side and Acorn and Wilf on the other.

In the midst of the **ROAR** of the soldiers watching us and the Mayor watching us, too, his uniform pressed and sharp and that look on his face you want to slap off, and the probes in the air broadcasting everything back to a projection on the hilltop for the crowds there to watch, and with everyone gathering behind me on the ramp, all of us ready to start this huge, huge thing–

In the midst of all this, Todd sees me and he says, "Viola."

And it's only then I really feel the weight of everything we're about to do.

I walk down the bay door, the eyes of the human world on us, the Spackle world, too, for all I know, and I brush past the Mayor's outstretched hand and let him give his greetings to everyone else.

I go straight to Todd, between the horses.

"Hey," he says, that crooked smile on his face. "Are you ready?"

"Ready as anyone could be," I say.

The horses chat to each other over us–**Boy colt, girl colt, lead, follow**–with all the warmth that one herd animal feels for another member of its herd, two happy walls boxing us in for a moment against the crowd.

"Viola Eade," Todd says. "Peacemaker."

I give a nervous laugh. "I'm so scared I can barely breathe."

He's a little shy of me, I think, after the last time we talked, but he takes my hand. Just that. "You'll know what to do," he says.

"How can you be so sure?" I say.

"Cuz you always have. When it's counted, you've always done just the right thing."

Not when I fired the missile, I think, and he must see it on my face because he squeezes my hand again and suddenly that's not enough, even though I still hate not hearing his insides, even though it's like talking to a photograph of the Todd I used to know, I push myself into him and he puts his arms around me. He presses his face into my hair, smelling God knows what awfulness of fever and sweat, but just to be close to him, to feel his arms around me and to be surrounded by all that I know of him, even if I can't hear him–

I just have to trust that it's still Todd in there.

And then, somewhere out in the world nearby, the Mayor starts his ruddy speech.

[TODD]

The Mayor's climbed up on a cart near the scout ship, standing above the crowd.

"Today is both a culmination and a new beginning!" he says, his voice booming thru the Noise of the soldiers gathered in the square, of the nonsoldiering men of the town gathered there, too, a Noise that amplifies his voice, so there ain't no one here who can't hear him, everyone looking back at him, weary but hopeful, even the women, some of 'em at the edges even holding kids, who they usually do their best to keep hidden away, but every face, young and old, wanting what the Mayor says to be true.

"We have fought our enemy with great cunning and bravery," he says, "and we have brought him to his *knees!*"

There's a cheer for this, even tho it ain't exactly what happened.

Mistress Coyle's watching him, her arms folded, and then we see her start walking over to the Mayor's cart.

"What's she doing?" Bradley says, coming over to me and Viola.

We watch as she pulls herself up on the cart till she's standing next to the Mayor, who shoots her a glance of death but don't stop his speech. "This day will be remembered by your children and your children's children!

"GOOD PEOPLE!" Mistress Coyle shouts right over the top of him. But she's not looking at the crowd; she's looking up into the probe broadcasting back to the hill. "TODAY IS A DAY WE WILL REMEMBER FOR THE REST OF OUR LIVES!"

The Mayor raises his voice to match hers. "THROUGH YOUR COURAGE AND SACRIFICE–"

"HARD TIMES WHICH YOU MET WITH FORTI-TUDE–" shouts Mistress Coyle.

"WE HAVE ACHIEVED THE IMPOSSIBLE–" shouts the Mayor.

"THE SETTLERS ON THEIR WAY WILL SEE THE WORLD WE'VE CREATED FOR THEM–"

"WE HAVE FORGED THIS NEW WORLD FROM OUR OWN BLOOD AND DETERMINATION–"

"We should leave," Viola says.

Me and Bradley look at her, surprised, but then I see a glint of mischief in his Noise. I ask Angharrad and Acorn to both kneel and I help Viola on the back of Acorn. Wilf gives Bradley a hand getting up on Angharrad. He don't look too sure on her, tho.

"Don't worry," I say. "She'll take good care of you."

Boy colt, she says.

"Angharrad," I say back.

"Todd," Viola says, echoing her.

And I look back at Viola and I say, "Viola."

That's all, just her name.

And we realize this is it.

This is it starting.

"A SHINING EXAMPLE OF PEACE IN OUR TIME–"

"I HAVE LED YOU TO A GREAT VICTORY–"

The horses start moving thru the square, past the speech cart, thru soldiers getting outta their way, heading towards the road, the one that leads to the Spackle hill.

The Mayor's voice falters a little as he sees what's happening. Mistress Coyle keeps bellering cuz she's looking up into the probe and don't see 'em yet, not till the Mayor says quickly, "AND WE SEND OUR AMBASSADORS OF PEACE ON THEIR WAY WITH FULSOME VOICES!"

The crowd cheers on cue, cutting Mistress Coyle off midstream, something she don't look too happy about.

"Viola'll be all right," Wilf says as we keep our eyes on her, shrinking down the road. "She always comes thru."

The crowd's still cheering but the Mayor hops off the cart and comes over to me and Wilf. "And they're off," he says, his voice a little peeved. "Rather earlier than I expected."

334

"You woulda talked all morning," I say. "And they've got danger waiting for 'em up that hill."

"*Mr.* President." Mistress Coyle grimaces as she passes by us on her way back up the ramp of the scout ship.

I keep watching Viola and Bradley until they disappear outta the square, then I move my eyes to the big projeckshun Simone set up while everyone was speechifying, hovering huge over the ruins of the cathedral, the same image broadcast back to the hilltop, the image of Viola and Bradley riding down the road, heading into the dead zone of the battlefield.

"I wouldn't worry, Todd," the Mayor says.

"I know," I say. "Any sign of funny business and the scout ship'll blow the Spackle sky-high."

"Yes, indeed," the Mayor says but in a way that makes me turn, that way he has like he knows more than he's saying.

"What?" I say. "What have you done?"

"Why do you always suspect I've done something, Todd?" he asks.

But he's still smiling that smile.

{VIOLA}

We ride out of the last edge of town and through a field of burned bodies, still here after the burning arrow attacks, scattered everywhere like felled trees.

"In a place of all this beauty and potential," Bradley says, looking around, "we just repeat the same mistakes. Do we hate paradise so much we have to be sure it becomes a trash heap?"

"Is that your idea of a pep talk?" I ask.

He laughs. "Think of it as a vow to do better."

"Look," I say. "They've cleared a path for us."

We near the bottom of the hill that leads up to the Spackle camp. Boulders and stones have been moved out of the way, along with Spackle bodies and the remains of their mounts, remains put there by artillery from the Mayor, a missile from me, and a bomb from Mistress Coyle, so we've all had a hand in it.

"It can only be a good sign," Bradley says. "A small welcome, making our path easier."

"Easier to walk into a trap?" I say, nervously gripping Acorn's reins.

Bradley makes to go up the path first, but Acorn puts himself in front of Angharrad, feeling her hesitation, trying to make her more comfortable by appearing confident. **Follow,** his Noise says, almost gently. **Follow.**

And she does. And up we go.

As we climb, we hear the hum of engines in the valley behind us as Simone pilots the ship into the air, where it'll watch us like a hawk hovering on an updraft, ready to swoop down with weapons if anything goes astray.

My comm beeps. I take it out of my pocket and see Todd looking back at me. *"You all right?"* he asks.

"I only just left," I say. "And Simone's already on her way."

"Yeah," he says. *"We can see you, bigger than life. Like yer the star of yer own vid."*

I try to laugh but it only comes out as coughing.

"*Any sign of danger,*" he says, more serious, "*any sign* at all *you get yerself outta there.*"

"Don't worry," I say. And then I say, "Todd?"

He looks at me through the comm, guessing what I'm about to say. "*You'll be okay,*" he says.

"If something happens to me–"

"*It won't.*"

"But if it does–"

"*It* won't." He says it almost angrily. "*I ain't saying good-bye to you, Viola, so don't even try. You get up there, you get peace, and you get back down here so we can make you well again.*" He leans in closer to the comm. "*I'll see you soon, all right?*"

I swallow a little. "All right," I say.

He clicks off.

"Everything okay?" Bradley asks.

I nod. "Let's get this over with."

We climb up the makeshift path, getting closer to the summit of the hill. The ship's high enough to see what's waiting for us. "*It looks like a welcoming party,*" Simone calls over Bradley's comm. "*Open ground with what has to be their leader sitting on one of their battlemore things.*"

"Anything threatening?" Bradley asks.

"*Nothing obvious. But there are an awful lot of them.*"

We ride on and, in the wreckage of the hill, I see we must be at about the point where Todd and I ran to get away from Aaron, leaping across to the ledge under the waterfall, the same ledge where the Spackle lined up and shot their fiery arrows, the same ledge that's not there anymore, not after I blasted it away.

We keep on past the place where I got shot and where Todd beat back Davy Prentiss Jr.–

And we near the last rise, only bits of it still there in its original shape, but close enough to the last place Todd and I thought we were safe, looking out onto what we thought was Haven.

But instead, it led us to this.

"Viola?" Bradley says, his voice low. "You all right?"

"I think the fever's rising again," I say. "I was drifting off there a little."

"Nearly there," he says gently. "I'll greet them. I'm sure they'll greet us back."

And then we'll see what happens, says his Noise.

We climb the last bit of the ruined zigzag road, climb over the top of the hill.

And into the camp of the Spackle.

[T O D D]

"They're nearly there," I say.

Me and Wilf and the Mayor and everybody else in the square are watching the big projeckshun above the ruins of the cathedral, watching as Viola and Bradley and two horses that suddenly look real small walk up into a waiting half circle of Spackle.

"That has to be their leader," the Mayor says, pointing to the one standing on the biggest battlemore in the row of 'em waiting there. We watch him as he sees Viola and Bradley crest the hill on the horses, that half circle of Spackle giving 'em nowhere to run except back the way they came.

"First they'll exchange greetings," the Mayor says, his eyes not leaving the picture. "That's how these things start. And then both sides will declare how strong they are and then finally they'll give an indication of intentions. It's all very formal."

We watch Bradley in the projeckshun, who seems to be doing exactly what the Mayor predicted.

"The Spackle's getting down," I say.

The leader of the Spackle slowly but gracefully swings a leg back over the animal. He gets down and takes off this helmet thing he was wearing, handing it to a Spackle next to him.

Then he starts walking cross the clearing.

"Viola's getting off her horse," Wilf says.

And she is. Acorn's kneeling to let her off and she gingerly steps to the ground. She turns from Acorn, readying to meet the leader of the Spackle, who's still coming toward her slowly, his hand outstretched–

"This is going well, Todd," the Mayor says. "Very well indeed."

"Don't say stuff like that," I say.

"Hey!" Wilf suddenly shouts, sitting forward–

And I see it–

There's a rumble thru the crowd of soldiers as they see it, too–

A Spackle is running from the half circle–

Breaking ranks and running toward the leader of the Spackle–

Heading straight for him–

And the leader of the Spackle is turning–

As if he's surprised—

And in the cold morning sunlight, we can see—

The Spackle who's running has got a blade—

"He's gonna kill the leader—" I say, getting to my feet—

And the ROAR of the crowd rises—

And the running Spackle reaches the leader, blade up—

Reaches him—

And goes past—

Past the leader whose arms move to stop him—

But he avoids 'em—

And keeps on running—

Running toward Viola—

And that's when I reckernize him—

"No," I say. *"No!"*

It's 1017—

Running flat out at Viola—

Carrying a blade—

He's gonna kill her—

He's gonna kill her to punish *me*—

"Viola!" I shout—

"VIOLA!"

The One in Particular

DAWN IS COMING, the Sky shows. *They will be here soon.*

He stands above me in his fullest armor, intricately sculpted clay covering his chest and arms, far too ornate and beautiful to ever be worn in battle. The ceremonial helmet teeters on his head like a spired hut, matched by an equally heavy ceremonial stone blade at his side.

You look ridiculous, I show.

I look like a leader, he shows back, not angry at all.

We do not even know if they will come.

They will come, he shows. *They will come.*

He heard my vow to defeat the peace. I know he did. I was too angry to try and hide it, though he would have probably heard it anyway. And yet he has kept me by his side, so unafraid of my insignificance that he cannot even pretend to see me as a threat.

Do not think I give away peace for nothing, he

shows. *Do not think they will have free rein to do with this world as they choose. There will be no repeat of the Burden, not while I am the Sky.*

And I see something in his voice, something deep down, flickers of something.

You have a plan, I sneer.

Let us say that I do not enter into these talks without preparing for every eventuality.

You only say that to keep me quiet, I show. *They will take all they can get and then they will take more by force. They will not stop until they have taken everything from us.*

He sighs. *The Sky asks again for the Return's trust. And to prove it, the Sky would very much like the Return by his side when the Clearing comes to us.*

I look up to him, surprised. His voice is truthful—

(—and my own voice yearns to touch his, yearns to know that he is doing right by me, by the Burden, by the Land, I want to trust him so badly it is like an ache in my chest—)

My promise to you remains, he shows. *The Source will be yours to do with as you please.*

I keep watching him, reading his voice, reading everything in it: the terrible and terrific responsibility he feels for the Land weighing on him every moment, awake or asleep; the concern he feels for me, for how I am eating myself alive with hate and revenge; his worry for the days to come and the weeks and months after that, how no matter what happens today, the Land will be forever changed, is already forever changing; and I see that, if forced, he will act without me; he will leave me behind if he must for the good of the Land.

But I see, too, how that would grieve him.

And I also see, hidden no doubt along the Pathways' End, that he has a plan.

I will come, I show.

The pinkness of the sun starts to show on the far horizon. The Sky stands in his battlemore's saddle. His top soldiers, also in ceremonial dress, also with ceremonial stone blades, are arranged in a broad half circle that encompasses the ragged lip of the hill. The Clearing will be allowed here, but no farther.

The voice of the Land is open, all of them watching the edge of the hill through their Sky. *We speak as one,* shows the Sky, sending it through them. *We are the Land and we speak as one.*

The Land repeats the chant, tying themselves together in a single bond, unbreakable as they face the enemy.

We are the Land and we speak as one.

Except for the Return, I think, because the band on my arm is hurting again. I push the lichen away to look at it, the skin around it stretched badly as it attaches itself to the metal, bloated and tight with scarring, painful every moment since it was first put on me.

But the physical pain is nothing compared to what is in my voice.

Because the Clearing did this to me. The *Knife* did it. It is the thing that marks me as the Return, the thing that keeps me forever separate from the Land as they chant around me, raising their single voice in a language the Clearing will understand.

We are the Land and we speak as one.

Except for the Return, who speaks alone.

*You do **not** speak alone,* the Sky shows, looking down at me from his steed. *The Return is the Land and the Land is the Return.*

The Land is the Return, comes the chant around us.

Say it, the Sky shows to me. *Say it so the Clearing know who they are dealing with. Say it so that we speak together.*

He reaches out a hand as if to touch me with it but he is too high, too far up on his battlemore. *Say it so that you **are** the Land.*

And his voice is reaching out to me, too, surrounding me, asking me to join him, to join the Land, to allow myself to become part of something bigger, greater, something that might—

The vessel of the Clearing suddenly rises into the air across from us, holding itself there and waiting.

The Sky looks out to it, the chant continuing behind us. *It is time,* he shows. *They come.*

I recognize her immediately. My surprise is so sharp the Sky looks down at me for a quick moment.

*They have sent **her**,* I show.

They have sent the Knife's one in particular.

My voice rises. Could he have come with her? Would he—?

But no. It is another of the Clearing, his voice as loud and chaotic as any of them. And it is chaotic with *peace.* The wish for it is all over him, hope for it, fear for it, courage around it.

They wish for peace, the Sky shows, and there is amusement in the voice of the Land.

But I look up to the Sky. And I see peace there, too.

The Clearing ride their mounts forward into the half circle but stop a distance away, looking at us nervously, his voice loud and hopeful, hers the silence of the voiceless.

"My name is Bradley Tench," he says through his mouth and his voice. "This is Viola Eade."

He waits to see if we understand his language and after a brief nod from the Sky, he says, "We come to make peace between us, to end this war with no further bloodshed, to see if we can correct the past and make a new future where our two peoples can live side by side."

The Sky shows nothing for a long moment, a quiet echo of the chant rolling unceasingly behind him.

I am the Sky, the Sky shows, in the language of the Burden.

The man from the Clearing looks surprised but we can tell from his voice that he understands. I watch the Knife's one in particular. She stares back at us, pale and shivery in the cold of early morning. The first sound she makes is a swarm of coughing into her fist. And then she speaks.

"We have the support of our entire people," she says, clicking her words only from her mouth, and the Sky opens his own voice a little to make sure he understands her. She gestures to the vessel still hovering out from the hill, ready no doubt to fire more weapons at the first sign of trouble from us. "Support to bring back peace," she says.

Peace, I think bitterly. *Peace that requires us to be slaves.*

Quiet, shows the Sky down at me. A command, softly shown but real.

And then he climbs down from his battlemore. He swings his leg behind him, stepping to the ground with a solid thud. He removes his helmet, handing it to the soldier nearest him, and he begins to walk toward the Clearing. Toward the man who, now that I can read his voice more closely, is only newly arrived, a forerunner of all those who are still to come. Still to come to push the Land out of its own world. Still to come to make *all* of us the Burden. And more will no doubt come after. And more after that.

And I think it would be better to die than let that happen.

One of the soldiers next to me turns, shock in his voice, telling me in the language of the Land to quiet myself.

My eyes fall on the ceremonial blade he carries.

The Sky makes his way slowly, ponderously, *leader-like* over to the Clearing.

Over to the Knife's one in particular.

The Knife who, though he no doubt fretted and worried about peace, though he no doubt *intended* to do the right thing, sent his one in particular instead, too afraid to face us himself—

And I think of him pulling me from the bodies of the Burden—

I think of my vow to strike him down—

And I find myself thinking, *No.*

I feel the voice of the Land on me, feel it reaching out to quiet me at this most important moment.

And again I think, *No.*

No, this cannot be.

The one in particular slides down from her mount to greet the Sky.

And I am moving before I even know I mean to.

I grab the ceremonial blade from the soldier next to me so fast he offers no resistance, only a surprised yelp, and I lift it high as I run. My voice is strangely clear, seeing only what is in front of me, the rocks on the path, the dry river-bed, the hand of the Sky reaching out to stop me as I pass him but too slow in his elaborate armor to do so—

I am crossing the ground toward her—

My voice is growing louder, a yell emerging from it, wordless in the languages of the Burden and the Land—

I know we are watched, watched from the vessel, watched from the lights that hover alongside it—

I am hoping that the Knife can see—

See as I race forward to kill his one in particular—

The heavy blade high in my hands—

She sees me coming and stumbles back toward her mount—

The man from the Clearing shouts something, his own mount trying to move between me and the Knife's one in particular—

But I am too fast, the space too short—

And the Sky is shouting behind me, too—

His voice, the voice of the entire *Land* booming behind me, reaching out to stop me—

But a voice cannot stop a body—

And she's falling back farther—

Falling against the legs of her own mount, who is also trying to protect her but is tangled up with her—

And there is no time—

There is only me—

Only my revenge—

The blade is up—

The blade is back—

Ready and heavy and dying to fall—

I take my final steps—

And I put my weight behind the blade to begin the end—

And she raises her arm to protect herself—

BARGAINING

{ V I O L A }

THE ATTACK COMES FROM NOWHERE. The leader of the Spackle, the *Sky*, as he calls himself, approaches us with greetings–

But suddenly there's another running toward him, a brutal stone blade in his hand, polished and heavy–

And he's going to kill the Sky–

He's going to kill his own leader–

At the peace talks, this is going to happen–

The Sky is turning, seeing the one with the sword come and he reaches out to stop him–

But the one with the sword ducks past him easily–

Ducks past him and runs toward me and Bradley–

Runs toward *me*–

"*Viola!*" I hear Bradley shout–

And he's turning Angharrad to come between us but they're two steps behind at least–

And the ground is empty between me and the one running–

And I'm stumbling back into Acorn's legs–

Girl colt! Acorn says–

And I'm falling back to the ground–

And there's no time–

The Spackle's on me–

The blade's in the air–

And I raise my arm in a hopeless attempt to protect myself–

And–

The blade doesn't fall.

The blade doesn't fall.

I glance back up.

The Spackle is staring at my arm.

My sleeve has dropped back and my bandage has come off as I've fallen and he's staring at the band on my arm–

The red, infected, sick-looking band with the number 1391 etched onto it–

And then I see it–

Halfway up his own forearm, as scarred and messy as mine–

A band reading 1017–

And this is *Todd's* Spackle, the one he set free from the Mayor's genocide at the monastery with a band all his own that's clearly infected him, too–

He's frozen his swing, the blade in the air, ready to fall but not falling, as he stares at my arm–

And then a pair of hooves strike him hard in the chest, sending him flying backward across the clear ground–

[TODD]

"VIOLA!"

I'm screaming my head off, looking for a horse to ride, a fissioncar, *anything* to get me up that hill–

"It's okay, Todd!" the Mayor shouts, looking at the projeckshun. "It's all right! Your horse kicked him away."

I look back to the projeckshun just in time to see 1017 hit the ground a buncha yards from where he was just standing, tumbling down in a heap, and Angharrad's hind legs coming back to the ground–

"Oh, good *girl!*" I yell. "Good horse!" And I grab my comm, shouting, "Viola! Viola, are you there?"

And now I see Bradley kneeling down to Viola and the Spackle leader grabbing up 1017 and pretty much *throwing* him back to the other Spackle, who drag him away, and I see Viola digging in her pocket for her comm–

"Todd?" she says.

"Are you okay?" I say.

"That was your Spackle, Todd!" she says. *"The one you let go!"*

"I know," I say, "if I ever see him again, I'm gonna–"

"He stopped when he saw the band on my arm."

"Viola?" Simone breaks in from the scout ship.

"Don't fire!" Viola says quickly. *"Don't fire!"*

"We're going to get you out of there," Simone says.

"NO!" Viola snaps. *"Can't you see they didn't expect that?"*

"Let her get you outta there, Viola!" I yell. "It's not safe. I *knew* I never shoulda let you–"

351

"Listen to me, both of you," she says. *"It's stopping. Can't you–?"*

She breaks off and in the projeckshun the leader of the Spackle has come near 'em again, his hands out in a peaceful way.

"He's saying he's sorry," Viola says. *"He's saying it's not what they wanted. . . ."* She breaks off for a second. *"His Noise is more pictures than words, but I think he's saying that one is crazy or something."*

I feel a little stab at this. 1017 crazy. 1017 driven crazy.

Course he would be. Who wouldn't be after what happened to him?

But that don't mean he gets to attack Viola–

"He's saying he wants the peace talks to continue," Viola says, *"and oh–"*

In the projeckshun, the leader of the Spackle takes her hand and helps her to her feet. He gestures to the Spackle in the half circle and they part and some more Spackle bring out these thin strips of wood woven into chairs, one for each of 'em.

"What's going on?" I say into the comm.

"I think he's–" she stops and the half circle parts once more and another Spackle comes thru, his arms full of fruits and fish and a Spackle next to him carries a woven-wood table. *"They're offering us food,"* Viola says and at the same time I hear Bradley say, *"Thank you"* in the background.

"I think the peace talks are back on," Viola says.

"Viola–"

"No, I mean it, Todd. How many chances are we going to get?"

I fume for a second but she's got a stubborn sound in her voice. "Well, you leave the comm open, you hear?"

"*I agree,*" Simone says on the other channel. "*And you be sure to tell their leader how close they came to being vapors and rubble just now.*"

There's a pause and in the projeckshun, the leader of the Spackle pulls up straight in his chair.

"*He says he knows,*" Viola says, "*and that—*"

And then we hear it, the words coming thru, and it's our language, in a voice that sounds kinda like us but like it's made of a million voices saying the exact same thing.

The Land regrets the actions of the Return, it says.

I look at the Mayor. "What's *that* sposed to mean?"

{VIOLA}

"The honest truth," Bradley says, "is that we can't leave. It was a one-way trip, decades long. Our forefathers saw this planet as a prime candidate for settlement, and the deep space probes"– he clears his throat in discomfort, though you can already see what he's going to say in his Noise–"the deep space probes didn't show any signs of intelligent life here, so–"

So the Clearing cannot leave, the Sky says, looking beyond us at the scout ship hovering there. *The Clearing cannot leave.*

"I'm sorry?" Bradley says. "The what?"

But the Clearing has much to answer for, the Sky says, and his Noise shows us a picture of the one who ran at us with a blade, the one with the band on his arm, the one that Todd knew–

And there's feeling behind it, communicated *directly* as feeling, outside of language, feelings of terrible sadness, not for us, not for the interruption to the peace talks, but for the one who attacked us, sadness coming now with images of the Spackle genocide, images of 1017 surviving it and finding the rest of the Spackle, feelings of how damaged he is, how damaged *we* made him–

"I'm not excusing that," I interrupt, "but that wasn't us."

The Sky stops his Noise and looks at me. And it feels as if every Spackle on the face of this planet is looking at me, too.

I choose my words carefully.

"Bradley and I are new here," I say. "And we're *very* eager not to repeat the mistakes of the first settlers."

Mistakes? says the Sky, and his Noise opens again with images of what can only be the first Spackle War–

Pictures of death on a scale I hadn't even imagined–

Pictures of Spackle dying by the thousands–

Pictures of atrocities at the hands of men–

Pictures of children, babies–

"We can't do anything about what's happened," I say, trying to look away but his Noise is everywhere, "but we *can* do something to keep it from happening again."

"Starting with an immediate ceasefire," Bradley adds, looking stricken under the weight of the pictures. "That's the first thing we can agree on. We'll make no further attacks on you, and you'll make no further attacks on us."

The Sky merely opens his Noise again, showing a wall of water ten times as tall as a man, rushing down the riverbed where we sit, wiping out all before it as it slams into the valley below, erasing New Prentisstown from the map.

Bradley sighs and then opens his own Noise with missiles from the scout ship incinerating this hilltop and then more missiles falling from orbit, falling from a height the Spackle couldn't hope to retaliate against, destroying the entire Spackle race in a cloud of fire.

The Sky's Noise gets a satisfied feeling, like we were just confirming what he already knew.

"So that's where we stand," I say, coughing. "Now what are we going to do about it?"

There's a longer pause and then the Sky's Noise opens again.

And we begin to talk.

[TODD]

"They've been at it for hours," I say, watching the projeckshun from the campfire. "What's taking 'em so long?"

"Quiet, please, Todd," the Mayor says, trying to catch every word over my comm. "It's important we know everything that's discussed."

"What's there to discuss?" I say. "We all stop fighting and live in peace."

The Mayor gives me a look.

"Yeah, okay," I say, "but she ain't well. She can't just sit up there in the cold all day."

We're around our campfire now, me and the Mayor, with Mr. Tate and Mr. O'Hare watching with us. Everyone in town's watching the projeckshuns, too, tho with less interest as time goes on cuz watching people talk for hours ain't that interesting, no matter how important. Wilf eventually said he needed to get back to Jane and took Mistress Coyle's ox-cart back to the hilltop.

"Viola?" we hear over the comm. It's Simone.

"Yes?" Viola answers.

"Just an update on our fuel, sweetheart," Simone says. *"The cells can keep us hovering here through the early part of the evening, but after that you're going to need to start thinking about coming back tomorrow."*

I press a button on my comm. "Don't you leave her there," I say. I see the Spackle leader and Bradley both look surprised in the projeckshun. "Don't you let her outta yer sight."

But it's Mistress Coyle who answers. *"Don't you worry, Todd,"* she says. *"They're going to know how strong and committed we are if we have to run this ship dry."*

I look baffled at the Mayor for a minute.

"Broadcasting for the folks on the hilltop, are we, Mistress?" he says raising his voice so the comm can hear.

"Would everyone shut up, please?" Viola says. *"Or I'm going to turn this thing off."*

This sets off another chain of coughing in her and I see how pale and thin and *small* she looks in the projeckshun. It's the smallness that hurts. Sizewise, she's always been just smaller than me.

But I think of her and I feel like she's as big as the world.

"You call me if you need anything," I say to her. "Anything at all."

"I will," she says.

And then there's a beep and we don't hear nothing more.

The Mayor looks surprised up into the projeckshun. Bradley and Viola are talking to the Spackle leader again but we can't hear nothing anyone's saying. She's cut off all sound.

"Thank you very much, Todd," Mistress Coyle says, all annoyed thru the comm.

"She wasn't shutting *me* up," I say. "It's you all trying to butt in."

"Stupid little cow," I hear Mr. O'Hare mutter from the other side of the campfire.

"WHAT did you say?" I shout, getting to my feet and staring bullets at him.

Mr. O'Hare stands, too, breathing heavy, looking for a fight. "Now we can't hear what's going on, can we? That's what you get for sending a little girl to—"

"You shut up!" I say.

His nostrils flare and his fists clench. "And what are you gonna do about it, boy?"

And I see the Mayor move to intervene—

But, "Step forward," I say—

And my voice is calm, my Noise is light—

I am the Circle—

And Mr. O'Hare steps forward without hesitating—

Right into the campfire.

He just stands there for a second, not noticing anything. Then he gives a yelp of pain and leaps straight into the air, the cuffs of his trousers on fire, already running to find water to put 'em out and I hear the Mayor and Mr. Tate laughing and laughing.

"Well, Todd," the Mayor says, "very impressive."

I blink. I'm shaking all over.

I coulda really hurt him.

I coulda, just by thinking it.

(and it kinda feels *good*–)

(shut up–)

"Now that we've obviously got some time to kill while the negotiations continue," the Mayor says, still laughing, "what do you say we engage in some light reading?"

And I'm only just recovering my breath, so it takes another long minute before I realize what he means.

{VIOLA}

"No," Bradley says, shaking his head again, his breath clouding up as the sun gets closer to setting. "We can't start with punishment. How we start sets the tone for everything that follows."

I close my eyes and remember him saying the exact same thing to me what seems like forever ago. And he was right. We started with disaster and it was pretty much disaster straight on through.

I put my head in my hands. I'm so tired. I know my fever's come up again, no matter how much medicine we might have brought, and even though the Spackle built a fire near us as the day got colder, I'm still shivering and coughing.

The day's gone really well, though, better than we expected. We've agreed to all kinds of things: a complete cease-fire on both sides while we talk, the setting up of a council to talk through all disputes, maybe even the beginnings to an agreement on land where the settlers can live.

But all day, there's been one stumbling block.

Crimes, the Sky says in our language. *Crimes is the word in the Clearing's language. Crimes against the Land.*

We've figured out that the Land is them and the Clearing is us, and that to them, even our *name* is a crime. But it's more specific than that. They want us to hand over the Mayor and his top soldiers to be punished for their crimes against a part of the Spackle they call the Burden.

"But you killed men, too," I say. "You killed hundreds of them."

The Clearing began this war, he says.

"But the Spackle aren't guiltless," I say. "There's been wrongdoing on both sides."

And immediately images of the Mayor's genocide reappear in the Sky's Noise–

Including one of Todd walking through piles of bodies toward 1017–

"NO!" I shout and the Sky sits back, surprised. "He had *nothing* to do with that. You don't *know*–"

"Okay, okay," Bradley says, his hands up. "It's getting late. Can we all just agree that this has been a very productive first day? Look how far we've come. Sitting at the same table, eating the same food, working toward the same purpose."

The Sky's Noise quiets down a bit, but I get that feeling again, that feeling of every eye of the Spackle on us.

"We'll meet again tomorrow," Bradley continues. "We'll talk to our people, you talk to yours. We'll all have a fresh perspective."

The Sky remains thoughtful for a moment. *The Clearing*

and the Sky will stay here tonight, he says. *The Clearing will be our guests.*

"What?" I say, alarmed. "No, we can't–" But more Spackle have already started bringing out three tents, so clearly this was planned from the start.

Bradley puts his hand on my arm. "Maybe we should," he says, his voice low. "Maybe it's a show of trust."

"But the ship–"

"The ship doesn't have to be in the air to fire its weapons," he says, a bit louder so the Sky can hear it, and we can tell from his Noise that he does.

I look into Bradley's eyes, into his Noise, see the kindness and hope that have always been there, that haven't been bashed out of him by this planet or the Noise or the war or anything that's happened so far. It's really more to keep that kindness in him rather than actually agreeing that I say, "Okay."

The tents, made of what looks like closely woven moss, are up in a matter of moments, and the Sky says a long formal good night to us before disappearing into his. Bradley and I get up and tend to the horses, who greet us with warm nickering.

"That actually went pretty okay," I say.

"I think the attack on you might have worked in our favor," Bradley says. "Made them more willing to show agreement." He lowers his voice. "Did you get that feeling, though? Like you were being watched by every living Spackle?"

"Yes," I whisper back. "I've been thinking that all day."

"I think their Noise is more than just communication," Bradley says, his whisper full of marvel. "I think it's who they are. I think they *are* their voice. And if we could learn to

speak it the way they do, if we could really learn to *join* their
voice . . ."

He trails off, his Noise vibrant and shimmering.

"What?" I say.

"Well," he says, "I wonder if we wouldn't be halfway to
becoming one people."

[TODD]

I watch Viola sleep in the projeckshun. I said no to her staying the night up there, so did Simone and Mistress Coyle.
She stayed anyway, and the scout ship flew back at nightfall.
She's left the front of her tent open to the fire and I can see
her in there, coughing, tossing and turning, and my heart
reaches out again for her, reaches out and wants to be there.

I wonder what she's thinking. I wonder if she's thinking
of me. I wonder how long this is all gonna take so we can
start living peaceful lives and get her well and I can take
care of her and hear her talk to me in person and not just
over a comm and she could read my ma's book to me again.

Or I could read it to her.

"Todd?" the Mayor says. "I'm ready if you are."

I nod at him and go into my tent. I take my ma's book
outta my backpack and run my hands over the cover like I
always do, over where Aaron's knife sliced into it on the night
it saved my life. I open up the pages to look at the writing,
the writing of my ma's own hand, written in the days after I
was born and before she was killed in the Spackle War or by
the Mayor himself or by the suicide lie he's been trying to
say is true and I boil a little at him again, boil at the anthill

361

of letters spilling cross the pages, dense and skittery, already changing my mind about having him do this and–

My dearest son, I read, the words suddenly there on the page, clear as anything, *Not a month old and already life is readying its challenges for you!*

I swallow, my heart beating fast, my throat clenching shut, but I don't take my eyes off the page, cuz there she is. There she *is*–

The corn crop failed, son. Second year in a row, which is a bad blow, since the corn feeds Ben and Cillian's sheep and Ben and Cillian's sheep feed all of us–

I can feel the low *hum,* feel the Mayor behind me at the opening of my tent, putting his learning inside my head, *sharing* it with me–

–and if that weren't bad enough, son, Preacher Aaron has started to blame the Spackle, the shy little creachers who never look like they eat enough. We've been hearing reports from Haven about Spackle problems there, too, but our military man, David Prentiss, says we should respect them, that we shouldn't look for scapegoats for a simple crop failure–

"You said that?" I say, not taking my eyes off the page.

"If your mother says I did," he says, his voice straining. "I can't keep this up forever, Todd. I'm sorry, but the effort it takes–"

"Just another second," I say.

But that's you waking up again in the next room. How funny that it's always you calling me from over there that stops me talking to you right here. But that means I always get to talk to you, son, so how could I be any happier? As always, my strong little man, you have–

And then the words slide off the page, outta my head, and I gasp from the shock of it and tho I can see what's coming next (*all my love,* she says; she says I have all her love), it gets harder, knottier, and thicker, the forest of words closing up in front of me.

I turn to the Mayor. He's got sweat across his brow and I realize I do, too.

(and again, there's that faint *hum* still in the air—)

(but it ain't bothering me; it ain't—)

"Sorry, Todd," he says, "I can only do it for so long." He smiles. "But I'm getting better."

I don't say nothing. My breath is heavy and so is my chest and my ma's words are crashing round my head like a waterfall and there she *was.* There she was talking to me, talking to *me,* saying her hopes for me, saying her love—

I swallow.

I swallow it away again.

"Thank you," I finally say.

"Well, that's fine, Todd," the Mayor says, keeping his voice low. "That's just fine."

And I'm realizing, as we're standing there in my tent, how tall I've been getting—

I can see nearly straight into his eyes—

And once more I'm seeing the man in front of me—

(the tiniest *hum,* almost pleasant—)

Not the monster.

He coughs. "You know, Todd, I could—"

"Mr. President?" we hear.

The Mayor backs outta my tent and I follow him quick in case something's happening.

"It's time," Mr. Tate says, standing there at attenshun. I look back at the projeckshun but nothing's changed. Viola's still asleep in her tent, everything else is like it was before.

"Time for what?" I say.

"Time," the Mayor says, pulling himself up straighter, "to win the argument."

"What?" I say. "What do you mean, *win the argument*? If Viola's in danger—"

"She is, Todd," he says, smiling. "But I'm going to save her."

{VIOLA}

"Viola," I hear, and I open my eyes and wonder for a moment where I am.

There's firelight coming from past my feet, warming me in the loveliest way, and I'm lying on a bed which seems to be made of woven shavings of wood but that doesn't even begin to describe how soft it is—

"Viola," Bradley whispers again. "Something's going on."

I sit up too fast, and my head spins. I have to lean forward with my eyes closed to catch my breath again.

"The Sky got up about ten minutes ago," he whispers. "He hasn't come back."

"Maybe he just had to go to the toilet," I say, my head starting to throb. "I'm assuming they *do*."

The fire is blinding us a little to the half circle of Spackle beyond it, most of them bedded down for the night. I pull the blankets around me tighter. They seem to be made of lichen, like the kind they grow on themselves for clothing, but it's

364

different up close than I expected, much more like cloth, heavier and very warm.

"There's more," Bradley says. "I saw something in their Noise. Not much more than an image. Fleeting and fast, but clear."

"What was it?"

"A group of Spackle," he says, "armed to the teeth and sneaking into town."

"Bradley," I say, "Noise doesn't really work that way. It's fantasies and memories and wishes and real things next to fake things. It takes a lot of practice to figure out what even *might* be true and not something the person *wants* to be true. It's mainly just mess."

He doesn't say anything, but the image he saw repeats in his own Noise. It's everything he said. It's also going out into the world, out across the half circle, over to the Spackle.

"I'm sure it's nothing," I say. "There was that one who attacked us, wasn't there? Maybe he wasn't the only one who didn't vote for peace–"

A loud beep from my comm makes both of us jump. I reach for it, under the blankets.

"*Viola!*" Todd shouts as I answer. "*Yer in danger! You gotta get outta there!*"

[TODD]

The Mayor knocks the comm right outta my hand.

"You'll endanger her worse by doing that," he says as I scramble after it. It don't look broke but it did shut off and I'm already clicking buttons to get her back. "I'm not kidding, Todd," he says, strong enough to make me stop and look at him. "If they get any hint we know what's going on, then I can't guarantee her safety."

"Tell me what's going on, then," I say. "If she's in danger–"

"She is," he says. "We all are. But if you trust me, Todd, then I can save us." He turns to Mr. Tate, who's still hovering there. "Everything ready, Captain?"

"Yes, sir," Mr. Tate says.

"Ready for what?" I say, looking twixt the pair of 'em.

"Now *that*," the Mayor says, turning to look at me, "is the interesting thing, Todd."

The comm beeps back into life in my hand. *"Todd?"* I hear. *"Todd, are you there?"*

"Do you trust me, Todd?" the Mayor says.

"Tell me what's going on," I say.

But he just asks me again. "Do you trust me?"

"Todd?" Viola says.

{ V I O L A }

"Viola?" I finally hear again.

"Todd, what's happening?" I say, looking worried up to Bradley. "What do you mean we're in danger?"

"Just . . ." and there's a pause. *"Hold tight for a second."* And he clicks off.

"I'll go get the horses," Bradley says.

"Wait," I say. "He said to hold tight."

"He also said we're in danger," Bradley says. "And if what I saw is true–"

"How far do you think we'd get if they wanted to hurt us?"

We can see some faces looking back at us now from the Spackle half circle, flickering in the firelight. It doesn't *feel* threatening, but I'm gripping the comm tight, hoping Todd knows what he's doing.

"What if this was their plan all along?" Bradley says, keeping his voice low. "To get us into negotiations and then make a demonstration of what they're capable of?"

"I didn't get any feeling from the Sky that we were in danger," I say. "Not once. Why would he do that? Why would he risk it?"

"To have more leverage."

I pause as I realize what he means. "The punishments."

Bradley nods. "Maybe they're going after the President."

I sit up farther, remembering the Sky's images of the genocide. "Which means they're going right for Todd."

[TODD]

"Make the final preparations, Captain."

"Yes, sir," Mr. Tate salutes.

"And wake Captain O'Hare, please."

Mr. Tate smiles. "Yes, sir," he says again and leaves.

"Tell me what's going on," I say, "or I go up there myself and get her down. I'm trusting you for now but that ain't gonna last—"

"I'm on top of things, Todd," the Mayor says. "You'll be pleased when you find out how much."

"On top of them how?" I ask. "How can you know anything about what's happening?"

"Let's put it this way," he says, his eyes flashing. "The Spackle we captured told us more than he thought."

"What?" I say. "What did he tell us?"

He smiles, almost like he can't believe it. "They're coming to get us, Todd," he says, his voice all amused-sounding. "They're coming to get me and you."

{VIOLA}

"What are we meant to be looking for?" Simone asks from the scout ship, still parked on the hilltop.

"Just anything unusual in the probes." I look at Bradley. "Bradley thinks he saw an attacking party in their Noise."

"It's a show of strength," Mistress Coyle says. *"Trying to prove they've still got the upper hand."*

"We think they might be going for the Mayor," I say. "They kept asking us to turn him over so they could punish him for his crimes."

"And that would be bad?" Mistress Coyle says.

"If they go for the President," Bradley says, meeting my eye. "Todd'll be right beside him."

"Oh," Mistress Coyle says. *"That's a bit more problematic for everyone, isn't it?"*

"We don't know any of this for sure," I say. "This could all be some misunderstanding. Their Noise isn't like ours, it's–"

"Wait," Simone says. *"I see something."*

I look out from the hilltop and see one of the probes flying toward the south of the town. I can hear from the Noise of the Spackle behind me that they see it, too. "Simone?"

"Lights," she says. *"Something's on the march."*

[TODD]

"Sir!" Mr. O'Hare says, face all puffy like he just woke up. "Lights have been spotted south of town! The Spackle are marching on us!"

"Are they?" the Mayor says, fake-surprised. "Then you'd better send some troops to meet our enemy, hadn't you, Captain?"

"I've already ordered squadrons to prepare to march, sir," Mr. O'Hare says, looking pleased and directing a sneer right at me.

"Excellent," the Mayor says. "I eagerly await your report."

"Yes, sir!" Mr. O'Hare salutes and trots away to meet his squadrons, ready to lead 'em into battle.

I frown. Something ain't right.

Viola's voice comes over my comm. *"Todd! Simone says there are lights on the road to the south! The Spackle are coming!"*

"Yeah," I say, still looking at the Mayor. "The Mayor's sending men out to fight 'em. You all right?"

"None of the Spackle are bothering us, but we haven't seen their leader for a bit." She lowers her voice. *"Simone's readying the ship to get back up in the air and prepping the weapons, too."* I hear disappointment creep into her voice. *"Looks like it won't be peace after all."*

I'm about to say something back when I hear the Mayor say, *"Now,* Captain," to Mr. Tate, who's been waiting patiently.

Mr. Tate picks up a burning torch from the campfire.

"Now what?" I say.

Mr. Tate raises the torch high above his head.

"Now *what*?"

And the world splits itself in two.

{VIOLA}

BOOM!

An explosion rings across the valley, echoing back on itself again and again, rumbling like thunder. Bradley helps me to my feet, and we look out. The moons are thin slivers in the night sky and it's hard to see anything but the campfires of the city.

"What happened?" Bradley's demanding. "What *was* that?"

I hear a surge of Noise and I look behind us. The half circle of Spackle is wide awake now, getting to their feet, coming closer to us, pressing toward the edge of the hill as they look into the valley, too–

Where we all see smoke rising.

"But–" Bradley starts to say.

The Sky bursts through the line of Spackle behind us. We hear him before we see him, his Noise a rush of sound and images and–

And surprise–

He's *surprised*–

He storms past us to the edge of the hill, looking into the city below–

"*Viola?*" I hear Simone say on the comm.

"Was that you?" I say.

"No. We weren't ready yet—"

"Who fired, then?" Mistress Coyle cuts in.

"And where?" Bradley says.

Because the smoke isn't coming from the south, where even now we can see lights in the trees and another set of lights heading out from the city to meet them.

The smoke and the explosion came from north of the river, up on the hillside in the abandoned orchards.

And then there's another.

[TODD]

BOOM!

The second is as loud as the first and it lights up the night just north and west of town and the soldiers are getting outta their tents at the sound of it and staring as the smoke starts to rise.

"I think one more should do it, Captain," says the Mayor.

Mr. Tate nods and raises the torch again. There's another man up in the rickety cathedral bell tower I can see now, who lit his torch when Mr. Tate raised his for the first time, passing the message on to men down the riverbank—

Men at the controls of the artillery the Mayor still commands—

The artillery taken outta use when we suddenly had a scout ship to protect us with bigger and better weapons—

But artillery that still works just fine, thank you very much—

BOOM!

I lift my comm again, which is squawking all over the place with voices, including Viola's, trying to figure out what's happened—

"It's the Mayor," I say into it.

"Where's he firing?" she says. *"That's not where the lights were coming from—"*

And then the comm is nicked right outta my hand by the Mayor, triumph all over his face, just glowing in the firelight—

"Yes, but that's where the Spackle actually *are*, dear girl," he says, spinning to keep me from taking the comm back. "Just ask your friend the Sky, why don't you? He'll tell you."

And I do get it back from him but the smile on his face is so unnerving I can barely look at it.

It's a smile like he's won something. Like he's won the biggest thing of all.

{VIOLA}

"What does he mean?" Mistress Coyle says over the comm in a panic. *"Viola, what does he mean?"*

The Sky is turning to us now, his Noise swirling so fast with images and feelings it's impossible to read anything.

But he doesn't look happy.

"I've got the probes where the President fired," Simone's voice says. *"Oh, my God."*

"Here," Bradley says, taking the comm from me. He

presses a few things and suddenly the comm is flashing up a smaller three-dimensional picture like the larger remote projectors we have down below and there, hovering in the night air, lit up by my small little comm–

Bodies.

Spackle bodies. Carrying all the weapons Bradley saw in the glimpse of Noise. Dozens of them, enough to wreak all kinds of havoc on the town–

Enough to take Todd and the Mayor, *kill* them both if they couldn't be taken–

And no lights to be seen anywhere.

"If those bodies are in the northern hills," I ask, "what are the lights to the south?"

[TODD]

"Nothing!" Mr. O'Hare shouts, running back into camp. "There's nothing there! A few torches left burning in the ground but nothing!"

"Yes, Captain," says the Mayor. "I know."

Mr. O'Hare pulls up short. *"You knew?"*

"Of course I did." The Mayor turns to me. "May I please use the comm again, Todd?"

He holds out his hand. I don't give it to him.

"I promised to save Viola, didn't I?" he says. "What do you think would have happened to her if the Spackle had been allowed to win their little victory tonight? What do you think would have happened to *us*?"

"How did you know they'd attack?" I ask. "How did you know it was a trick?"

"How did I save us all, you mean?" He's still holding out his hand. "I'll ask you one more time, Todd. Do you trust me?"

I look at his face, his completely untrustworthy, unredeemable face.

(and I hear the *hum*, just a little bit–)

(and okay, I *know*–)

(I know he's in my head–)

(I ain't no fool–)

(but he did save us–)

(and he gave me my ma's words–)

I hand him the comm.

{VIOLA}

The Sky's Noise whirls like a storm. We've all seen what's happened in the projection. We can all hear the cheering of the soldiers down in the town. We can all feel the distant rumble of the scout ship as it rises and recrosses the valley.

I wonder what's going to happen to me and Bradley. I wonder if it'll be quick.

Bradley's still arguing, though. "You attacked us," he says. "We came here in good faith and you–"

The comm beeps, much louder than usual.

"I think it's time my voice was heard, Bradley."

It's the Mayor again, and somehow his face, too, big and gloating and smiling in the hovering picture projected from it. He's even turned as if he's facing the Sky.

As if he's looking him right in the eye.

"You thought you'd learned something, didn't you?" he asks.

"You thought your captured soldier had looked into me and saw that I could read Noise as deeply as you, isn't that right? So you thought to yourself, here's something I can use."

"How's he doing this?" we hear Mistress Coyle on a voice-only line. *"He's broadcasting out to the hilltop–"*

"So you sent him back to us as a peace envoy," the Mayor goes on, like he didn't hear her, *"and had him show me just enough to make me think I discovered your plan to attack us from the south. But there was another plan below, wasn't there? Buried far too deep for any"*–he pauses for effect–*"Clearing to read."*

The Sky's Noise flares.

"Get that comm away from him!" Mistress Coyle's voice shouts. *"Cut him off!"*

"But you didn't count on my abilities," the Mayor says. *"You didn't count that I can read deeper perhaps than even any Spackle, deep enough to see the* real *plan."*

The Sky's face is expressionless but his Noise is loud and open and stirring with anger.

Stirring with the knowledge that the Mayor's words are all true.

"I looked into the eyes of your peace envoy," the Mayor says, *"Into* your *eyes and I read everything. I heard the voice speak and I saw you coming."* He brings the comm forward so his face looms larger in the projection. *"So know this, and know it well,"* he says. *"If it comes to battle between us, the victory will be mine."*

Then he's gone. His face and the image blink out so that the Sky is staring back at only us. We hear the scout ship's engines, but they're still half the valley away. The Spackle here are heavily armed, but that hardly matters because the

375

Sky himself could take out me and Bradley on his own if he needed to.

But the Sky remains still, his Noise spinning and swirling darkly, again as if every eye of the Spackle is in him, watching us and considering what's happened–

And deciding his next move.

And then he takes a step forward.

I step back without meaning to, bumping into Bradley, who puts a hand on my shoulder.

So be it, the Sky says.

And then he says, *Peace*.

[TODD]

Peace, we hear from the leader of the Spackle's own Noise, boomed across the square, just like the Mayor's voice did, his face filling the projeckshun–

And the cheering around us is as loud as the world.

"How did you do that?" I say, looking down at my comm.

"You do have to sleep sometimes, Todd," he says. "Can you blame me if I'm curious about new technologies?"

"Congratulations, sir," Mr. Tate says, shaking the Mayor's hand. "That showed 'em."

"Thank you, Captain," the Mayor says. He turns to Mr. O'Hare, who's looking way more grudging about being sent running for nothing.

"You did fine work," the Mayor says. "We had to look convincing. That's why I couldn't tell you."

"Of course, sir," says Mr. O'Hare, not sounding like it's very fine at all.

And then the soldiers crowd in, each wanting to shake the Mayor's hand, too, each one telling him how he outsmarted the Spackle, each one saying that the Mayor's the one who won the peace, that he did it without the help of the scout ship, that he really showed 'em, didn't he?

And the Mayor just takes it all in, accepting every word of it.

Every word of praise for his victory.

And for a second, just for a second—

I feel a little bit proud.

I Raise My Knife

I RAISE MY KNIFE, the one I stole from the cook-
ing huts on my way here, a knife used for the butchery of
game, long and heavy, sharp and brutal.

I raise it over the Source.

I could have made peace impossible, I could have made this
war unending, I could have torn the life and heart out of
the Knife—

But I did not.

I saw her band.

Saw the pain obvious even in one of the voiceless
Clearing.

She had been marked, too, just as they marked the
Burden, with what seemed to be the same effect.

And I remembered the pain of the banding, the pain
not only in my arm but in the way the band encircled my

self as well, took what was me and made it smaller, so that all the Clearing ever saw was the band on my arm, not me, not my face, not my voice which was also taken—

Taken to make us like the Clearing's own voiceless ones.

And I could not kill her.

She was like me. She was banded like me.

And then the beast reared up its hind legs and kicked me across the ground, probably breaking more than one bone in my chest, bones that ache even now, which did not stop the Sky from grabbing me up and flinging me into the arms of the Land, showing, *If you do not speak with the Land, then it is because **you** have chosen it.*

And I understood. I was being properly exiled. The Return would not return.

The Land took me from the peace grounds and deep into the camp, where they roughly sent me on my way.

But I was not going to leave without the Sky's final promise.

I stole a knife and came here—

Where I stand ready to kill the Source.

I look up as the news of the Sky's attempts to secretly attack the Clearing flashes through the Pathways' End. So *that* was his plan, one that would show the Clearing just how effective an enemy we are, how we could walk into their stronghold during peace talks, take the specific enemies we wanted and give them the justice they deserve. The peace that would flow from that, if peace it was, would be one that *we* dictated.

That was why he asked me to trust him.

But he has failed. He has admitted defeat. He has called for peace. And the Land will cower under the Clearing and the peace will not be a peace of strength for the Land. It will be a peace of weakness—

And I stand over the Source with my knife. I stand ready to take the revenge long since denied me.

I stand ready to kill him.

I knew this is where you would go, the Sky shows, entering the Pathways' End behind me.

Have you not a peace to be making? I show back, not moving from where I stand. *Have you not a Land to betray?*

Have you not a man to be killing? he shows.

You promised me this, I show. *You promised he would be mine to do with as I pleased. And so I will do this thing and then I will go.*

And then the Return will be lost to us, the Sky shows. *Will be lost to himself.*

I look back at him, pointing at the band with my knife. *I was lost to myself when they put this on me. I was lost to myself when they killed every other member of the Burden. I was lost when the Sky refused to take revenge for my life.*

So take it now, the Sky shows. *I will not stop you.*

I stare into him, into his voice, into his *failure.*

And I see, here in the Pathways' End where secrets live, I see that it is a bigger failure than even that.

You were going to give me the Knife, I marvel. *That was your surprise. You would have given me **the Knife.***

My voice begins to burn at the realization. That I could have had the Knife. I could have had the Knife himself—

But you failed at even that, I show, furious.

And so you will have your revenge on the Source, he shows. *Again, I will not stop you.*

No, I nearly spit at him. *No, you will **not.***

And I turn back round to the Source—

And I raise my knife—

He lies there, his voice burbling in the way of dreams. It has given up all its secrets here at the Pathways' End, lying here all these weeks and months, open and useful, returning from the brink of silence, immersed in the voice of the Land.

The Source. The father of the Knife.

How the Knife will weep when he hears. How he will wail and moan and blame himself and hate me, as I take someone beloved from him—

(And I feel the Sky's voice behind me showing me my own one in particular, but why now—?)

I will have my revenge—

I will make the Knife hurt like I do—

I *will*—

I will do it *now*—

And—

382

And—

And I begin to roar—

Rising up through my voice and out into the world, a roar of my whole self, my whole voice, my every feeling and scar, my every wound and hurt, a roar of my memories and my lostness, a roar for my one in particular—

A roar for myself—

A roar for my weakness—

Because—

I cannot do it—

I cannot do it—

I am as bad as the Knife himself.

I cannot do it.

I collapse to the ground, the roar echoing round the Pathways' End, echoing in the voice of the Sky, echoing for all I know through the Land outside and back through the emptiness that has opened in me, the emptiness big enough to swallow me whole—

And then I feel the voice of the Sky on me, gently—

I feel him reaching under my arm, raising me to my feet—

I feel warmth around me. I feel understanding.

I feel love.

I shake him off and step away. *You knew,* I show.

The Sky did not know, he shows back. *But the Sky hoped.*

You did this to torture me with my own failure.

It is not failure, he shows. *It is success.*

I look up. *Success?*

Because now your return is complete, he shows back. *Now your name is true at the exact moment it becomes a lie. You have returned to the Land and are no longer the Return.*

I look at him, mistrustful. *What are you talking about?*

It is only the Clearing who kill for hate, who fight wars for personal reasons. If you had done this, you would have become one of them. And you would never have returned to the Land.

You have killed the Clearing, I show. *You have killed them in their hundreds.*

Never when the lives of the Land were not at stake.

But you agreed to their peace.

I want what is best for the Land, he shows. *That is what the Sky must **always** want. When the Clearing killed us, I fought them, because that was best for the Land. When the Clearing wanted peace, I gave them peace, because that was best for the Land.*

You attacked them tonight, I show.

To bring you the Knife and to bring their leader to justice for his crimes against the Burden. These are also in the best interest of the Land.

I look at him, thinking. *But the Clearing might still give the leader up. We have seen their disagreements.*

They might give him to you yet for his crimes.

The Sky wonders what I am asking. *Possibly.*

But the Knife, I show. *They would have fought for him. If you had brought him here—*

You would not have killed him. You have just shown this.

But I **might** *have. And then the war would be unending. Why risk so much for me? Why risk* **everything** *for me?*

Because sparing the Knife would show the Clearing our mercy. It would show we could choose not to kill even when we had reason to do so. It would be a powerful gesture.

I stare at him. *But you do not* **know** *what I would have done.*

The Sky looks over to the Source, still sleeping, still alive. *I believed you would not.*

Why? I show, pressing. *Why is it so important what I do?*

Because, he shows, *this is knowledge you will need when you are the Sky.*

What did you say? I show after a long, heavy moment.

But he is moving now, over to the Source, placing his hands over the Source's ears and looking down into the Source's face.

When I am the Sky? I show loudly. *What do you mean?*

I think the Source has served his function. He looks

back to me, a twinkle in his voice. *I think the time has come to wake him.*

But **you** *are the Sky,* I sputter. *Where are you going? Are you ill?*

No, he shows, looking back to the Source. *But I will go one day.*

My mouth hangs open. *And when you do—*

Wake, shows the Sky, sending his voice down into the Source like a stone dropped in water—

Wait! I show—

But already the Source's eyes begin to blink open as he takes a loud breath. His voice quickens and quickens again, brightening with a thick wakefulness, and he blinks some more, looking at me and the Sky with surprise—

But not fear.

He sits up, falling at first out of weakness, but the Sky helps him rise to his elbows and he looks at us further. He puts a hand to the wound on his chest, his voice singing baffled remembrance, and he looks at us again.

I've had the strangest dream, he shows.

And though he shows it to us in the language of the Clearing.

He shows it in the perfect, unmistakable voice of the Land.

LIFE DURING PEACETIME

THE DAYS OF GLORY

{VIOLA}

"LISTEN TO THEM," Bradley says, as even from this distance, the ROAR from the town is loud enough to make him raise his voice. "Finally cheering something *good*."

"Do you think it'll snow?" I say, looking up from Acorn's saddle into the clouds that have rolled in, a rare sight in what's been a clear and cold winter. "I've never seen snow."

Bradley smiles. "Me neither." And his Noise is smiling, too, at the randomness of my comment.

"Sorry," I say. "This fever."

"We're nearly there," he says. "We'll get you warm and snug."

We're heading back from the zigzag hill, heading down the road that leads to the square.

Heading back the morning after last night's artillery attack.

The morning after we secured peace. For real, this time.

We did it. Even if it was the Mayor's action that clinched

it—something Mistress Coyle won't be at all happy about—we actually did it. In two days' time, we'll have the first meeting of a human-Spackle council to set out all the details. So far, the council's made up of me, Bradley, Simone, Todd, and the Mayor and Mistress Coyle, and the six of us are going to have to somehow work together to make this a new world with the Spackle.

Something that might actually make us work *together*.

I wish I felt better, though. Peace is here, real peace, all that I wanted, but my head throbs so much and my cough is so bad—

"Viola?" Bradley asks, concern in his voice.

And then, down the road, I see Todd running to meet us and my fever is so bad it feels like he's surfing here on a wave of cheering and the world goes really bright for a second and I have to close my eyes and Todd is next to me, his hands reaching up—

"I can't hear you," I say.

And I fall right out of Acorn's saddle and into his arms—

[TODD]

"This glorious new day," the Mayor's voice booms, *"this day when we have beaten our enemy and begun a new era!"*

And the crowd below us cheers.

"I've had just about enough of this," I mutter to Bradley, holding Viola next to me on the bench where we're sitting. We're up on a cart, in front of a square filled with people, the Mayor's face not just in the hovering projeckshun behind us but on the sides of two buildings as well. Another thing he figured out how to do on his own. Bradley's frowning as the Mayor drones on. Mistress Coyle and Simone are on the other side of us, frowning even harder.

I feel Viola turn her head. "Yer awake," I say.

"Was I sleeping?" she says. "Why didn't anybody put me to bed?"

"*Exactly,*" I say. "The Mayor said you had to be here first, but he's got about two more seconds before I–"

"*Our peacemaker has recovered!*" the Mayor says, looking back at us. He's got a microphone in front of him, but I'm pretty sure he don't even need it. "*Let's give her the thanks she's owed for saving our lives and ending this war!*"

And it suddenly feels like we're drowning in the rising ROAR of the crowd.

"What's going on?" Viola says. "Why's he talking about me like that?"

"Because he needs a hero that isn't me," Mistress Coyle hisses.

"*Not forgetting of course the very formidable Mistress Coyle,*" the Mayor says, "*who was so helpful in my campaign against the Spackle insurgency.*"

Mistress Coyle's face goes so red it looks like you could fry eggs on it. "*Helpful?*" she practically spits.

But you can hardly hear her over the Mayor.

"*Before I hand you over to the mistress for her own address to you,*" the Mayor says, "*I have an announcement to make. One that I especially wanted Viola to hear.*"

"What announcement?" Viola says to me.

"No idea," I say.

And I really don't know.

"We've made a breakthrough," the Mayor says. *"This very day we have made a breakthrough on the terrible, unanticipated problem of the identification bands."*

I grip Viola harder without meaning to. The crowd's fallen silent, as silent as it can get. The probes are sending this back to the hilltop, too. The Mayor has every human on this planet listening to him.

And he says, *"We've found a cure."*

"WHAT?" I shout, but I'm already being drowned out by the uproar.

"How appropriate that this should come on our day of peace," the Mayor's saying. *"How wonderful and blessed that on the threshold of a new era, I can also announce to you that the sickness of the bands is over!"*

He's talking up into the probes now, straight back to where most of the women are sick, to where the mistresses haven't been able to heal 'em.

"There's no time to waste," he says. *"We'll begin distributing the cure without delay."*

Then he turns back to me and Viola again. *"And we'll start with our very own peacemaker."*

{VIOLA}

"He's taken *all* the credit!" Mistress Coyle shouts, stomping around the healing room of the scout ship as we fly back. "He had them eating out of his *hands!*"

"You're not even going to *try* the cure?" Bradley says.

Mistress Coyle looks at him like he's just asked her to take off all her clothes. "You honestly think he just *discovered* it?

He's had it all along! If it's even a cure at all and not another little time bomb."

"But why would he do that," Bradley says, "if curing all the women makes him even more popular?"

"He's a genius," Mistress Coyle says, still ranting. "Even I have to admit that. He's a terrible, savage, brutal genius."

"What do *you* think, Viola?" Lee asks from the next bed.

I can only cough by way of answer. Mistress Coyle stepped in front of me when the Mayor tried to give me the new bandages and refused to let him touch me with them until she and the other mistresses tested them thoroughly first.

And the crowds booed her, actually *booed*.

Especially when the Mayor brought up three women with bands. Three women with no signs of infection at all. "We haven't figured out a way to remove the bands safely yet," the Mayor said, "but the early results are obvious."

Things kind of disintegrated from there and Mistress Coyle didn't even get to give her speech, though they probably would have kept booing her anyway. After we got off the cart, Todd said he didn't know any more than we did. "Mistress Coyle can do her tests," he said to me, "and I'll see what I can find out."

But he was gripping my arms tight, whether in hope or fear, I don't know.

Because I couldn't hear him.

The rest of us finally went back to the scout ship, Mistress Lawson coming with us to help test the Mayor's cure.

"I don't know what to believe," I say now, "only that it *would* be in his interests to save us."

"So we have to base our decision on what suits him best?" Mistress Coyle says. "Brilliant, just brilliant."

"We're coming in for a landing," Simone says over the comm system.

"I'll tell you one thing," Mistress Coyle says. "When we're on that council together, he'll learn that his days of outmaneuvering me are *over*." There's a judder as we touch down. "And now," she says, her voice burning with heat, "I've got my own speech to give."

Before the engines are even properly off, she's marched out of the room, down the bay door and into the crowds that wait for us, crowds I can see on the monitors.

She's greeted by a few cheers.

But only a few.

And nothing at all like what the Mayor got back in town.

And then this crowd, led by Ivan and other voices, begins to boo her, too.

[TODD]

"Why would I harm the women?" the Mayor says to me across the campfire, as night begins to fall on his day of glory. "Even if you still somehow believe I'm bent on killing every one of them, why would I do it *now*, at my moment of biggest triumph?"

"Why didn't you tell me, tho?" I say. "That you were so close to a cure?"

"Because I didn't want to risk your disappointment if I failed."

He looks at me for a long time, trying to read me, but

394

I'm so good at it now I don't think even *he* can hear me.

"Can I make a guess at what you believe?" he finally says. "I think you want to get that cure to Viola as soon as possible. I think you're worried Mistress Coyle won't move fast enough on her tests because she won't want me to be right."

And I do think this. I *do*.

I want the cure to be true so bad I could almost choke.

But it's the Mayor.

But it could save Viola.

But it's the *Mayor*—

"I also think you want to believe me," he says. "That I'd really do this for real. If not for her, then for you."

"Me?" I say.

"I think I've figured out your special talent, Todd Hewitt. Something that should have been obvious from the behavior of my son."

My stomach tenses, with anger, with grief, like it always does when Davy's mentioned.

"You made him better," the Mayor continues, his voice soft. "You made him smarter and kinder and more aware of the world and his place in it." He sets down his coffee cup. "And whether I like it or not, you've done the same for me."

And there's that faint *hum*—

Connecting us—

(but I know it's there and it ain't affecting me—)

(it ain't—)

"I regret what happened with David," he says.

"You shot him," I say. "It weren't nothing that just *happened*."

395

He nods. "I regret it more with every passing day. With every day that I'm with *you,* Todd. Every day, you make me better. Knowing that I've got you to watch what I do." He lets out a sigh. "Even today, in what is arguably the greatest victory I've ever had, my first thought was, *What will Todd think?*"

He gestures to the darkening sky above us. "This world, Todd," he says. "This world and how it *talks,* how loud its voice is." He drifts a little, his eyes unfocused. "Sometimes it's all you can hear, as it tries to make you disappear into it, to make you *nothing.*" He's almost whispering now. "But then I hear *your* voice, Todd, and it brings me back."

I don't know what he's talking about, so I just ask, "Have you had the cure for the bands all this time? Have you just been holding it back?"

"No," he says. "I've been having my men work round the clock so I could save Viola for *you,* Todd. To show you how much you've come to mean to me." His voice is forceful now, almost emoshunal. "You've *redeemed* me, Todd Hewitt. Redeemed me when no one else would have thought it possible." He smiles again. "Or even desirable."

I still don't say nothing. Cuz he ain't redeemable. Viola even said so.

But–

"They'll test it," he says. "They'll find it's a cure, and then you'll see that I tell you the truth. It's so important, I won't even ask you to trust me."

He waits again for me to say something. I still don't.

"And now," he says, slapping his hands on his thighs, "it's time to start preparing for our first council meeting."

He gives me a final look, then heads back into his tent. I get up after a minute and go over to Angharrad, tethered with Juliet's Joy by my own tent, eating her heart's delight of hay and apples.

She saved Viola's life up on that hill. I ain't never forgetting that.

And now the Mayor's offering to do it down here.

And I wish I could believe him. I *want* to.

(redeemed–)

(but how far–?)

Boy colt, Angharrad says, nuzzling my chest.

Submit! Juliet's Joy snaps, her eyes wide.

And before I can say anything, Angharrad snaps back **SUBMIT!** even louder.

And Juliet's Joy lowers her head.

"*Girl!*" I say with amazement. "*That's* my girl."

Boy colt, she says, and I hold on to her, feeling her warmth, her fuggy horse smell tickling my nose.

I hold on to her and I think about redempshun.

{VIOLA}

"You are *not* going to be on the council with the Spackle, Ivan," Mistress Coyle says, Ivan clomping in behind her into the scout ship. "And you are *not* allowed in here."

It's the day after we came back from town, and I'm *still* on my bed, feeling worse than ever, the fever not responding at all to Mistress Lawson's newest combination of antibiotics.

Ivan stands there a moment, looking defiantly at Mistress Coyle, at me, at Lee on the other bed, at Mistress Lawson

where she's removing Lee's final bandages. "You're still acting like you're in charge here, Mistress," Ivan says.

"I *am* in charge here, *Mr.* Farrow," Mistress Coyle seethes
back at him. "As far as I know, no one's appointed you their
new Mistress."

"Is that why people are returning to the town in droves?"
he says. "Is that why half the women are already a-taking the
Mayor's new cure?"

Mistress Coyle spins round to Mistress Lawson. *"What?"*

"I only gave it to the dying, Nicola," Mistress Lawson says,
slightly sheepish. "If you have to choose between certain
death and possible death, it's no choice at all."

"It's not just the dying now," Ivan says. "Not when the rest
saw how well it works."

Mistress Coyle ignores him. "And you didn't *tell* me?"

Mistress Lawson looks down. "I knew how upset you'd
be. I've tried to talk the others out of it–"

"Your own mistresses are doubting your authority," Ivan
says.

"You shut your mouth, Ivan Farrow," Mistress Lawson
barks.

Ivan licks his lips, sizing us all up again, and then he
leaves, heading back to the crowd outside.

Mistress Lawson immediately starts apologizing. "Nicola,
I'm so sorry–"

"No," Mistress Coyle stops her. "You were right, of course.
Those worst off, those who had nothing to lose . . ." She rubs
her forehead. "Are people really going back to town?"

"Not as many as he said," Mistress Lawson says. "But
some."

Mistress Coyle shakes her head. "He's winning."

And we all know she means the Mayor.

"You've still got the council," I say. "You'll be better at that than he is."

She shakes her head again. "He's probably planning something right now." She sighs out through her nose, and then she leaves, too, without another word.

"He won't be the only one planning something," Lee says.

"And we've seen how well her plans have worked in the past," I say.

"You two hush up," Mistress Lawson snaps. "A lot of people are alive today because of her."

She tears the last bandage off Lee's face with more vigor than is strictly necessary. Then she bites her bottom lip and glances up at me. Over the bridge of Lee's nose, there's just bright pink scar tissue where his eyes used to be, the sockets covered now with livid skin, the blue eyes that used to look back gone forever.

Lee can hear our silences. "Is it that bad?"

"Lee—" I start to say, but his Noise says he isn't ready and he changes the subject.

"Are you going to take the cure?" he asks.

And I see all the feelings he has for me right at the front of his Noise. Pictures of me, too. Way more beautiful than I ever could be.

But the way he'll see me forever now.

"I don't know," I say.

And I really *don't* know. I'm not getting better, not at all, and the convoy is still weeks away, if they'll even be able to help when they get here. *Fatal,* I keep thinking, and now it doesn't just feel like Mistress Coyle trying to scare me. I wonder if I'm one of those women Mistress Lawson mentioned who have to choose between certain death and possible death.

"I don't know," I say again.

"Viola?" Wilf says, appearing in the doorway.

"Ah," Lee says, his Noise reaching out to Wilf's, almost unwillingly seeing what Wilf's seeing–

Seeing his own scarred eyes.

"Phew," he whistles, but you can hear the nervousness, the fake bravery. "That's not so bad. You two made it seem like I was practically Spackle."

"Ah brought Acorn back from town," Wilf says to me. "Stabled him wi' my oxes."

"Thank you, Wilf," I say.

He nods. "And young Lee there," he says. "If ya ever need me to see for ya, ya just gotta say."

There's a flood of surprised and touched feeling in Lee's Noise, bright enough for Wilf to see his answer.

"Hey, Wilf?" I say, getting an idea, one that feels better by the second.

"Yeh?" he says.

"How would like you be on the new council?"

[TODD]

"It's a ruddy *great* idea," I say, watching Viola's face in my comm. "Every time they wanna do something stupid, Wilf won't even say no, he'll just say what we should obviously do instead."

"*That's what I thought,*" she says and doubles up coughing again.

"How are them tests coming along?" I say.

"*The women who've taken it haven't shown any problems
so far, but Mistress Coyle wants to do more checks.*"

"She ain't never gonna approve it, is she?"

Viola don't disagree. "*What do you think about it?*"

I take a long deep breath. "I don't trust him," I say, "no
matter how much he says he's redeemed."

"*He says that?*"

I nod.

"*Well, that's exactly the kind of thing he* would *say.*"

"Yeah."

She waits for me to say more. "*But?*"

I look back into her eyes, back thru the comm to her,
there, on the hilltop, on this same world as me but so far
away. "He seems to *need* me, Viola. I don't know why, but
it's like I'm important to him somehow."

"*He called you his son once before, when we were fighting
him. Said you had power.*"

I nod. "I don't trust him to do any of this outta the goodness of the heart he ain't got." I swallow. "But I think he'd
do it to get me on his side."

"*Is that enough reason to risk it?*"

"Yer dying," I say, and then keep talking cuz she's already
talking over me. "Yer dying and yer lying to me that yer not
and if something happened to you, Viola, if something *happened—*"

My throat chokes up hard, like I really can't breathe.

And I can't say nothing more for a second.

(I am the Circle–)

"*Todd?*" she finally says, for the first time not denying she's sicker than she's said. "*Todd, if you tell me to take it, I will. I won't wait for Mistress Coyle.*"

"But I don't *know*," I say, my eyes still flooded.

"*We fly in tomorrow morning,*" she says. "*To ride up for the first council.*"

"Yeah?"

"*If you want me to do it,*" she says, "*I want you to put the bandages on me yourself.*"

"Viola–"

"*If it's you doing it, Todd,*" she says, "*nothing can go wrong. If it's you doing it, I know I'm safe.*"

And I wait for a long minute.

And I don't know what to say.

And I don't know what to do.

{VIOLA}

"So you're taking it, too, then?" Mistress Coyle says from the doorway after I click off with Todd.

I'm about to complain about her listening to a private conversation again but she's done it so often I'm not even really mad. "It's not decided yet."

I'm alone with her. Simone and Bradley are preparing for tomorrow's meeting, and Lee is out with Wilf, learning about the oxes, whose Noise he can see.

"How are the tests coming?" I ask.

"Excellent," she says, not uncrossing her arms. "Aggressive antibiotics combined with an aloe Prentiss says he found in the weapons of the Spackle that allows for a dispersal of the medicine ten or fifteen times faster than we'd been doing it. Hitting it so fast it doesn't have time to regroup. It's quite brilliant, really." She looks me square in the eye, and I swear I see sadness there. "A real breakthrough."

"But you still don't trust it?"

She sits down next to me with a heavy sigh. "How can I? After all he's done? How can I not just sit here in despair at all the women who keep reaching for the cure, all the while sick with worry that they're just walking into a trap?" She bites her lip. "And now you."

"Maybe," I say.

She takes a long breath and lets it out. "Not all the women are taking it, you know. There are some, a good number, who'd rather trust me to find a better cure for them. And I will, you know. I will."

"I believe you," I say. "But fast enough?"

She gets a look on her face so unusual for her that it takes me a second to realize what it is.

She looks almost defeated.

"You've been so sick," she says, "trapped in this little room, that you don't really realize what a hero you are out there."

"I'm not a *hero*," I say, surprised.

"Please, Viola. You faced down the Spackle and won. You're everything they want to be themselves. A perfect symbol for the future." She shifts her weight. "Not like those of us left in the past."

"I don't think that's true−"

"You went up a girl and came down a woman," she says.

"I get asked five hundred times a day how the Peacemaker is doing."

And it's only then I see the importance of what she's saying.

"If I take the cure," I say, "you think everyone else will, too."

Mistress Coyle says nothing.

"And he'll have completely won," I continue. "That's what you think."

She still says nothing, looking at the floor. When she does speak, it's unexpected. "I miss the ocean," she says. "On a fast horse, I could leave right now and make it there by sundown, but I haven't even seen it since we failed to make a fishing village. I moved to Haven and never looked back." Her voice is quieter than I've ever heard it. "I thought that life was over. I thought in Haven there were things worth fighting for."

"You still *can* fight for them," I say.

"I think I may be already beaten, Viola," she says.

"But–"

"No, I've had power slip away from me before, my girl. I know what it feels like. But I always knew I'd come back." She turns to me, her eyes sad but otherwise unreadable. "But you aren't beaten, are you, my girl? Not yet."

She nods, as if to herself, then she does it again and gets up.

"Where are you going?" I call after her.

But she keeps on and doesn't look back.

[TODD]

I hold up my ma's book. "I wanna read the end."

The Mayor looks up from his reports. "The end?"

"I wanna find out what happened to her," I say. "In her own words."

The Mayor leans back. "And you think I'm afraid to have you hear it?"

"Are you?" I say, keeping his gaze.

"Only in how sad it will be for you, Todd."

"Sad for *me*?"

"Those were terrible times," he says. "And there's no version of that history, not mine, not Ben's, not your mother's, where there's a happy ending."

I keep staring at him.

"All right," the Mayor says. "Open it to the end."

I look at him for another second, then I open her book, flipping thru the pages till I get to the last entry, my heart skipping a little at what I'll find there. The words are the usual scramble, spilling out everywhere like a rock slide (tho I'm getting better at picking some of 'em out, it's true) and my eyes go right to the end, the very last paragraphs, to the very last things she ever wrote to me–

And then suddenly, almost before I'm ready–

This war, my dearest son–

(there she is–)

This war that I hate *because of how it threatens all yer days to come, Todd, this war that was bad enough when we were just fighting the Spackle, but now there are divisions forming, divisions twixt David Prentiss, the head of our little*

army here, and Jessica Elizabeth, our Mayor, who's been
rallying the women and many of the men to her side, Ben and
Cillian included, over how the war's being conducted.

"You were dividing the town?" I say.

"I wasn't the only one," the Mayor says.

And oh it makes my heart sick, Todd, to see us split like
this, split before we've even made peace, and I wonder how
this can be a real New World when all we do is bring our old
quarrels to it.

The Mayor's breathing is light and I can somehow tell
he ain't struggling half as hard as he used to.

(and the faint *hum* there, too—)

(that I know is him connecting us—)

But then there's you, son, as of right now the youngest boy
in town, maybe even in this whole world, and yer gonna have
to be the one who makes it come right, you hear? Yer a native
born New Worlder, so you don't have to repeat our mistakes.
You can shake off the past and maybe, just maybe, you'll bring
paradise to this place.

And my stomach pulls a little cuz she's wished that for
me from the very first page.

But that's probably enough responsibility for one day, huh? I
have to leave now for that secret meeting Mayor Elizabeth's called.

And oh, my beautiful boy, I'm afraid of what she's going to
suggest.

And that's it.

After that, it's just blank.

Nothing more.

I look up to the Mayor. "What did Mayor Elizabeth
suggest?"

"She suggested the attack on me and my army, Todd," he says. "An attack which they lost, as much as we tried not to make it a dangerous fight. And then they killed themselves to ensure our doom. I'm sorry, but that's what happened."

"No, it ain't," I say, starting to boil. "*My* ma wouldn't do that to me. Ben said–"

"I can't convince you, Todd," he says, frowning sadly. "There's nothing I can say that ever will, I know that. And I'm certain I made mistakes back then, maybe even mistakes that led to worse consequences than I'd ever intended. Maybe that's even true." He leans forward. "But that was before, Todd. That's not now."

My eyes are still wet, thinking of my ma, signing off.

Being afraid of what was to come.

Whatever it was.

Cuz the answer ain't there. What really happened ain't there. I know as much about the Mayor as before.

"I am a bad man, Todd," the Mayor says. "But I'm getting better."

I touch my fingertips to the cover of my ma's journal, feeling along the knife mark. I don't believe his verzhun of the story, I just don't and never will.

I believe *he* believes it, tho.

I believe he might even be sorry.

"If you ever hurt Viola," I say, "you know I'd kill you."

"One of the many reasons why I never would."

I swallow. "The cure will make her well? It'll save her life?"

"Yes, Todd, it will." And that's all he says.

I look up into the sky, into another freezing night, cloudy

still, but no snow yet. Another night with little or no sleep, the night before the first big council meeting. The night before we start making the new world for real.

Just like my ma said.

"Bring me the bandages," I say. "I'll put 'em on her myself."

He makes a low sound, almost as if in his Noise, and his face is holding back a smile, a real, true, and feeling smile.

"Thank you, Todd," he says.

And he sounds like he means it.

I wait a long time before I say it–

But I do finally say it.

"Yer welcome."

"Mr. President?" we hear. Mr. O'Hare's come up to us, waiting to interrupt.

"What is it, Captain?" the Mayor says, still looking at me.

"There's a man here," Mr. O'Hare says, "been hassling the men all night about a meeting with you. Wants to pledge his support."

The Mayor don't even try to hide his impayshunce. "If I have to listen to every man on this planet pledge his support–"

"Said to tell you his name is Ivan Farrow," Mr. O'Hare says.

And the Mayor looks surprised.

And then he gets a different kinda smile on his face.

Ivan Farrow. Who goes where the power is.

{ VIOLA }

"*Look how beautiful,*" Simone says over the comm system as we feel the scout ship rise slowly into the air. There's a click and all the screens in the healing room show the sun, rising pink over the far ocean.

It's only there for a brief moment before the clouds cover it away again.

"Sunrise," Bradley says, his Noise reaching out to Lee to show it to him.

"A good omen," Lee says. "Sun peeking through on a gray morning."

"We fly down to make a new world," Bradley says, his Noise warm and excited. "A *real* new world this time." He smiles and the room fills up with it.

Wilf is the only one not with us, because he's riding Acorn down to town for me and will meet us there. Mistress Coyle is sitting on the chair next to my bed. She was gone all night, no doubt off thinking of the best way to get back on top in her fight with the Mayor.

Or maybe accepting her defeat.

Which makes me surprisingly sad.

"Have you decided if you'll take the cure yet, Viola?" she asks, just to me, keeping her voice low.

"I don't know," I say. "I'll talk to Todd about it. But it won't be because I'm trying to spite *you*. It doesn't have to change anything–"

"But it will, my girl." She turns to me. "Don't misunderstand me. I've made my peace with it. Part of being a leader is knowing when to hand over the reins."

I try and sit up. "I don't want to take anyone's *reins*-"

"You've got the people's goodwill, Viola. With a little skill, you could easily turn that into strength."

I cough. "I'm not really feeling up to-"

"This world needs you, my girl," she says. "If you're the face of opposition, then that's fine with me. As long as the opposition *has* a face."

"I'm just trying to make the best world we can."

"Well, you keep on doing that," she says, "and everything will be fine."

She doesn't say anything more, and we land shortly after, the ramp dropping down into the square, the **ROAR** of the crowd rising up to greet us.

"The Spackle are expecting us at midday," Simone says as we walk out, Bradley helping me along. "The President's promised horses for us all and enough time this morning to talk through the agenda."

"Todd says the Mayor's agreed to keep the speeches to the crowd short," I say, turning to Mistress Coyle. "And to make sure you've got a chance to say something this time."

"Thank you very much, my girl," she says. "Though you might also want to think of what *you're* planning on saying."

"Me?" I say. "But I don't-"

"And there he is," she says, looking down the ramp.

Todd is coming toward us through the crowd.

And he's carrying a roll of bandages under his arm.

Under her breath, I hear Mistress Coyle say, "So be it."

"I don't really know what I'm doing," I say, unrolling the bandages the Mayor gave me.

"You just wrap them round like a cloth," Viola says. "Tight, but not too tight."

We're in my tent, sitting on my cot and the world outside is going on with its loud, ROARing business. The Mayor and Mistress Coyle and Bradley and Simone and Wilf and Lee, who's sorta invited himself on the council, too, are all arguing about who's gonna talk first to the Spackle and what they're gonna say and blah blah blah.

"What are you thinking?" Viola asks, staring at me hard.

I smile a little. "I'm thinking, *I don't really know what I'm doing.*"

She smiles a little back. "If this is you now, I guess I'll just have to get used to it."

"You don't hate it no more?"

"Yeah, but that's my problem, not yours."

"I'm still me," I say. "I'm still Todd."

She looks away, letting her eyes fall to the bandages. "Are you sure about this?" she asks. "You're sure none of this is a lie?"

"He knows I'd kill him if he hurt you," I say. "And the way he's been acting–"

She looks up. "But it probably *is* just acting–"

"I think *I'm* the one changing *him,* Viola," I say. "Enough for him to want to save you for me, anyway."

She keeps looking, keeps trying to read me.

I don't know what she sees.

And after a minute, she holds out her arm.

"Okay," I say. "Here we go."

I start unwinding the old bandages still on the wound. I take off one, then another, and then there's the band, 1391, exposed to the air. It looks bad, worse than I even expected, the skin around it red and raw and pulled tight in an ugly-looking way and the skin beyond is darkened in wrong shades of purple and yellow and there's a smell, too, a smell of sickness and badness.

"Jesus, Viola," I whisper.

She don't say nothing but I see her swallow so I just take the first new bandage and wrap it right over the top of the band. She gives out a little gasp as the first jolt of medicine enters her system.

"Does it hurt?" I say.

She bites her lip and nods quickly, then gestures for me to do more. I unroll the second bandage and the third, wrapping them round the edges of the first like the Mayor told me, and she gasps again.

"Look, Todd," she says, her breathing fast and shallow. The bruises and darkness on her arm are already fading and you can actually see the medicine moving thru her, doing battle with the infeckshun right there under her skin.

"How does it feel?" I ask.

"Like burning knives," she says, a tear dropping from each eye—

And I reach out—

And I touch my thumb to her cheek—

Just gentlelike—

Brushing one of the tears away—

412

Feeling her skin under my hand—

Feeling the warmth of it, the softness—

Feeling like I wanna just go on touching her forever—

And I'm embarrassed to think this—

And then I realize she can't hear it—

And I start to think how awful that must be for her—

And then I feel her press her cheek more strongly into my fingers—

Turning her head, so the palm of my hand is holding her—

Holding her there—

And another tear falls down—

And she turns more—

Turns so her lips are pressing against my palm—

"Viola," I say—

"We're ready to go," Simone says, sticking her head in the tent.

I pull my hand away quick, tho I know we ain't doing nothing wrong.

And after a long awkward second, Viola says, "I feel better already."

{VIOLA}

"Shall we?" the Mayor says, a wide smile across his face, his uniform with the gold stripes down the sleeves looking somehow brand-new.

"If we must," Mistress Coyle says.

Wilf has joined us and we're gathered in front of the ruins of the cathedral, back from a cart with a microphone on top

413

for Mistress Coyle to be heard. Projections of it are being sent back to the hilltop, shown on the two building sides again and hovering above the rubble behind us.

The crowds are already cheering.

"Viola?" the Mayor asks, reaching out to take my hand to lead me to the stage. Todd gets up to follow me.

"If no one else minds," Mistress Coyle says, "I wonder if this might just be very short addresses by President Prentiss and myself this morning?"

The Mayor looks surprised, but I speak first. "That's a good idea," I say. "It'll make it go a lot quicker."

"Viola–" the Mayor says.

"And I'd like to sit for a minute and let the cure work some more, too."

"Thank you," Mistress Coyle says, weight in her voice. "You'll make a very good leader, Viola Eade." And then, as if to herself, "Yes, you will."

The Mayor's still looking for a way to get what he wants but Simone and Bradley aren't moving and he finally agrees. "All right, then," he says, holding his elbow out to Mistress Coyle. "Shall we address the populace?"

Mistress Coyle ignores the elbow and starts walking toward the stage. The Mayor follows quickly so he can get in front of her and have the crowds see him let her go up first.

"What was that all about?" Todd says, watching them go.

"Yeah," Bradley says, his Noise quizzical. "When did you start letting her get her way?"

"A little nicer to Mistress Coyle, please," Simone says. "I think I see what Viola's doing."

"And what's that?" Todd says.

414

"*Good people of New World,*" we hear Mistress Coyle's voice start to boom over the speakers. "*How far we've all come.*"

"Mistress Coyle thinks her days as leader are coming to an end," Simone says. "This is her way of saying good-bye."

Wilf gets a funny look on his face. "Good-bye?"

"*How far President Prentiss has taken us,*" Mistress Coyle is saying. "*To places we never even knew existed.*"

"But she's still leader," Lee says, sitting behind us. "There are a lot of people, a lot of *women–*"

"The world's changing, though," I say. "And she wasn't the one who changed it."

"And so she's going out on her own terms," Simone says, some emotion in her voice. "I admire her for it. Knowing when to leave the stage."

"*Taken us from the edge of one abyss,*" Mistress Coyle says, "*and right to the edge of another.*"

"Good-bye?" Wilf says again, more strongly.

I turn to him, hearing the concern in his Noise. "What is it, Wilf?"

But now Todd's figuring it out, too, his eyes opening wider.

"*Who has killed to protect us,*" Mistress Coyle says. "*Killed and killed and killed.*"

And there's uncomfortable murmuring from the crowd, rising higher.

"She thinks this is the end, Viola," Todd says, alarm entering his voice. "She thinks this is the *end.*"

And I turn back to the stage.

And I understand, too late, what Mistress Coyle has done.

415

I'm running before I even know exactly why, just knowing that I gotta get to the stage, gotta get there before–

"Todd!" I hear Viola call out behind me and I turn as I'm running to see Bradley grabbing her shoulder to hold her back and Simone and Wilf are running after me, running toward the stage–

Running to where Mistress Coyle's speech ain't going down too well with the crowd–

"A *peace bathed in blood,*" she's saying into the microphone. "A *peace paved with the corpses of women–*"

The crowd's booing now and I reach the back edge of the platform–

The Mayor's smiling at Mistress Coyle and it's a dangerous smile, a smile I know all too well, a smile that's gonna let her go ahead and make things worse and worse for herself–

But that ain't the idea that's dawning in me–

And I'm leaping onto the back of the platform, Mistress Coyle on my right, the Mayor on my left–

And Simone's jumping up after me on my right, Wilf behind her–

"A *peace,*" Mistress Coyle says, "*that he's seized with two bloody fists–*"

And the Mayor looks to see what I'm doing–

Just as Mistress Coyle is turning toward him–

Saying, "*But there are still those of us who care too much for this world to let that happen–*"

And she's opening the buttons of her coat–

Exposing the bomb she's got strapped round her waist–

416

{Viola}

"Let me go!" I yell, still trying to twist away from Bradley as Todd leaps onto the platform, Simone and Wilf right behind him.

Because I'm getting it, too–

You'd be surprised at how powerful a martyr can be, Mistress Coyle once told me–

How strongly people will fight in the name of the dead–

And I hear the gasp of the crowd as they see the projection–

As Bradley and I see it, too–

Mistress Coyle, large as life, face as calm as a saucer of milk, opening her coat to show the bomb she's wearing, draped around her torso like a corset, enough explosives to kill her, kill the Mayor–

Kill Todd–

"TODD!" I scream–

[Todd]

"TODD!" I hear Viola scream from behind us–

But we're too far from Mistress Coyle–

There's too many steps across the platform to stop her–

As her hand moves to a button on the bomb–

"JUMP!" I scream. "GET OFF THE CART!"

And I'm jumping as I scream it–

Jumping outta the way–

Over the side–

Grabbing Simone's jacket to take her with me–

417

"For a New World," Mistress Coyle says, the microphone still booming. *"For a better future."*

And she presses the button–

{VIOLA}

Flames explode out from Mistress Coyle in all directions, so fast the heat blows me right back into Bradley, who hisses in pain as my skull hits his chin, but I'm keeping to my feet and pressing forward into the blast wave, seeing the fire cascading out and I'm screaming, *"TODD!"* because I saw him jumping off the cart, dragging someone with him, and oh please oh please oh please and the initial blast's billowing up into the air in smoke and fire and the cart's burning and people are screaming and the *Noise* of it all and I'm breaking free from Bradley and I'm running–

"TODD!"

[TODD]

"TODD!" I hear again, my ears ringing, my clothes hot and burning–

But I'm thinking about Simone–

418

I grabbed her and threw us both off the side of the cart as the fire *whooshed* round us but we spun as we fell and I know she got the brunt of it, the fire hitting her full on and I'm patting her clothes to put 'em out and the smoke's blinding me and I'm yelling, "Simone! Are you all right? *Simone!*"

And a voice, grunting with pain, says, "Todd?"

And—

And it ain't Simone's voice.

The smoke starts to clear.

It ain't Simone.

"You *saved* me, Todd," says the Mayor, lying there, bad burns all over his face and hands, his clothes smoking like a brush fire. "You saved my life."

And his eyes are full of the wonder of it—

That in the rush of the explozhun the person I chose to save—

The one I chose without even thinking—

(without there even being time for him to control me—)

(no time for him to *make* me do it—)

Was the Mayor.

"TODD!" I hear Viola shout—

And I turn round to look—

Wilf is struggling to his feet from where he jumped off the back of the cart—

And there's Viola, still running—

Looking at me and the Mayor on the ground, the Mayor still breathing, still *talking*—

"I think I need a healer, Todd," he's saying—

And Simone's nowhere to be found—

Simone, who was standing right in front of Mistress Coyle when the bomb went off—

Simone, who was within my reach—

"Todd?" Viola asks, stopping a bit away from us, Wilf coughing but staring, too, Bradley running up behind 'em—

Everyone seeing that I saved the Mayor—

And not Simone—

And Viola says it again—

"Todd?"

And she's never looked farther away from me.

The Source

THROUGH THE CIRCLE of the Pathways' End around us, we see a brief glimpse of pink sun rising in the east before it disappears behind the blanket of gray cloud that has hung over us for the past two days.

Hung over me and the Source, as we waited for the council of peace.

This was the Sky's wish while he prepared for the council meeting, for me to stay here, bringing the Source his food and getting him to his feet again to regain the strength to walk after his long sleep, getting him washed and clothed and shaved in the Clearing fashion, and all the while showing him everything that happened while he served as the Source for the Land.

While, it seems, he *became* the Land.

He opens his voice, showing me other sunrises he has seen, where the fields turned golden and the Source and his one in particular stood up from their early morning labors to watch it rise, a memory as simple as that, yet covered in joy and loss and love and grief—

And hope.

All shown perfectly in the voice of the Land and with the same perplexing cheerfulness he has had since waking.

And then his voice shows *why* he is hopeful. The Source will be returned to the Clearing today as a surprise gesture of goodwill.

He is going to see the Knife again.

He looks at me, the warmth overflowing his voice, warmth I cannot help but feel, too.

I stand up quickly to get away from it. *I will get us breakfast,* I show.

Thank you, he shows as I go to the cook fire.

I do not show anything back.

We have listened to his voice these past months, the Sky showed me that first night when we woke the Source. *He can only have been listening back, learning to speak our voice, adapting to it, finally embracing it. The Sky's own voice changed shape around me. Much as the Sky hoped the Return would.*

*I **have** embraced it,* I showed back. *As much as I can.*

The Source speaks the language of the Land as if it were his own, but you still speak only the language of the Burden.

It is my first language, I showed and then I looked away. *It was the language of my one in particular.*

422

I was at the cookfire then, too, making the Source's first proper meal after months of being fed liquids through shunts down his throat. *And just because he speaks with our voice,* I showed, *does not mean he is one of us.*

Does it not? The Sky asked. *What is the Land if not its voice?*

I looked back at him. *Surely you are not suggesting—?*

*I merely suggest that if this one can immerse himself so far into the Land with such obvious understanding and feel **himself** part of the Land—*

Does that not make him dangerous? I showed. *Does that not make him a threat to us?*

Or does it make him an ally? the Sky showed back. *Does it provide us more hope for the future than we ever thought possible? If he can do it, can others? Is there more understanding possible?*

I had no answer and he made to leave.

What did you mean about me becoming the Sky? I showed. *Why me of all of the Land?*

At first I thought he would not answer. But he did.

Because you of all the Land understand the Clearing, he showed. *You of all the Land understand most fully what it would mean to invite them into our voice should that day ever come. And of all the Land, you are the one who would choose war most readily. And so when you choose **peace,*** his voice grew stronger, *it will mean all the more.*

I take the Source his breakfast, a fish stew unlike anything

423

I have ever seen the Clearing eat, but the Source does not complain.

He does not complain about *anything*.

Not about us holding him as a sleeping prisoner for all this time, instead thanking us, thanking *me* as if I did it personally, for healing the bullet wound in his chest, a bullet wound put there, to my astonishment, by the loud friend of the Knife, the same one who put the band on my arm.

He also does not complain that we read his voice for every advantage we could get. Though he is sad that so many of his kind have died in the war, he is happy on the one hand to have done something for victory over the leader of the Clearing and happier on the other that it has led to peace.

I don't complain because I've been transformed, he shows as I hand him his breakfast. *I hear the voice of the Land. It's very strange, because I'm still* **me,** *still an individual, but I'm also* **many,** *part of something bigger.* He takes a bite of his breakfast. *I think I might be the next evolutionary step for my people. Much as you are.*

I sit up, startled. **Me?**

You're one of the Land, he shows, *but you can conceal and muddy your thoughts like a man. You're one of the Land but you speak my language better than I do, better than any man I've ever met. We're the bridges twixt our two peoples, you and I.*

I bristle. *There are some bridges that should never be crossed.*

424

And still he smiles. *That's the thinking that's kept us so long at war.*

*Stop being so **happy**,* I show.

Ah, yes, but today, he shows, *today I'll see Todd again.*

The Knife. He has shown me the Knife, over and over again, so much so it is often as if the Knife is standing in Pathways' End with us, a third presence. And how brilliant he looks in the Source's voice, how young and fresh and strong. How loved.

I have told the Source every bit of the story up until his waking, including every action the Knife took and did not take, but instead of disappointment, the Source is *proud*. Proud of how the Knife has come through difficulty. Understanding and grieving over everything the Knife has suffered, every mistake the Knife has made. And every time the Source thinks of the Knife, a strange Clearing melody accompanies it, a song sung to the Knife when he was young, a song that binds the Knife to the Source—

"Call me Ben, please," the Source says through his mouth. "And the Knife is called Todd."

The Land do not use names, I show back. *If you understand us, then you understand that.*

Is that what the Return thinks? he shows, smiling through a mouthful of stew.

And again, my voice is filled with warmth and humor when I do not want it to be.

You're determined to dislike me, aren't you? he shows.

425

My voice hardens. *You killed my people. You killed them and enslaved them.*

He reaches out with his voice, in a gentle way I have never felt from the Clearing. *Only some of us acted that way. The man you fight killed my one in particular, too, and so I fight him with you.*

I stand up to go but he shows, *Please, wait.* I pause. *We,* he shows, *my people, have done you a great wrong, I know that, and anyone could argue that your people have done me wrong by keeping me here all this time. But I personally have done you no wrong. And **you've** done no wrong to **me.***

I try to keep my voice clear of when I held the knife over him.

And then I do not. I show him what I could have done to him. What I *wanted* to do—

But you stopped, he shows. *And surely this here, this understanding between the two of us, one single voice of a man reaching out to one single voice of the Land, surely **that's** the beginning of real peace.*

It is indeed, shows the Sky, entering the Pathways' End. *It is the best beginning of all.*

The Source sets down his meal. *It's time?* he shows.

It is time, the Sky agrees.

The Source lets out a happy sigh and once more his voice is filled with the Knife. "Todd," he says in the Clearing's chirps.

And that is when we hear the explosion in the distance.

* * *

We all turn quickly to face the horizon even though there is no chance of seeing anything with our physical eyes.

What's happened? asks the Source. *Have we been attacked?*

"*We*"? I show back to him.

Wait, shows the Sky. *It will come—*

And it does a moment later, the voices of the Pathways' receiving the voices of the Land from down below, showing us the explosion in the middle of the city, an explosion at the head of a great crowd of the Clearing, though the eyes we are seeing it through are high above the city on the lip of the hill, and all we can really see is a flash of fire and a column of smoke.

Is that the Land? the Source asks. *Has the Land done this?*

It has not, shows the Sky. He steps quickly out of the Pathways' End, gesturing us to follow. We go to the steep path, which I will have to help the still-weak Source climb down, and as we reach it, the Source's voice is filled with one thing—

Fear.

Not for himself, not for the peace process—

Fear for the Knife. All his voice can show is how much he fears losing the Knife on the very morning they were to be reunited, fear that the worst has happened, that he has lost his son, his most beloved son, and I can feel his heart aching with worry, aching with love and concern—

An ache I know, an ache I have felt—

An ache that passes from the Source to me as we climb down—

The Knife—

Todd—

Standing in my voice, as real and fragile and worthy of life as any other—

And I do not want it.

I do not want it.

SEPARATIONS

[TODD]

A SMALL INTAKE OF BREATH is all the Mayor gives when Mistress Lawson presses the bandages against the back of his scalp, tho the burns there are horrible to see.

"Severe," Mistress Lawson says, "but shallow. The flash was so fast it didn't go very deep. You'll scar, but you'll heal."

"Thank you, Mistress," the Mayor says as she wipes a clear gel over the burns on his face, which ain't as bad as on the back of his head.

"I'm merely doing my job," Mistress Lawson says sharply. "And now there are others to be treated."

She leaves the healing room of the scout ship, taking a pile of bandages with her. I'm sitting in a chair near the Mayor, burn gel on my hands, too. Wilf is on the other bed, burned up his front but still alive cuz he was already falling when the bomb went off.

Outside is another story. Using the Noise of the crowd, Lee's out there helping the dozens of people who were burned and injured in Mistress Coyle's suicide.

Killed, too. At least five men and one woman in the crowd.

And Mistress Coyle herself, of course.

And Simone.

Viola ain't spoken to me since the bomb. She and Bradley are off doing something.

Something away from me.

"It'll be all right, Todd," the Mayor says, seeing me keep checking the door. "They'll realize you had to make a split-second decision and I was closest—"

"No, you weren't," I say. I clench my fists and wince at the pain from the burns. "I had to reach farther to grab you."

"And you *did* grab me," the Mayor says, marveling a little.

"Yeah, yeah, all right," I say.

"You *saved* me," he says, almost to himself.

"Yeah, I *know*—"

"No, Todd," he says, sitting up on the bed, tho it obviously pains him. "You saved *me*. When you didn't have to. I can't tell you how much that means to me."

"You sure keep trying."

"I'll never forget this, that you think of me as worth saving. And I *am*, Todd. And it's you who's made me that way."

"Quit talking like that," I say. "Other people are dead. Other people I didn't save."

He just nods, nods and lets me feel like crap all over again for not saving Simone.

And then he says, "She won't have died in vain, Todd. We'll make sure of that."

And he sounds truthful, like he always does.

(it sure *feels* true–)

(and the faint *hum*–)

(it's glowing with *joy*–)

I look over to Wilf. He's staring up at the ceiling, soot-covered skin poking out thru white bandages. "Ah think you mighta saved me, too," he says. "Yoo said, *Jump*. Yoo said, *Get offa the cart*."

I clear my throat. "That ain't really saving you, Wilf. It didn't save Simone."

"Yoo were in mah head," Wilf says. "Yoo were in mah head sayin, *Jump* and my feet were jumpin afore Ah even tole 'em to. Yoo *made* me jump." He blinks at me. "How d'yoo do that?"

I look away at the thought of it. I probably did do it, reached out and controlled him, and if Simone didn't have Noise, she wouldn't have responded to it.

But the Mayor might have. I might not have even *needed* to grab him.

The Mayor sets both feet on the floor and painfully, slowly, brings himself to standing.

"Where do you think yer going?" I say.

"To address the crowds," he says. "We need to tell them that the peace process doesn't end because of the actions of one mistress. We need to show them that *I* am still alive and that *Viola* is." He puts a hand gingerly to the back of his neck. "This peace is fragile. The *people* are fragile. We need to tell them there's no reason to give up hope."

I wince a little at his last word.

Mr. Tate comes thru the door carrying a pile of clothes. "As requested, sir," he says, handing 'em to the Mayor.

"Yer putting on clean clothes?" I say.

"So are you," he says, handing me half the pile. "We certainly can't go out there in burned rags."

I look down at my own clothes, what's left of 'em after Mistress Lawson peeled the burned ones off my skin.

"Put them on, Todd," the Mayor says. "You'll be surprised at how much better they make you feel."

(and the faint *hum*–)

(the joy of it–)

(it's kinda making me feel not so terrible–)

I start putting on the new clothes.

{ V I O L A }

"There." Bradley points at the screen in the cockpit. "He *is* closer to Simone, but Prentiss is closer to the edge of the platform."

He slows down the recording and stops it at the point where Mistress Coyle is about to press the button on the bomb. The point where Simone is still heading straight for her and where Wilf is stepping backwards to jump off the cart.

And where Todd is already reaching for the Mayor.

"He wouldn't have even had a chance to think," Bradley says, his voice thick, "much less choose."

"He went right for the Mayor," I say. "He didn't *have* to think."

We watch the explosion again, an image that was broadcast to the town outside and to the people watching on the hilltop, who are thinking God *knows* what right now.

We watch as the Mayor is saved again.

And Simone isn't.

Bradley's Noise is so sad, so *broken*, I can barely look at it.

"You told me," he says, closing his eyes, "that whoever else I doubted on this planet, Todd was the one I could trust. *You* said that, Viola. And you've been right every time."

"Except this time." Because I can read Bradley's Noise, read what it *really* thinks. "You blame him, too."

He looks away from me, and I see his Noise struggling with itself. "Todd obviously regrets it," he says. "You can see it all over his face."

"But you can't *hear* it. Not in his Noise. Not the truth."

"Have you asked him?"

I just look again at the screen, at the fire and chaos that followed Mistress Coyle blowing herself up.

"*Viola–*"

"Why did she do it?" I say, too loud, trying to ignore the sudden Simone-shaped hole in the world. "Why, when we had peace?"

"Maybe with the both of them gone," Bradley says sadly, "she hoped the planet would rally around someone like you."

"I don't *want* that responsibility. I didn't ask for it."

"But you could probably have it," he says. "And you'd use it wisely."

"How do you know?" I say. "*I* don't even know that. You said war should never be personal, but that's all it's *ever* been for me. If I hadn't fired that missile, we wouldn't even be here. Simone would still be–"

"Hey," Bradley says, stopping me because I'm getting even more upset. "Look, I need to contact the convoy, tell them what happened." His Noise folds with grief. "Tell them we've lost her."

I nod, my eyes wetting further.

"And you," he says, "you need to talk to your boy." He lifts my chin. "And if he needs saving, then you save him. Isn't that what you told me you did for each other?"

I let go a few more tears but then I nod. "Over and over again."

He gives me a hug, a strong and sad one, and I leave him so he can call the convoy. I walk the short hallway back to the healing room as slow as I can, feeling like someone's torn me in two. I can't believe Simone is dead. I can't believe *Mistress Coyle* is dead.

And I can't believe Todd saved the Mayor.

But it's Todd. Todd, who I trust with my life. *Literally*. I trusted him to put these bandages on me, which frankly have me feeling better than I have in months.

And if he saved the Mayor, then there must be a reason. There *must* be.

I take a deep breath outside the door of the healing room.

Because that reason is *goodness*, isn't it? Isn't that what Todd basically is? Despite the mistakes, despite killing the Spackle by the riverside, despite the work he did for the Mayor, Todd is essentially good, I know this, I've seen it, I've *felt* it in his Noise–

But I can't feel it anymore.

"No," I say again. "It's Todd. It's *Todd*."

I push the panel to open the door.

And see Todd and the Mayor wearing matching uniforms.

[TODD]

I see her in the doorway, see how healthy she's looking—

See her see the clothes me and the Mayor are wearing, the same right down to the gold stripe on the sleeves of the jackets.

"It's not what you think," I say, "my clothes were all burned—"

But she's already stepping back from the door, stepping away—

"*Viola,*" the Mayor says, strong enough to stop her. "I know this is a tough time for you, but we must address the people. We must reassure them that the peace process will go forward as planned. And as soon as we can, we must send a delegation to the Spackle to assure them of the same thing."

Viola looks him square in the eye. "You say *must* way too easy."

The Mayor tries to smile thru his burns. "If we don't talk to the people right now, Viola, things could fall apart. The Answer might wish to finish Mistress Coyle's action and use this moment of chaos to do so. The Spackle could attack us for the same reason. My own men might even get it into their heads that I'm incapacitated and decide to stage a coup. I trust that these are not outcomes you would want."

435

And I can see that she feels it, too.

The weird joy coming from him.

"What would you say to them?" she says.

"What would you like me to say?" he asks. "Tell me and I'll repeat it word for word."

She narrows her eyes. "What are you playing at?"

"I'm not playing at anything," he says. "I could have died today and I did not. And I did not because Todd saved me." He steps forward, eagerness in his voice. "It may not have been what you wanted, but if Todd saved me, then I'm worth saving, don't you see? And if I'm worth saving, then we all are, this whole place, this whole *world*."

Viola looks to me for help.

"I think he's in shock," I say.

"I think you may be right," the Mayor says, "but I'm not wrong about talking to the crowds, Viola. We need to do it. And quickly."

Viola's looking at me now, looking at the uniform I'm wearing, searching for some truth. I try to make my Noise heavy, to let her see how I'm feeling, to show her how every-thing's spun outta control, how I didn't mean for this to happen, but now that it has, maybe—

"I can't hear you," she says quietly.

And I try to open up again but it feels like something's blocking me—

She glances over to Wilf, and her face gets even frownier.

"All right," she says, not looking at me. "Let's go talk to the people."

{Viola}

"Viola," Todd calls after me down the ramp. "Viola, I'm *sorry*. Why won't you even let me say that?"

And I stop there, trying to read him.

But there's still just silence.

"Are you really sorry?" I say. "If you had to choose all over again, are you sure you wouldn't do the same thing?"

"How can you even ask that?" he says, frowning.

"Have you seen what you're *wearing* lately?" I look back up at the Mayor, walking slowly to the top of the ramp, taking care with his injuries but still smiling through the burn gel on his face, still wearing an impossibly clean uniform.

Just like Todd.

"You could be father and son."

"Don't say that!"

"It's true, though. Look at yourselves."

"Viola, you *know* me. Out of everyone left alive on this planet, yer the one who *does*."

But I'm shaking my head. "Maybe not anymore. Since I stopped being able to hear you–"

He *really* frowns at this. "So that's what you want, is it? I'm fine as long as you can hear everything I think but not the other way round? We're friends as long as you got all the power?"

"It's not about *power*, Todd. It's about trust–"

"And I ain't done enough for you to *trust* me?" He points up the ramp at the Mayor. "He's fighting for peace now, Viola. And he's doing that cuz of *me*. Cuz I changed him."

"Yeah," I say, flicking the gold stripe on his sleeve. "And

how has he changed *you*? Enough so you save *him* and not Simone?"

"He hasn't *changed* me, Viola–"

"Did you control Wilf to get him to jump off the cart?"

His eyes open wide.

"I saw it in his Noise," I say. "And if it bothered Wilf, it can't be a good thing."

"I saved his *life!*" he shouts. "I was doing it for *good*–"

"So that makes it okay? That makes it okay that you said you couldn't do it? That you *wouldn't* do it? How many other people have you controlled *for their own good*?"

He fights with his words for a minute and I can see some real regret in his eyes, regret over something he hasn't told me, but which I still can't see in his complete lack of Noise–

"I'm doing all this for *you!*" he finally shouts. "I'm trying to make this a safe world for *you!*"

"And I've done it for *you,* Todd!" I shout back. "Only to find out that maybe you're not *you* anymore!"

And his face is so angry but also so horrified, so shocked and hurt by what I'm saying I can almost–

For a second I can almost–

"IT'S HIM!"

A single voice, cutting thru the ROAR of the crowd gathered round the scout ship.

"IT'S THE PRESIDENT!"

Other voices follow, one, then a hundred, then a thousand, and the ROAR gets higher and louder, until it feels like we're in an ocean of Noise, surging up the ramp and lifting the Mayor above it all. He starts walking slowly down, his head up, his face beaming, his hand reaching out to the crowd to show them that, yes, he's all right, he's survived, he's still their leader.

Still in charge. Still the victor.

"Come, Todd, Viola," he says. "The world awaits."

[TODD]

"The world awaits," the Mayor says, taking my arm, pulling me away from Viola, his eyes on the crowd cheering him, **ROAR**ing for him, and I see that the projeckshuns are still running, the probes still programmed to follow us, follow *him,* and there we are on the walls of the buildings around the square, the Mayor leading the way, me being pulled along behind him, Viola still standing on the ramp with Bradley and Wilf coming down behind her–

"Listen to them, Todd," the Mayor says to me and again I feel the *hum*–

The *hum* of joy–

I feel it even in the **ROAR** of the crowd–

"We can really do it," he's saying as the crowd parts before us, giving us room to walk to a new platform Mr. Tate and Mr. O'Hare musta cobbled together. "We can really rule this world," the Mayor says. "We can really make it a better place."

"Let me go," I say.

But he don't let go.

He don't even look at me.

I turn back to find Viola. She ain't moved from the ramp. Lee's come thru the crowd to her and they're all watching me let myself get dragged away by the Mayor,

439

both of us wearing the same uniform—

"Let me *go*," I say again, pulling away.

The Mayor turns round, grabbing me hard by the shoulders and the crowds are closing up the pathway twixt me and Viola—

"Todd," the Mayor says, the *hum* of joy coming off him like sunshine. "Todd, don't you see? You've done it. You've led me down the road to redemption and we've arrived."

The crowd is still ROARing, loud as anything now that the Mayor's among them. He stands up straighter, looks round at the soldiers and townsfolk and even women round us all cheering, and with a smile on his face, he says, "Quiet, please."

{VIOLA}

"What the *hell*?" I say, as the ROAR of the crowd vanishes almost instantly, spreading out in circles till the cheering stops, in voice and in Noise, as near as this place ever comes to silence. Even the women as they see how quiet the men have gone.

"I heard it," Bradley whispers.

And Wilf whispers, "Ah heard it, too."

"Heard *what*?" I say, too loud in the new quiet, causing faces from the crowd to look back and *shush* me.

"Just the words *Quiet, please*," Bradley whispers. "Right in the middle of my head. And I swear my Noise is quieter, too."

"And mine," Lee says. "It's like I've gone blind all over again."

"How?" I say. "How can he have that much power?"

"There's something funny bout him since the blast," Wilf says.

"Viola," Bradley says, putting his hand on my arm. "If he can do that to a thousand people at once—"

I look out and see the Mayor standing in front of Todd, looking right into his eyes.

I start forward toward the crowd.

[TODD]

"I've been waiting for this my entire life," the Mayor's saying to me and I'm finding I can't look away.

I'm finding I don't really want to.

"I didn't even know it, Todd," he's saying. "All I wanted was to bring this planet under my thumb and, failing that, to destroy it completely. If I couldn't have it, then no one else could either."

The Noise around us is almost a complete hush. "How are you doing this?" I ask.

"But I was wrong, you see?" he says. "When I saw what was going to happen with Mistress Coyle, when I saw that I had failed to predict it but that *you* had, Todd, and you *saved* me—" He stops and I swear it's cuz his voice is too filled with emoshun to go on. "When you *saved* me, Todd, that's when everything changed. When everything fell into place."

(and the *hum*, gleaming like a lighthouse in my head—)

(that *joy*—)

(it feels *good*—)

"We could make this world better," he says. "You and I could make it better *together*. With your goodness, with everything about you that feels and hurts and regrets and refuses to fall no matter what you've done, Todd, if we combined that with how I can lead men, how I can control them–"

"They don't wanna be controlled," I say.

His eyes, I can't look away from 'em–

"Not *that* kind of control, Todd," he says. "*Peaceful* control, benevolent control–"

And the joy–

I *feel* it–

"Like the leader of the Spackle has over his own people," the Mayor keeps saying. "That's the voice I've been hearing. The *one* voice. They're him and he's them and that's how they survive, that's how they learn and grow and *exist*." He's breathing heavy now, the burn gel on his face making him look like he's coming up from underwater. "I can be that for the people here, Todd. *I* can be their voice. And you can help me. You can help me be *better*. You can help me be *good*."

And I'm thinking–

I *could* help him–

I *could*–

(*no–*)

"Let me go," I say–

"I've known you were special since Prentisstown," he says, "but it's only today, only when you saved me, that I realized exactly why."

He grips me harder.

"You're my *soul*, Todd," he says, the crowd around us swooning at how strong he says it and their Noise confirming it and answering it back. "You're my soul and I've been looking for you without even knowing it." He smiles at me wonderingly. "And I've found you, Todd. I've *found* you–"

And then there's a sound, a different sound, coming from somewhere at the edges of the crowd, a murmuring in their Noise, rumbling its way from the far end of the square towards us.

"A Spackle," the Mayor whispers, seconds before I see it, surprisingly clear in the Noise of the crowd.

There's a Spackle coming up the road on a battlemore.

"And . . ." the Mayor says, frowning slightly and standing up to look.

"And what?" I say–

But then I see it in the crowd Noise, too–

The Spackle's not alone–

There are *two* battlemores–

And then I hear it–

I hear the sound that turns the entire world upside down–

{VIOLA}

I press hard through the crowd, caring less and less if I'm stepping on people or shoving them out of the way, especially since most of them barely seem to notice. Even the women, who seem caught up in the moment, their faces filled with the same strange anticipation–

"*Move,*" I say through gritted teeth.

Because I'm realizing it now, too late, too late, that of course the Mayor's got inside Todd, of *course* he has, and

443

maybe Todd *has* changed him, changed him for the better, no doubt, but the Mayor's always been stronger, always been smarter, and changing for the better doesn't mean that he's ever going to reach good and of *course* he's been changing Todd, too, of course he has, how could I be so stupid not to see it, not to talk to him–

Not to *save* him–

"Todd!" I call–

But it's drowned out by a surge in the Noise of the crowd, images from the far side, where something's happening, something that's being passed along through the Noise of the people seeing it, spreading through the crowd–

Noise that shows two Spackle coming up the road–

Two Spackle on battlemores, one of them sitting rather than standing–

And with a jolt, I see that the standing one is the same Spackle who attacked me–

But there's no time for that feeling, because the Noise suddenly corrects itself–

And the seated Spackle isn't a Spackle–

It's a *man*–

And in the Noise of the crowd, passed along like a baton in a race, I can hear it–

The man is singing–

[TODD]

My stomach drops outta the bottom of my feet and my breath feels like I'm choking and my legs are moving and

I'm tearing outta the Mayor's grip, feeling the bruises as he don't wanna let me go–

But I'm going–

Oh, Christ, I'm *going*–

"*Todd!*" he calls after me, real shock in his voice, real *pain* that I'm running from him–

But I'm running–

There ain't nothing gonna stop me from running–

"*MOVE!*" I shout–

And the soldiers and men in front of me move right outta the way, like they didn't even decide for themselves–

Cuz they didn't–

"Todd!" I hear the Mayor behind me still, but getting farther behind–

Cuz up ahead–

Oh, Jesus, I don't believe it I don't believe it–

"*MOVE IT!*"

And I'm trying to listen, trying to listen for the sound again, trying to listen for the *song*–

And the crowd keeps moving, getting outta my way like I'm a fire come to burn 'em–

And the Spackle's coming thru their Noise, too–

It's 1017–

The Spackle is *1017*–

"NO!" I call and run even harder–

Cuz I don't know what it means that 1017 is here–

But there he is in the Noise of the crowd–

Getting brighter and clearer as I get closer–

Way clearer than Noise usually is–

"Todd!" I hear behind me—

But I don't stop—

Cuz as I'm getting closer even the rising Noise of the crowd can't cover it up—

The song—

Clear as the air—

Ripping my heart right in two—

The song, *my* song—

Early one mo-o-rning, just as the sun was rising . . .

And my eyes are wetting and the crowd is thinning and the path they're clearing for me is meeting the path they're clearing for the Spackle—

And just a few more people—

Just a few more—

And the crowd opens up—

And there he is—

There he is in front of my eyes—

And I have to stop—

I have to stop cuz it feels like I can't even stand up—

And when I say his name, it barely comes out as more than a whisper—

But he hears it—

I know he hears it—

"Ben."

{ V I O L A }

It's *Ben.*

I can see him as clearly in the Noise of the crowd as if he were standing right in front of me. There's the Spackle that tried to kill me, 1017, riding a battlemore, and Ben's sitting behind him on another one, the song he's singing coming clear: *I heard a maiden call from the valley below—*

But his mouth isn't moving—

Which must be a mistake of the crowd Noise—

But he's there, riding up the road, and since no one here can know him, his face must be accurate. It must really be Ben—

And I can feel the Mayor's medicine surging through me and I use my new strength to start shoving people out of the way even harder—

Because in their Noise, I can see the Mayor pushing forward ahead of me, too—

And I see that Todd's reached Ben—

See it like I'm right there—

Feel it like I'm right there because Todd's own Noise has opened, as he's gotten farther away from the Mayor and closer to Ben, his own Noise is opening as wide as it used to be, opening with astonishment and joy and so much love you can hardly bear to look at it and those feelings are surging back along the crowd like a wave and the crowd is staggering under it, staggering under the feeling that Todd's transmitting to them—

Transmitting it just like the Mayor can—

[TODD]

I can't even say nothing, I just can't, there ain't no words for it as I'm running to him, running right past 1017, and Ben's coming down off his battlemore and his Noise is rising to greet me with everything I know about him, everything since I was a baby, everything that means he's really Ben—

And he ain't quite saying it in words—

And he's opening up his arms and I'm throwing myself into 'em and I'm hitting him so hard we fall back against the beast he was riding and—

How big you've gotten, he says—

"Ben!" I say, gasping the words, "Aw, Jesus, *Ben—*"

You're as tall as me, he says. *Big as a man.*

And I'm barely noticing that he says it a bit strange cuz I'm just holding him tight and my eyes are leaking water and I can barely speak as I feel him here, right *here,* right *here* in the flesh, alive and alive and alive—

"How?" I finally say, pulling back a little but still holding on to him and I can't say no more but he knows what I mean—

The Spackle found me, he says. *Davy Prentiss shot me—*

"I know," I say and my chest gets heavier, my chest weighing down and my Noise feeling heavier, too, heavy like it ain't felt in a good long while, and Ben can see it and he says—

Show me.

And I do, right there before I can even get any proper words out, I show him the whole terrible story of what happened after we left him and I'd swear he was helping me do it, helping me show him the death of Aaron, the wounding of Viola, our separation, the attacks by the Answer, the banding of the Spackle, the banding of the women, the *deaths* of the Spackle, and I look over to 1017 still up on his battlemore and I show Ben all about that, too, and everything that followed, Davy Prentiss coming round to being human and then dying at the Mayor's hand and the war and more deaths—

It's all right, Todd, he says. *It's all over. The war is over.*

And I can tell—

I can tell he forgives me.

He forgives me for all of it, tells me I don't even need to be forgiven, tells me I did the best I could, that I made mistakes but that's what makes me human and that it's not the mistakes I made but how I responded to 'em and I can feel it from him, feel it from his Noise, telling me how I can stop now, how everything's gonna be all right—

And I realize he ain't telling me with words. He's sending it right into the middle of my head. Actually, no, he *ain't*; he's *surrounding* me with it, letting me sit in the middle of it, knowing it to be true, the forgiveness, the— and here's a word I don't even know but suddenly do— *absolushun*, absolushun from him if I want it, absolushun for everything—

"Ben?" I say, feeling puzzled, feeling *more* than puzzled. "What's going on? Yer *Noise*—"

There's a lot we need to talk about, he says, again not with his mouth, and I start to feel weird about it but the warmth of it is all round me, the *Ben* of it's all there, and my heart just breaks open again and I smile back at the smile he's giving me—

"Todd?" I hear behind us.

We turn to look.

The Mayor stands at the edge of the crowd, watching us.

449

"Todd?" I hear the Mayor say as I stop right beside him—

Because it *is* Ben, it *is*. I don't know how, but it really is him—

And he and Todd turn to look, a dazed cloud of happy Noise swirling round them, expanding over everything, including the Spackle still up on the battlemore next to them, and I move toward Ben, my own heart surging—

But I glance at the Mayor's face as I run past—

And I see *pain* there, just for a second, fleeting across his gel-shiny features, and then it's gone, replaced with the face we know so well, the face of the Mayor, bemused and in charge—

"Ben!" I call and he opens an arm to receive me. Todd steps back but the feelings from Ben are so good, so strong that after a second Todd embraces both of us together and I feel so happy about it I start to cry.

"Mr. Moore," the Mayor calls from a distance away. "Reports of your death seem to have been exaggerated."

As have reports of yours, Ben says, but in the strangest way, not using his mouth, using his Noise more directly than I've ever heard—

"This is most unexpected," the Mayor says, glancing at Todd, "but joyful of course. Very joyful indeed."

But I don't see much joy behind the smile he's giving.

Todd doesn't seem to notice, though. "What's with yer Noise?" he says to Ben. "Why are you talking like that?"

"I believe I have an idea," the Mayor says.

But Todd isn't listening.

"I'll explain everything," Ben says, using his mouth for the first time, though his voice is scratchy and clogged, as if he hasn't used it in ages. *But let me say first,* he says, back through his Noise, reaching up to the Mayor and the crowd behind him, *that peace is still with us. The Land still wants it. A real new world is still open to all of us. That's what I came to tell you.*

"Is that so?" the Mayor says, still smiling his cold smile.

"Then what's *he* doing here?" Todd says, nodding at 1017. "He tried to kill Viola. He don't care about peace."

The Return made a mistake, Ben says, *for which we must forgive him.*

"The who did what now?" Todd says, perplexed.

But 1017 is already turning his battlemore back toward the road without acknowledging us, riding back through the crowds on his way out of the city.

"Well, now," the Mayor says, his smile still stuck there. Ben and Todd lean into each other, the feelings rolling off them in waves, waves that make me feel great in spite of all my worries. "Well, now," the Mayor says again, a little louder, trying to make sure he has all our attention. "I would very, very much like to hear what Ben has to say."

I'm sure you would, David, Ben says in that weird Noise way. *But first I've got a lot of catching up to do with my son.*

And there's a surge of feeling from Todd—

And he doesn't see the glimmer of pain flash again on the face of the Mayor.

"But I don't unnerstand," I say, not for the first time. "Does that make you Spackle now or something?"

No, Ben says, thru his Noise, but way clearer than Noise speech ever usually is. *The Spackle speak the voice of this planet. They live within it. And now, because of how long I was immersed in that voice, I do, too. I've connected with them.*

And there's that *connected* word again.

We're in my tent, just me and him, Angharrad tied outside in a way that blocks the opening. I know the Mayor and Viola and Bradley and all them are out there waiting for us to come out to tell 'em what the hell's going on.

But let 'em wait.

I got Ben back and I ain't letting him outta my sight.

I swallow and think for a minute. "I don't unnerstand," I say again.

"I think it could be the way forward for all of us," he says with his mouth, croaky and crackling. He coughs and lets his Noise take over again. *If we can all learn to speak this way, then there won't be any more division twixt us and the Spackle; there won't be any division twixt humans. That's the secret of this planet, Todd. Communication, real and open, so we can finally understand each other for once.*

I clear my throat. "Women don't got Noise," I say. "What'll happen to them?"

He stops. *I'd forgotten,* he says. *It's been so long since I've really been around them.* He brightens again.

*Spackle women have Noise. And if there's a way for men to **stop** having Noise*—he looks at me—*there must be a way for women to start.*

"The way things've gone round here," I say, "I don't know that yer gonna have much success with that kinda talk."

We sit quietly for a moment. Well, not quietly, cuz Ben's Noise churns around us constantly, taking my own Noise and mixing it in like the most natural thing in the world, and in any instant I can know anything and everything about him. Like how, after Davy shot him, he stumbled into the undergrowth to die and lay there for a day and a night before he was found by a hunting party of Spackle and then what followed was months of dreaming where he was nearly dead, months away in a world of strange voices, learning all the knowledges and histories of everything the Spackle know, learning new names and feelings and unnerstandings.

And then he woke up and was changed.

But was still Ben, too.

And I tell him, thru the best use of my Noise, which feels open and free again like it ain't done for months, about everything that happened here and how I still don't quite unnerstand how I ended up wearing this uniform—

But all he asks is, *Why isn't Viola in here with us?*

{ VIOLA }

"Don't you feel excluded?" the Mayor says, pacing around the campfire one more time.

"Not really," I say, watching him. "It's his father in there."

"Not his *real* father," says the Mayor, frowning.

453

"Real enough."

The Mayor keeps pacing, his face hard and cold.

"Unless you mean–" I say.

"If they ever do emerge," he says, nodding at the tent where Ben and Todd are talking, where we can hear and see a cloud of Noise spinning denser and more intricately than any usual man's Noise, "please send Todd to retrieve me."

And off he goes, Captain O'Hare and Captain Tate following him.

"What's with him?" Bradley asks, watching the Mayor leave.

It's Wilf who answers. "He thinks he's lost his son."

"His son?" Bradley asks.

"The Mayor's somehow got it into his head that Todd's a replacement for Davy," I say. "You saw how he was talking to him."

"I heard some of it through the crowd," Lee says, from where he's sitting by Wilf. "Something about Todd transforming him."

"And now Todd's *real* father's here," I say.

"At the worst possible moment," Lee says.

"Or just in the nick of time," I say.

The curtain of the tent opens and Todd pokes his head out.

"Viola?" he says.

And I turn to look at him–

And when I do, I can hear everything he's thinking.

Everything.

Clearer than before, clearer than seems possible–

And I'm not even sure I'm supposed to, but I look him in the eyes and I see it–

454

In the middle of everything he's feeling–
Even after we fought–
Even after I doubted him–
Even after I *hurt* him–
I see how much he loves me.
But I see more, too.

[TODD]

"So what happens now?" Viola says to Ben, sitting next to me on my cot. I've taken her hand. Didn't say nothing about it, just took it, and she let me and we sit side by side.

Peace is what happens, Ben says. *The Sky sent me to find out about the explosion, to see if peace was still possible.* He smiles and again it's thru his whole Noise, reaching out to us so that it's hard not to smile yerself. *And it is possible. That's what the Return is telling the Sky right now.*

"What makes you think 1017 is trustworthy?" I say. "He attacked Viola."

I squeeze Viola's hand.

She squeezes it back.

Because I know him, Ben says. *I can hear his voice, hear the conflict in it, hear the good that wants to come. He's like you, Todd. He can't kill.*

I look at the floor at that.

"I think you need to talk to the Mayor," Viola says to Ben. "I don't think he's too happy that you're back."

No, Ben says. *I got that impression too, though he is very difficult to read, isn't he?* He stands. "But he needs to know the war is over," he rasps in his spoken voice.

He looks at me and Viola sitting there, gives another little smile, and then leaves us in the tent.

We don't say nothing for a minute.

Or for another minute more.

And then I tell her the thought that's been coming ever since I saw Ben.

{VIOLA}

"I wanna go back to old Prentisstown," Todd says.

"What?" I say, surprised, even though I'd seen it swirling in his Noise.

"Maybe not old Prentisstown itself," he says. "But not here."

I sit up. "Todd, we've barely started–"

"But we *will* start and soon," he says, still holding my hand. "The ships'll come and the settlers will wake up and then there'll be a new city. With all new people." He looks away. "After living in one for a while, I don't think I like cities much."

His Noise is getting quieter now that Ben's left, but I can still see him imagining life after the convoy, things getting back to normal, people spreading up the river again. "And you want to go," I say.

He looks back to me. "I want you to come with me. And Ben. And Wilf and Jane, maybe. Bradley, too, if he wants, and that Mistress Lawson seems nice. Why couldn't we all make a town of it? A town far away from all this." He sighs. "A town far from the Mayor."

456

"But he needs to be watched—"

"There'll be five thousand new people who'll know all about what he is." He looks down at the ground again. "Besides, I think maybe I've done all I can for him," he says. "And I'm tired."

The way he says it makes me realize how tired I am, too, how tired I am of all of this, and how tired he must be, how tired he *looks,* how worn out and through with it all, and my throat starts to clench with the feeling of it.

"I want to go away from here," he says. "And I want you to come with me."

And we sit there in silence for a good long while.

"He's in your head, Todd," I finally say. "I saw him there. Like you're connected somehow."

Todd sighs again at the word *connected.* "I know," he says. "That's why I wanna go. I came close but I ain't forgot who I am. Ben reminded me of all I ever need to know. And, yeah, I'm connected to the Mayor, too, but I've pulled him away from all this war stuff."

"Did you *see* what he did with the crowd?"

"It's almost over," Todd says. "We'll have peace, he'll have his victory, and he won't need me, even tho he thinks he does. The convoy'll come, he'll be the hero but he'll be out-numbered, and we'll get the hell outta here, okay?"

"Todd—"

"It's almost over," he says again. "And I can hang on till it is."

And then he looks at me in a different way.

His Noise keeps getting quieter, but I can see it there still—

457

See how he feels the skin of my hand against his, see how he wants to take it and press it to his mouth, how he wants to breathe in the smell of me and how beautiful I look to him, how strong after all that illness, and how he wants to just lightly touch my neck, just *there,* and how he wants to take me in his arms and–

"Oh, God," he says, looking away suddenly. "Viola, I'm sorry, I didn't mean–"

But I just put my hand up to the back of his neck–

And he says, "Viola–?"

And I pull myself toward him–

And I kiss him.

And it feels like, *finally.*

[TODD]

"I'm in complete agreement," the Mayor says to Ben.

You are? Ben says, surprised.

We're all gathered round the campfire, Viola sitting next to me.

Holding my hand again.

Holding like she ain't never gonna let it go.

"Of course I am," the Mayor says. "As I've said many times, peace is what I want. It's what I *genuinely* want. Believe it out of self-interest if nothing else."

Excellent then, Ben says. *We'll continue with the council as planned. That is, if your injuries will allow you to take part?*

The Mayor's eyes spark a little. "What injuries would those be, Mr. Moore?"

There's a stillness as we all see the burn gel covering his face and the bandages on the back of his neck and head.

But no, he don't look like he's feeling any injuries at all.

"In the meantime," the Mayor says, "there are certain things that need to be done right away, certain assurances to be made."

"Assurances to who?" Viola asks.

"The people on the far hilltop, for one," the Mayor says. "They may not be gathering themselves into the Army of the Martyress just yet, but I would feel no surprise if Mistress Coyle had left instructions with Mistress Braithwaite should she fail. Someone needs to go back up there and settle things."

"I'll go," Mistress Lawson says, frowning. "The mistresses will listen to me."

"Me, too," says Lee, aiming his Noise away from me and Viola.

"And our friend Wilf to drive them," says the Mayor.

We all look up at that. "I'll *fly* them," Bradley says.

"And be gone all night?" the Mayor asks, looking at him hard (and I wonder if I hear the *hum*–) "Not to return until morning with a burn unit far surpassing anything we have in the city? Plus, I think you, Bradley, need to go back to the Spackle *today*, right now, with Ben and Viola."

"*What?*" Viola says. "But we agreed on tomorrow–"

"By tomorrow, the schism Mistress Coyle wanted may have taken firmer hold," the Mayor says. "How much better if you, hero of the first talks, come back tonight with matters already settled? With, for example, a river flowing slowly down the banks?"

459

"I wanna go with Ben," I say. "I don't—"

"I'm sorry, Todd," the Mayor says, "I really am, but you have to stay here with me, as usual, and make sure I don't do anything anyone would disapprove of."

"No," Viola says, surprisingly loud.

"All this time and you're worried *now*?" the Mayor says to her, smiling. "It's only a few hours, Viola, and with Mistress Coyle gone, the credit for winning this war falls solely to me. I've got plenty of reason to behave, believe me. The convoy may just crown me king."

There's a long pause where everyone looks at one another, considering this.

I have to say that all sounds rather sensible, Ben finally says. *Aside from the king part, obviously.*

And I watch the Mayor as everyone starts talking it thru. He looks right back at me. I expect to see anger.

But all I see is sadness.

And I realize—

He's saying good-bye.

{ V I O L A }

"That Ben's Noise is amazing," Lee says as I help him up on the cart that will take them back to the hilltop. "It's like the whole world in there, and everything is so *clear*."

We decided, after a bit more debate, to go with the Mayor's plan. Bradley, Ben, and I will ride up to the Spackle now. Lee, Wilf, and Mistress Lawson will go to the hilltop to calm things down. Todd and the Mayor will stay in town to hold things together here. And we'll all try to get back together as fast as we can.

Todd says he thinks the Mayor just wants to say goodbye to him in private, now that Ben's come back, and that it would probably be more dangerous for Todd *not* to be there. I still argued against it until Ben agreed with Todd, saying it was the last hours before real peace and whatever good influence Todd had over the Mayor, now was when it would be needed most.

I'm still worried, though.

"He says it's how all the Spackle talk," I say to Lee. "How all the Spackle *are*, how they evolved. To fit the planet perfectly."

"And us not so much?"

"He said we could learn if *he* did."

"And the women?" Lee asks. "What about them?"

"What about the Mayor? He doesn't have Noise anymore."

"Neither does Todd," Lee says, and he's right. The farther Todd gets away from Ben, the quieter he is. And then I see Todd in Lee's Noise, see me and Todd in Todd's tent, see me and Todd–

"Hey!" I say, blushing red. "That didn't happen!"

"Something did," he mumbles. "You were in there for ages."

I don't say anything, just watch Wilf yoke up oxes to the front of the cart and Mistress Lawson fuss over supplies she wants to take back to the hilltop.

"He asked me to go away with him," I say after a long minute.

"When?" Lee asks. "*Where?*"

"When this is all over," I say. "As soon as we can."

"And will you?"

I don't answer.

"He loves you, you idiot," Lee says, not unkindly. "Even a blind man can see that."

"I know," I whisper, looking back over to the campfire, where Todd's saddling up Angharrad for Bradley to ride.

"We're ready," Wilf says, coming over.

I embrace him. "Good luck, Wilf," I say. "I'll see you tomorrow."

"Yoo too, Viola."

I embrace Lee as well, who whispers in my ear, "I'll miss you when you go."

I pull away and even hug Mistress Lawson. "You're looking so healthy," she says. "Like a new girl."

Then Wilf strikes the reins and the cart starts making its way around the ruins of the cathedral, around the lonely bell tower, still standing after all this time.

I watch them until they disappear.

And then a snowflake lands on the tip of my nose.

[TODD]

I'm smiling like a loon as I hold out my hand to catch the flakes as they fall. They land like perfect little crystals before almost instantly melting on my palm, where the skin from my burns is still red.

"First time in years," the Mayor says, looking up like everyone else, into the snow dropping down like white feathers, everywhere and everywhere and everywhere.

462

"Ain't that something?" I say, still smiling. "Hey, Ben!" I start over to where he's introducing Angharrad to his battlemore.

"Wait for a moment, Todd," the Mayor says.

"What?" I say, a little impayshuntly cuz I'd much rather be sharing snow with Ben than the Mayor.

"I think I know what happened to him," the Mayor says and we both look over to Ben again, still talking to Angharrad and the other horses now, too.

"Nothing *happened* to him," I say. "He's still Ben."

"Is he?" the Mayor asks. "He's been opened up by the Spackle. We don't really know what that will do to a man."

I frown and feel a roil in my stomach. It's anger.

But there's a little bit of fear there, too.

"He's fine," I say.

"I say this out of concern for you, Todd," he says, sounding sincere. "I can see how happy you are to have him back. How much it means to have your father again."

I stare at him, trying to figure him out, keeping my own Noise light, so we're just two stones giving nothing away to each other.

Two stones getting slowly covered in snow.

"You think he may be in danger?" I finally say.

"This planet is information," the Mayor says. "All the time, never-ceasing. Information it wants to give you, information it wants to take from you to share with everyone else. And I think you can respond to that in two ways. You can control how much you give it, as you and I have done in shutting off our Noise—"

"Or you can open yourself up to it completely," I say, looking back at Ben, who catches my eye and smiles back.

"And which way is the proper way," the Mayor says, "well, we'll have to see. But I'd keep an eye on your Ben if I were you. For his own good."

"You don't have to worry about that," I say, turning back to him. "I'll be keeping an eye on him the rest of his life."

And I'm smiling as I say it, still warm from Ben's smile to me, but I catch a glint in the eye of the Mayor, brief and vanishing, but there.

And it's a glint of pain.

But then it's gone.

"I hope you'll be around to keep an eye on me, too," he says, his own smile returning. "Keep me on the straight and narrow."

I swallow. "You'll do fine," I say. "With or without me."

And there's the pain again. "Yes," he says. "Yes, I expect I will."

{VIOLA}

"You look like you've rolled in flour," I say down to Todd as he approaches.

"So do you," he says.

I give my head a shake and bits of snow fall down around me. I'm already up on Acorn and I can hear the horses greeting Todd, Angharrad especially, standing underneath Bradley.

She's a beauty, Ben says, next to us on his battlemore. *And I think she's got a little crush.*

Boy colt, Angharrad says, ducking her head at the battlemore and looking away.

"I suggest your first order of business be reassurance," the

Mayor says, coming over. "Tell the Spackle we're more committed to peace than ever. And then see if you can get some demonstrable action from them right away."

"Like the river being released," Bradley says. "I agree. Show the people they've got something to hope for."

"We'll do our best," I say.

"I'm sure you will, Viola," the Mayor says. "You always have."

But I notice he keeps his eyes steady on Todd and Ben as they say their good-byes.

It's only a few hours, I hear Ben say, his Noise bright and warm and reassuring.

"You keep yerself safe," Todd says. "I ain't losing you a third time."

Well, that would just be terrible bad luck, wouldn't it? Ben smiles.

And they embrace, warm and strong, like a father and son.

I keep watching the Mayor's face.

"Good luck," Todd says, coming up to my saddle. He lowers his voice. "You keep thinking bout what I said. You just keep thinking bout the future." He grins shyly. "Now that we actually have one."

"Are you *sure* about this?" I ask. "Because I can stay. Bradley can–"

"I told you," he says. "I think he just wants to say good-bye. That's why it all feels so weird. It's actually over."

"Are you sure you'll be all right?"

"I'll be fine," Todd says. "I've managed all this time with him. I can last a couple more hours."

And we squeeze hands again, holding it a second longer.

"I'll do it, Todd," I whisper. "I'll come with you."

And he doesn't say anything, just squeezes my hand harder and brings it up to his face like he wants to breathe me in.

[TODD]

"The snow's getting thicker," I say.

Viola and Ben and Bradley have been on the road for a little while now and I'm watching the projeckshun as they start up the hill to the Spackle, riding slowly in the weather. Viola said she'd call me when she got there but there ain't no harm in checking their progress, is there?

"The flakes are too big to be much of a worry," says the Mayor. "It's when they're small and coming down like rain that you've got a proper blizzard on the way." He brushes them off his sleeve. "These are just a false promise."

"It's still snow," I say, watching the horses and the battlemore in the distance.

"Come, Todd," the Mayor says. "I need your help."

"My help?"

He gestures around his face. "I may say I have no injuries, but the burn gel makes it easier to believe."

"But Mistress Lawson–"

"Has gone back up to the hilltop," he says. "You can put some on your hands at the same time. It's efficient."

I look down at my hands, starting to sting again as the medicine wears off. "Okay," I say.

We head on over to the scout ship, landed in a corner

of the square not far from us, get ourselves up the ramp and into the room of healing, where the Mayor sets himself down on a bed, takes off his uniform jacket, and folds it next to him. He starts peeling off the bandages from the back of his head and neck.

"You should keep those on," I say. "They're still fresh."

"They're binding," the Mayor says. "I'd like you to put new ones on a little more loosely, please."

I sigh. "Fine." I go to the treatment drawers and take out some burn bandages, as well as a canister of the burn gel for his face. I unpeel the bandage wrappers and tell him to lean forward, placing them loosely on the horrible burned stretch on the back of his head. "This don't look too good," I say, setting the bandage down lightly.

"It'd be worse if you hadn't saved me, Todd." He sighs in relief as the medicine reaches into the burn, moving thru his system. He sits up for the gel, showing me his face, which has a smile on it, a smile that looks almost sad. "Remember when I bandaged you, Todd?" he asks. "All those months ago."

"I ain't likely to be forgetting," I say, spreading the gel on his forehead.

"I think that was the moment we first really understood one another," he says. "Where you saw that maybe I wasn't all bad."

"Maybe," I say, carefully, using two fingers to slop it across his red cheekbones.

"That was the moment where this all really started."

"It started a hell of a lot earlier for *me*."

"And now here you are bandaging me in return," he says.

467

"At the moment where it ends."

I stop, hands still in the air. "Where what ends?"

"Ben's returned, Todd. I'm not ignorant of what that means."

"What does it mean?" I say, looking at him all wary.

He smiles again and this time there's sadness all over it. "I can still read you," he says. "Nobody else can but then nobody else on this whole planet is like me, are they? I can read you even when you're as silent as the black beyond."

I lean back from him.

"You want to go with Ben," he says, shrugging a little. "Perfectly understandable. When this is all over, you want to take Ben and Viola and start a new life away from here." He grimaces a little. "Away from me."

His words ain't threatening; they're actually the good-bye I was expecting, but there's this feeling in the room, this weird feeling–

(and the *hum*–)

(I'm noticing now for the first time–)

(it's completely gone from my head–)

(which is somehow even more frightening than it being there–)

"I ain't yer son," I say.

"You might have been," he says, almost in a whisper. "And what a son you would have made. Someone I could have finally handed over to. Someone with *power* in their Noise."

"I ain't like you," I say. "I ain't never gonna *be* like you."

"No, you won't," he says. "Not with your real father here. Even though our uniforms match, eh, Todd?"

I look down at my uniform. He's right. It's even nearly the same *size* as the Mayor's.

Then he turns his head slightly, looking past me. "You can come out now, Private. I know you're there."

"What?" I say, turning toward the door.

In time to see Ivan step into it. "The ramp was down," he says, looking sheepish. "I was just a-making sure no one was in here who shouldn't be."

"Always seeking where the power is, Private Farrow," the Mayor says, smiling sadly. "Well, I'm afraid it's not in here anymore."

Ivan gives me a nervous glance. "I'll just be a-going, then."

"Yes," says the Mayor. "Yes, I think you finally will."

And he reaches calmly for his uniform jacket, folded nicely on the bed, and me and Ivan just stand there and watch as he reaches inside a pocket, takes out a gun, and without changing the expresshun on his face, shoots Ivan thru the head.

{ V I O L A }

We're right at the top of the hill when we hear it, taking the first steps into the Spackle camp, the Sky and 1017 waiting to greet us.

I turn round in the saddle, looking back toward the city.

"Was that a gunshot?" I say.

[TODD]

"Yer mad," I say, my hands up now, edging toward the door, where Ivan's body is spilling blood everywhere. He didn't move, didn't even flinch when the Mayor raised the gun, didn't do nothing to stop his own death.

And I know why.

"You can't control me," I say. "You can't. I'll fight you and I'll win."

"Will you, Todd?" he says, his voice still low. "Stop right there."

And I stop.

My feet feel like they're frozen to the ground. My hands are still up and I ain't going nowhere.

"All this time, you really believed you had the upper hand?" The Mayor rises from the sickbed, still holding the gun. "That's almost sweet." He laughs, as if fond of the sweetness. "And you know what? You *did*. You did have it. When you were acting like a proper son, I would have done anything you asked, Todd. I saved Viola, I saved this town, I fought for *peace*, all because you asked."

"Back off," I say, but my feet still ain't moving, I still can't get them off the goddam ground.

"And then you saved my *life*, Todd," he says, still coming toward me. "You saved me instead of that woman and I thought, *He's with me. He's really with me. He really is all I've ever wanted in a son.*"

"Let me go," I say, but I can't even put my hands to my ears.

"And then Ben comes to town," he says, a flash of fire in

470

his voice. "Right at the moment when everything was complete. The moment where you and I had the fate of this world in the palm of our hands." He opens his palm as if to show me the fate of the world. "And then it melted away just like the snow."

VIOLA, I think at him, right at his head.

He smiles back. "Not quite as strong as you used to be, are you?" he asks. "Not quite as easy to do when your Noise is silent."

My stomach drops as I realize what he's done.

"Not what *I've* done, Todd," he says, stepping right up to me. "What *you've* done. This is about what *you* have done."

He raises the gun.

"You broke my heart, Todd Hewitt," he says. "You broke a father's heart."

And he slams the butt of the gun against my temple and the world goes black.

The Future Arrives

THE SKY RIDES OVER TO ME through the ice falling gently from the clouds above. It comes down like white leaves, already spreading a blanket of itself across the ground, coating us, too, on the battlemores we still ride.

It is a messenger of things to come, the Sky shows happily. *A sign of a new beginning, the past wiped clean so that we can start a new future.*

Or maybe it is just the weather, I show.

He laughs. *That is exactly how the Sky must think. Is it the future or is it just the weather?*

I ride forward to the lip of the hill, where I can see more clearly the group of three crossing the last empty field before the climb. They are coming *now*, not waiting until tomorrow, eager no doubt for further signs of peace to calm the dissension that is tearing them apart. The Sky already has the Land prepared where we blocked the river, as we know they will ask for it to be released, slowly, letting it resume its natural course.

And we will give it to them. After negotiation, but we will give it to them.

How do you know I will be the Sky? I ask. *You cannot tell the Land who to choose. I have seen it in their voices. The Land comes to an agreement after the Sky has died.*

Correct, the Sky shows, pulling his lichen cloak around him tighter. *But I can see no other choice they would make.*

I am not qualified, I show. *I am still angry with the Clearing, and I cannot kill them, even when they deserve it.*

And do you not think that conflict is what makes the Sky? he shows. *To seek a third choice when the two offered seem impossible? You alone know what it is like to carry that weight. You alone have already made these choices.*

Looking down, I can see now that, in addition to the Source, it is the two of the Clearing who were here before, the noisy man with the darker skin—

And the Knife's one in particular.

And what do you make of the Knife, the Sky asks, *now that you have seen him again in the flesh?*

Because there he was.

Running toward the Source, seeing me but not even slowing, greeting the Source with so much joy, so much love, that I very nearly had to ride away right then. And the Source's voice opened up so wide with the same feelings that it expanded out around everyone nearby.

Including the Return.

And for a moment, I was in that joy, I was inside that love and happiness, inside the reunion and the reconnection, and I saw the Knife again for the flawed Clearing that he was, and as the Source forgave the Knife, as the Source provided absolution for everything the Knife had done—

For everything *Todd* had done—

I felt my voice provide it, too, I felt my voice join with the Source's and offer my own forgiveness, offer to let go and forget every wrong he had done to me, every wrong he had done to our people—

Because I could see through the Source's voice how the Knife punishes himself for his crimes more than I ever could—

He is just one of the Clearing, I show to the Sky. *As unremarkable as any of them.*

He is not, the Sky shows gently. *He is as remarkable among them as the Return is among the Land. And that is why you could not forgive him when you arrived here. That is why your forgiveness of him now, even if only through the voice of the Source—*

I do not forgive him on my own—

But you have seen how it is possible. And that in itself marks you yet again as remarkable.

I do not feel remarkable, I show. *I only feel tired.*

Peace is here at last, the Sky shows, reaching over to place a hand on my shoulder. *You will rest. You will be happy.*

His voice is surrounding me now and I take a breath in surprise—

For the future is in the Sky's voice, a future he rarely speaks of, because it has been so dark lately—

But here it is as bright as the falling flakes of ice—

A future where the Clearing keeps its word and stays within its borders and where the body of the Land that surrounds us now on this hilltop can live unbothered by war—

But one where the Clearing can learn to speak the voice of the Land, too, one where understanding is not only possible, but desired—

A future where I work by the Sky's side, learning what it is to be a leader—

A future where he guides and teaches me—

A future of sunlight and rest—

A future with no more death—

The Sky's hand squeezes my shoulder ever so slightly.

The Return has no father, he shows. *The Sky has no son.*

And I understand what he is saying, what he is asking—

And he sees my indecision—

Because if he was lost to me like my one in particular—

It is one possible future, he shows, warmth still in his voice. *There may be others.* He looks up. *And here one arrives now.*

***

The Source leads them, happiness and optimism in his voice preceding him and greeting us as he crests the hill. The Clearing man is second, "Bradley" in their language, his own voice louder and harsher and much less far-reaching than the Source.

And finally her. The Knife's one in particular.

Viola.

She rides up over the hill, her steed leaving hoofprints in the gathered white of the ice. She looks far healthier than before, almost well, and I wonder for a moment at the change, I wonder if they have found a cure for the band, the one that still stings and burns on my own arm—

But before I can ask, before the Sky can properly greet them, a *crack* resounds over the valley, strangely muffled under the blanket of white.

A *crack* that is unmistakable.

The Knife's one in particular turns around quickly in her saddle.

"Was that a gunshot?" she asks.

A cloud immediately comes over the voice of the Source and the man of the Clearing, too.

And the Sky. *It could be nothing,* he shows.

"When has it ever been nothing in this place?" the man of the Clearing says.

The Source turns to the Sky. *Can our eyes see it?* he asks. *Are we near enough to see?*

"What do you mean?" the man of the Clearing asks. "See what?'

Wait a moment, the Sky says.

The Knife's one in particular is holding a small box she has taken from her pocket. "Todd?" she says into it. "Todd, are you there?"

But there is no answer.

Not before we all hear a familiar sound—

"That's the *ship*!" the man from the Clearing says, spinning his steed round to see the vessel rising from the valley floor.

"Todd!" the Knife's one in particular yells into the metal box—

But again there is no answer.

What is happening? shows the Sky, command in his voice. *We thought the pilot of the ship was killed—*

"She *was*," the man from the Clearing says. "And I'm the only other one who knows how to fly it—"

But there it is, lumbering into the air from the center of their city—

And beginning to fly right toward us—

With increasing speed—

"Todd!" the Knife's one in particular is saying in increasing panic. "Answer me!"

It's Prentiss, the Source shows to the Sky. *It can only be him.*

"But *how*?" the man from the Clearing demands.

It doesn't matter now, the Source shows. *If it's the Mayor—*

We need to run, finishes the Sky, turning to the

Land and sending out the order instantly, run and run and
RUN—

And there is a *whisking* sound from the vessel, the
vessel that is almost upon us, a *whisking* sound that makes
us turn from where we have already started to flee—

The vessel has fired its biggest weapons—

Fired them right at us—

THE END OF
NEW WORLD

THE FINAL BATTLE

[TODD]

"*WAKE UP, TODD,*" says the Mayor's voice over the comm system. *"You'll want to see this."*

I groan and roll over—

And bump into the body of Ivan, streaks of his blood spilling cross the floor as the ship rocks and rolls—

As the ship *rocks*—

I look up at the monitors. We're in the air. We're up in the effing *air*—

"What the *hell*?!" I yell—

The Mayor's face pops up on one of the screens. *"How do you like my flying?"* he says.

"How?" I say, getting to my feet. "How do you know—?'

"The exchange of knowledge, Todd," he says and I see him adjust some controls. *"Did you not listen to anything I told you? Once you're connected to the voice, you know everything it knows."*

"Bradley," I say, realizing. "You reached into him and

took out how to fly the ship."

"*Quite so,*" he says and there's that smile again. "*It's surprisingly easy. Once you know the knack.*"

"Put us down!" I shout. "Put us down right now—"

"*Or you'll do what, Todd?*" he asks. "*You made your choice. Made it perfectly clear.*"

"It ain't about *choosing*! Ben's the only father I ever had—"

Which, as soon as it's outta my mouth, I know is the wrong thing to say cuz the Mayor's eyes go darker than I ever seen 'em, and when he speaks, it's like the black beyond coming down from above and outta his mouth.

"*I was your father, too,*" he says. "*I formed you and taught you and you would not be who you are today if it weren't for me, Todd Hewitt.*"

"I didn't mean to hurt you," I say. "I didn't mean to hurt nobody—"

"*Intentions do not matter, Todd. Only actions. Like this one, for instance—*"

He reaches forward and presses a blue button.

"*Watch now,*" he says—

"No!" I shout—

"*Watch the end of this New World—*"

And in the other screens—

I see two missiles fired outta the side of the scout ship—

Fired right at the top of the hill—

Right where *she* is—

"Viola!" I scream. "VIOLA!"

{Viola}

There's no place to run, nowhere we can possibly get away from the missiles *whooshing* toward us at impossible speed, streaks of steam through the falling snow–

Todd, I have a split second to think–

And then they hit with two huge *cracks* and the Spackle Noise screams and debris flies into the air–

And–

And–

And we're still here–

No waves of heat and death, no top of the hill obliterated with us still standing on it–

What happened? Ben asks as we all lift our heads again.

There's a gash in the riverbed and some smoke from where the missile hit but–

"It didn't explode," I say.

"Nor that one," Bradley says, pointing to the hillside, where a streak of brush and shrubs has been torn out but where you can also see the casing from the missile broken up into pieces.

Broken up by the impact with the rock, *not* by an explosion.

"They can't be duds," I say, "not both of them." I look at Bradley and feel a rush of excitement. "You disconnected the warheads!"

"Not me," he says, looking back up to the scout ship, hovering there, the Mayor no doubt wondering as much as we are how we're all still standing here. "Simone," Bradley says.

He looks back at me. "We never quite got over me having Noise and I thought she was too close to Mistress Coyle, but . . ." He looks back up at the scout ship. "She must have seen the potential harm." I can see his Noise choking up. "She saved us."

The Sky and 1017 are watching, too, and you can hear their surprise that the missiles didn't kill everyone.

Are those the only weapons on the ship? Ben asks.

I look back up and the scout ship is already turning in the air–

"The hoopers," I say, remembering–

[TODD]

"What the HELL?" the Mayor growls–

But I'm watching the screens that show the hilltop–

Where the missiles ain't exploded–

They just crashed and that was that, causing no more damage than throwing a really big rock–

"Todd!" the Mayor shouts into the camera. *"What do you know of this?"*

"You fired at *VIOLA!*" I shout back. "Yer life ain't worth nothing, you hear me? NOTHING!"

He makes another growling sound and I run to the door of the healing room but of course it's locked and then the whole floor lurches back as he powers the ship forward. I fall into the beds, slipping on Ivan's blood, trying to keep my eyes on the screens, trying to see her anywhere on the hilltop–

And with one hand I'm patting my pockets down for the comm but of course he took that–

But then I start looking round the room cuz Simone used to talk to us from the ship, didn't she? And if the comm system comes down here from the cockpit, maybe it can go *outta* here as well–

I hear two more *whooshing* sounds–

In the screens, two more missiles are headed for the hilltop, at closer range this time, and they both slam hard into the crowds of Spackle fleeing down the riverbed–

But still no proper explozhuns–

"Very well, then," I hear the Mayor say in that measured way that means he's *really* angry.

And we're flying right over the top of the Spackle–

And god*dam* if there ain't a lot of 'em–

How in the living hell did we ever think we could fight an army that big?

"I do believe there's another class of weapon on this ship," the Mayor says–

And the screens show a view from above as the cluster bombs drop onto the fleeing Spackle–

Drop and fall and not explode neither–

"DAMMIT!" I hear the Mayor yell–

I lurch over to the comm panel where the Mayor's voice is coming out. I touch the screen beside it and a whole list of words pops up–

"So be it," seethes the Mayor on the screen behind me. *"We'll just have to do things the old-fashioned way."*

And I'm looking at the words on the screen and I'm forcing my concentrayshun on 'em, forcing everything the Mayor taught me–

And slowly, slowly, slowly, they start to make sense–

"We wanted peace!" Bradley shouts at the Sky, as we watch the hoopers fall with almost no effect except for the poor Spackle just beneath them. "This is the action of one man!"

But the Sky's Noise has no words, just *anger,* anger that he's been duped, anger that his position is weak because he's proposed peace, anger that we've betrayed him.

"We haven't!" I shout. "He's trying to kill us, too!"

And my heart's beating out of my chest worrying what the Mayor's done to Todd–

"Can you help us?" Bradley says to the Sky. "Can you help us stop him?"

The Sky looks over to him, surprised. The Spackle behind him still run but the trees on the riverbanks are starting to disguise their numbers as they flee the scout ship, which has stopped dropping the disarmed hoopers and is hovering ominously in the still-falling snow.

"Your burning fire-bolt things," I say. "Those things you shoot from the bows."

Would they work against an armored vessel? The Sky asks.

"In large enough numbers, maybe," Bradley says. "While the ship's still low enough to be hit."

The ship is turning now, still hovering at the same height, and we hear a change to the pitch of its engines.

Bradley looks up sharply.

"What is it?" I say.

Bradley shakes his head. "He's changing the fuel mixture," he says and his Noise cranks up, confused but alarmed, as if it's remembering something just a little out of reach–

"He's the last obstacle to peace here," I say to the Sky. "If we can stop *him*–"

Then someone else will pop up in his place, says the Sky. *That has always been the evil of the Clearing.*

"Then we'll just have to work that much *harder!*" I say. "If we managed to get this far against the man in that ship, don't you think that at least shows how much it means to *some* of us?"

The Sky looks back up and I can see the rumblings of agreement there, rumblings that what I say is true against the other truth of the ship hanging in the air–

And of the ships to come–

The Sky turns to 1017. *Send a message along the Pathways,* he says. *Order the weapons to be prepared.*

(1 0 1 7)

Me? I show.

The Land will need to learn to listen to you, the Sky shows. *They can begin right now.*

And he opens his voice to me and I am sending out his orders in the language of the Land almost before I know I am doing it–

I let it flow through me, as if I am merely a channel–

Flow through me and out into the Pathways, into the soldiers and the Land waiting around us, and it is not my voice, not even the Sky's voice nearby speaking through me, but a voice of the bigger Sky, the Sky that exists apart from whatever individual goes by the name, the Sky which is the agreement of the Land, the accumulated voice of all of us, the voice of the Land speaking to itself, the voice that keeps it alive and safe and ready to face the future, it is *that* which speaks through me—

That is the voice of the Sky—

And it urges the soldiers to battle, urges the rest of the Land to fight as well, to gather the spinning fire and the weapons on the backs of the battlemores in our hour of need—

It's working, the Source shows to the people from the Clearing. *Help is coming*—

And then there is a hissing sound from above and we all look up—

To see a waterfall of fire pouring out of the engines of the vessel—

Pouring down like blood from a wound, smoke and steam billowing around it in the cold air, pouring down onto the Land and setting it ablaze and as the vessel starts to fly a wide circle around us, the fire roars up from the ground in walls, burning everything that can burn, trees, secreted huts, the Land, the world—

"Rocket fuel," the man from the Clearing says.

"He's trapping us here," the Knife's one in particular says, spinning round on her beast, which calls out in alarm at the flames that face us on all sides.

The vessel rises higher in the air, its circle arcing wider, the fire still pouring out of it—

He's destroying everything, the Source says. *He's setting the whole valley ablaze.*

[TODD]

The ship pitches this way and that and I can hardly stand up straight in front of the comm panel.

And on the screens, there's fire everywhere–

"What're you *DOING*?" I shout, trying not to panic as I sweat thru the words on the panel–

"Old pilot's trick that Bradley forgot his grandfather taught him," the Mayor says. *"You change the mixture of the fuel, oxygenate it, and it just burns and burns and burns."*

I look up and see us higher in the sky, swooping across the rim of the upper valley, circling round and pouring the rain of fire down onto the trees below, and the fire is sticky and super-hot, kinda like the Spackle fire bolts, and even tho there's snow coming down, the trees are just *exploding* in the heat, catching other trees, the fire just *zooming* thru 'em, faster than the Spackle can run, and the screens show a massively expanding band of flames following us as we fly, circling the valley, trapping 'em inside–

He's setting the whole world on fire.

I look back at the comm screen. There's a bunch of boxes I could press but I'm still trying to read the top one. *Rekent,* I think it says. *Rekent Comms.* I breathe in, close my eyes, try to lighten my Noise, try to feel it like when the Mayor was in there–

"Watch as the world burns, Todd," the Mayor says. *"Watch as the last war begins."*

Recent Comms. That's what it says, *Recent.*

I press it.

"Todd?" the Mayor says. *"Are you watching?"*

491

I look up at his face on the screen. I realize he can't see me. I look back to the comm box. There's a red circle on the bottom right saying *Visuals Off*.

Which I read first time thru.

"You don't care who wins, do you?" I say. He's flying a wide circle round New Prentisstown now, soaking the forests to the south *and* the north in a fire that can't help but eventually reach the city. I can already see an arm of it shooting thru a row of outlying houses.

"You know, Todd?" he says. *"I find that I really don't care, no. Isn't that something? Just so it's over. Just so that it's all finally over."*

"It coulda *been* over," I say. "It coulda been peace."

The comm screen is now a list of the *Recent Comms* I guess and I'm working my way down it—

"We could have made peace together, Todd," the Mayor says. *"But you decided that wasn't for you."*

Comm, I read, *comm, commoony, communicay—*

"For which I must thank you," he says. *"For returning me to my true purpose."*

Communicaytor 1. Communicator 1. That's what it says, *Communicator 1.* The whole thing's a list of communicators. Going down from 1 to 6, tho not in order. 1's at the top, then 3 (I *think* it's 3), then 2 maybe, then whatever the others are—

"You said you were transformed," I say, sweating as I look at the panel. "You said you were a different man."

"I was wrong. Men can't be transformed. I will always be who I am. And you'll always be Todd Hewitt, the boy who can't kill."

"Yeah, well," I say, with feeling. "People change."

The Mayor laughs. *"Have you not been listening? They don't change, Todd. They do not change."*

The ship lurches again as he makes another pass, torching the world below us. I'm still sweating over the comm panel. I don't know which number is Viola's but if these are recent and in order then she must be 1 or 3 cuz–

"What are you up to in there, Todd?" the Mayor says.

And the comm panel goes blank.

{Viola}

The scout ship's hardly visible now through the smoke that's rising everywhere. We're safe so far in the middle of the rocky riverbed, but there's no way to get out with fires all around. The Mayor's flown around the whole valley, which is burning so bright it's difficult to look at directly–

*How can there be so **much** of it?* Ben asks as we watch the fire rage through the forests, spreading almost impossibly fast.

"A few drops of it was enough to blow up a bridge," I say. "Imagine what a whole shipful can do."

Can you not contact the vessel? the Sky asks me.

I hold up my comm. "No answer," I say. "I keep trying."

Then, as the vessel is out of reach of our weapons, the Sky says, his Noise resolving into a decision, *there is only one course of action.*

We all stare at him for a moment as we realize what he means.

"The river," I say.

493

And there's a roar in the air that makes us turn–

"He's coming back round!" Bradley yells–

And we see, in a parting of the smoke, the scout ship flying up over the lip of the hill, screaming out of the sky like judgment–

Coming straight for us–

[TODD]

The screens are nothing but fire now, fire everywhere, ringing the valley, ringing New Prentisstown, blazing on the hilltop where Viola still is, somewhere in all that burning–

"I'll kill you!" I shout. "You hear me? I'll KILL YOU!"

"*I should finally hope so, Todd,*" the Mayor says, a weird smile on his face in the screen he's left up of himself. "*You've waited long enough.*"

But I'm already looking round for some other way to contact Viola (please please please). The comm panel won't come back on but I swear I saw Mistress Lawson doing something on one of the screens by the healing beds. I go over and press one.

It lights up at my touch with a whirl of words.

And one of 'em begins with *Comm*.

"*I should probably tell you what'll happen next, Todd,*" the Mayor says. "*It's important that you know.*"

"Shut up!" I say, pressing the *Comm* box on the screen. Up pops another set of boxes and a whole lot of 'em begin with *comm* this time. I take a deep breath and try to make my Noise into its reading shape. If the Mayor can steal learning, then so can I.

"I've ordered Captain O'Hare to lead a small force into battle with the Spackle that will inevitably attack the city," the Mayor continues. "A suicide mission obviously, but then Captain O'Hare always was expendable."

Communicayteeons Hoob, I read. I squint and breathe again. Please please please. *Communicayteeons Hoob.* I ain't got no idea what it means so I breathe deep a third time and close my eyes (*I am the Circle and the Circle is me*). I open 'em again. *Communications Hub.* There it is, that's what it says. I press it.

"Captain Tate will already be leading the rest of the army to the Answer on the hilltop," the Mayor rattles on, "to dispose of the remnants of the rebellion—"

I look up. "What?"

"Well, we can't go around risking me being blown up by terrorists, can we?" he says.

"You effing *monster!*"

"And then Captain Tate will be leading the army to the ocean."

I *really* look up at this. "The ocean?"

"Where we will make our last stand, Todd," the Mayor says and I can see him grinning. "The ocean at our backs, the enemy at our fronts. What better war could you ask for? Nothing to do but fight and die."

I look back at the comm screen.

And there it is. *Recent Comms.* I press it. More boxes pop up.

"But it has to start with the death of the leader of the Spackle," the Mayor's saying. "And I'm sorry to say that also means all who are near him."

495

I look up again. We're right near the lip of the hill, flying up over it and down the dry riverbed toward the fleeing Spackle—

Toward Viola—

Who I can see on the screens now—

See that she's still riding Acorn, Bradley and Ben next to her, the Spackle leader behind 'em, urging 'em all to run—

"NO!" I scream. *"NO!"*

"I'll be sorry to lose her," the Mayor says as we bear down on 'em, fire trailing out behind us. *"Less sorry to lose Ben, if I'm honest."*

I press the top button on the comm screen, the one that says *Communicator 1,* and I scream "VIOLA!" into it, my voice breaking with the volume, *"VIOLA!"*

But in the screens, we're already over the top of 'em—

(1 0 1 7)

The Sky turns his battlemore hard, corralling the beasts of the Clearing to the side, pushing them out of the path of the vessel, toward trees that are burning on the riverbank—

But the beasts of the Clearing are resisting—

Fire, I can hear them call wildly, *Fire!*

The vessel is coming! I show, not just at the Sky but at the Land around me, radiating the warning in all directions and I am pulling my own beast back toward the burning trees, where there is a small space we might use as cover—

GO! I hear from the Sky, and my battlemore responds, whirling round toward the fire as the beasts of the Clearing do the same, and here come the Source, the man from the

Clearing, and the Knife's one in particular—

Ben and Bradley and Viola—

Their beasts racing toward me now, toward the small space in the burning trees, where we will not be able to stay for long but which might just avoid the vessel still screaming down—

And all around us the Land's fear courses through me, their terror, their *deaths,* and I feel more than just the ones I can see, the ones running by my charging battlemore, I can feel them *all.* I feel the soldiers remaining to the north of the valley and the soldiers to the south, trying to save themselves in a forest where every tree blazes, where the fire keeps leaping from branch to branch, even in the falling ice, leaping faster than many of them can run and I feel the Land up the river, too, away from this inferno, watching it roar up the valley toward them, overtaking some of those who flee, and I see it all, too, see through the eyes of every Land—

I see the eyes of this planet, watching itself burn—

And *I* burn, too—

"HURRY!" I hear the Knife's one in particular shout and I turn again and I see she is screaming for the Sky, whose battlemore has fallen a step or two behind as the Sky sends out orders to the Land to save themselves—

The vessel flies directly overhead—

Raining fire down the riverbed—

And the Sky's eyes meet mine—

They meet mine across the smoke and fire and falling ice—

No, I show—

No!

And he disappears in a wall of flame—

{Viola}

The horses leap forward as the wall of flame WHOOSHES up the riverbed behind us—

And there's hardly anywhere to get away from it, the trees in front of us are ablaze and the rocks on the hillside above are somehow burning, too, even the snowflakes are evaporating in midair, leaving little wisps of steam where they were hanging, and we're away from the first attack but if he comes back, there's nowhere to go, there's nowhere at all to go—

"Viola!" Bradley yells, bumping Angharrad into Acorn and they greet each other with terrified whinnies—

"How do we get out of here?!" I say, coughing in the smoke, and I turn to see a thirty-foot wall of fire burning down the dry riverbed where we were just standing—

"Where's the Sky?" Bradley says.

We turn to look at Ben and I realize for the first time that we can't hear his Noise, that's it's focused away from us, that all the Spackle nearby have stopped as well, as if frozen, a sight beyond eerie in the middle of an inferno, even though there's nowhere to run—

"Ben?" I say—

But he's staring at the wall of flame down the riverbed—

And then we hear it—

A tearing sound, like the air being ripped in two, approaching from behind us—

1017—

Off his battlemore and on foot–

Racing toward the flames, which are already decreasing on the bare rocks–

Leaving burning piles of ash–

Like on the battlefield before when the Spackle shot the fire bolts–

Except this time it's just two–

1017 races for them, his Noise making a sound more horrible, more full of rage and grief than anything I've ever heard in my entire life–

As he rushes toward the blackened corpses of the Sky and his battlemore–

(1 0 1 7)

I run–

No thought in my head–

No sound in my voice except a wail I can barely hear myself–

A wail demanding that it be taken back–

A wail refusing to believe what I have seen, refusing to accept what has happened–

I am only vaguely aware of the Clearing and the Source as I run by them–

Vaguely aware of the *roar* forming in my ears, in my head, in my heart–

In my voice–

The rocks in the riverbed still burn but the fire is lifting off them even as I approach, so this attack was a waste in terms of setting more things ablaze–

But not a waste because it clearly had a single target—

I plunge into the flames, feeling them blister my skin, some of the rocks blazing red as coals—

But I do not care—

I reach where the Sky was riding his beast—

Reach where he has fallen to the stones—

Where he and the beast still burn—

And I am beating at the flames, trying to put them out with my bare hands, the wail getting louder, reaching beyond me, out of me, out into the world, out into the Land, trying to erase everything that has happened—

And I grab under the Sky's burning arms and pull him from his burning steed—

And I show it out loud, *No!*

And my skin is burning on the rocks, my own lichen smoldering from the heat—

NO!

But he is a dead weight in my hands—

And—

And—

And then I *hear* him—

And I freeze—

I cannot move at all—

The Sky's body is in my hands—

But his voice—

Removed from his body—

Hanging in the air as he leaves his body behind—

But pointed at me—

Showing—

The Sky—

He shows to me, *The Sky*—
And then he is gone—
And in the next instant, I hear them—
I hear the voices of all the Land—
Every one of them frozen—
Frozen though some of us burn—
Frozen though some of us die—
Frozen like I am, holding the body of the Sky—
Except it is no longer the body of the Sky—
The Sky, I hear—
And it is the Land speaking now—
The Land's voice, twining together as one—
The Sky is the voice of the Land and for a moment it
was cut off, freed from itself, lost and out in the world,
without a mouth to speak it—
But only for a moment—
The Sky, I hear—
And it is the Land—
Speaking to me—
Their voice entering me—
Their *knowledge* entering me, the knowledge of all
the Land, of all the Skies that have ever been—
Their language entering me in a rush, too, in a way
I see now that I have always resisted, always *wanting* to
keep myself apart, but in an instant I know it all—
I know them all—
I know *us* all—
And I know it was him—
He passed it on to me—
The Sky is chosen by the Land—

But in times of war, there must be no delay—

The Sky, he told the Land as he died—

And *The Sky,* the Land says into me—

And I answer back—

I answer back, *The Land*—

And I rise, leaving the old Sky behind, leaving my grief to wait—

Because the burden falls to me *immediately*—

The Land is in peril—

And the good of the Land *must* be the thing that comes first—

And so there is only one thing to do—

I turn back to the Land, back to the Source, who is calling me *The Sky,* too, back to the man from the Clearing and the Knife's one in particular, all eyes on me, all voices on me—

And I am the Sky—

And I speak the language of the Land—

(but my own voice is there, too—)

(my own voice, full of *rage*—)

And I tell the Land to release the river—

All of it at once—

{VIOLA}

"It'll destroy the town!" Bradley says before Ben even tells us what's happening-

Because we could see it in the Noise all around us, see 1017 telling them to release the river-

"There are still innocent people down there," Bradley

says. "The force of a river pent up this long will wipe them off the planet!"

It's already done, Ben says. *The Sky has spoken and it's already started—*

"The Sky?" I say–

The new Sky, he says and looks behind us–

We turn. 1017 is walking forward out of the shimmering haze over the hot rocks of the riverbed, a look in his eye different from before.

"*He's* the new Sky?" Bradley asks.

"Oh, shit," I say.

I can talk to him, Ben says. *I'll try to help him see the right thing but I can't stop the river from coming—*

"We have to warn the town," Bradley says. "How much time do we have?"

Ben's eyes unfocus for a moment and in his Noise we see the Spackle dams holding back an impossible amount of water, backed up on the plain where Todd and I once saw that herd of creatures calling **Here** to one another, stretched horizon to horizon, now filled with water, a whole inland *sea* of it. *It's way back,* Ben says, *and there's work to do to release it.* He blinks. *Twenty minutes, if that.*

"That's not enough!" Bradley says.

That's what you've got, Ben says.

"Ben–" I say.

Todd's up there, Ben says, looking into my eyes, his Noise feeling like it's going right into me and I can hear it in a way I've never heard from a man on this planet. *Todd's up there and still fighting for you, Viola.*

"How do you know?"

I can hear his voice, Ben says.

"What?"

Not clearly, Ben says, sounding as surprised as I am, *not anything specific, but I could feel him up there. I could feel **everyone** as we chose the Sky.* His eyes widen. *And I heard Todd. I heard him fighting for you.* He rides closer on his battlemore. *You have to fight for **him**.*

"But the Spackle are dying," I say. "And the people in town–"

If you fight for him, you fight for us all.

"But war can't be personal," I say, almost asking it–

If it's the person who'll end the war, Ben says, *then that's not personal; it's universal.*

"We need to go," Bradley says. "Right now!"

I take a last second and nod at Ben and then we're turning the horses around to try and find a safe path through the fire–

And see 1017 standing in our way.

"Let us go," Bradley says. "The man in the ship is the enemy of us both. He's the enemy of every creature on this planet."

And as if on cue, we can hear the roar of the scout ship coming back this way, ready for another pass–

"Please," I beg.

But 1017's keeping us right there–

And I can see us in his Noise–

See us *dying* in his Noise–

No, Ben says, riding forward. *There's no time for*

revenge. *You must get the Land out of the way of the river—*

But we can see the fight in 1017, see his Noise twist this way and that, wishing revenge but wishing to save his people, too—

"Wait," I say, because I'm remembering—

I pull up my sleeve, exposing the band, pink and healing and no longer killing me, but there forever—

I feel the surprise in 1017's Noise but he still doesn't move—

"I hate the man who killed your Sky as much as you do," I say. "I'll do *everything* I can to stop him."

He watches us for a moment longer, the fires still raging around us, the scout ship still coming back down the valley—

Go, he says. *Before the Sky changes his mind.*

[T O D D]

"VIOLA!" I scream but still no answer on Communicator 1 or Communicator 3 as I feel the floor pitch below me. I look up at the screens and see us coming round after having left a scorching fire down the riverbed—

But there's too much smoke and I can't see her or Ben—

(please please please—)

"Look at the Spackle, Todd," the Mayor says over the comm, sounding intrigued. *"They're not even running."*

I'll kill him, I'll effing *kill* him—

And then I think, stopping him is something I *want*. It's something I *desire* more than anything and if it's all about desire—

Stop the attack, I think, concentrating hard thru the rocking and rolling of the ship, trying to find him up there in the cockpit. *Stop the attack and land the ship.*

"Is that you I feel knocking on my door, Todd?" The Mayor laughs.

And there's a flash in the middle of my head, a flash of white burning pain and the words he's used since the beginning, YER NOTHING YER NOTHING YER NOTHING and I stagger back, my eyes blurry, my thoughts a mess–

"And you didn't need to try anyway," the Mayor says. *"It looks as if our Viola has survived."*

I blink at the screens and see us flying toward two figures on horseback, one of 'em Viola–

(thank god thank god–)

Riding toward the lip of the hill in full fury, avoiding fire where they can, jumping thru it where they can't–

"Don't worry, Todd," the Mayor says. *"My work here is done. If I'm not mistaken, the river will be on its way and we shall await our fates at the ocean shore."*

I'm still breathing heavy but I stumble back to the comm panel.

Maybe *my* comm was Communicator 1 but it was Mistress Coyle who was number 3–

I reach up and press Communicator 2.

"Viola?" I say.

And on the screen where I can see her, all small and tiny on Acorn's back as they reach the lip of the burning hill and fly right over to the jagged path below–

I see her flinch in surprise, see her and Acorn stumble to a halt, see her reach in her cloak–

506

"Todd?" I hear, clear as anything–

"What was that?" I hear the Mayor say–

But I'm still pressing the button–

"The ocean, Viola!" I yell. "We're going to the ocean!"

And I'm hit with another blast of Noise–

{VIOLA}

"The ocean?" I yell back into the comm. "Todd? What do you mean–?"

"Look!" Bradley calls, a little farther down the wrecked zigzag road on Angharrad. He's pointing at the scout ship–

Which is hurtling through the valley away from us, heading east–

Heading toward the ocean–

"Todd?" I say again, but there's no response from the comm. *"Todd!?"*

"Viola, we have to *go*," Bradley says and gees Angharrad back down the hill. There's still no sound from the comm but Bradley's right. There's a wall of water coming and we've got to warn who we can–

Even though I know as Acorn charges down the hill once more that there are probably going to be very few lives we can save–

Maybe not even our own–

[TODD]

I groan and pick myself up from the floor, where I fell on Ivan's body. I glance back up at the screens but I don't reckernize nothing now, don't even see no fires, just green trees and hills below us—

So we're on our way to the ocean—

For the end of it all—

I wipe Ivan's blood off on my coat, the stupid uniform coat that matches the Mayor's exactly, and even the thought of us looking the same fills me with shame—

"Ever seen an ocean, Todd?" he asks.

And I can't help but look—

Cuz there it is—

The ocean—

And for a second, I can't take my eyes off it—

Filling all of the screens at once, filling 'em and filling 'em and filling 'em, a stretch of water so huge it ain't got no end, just the beach at the start, covered in sand and snow, and then water forever and ever into the cloudy horizon—

It makes me so dizzy I gotta look away—

I go back to the comm screen where I got thru for a second to Viola but of course it's off, the Mayor shutting down anything and everything I might use to talk to her.

It's just me and him now, flying to the ocean—

Just me and him for the final reckoning—

He went after Viola. He went after Ben. If the fire didn't kill 'em, the flood might, and so yeah, we'll have an effing reckoning—

Yes, we will—

And I start thinking her name. I start thinking her name good and hard, to practice it, to warm it up in my mind, in my *Noise*—

Feeling my anger, feeling my worry for her—

508

He may have made it harder to fight by making my Noise quiet, but if he can still punch with his Noise, then so can I—

Viola, I think.

VIOLA—

(THE SKY)

I must send the Land through fire to save it. I must send them climbing up the burning hills of the valley, through trees that blaze, through secreted huts that collapse and explode. I must send them through great peril to escape an even greater peril now rushing down the riverbed—

A greater peril that *I* set on them—

A greater peril that *the Sky* deemed necessary—

Because these are the choices of the Sky, these are the choices the Sky has to make for the good of the Land. Huge numbers of us would burn to death if we let the fire keep raging through the forest, huge numbers of us might still burn to death as we make our escape—

But at least if the second option happens, we will take many hundreds of the Clearing with us—

No, I hear the Source show, clambering up the steep hill behind me. We are on our battlemores, trying to find a way through the burning to get far enough above the riverbed before the water hits. The battlemores are suffering as we go but we have to press on, hoping their armor will save them.

The Sky can't think that way, the Source shows. *War against the Clearing will only destroy the Land. Peace must still be possible.*

I turn to him from where I stand in my saddle, looking down to where he sits on his, like a *man* does. **Peace?** I show, outraged. *You expect* **peace** *after what they've done?*

After what **one** *of them has done,* the Source shows. *Peace is not only possible; it's* **vital** *to our future.*

Our *future?*

He ignores this. *The only alternative is complete mutual destruction.*

And the problem with that would be what?

But his own voice is already glowing with anger. *That's not something the Sky would ask.*

And what do you know of the Sky? I show. *What do you know of any of us? You have spoken in our voice for a fraction of your life. You are not us. You will never be us.*

As long as there is an us and them, he shows back, *the Land will never be safe.*

I make to answer but the voice of the Land calls down from the valley to the west, warning us. Our steeds begin to climb even faster. I look up the valley, through the flakes of ice still falling, through the fires that burn on either side, the smoke that rises into the clouds above—

And down the riverbed comes a bank of steaming fog, racing ahead of the river like the whistle before an arrow—

Here it comes, I show.

The fog rushes by us and up, coating the world in white.

I give the Source one last look—

And then I open my voice—

I open it to all the Land that can hear it, seeking out

Pathways to pass it on, until I know that I am speaking to *all* Land, everywhere—

And I hear it, the echoes of the first command I sent, the command to gather weapons—

Sitting there as if a destiny to be fulfilled—

I seize on it in the voice and send it again, send it farther and wider than before—

Prepare yourselves, I tell the Land.

Prepare yourselves for war—

NO! the Source shouts again—

But his words are lost as water as tall as a city crashes through the valley below us, swallowing everything in its path—

{V I O L A}

We pound up the road into town, Acorn running so fast I can barely keep hold of his mane—

Girl colt hang on, Acorn says and manages to speed up even more—

Bradley's up ahead of me on Angharrad, the falling snow whipping around us as we cut through it. We're rapidly nearing the outskirts of town, where the road meets the first houses—

What the hell—? I hear Bradley yell in his Noise—

There's a small group of men marching down the road. They're in formation, led by Captain O'Hare, weapons raised and apprehension rising through their Noise like the smoke billowing up on the north and south horizons.

"TURN BACK!" Bradley yells as we get closer to them. "YOU'VE GOT TO TURN BACK!"

Captain O'Hare stops, his Noise puzzled, the men behind him stopping, too. We reach them, the horses skidding to a halt–

"There's a Spackle attack coming," Captain O'Hare says. "I've got orders–"

"They've released the river!" I shout.

"You've got to get to higher ground!" Bradley says. "You've got to tell the townsfolk–"

"Most of them have left already," Captain O'Hare says, his Noise rising red. "They're following the army up the road at full fast march."

"They're doing *what*?" I say.

But Captain O'Hare's looking angrier and angrier. "He knew," he says. "He *knew* this was suicide."

"Why is everyone else marching up the road?" I demand.

"They're going to the mistresses' hilltop," Captain O'Hare says, bitterness in his voice. "To *secure* it."

And we see in a flash of his Noise just what *secure* means.

I think of Lee on that hilltop. I think of Lee unable to see.

"Bradley!" I shout, slapping Acorn's reins again.

"Get your men to higher ground!" Bradley shouts as we ride around the soldiers and back down the road. "Save as many people as you can!"

But then we hear the *roar*–

Not the ROAR of the Noise of a group of men–

The *roar* and *crash* of the river–

We look back–

To see an impossibly massive wall of water obliterate the top of the hill–

[TODD]

The screens change. The ocean disappears and up pop the probes from the town. The Mayor's got one of 'em pointed right at the empty waterfall–

"Here it comes, Todd," he says–

"Viola?" I whisper frantically, trying to find her in the screens, trying desperately to see if any of the probes are watching her ride thru the city–

But I don't see nothing–

Don't see nothing but the huge wall of water come shooting out over the hilltop, pushing a town-sized cloud of fog and steam before it–

"Viola," I whisper again–

"Here she is," the Mayor's voice says–

And he switches to a probe view that's her and Bradley on their horses, racing for their lives up the road thru town–

And there are people running, too, but there ain't no way under heaven they're gonna outrun the water smashing into the bottom of the falls and flinging its way forward, thru clouds of steam and fog–

A wave heading right for the city–

"Faster, Viola," I whisper, pressing my face close to the screen. *"Faster."*

{ VIOLA }

"Faster!" Bradley calls ahead of me–

But I can barely hear him–

The *roar* of the water behind us is literally deafening–

"FASTER!" Bradley screams again, looking back–

I look back, too–

Holy God–

It's almost a solid thing, a solid white wall of raging water, higher than the highest building in New Prentisstown, smashing into the river valley, obliterating the battlefield at the bottom of the hill instantly and *roaring* forward, eating everything in the way–

"Come ON!" I shout to Acorn. *"COME ON!"*

And I can feel the terror coursing through him. He knows exactly what's coming after us, what's blasting the first houses of New Prentisstown to splinters and no doubt Captain O'Hare and all his men, too–

And there are other people running, screaming out of houses and running for the hills to the south, but they're too far away, much too far to reach on foot, and all these people are going to die–

I turn away, spurring Acorn again with my ankles out of pure fright. His mouth is spitting foam from the effort–

"Come on, boy," I say between his ears. "Come *on!*"

But he doesn't answer me, just runs and runs and we're through the square and past the cathedral and onto the road out of town and I sneak another look behind me and see the wall of water smash through the buildings at the far edge of the square–

"We're not going to make it!" I yell to Bradley–

He looks at me and then back behind me–

And his face tells me I'm right–

[TODD]

Outta the corner of my eye, I see a screen showing that we're landing on the shore and there's snow and sand and endless water, waves crashing in and dark shadows moving thru 'em just under the surface–

But my attenshun is on the probe following Viola and Bradley–

Following 'em as they ride thru the square, thru the people left behind, past the cathedral and onto the road outta town–

But the water's too fast, too high, too powerful–

They ain't gonna make it–

"No," I say, my heart just ripping in my chest. "Come on! *Come on!*"

And the wall of water slams into the ruins of the cathedral, finally knocking over the bell tower that stood on its own–

It disappears in a flash of water and brick–

And I'm realizing something–

The water's slowing–

As it tears thru New Prentisstown, as it *erases* New Prentisstown, all the junk and the buildings are slowing it down, just a little, just a bit, making the wall of water a little bit shorter, a little bit slower–

"But not nearly enough," the Mayor says–

And he's in the room behind me–

I whirl round to face him–

"I'm sorry that she'll die, Todd," he says. "I truly am."

And I hit him with a **VIOLA** that's packed with everything I got–

"No," I feel myself whispering as New Prentisstown is torn to pieces behind us, as the wall of water is now filled with timber and brick and trees and who knows how many bodies–

And I'm looking back–

And it's slowing down–

Choking some on all the debris–

But not enough–

It's reached the stretch of road just behind us, still coming quick, still coming full and hard and brutal–

Todd, I think–

"Viola!" Bradley calls back to me, his face twisted–

And there's no way–

There's just no way–

Girl colt, I hear–

"Acorn?"

Girl colt, he says, his Noise ragged with the force he's putting out–

Angharrad, too, I can hear her ahead–

Follow! she says–

"What do you mean, *follow*?" I say, alarmed, looking back at the water not a hundred yards behind us–

Ninety–

Girl colt, Acorn says again.

"Bradley?" I call but I see him gripping Angharrad's mane tight just as I'm grabbing Acorn's–

And **Follow!** she bellows again–

Follow! Acorn answers–

HOLD! they yell together–

And I'm nearly knocked off his back by an impossible burst of speed–

A burst of speed that can only be tearing the muscles in his legs, that can only be bursting his lungs–

But we're doing it–

I look back–

We're outrunning the flood–

[TODD]

VIOLA! I think right at him–

Hitting him with all the rage that she's in so much danger, all the rage that I don't know what's happened to her, all the rage that she might be–

All *that* rage–

VIOLA!

And the Mayor flinches and rocks back on his heels–

But doesn't fall–

"I told you you've gotten stronger, Todd," he says, steadying himself and giving me a smile. "Not strong enough, though."

And there's a flash of Noise in my head so hard I fall back over a bed and crumple to the floor, the world reduced to nothing but the Noise echoing thru me, YER NOTHING YER NOTHING YER NOTHING and everything shrinks to just that sound–

But then I think *Viola*–

I think of her out there–

And I push it back–

I feel my hands on the floor–

I use them to rise to my knees—

I lift my head—

To see the Mayor's surprised face only a yard or so away, coming toward me, something in his hand—

"Goodness," he says, sounding almost cheerful. "Even stronger than I thought."

And I know another blast's coming so I do it the old-fashioned way before he can gather himself—

I jump at him, pushing hard with my feet and leaping out—

He ain't expecting it and I hit him about waist-height, knocking us back into the screens—

(where the river's still shooting down the valley—)

(where Viola ain't nowhere to be seen—)

And he slams into 'em with a grunt, my weight against him, and I pull back my fist to punch him—

And there's a light tap on my neck—

Just light as a touch—

And there's something sticking to me and I put my hand to it—

A bandage—

The thing he was carrying—

"Sleep tight," he grins down at me—

And I fall to the floor and the screens full of water are the last things I see—

{VIOLA}

"Acorn!" I shout into his mane—

But he ignores me, just keeps up his insane run,

Angharrad, too, with Bradley up ahead–

And it's working, we've reached a curve in the road and the river behind us is still coming, still full of wreckage and trees–

But it's slowing more, lowering its height some, keeping more to the riverbed–

And still the horses run–

Down the road and away, a rushing fog reaching out to us, its tendrils licking at the horses' tails–

And the river still coming–

But getting farther behind–

"We're doing it!" Bradley shouts back to me–

"A little farther, Acorn," I say between his ears. "We're almost out of it."

He doesn't say anything back, just keeps running–

The road is becoming thicker with trees, half of them burning, slowing down the river even more, and I recognize where we're getting to. We're nearing the old house of healing where I was kept for so long, the house of healing I ran from–

And found the hilltop with the communications tower–

The hilltop where the army's marching somewhere ahead of us–

Maybe already even there–

"I know a back way!" I shout. I point up the road, to a little farm off to the right, up a hill with a forest above it where the fire hasn't reached. "Up there!"

Girl colt, I hear Acorn say in acknowledgment and the horses turn for it, skirting the corner and shooting up the drive, heading for the narrow path I know is there through the woods–

There's a huge *crash* behind us as the river comes pounding down the road we just left, sloshing water and trees and debris everywhere, dousing the fire but drowning everything else, surging up the drive behind us, swallowing the little farmhouse–

But we're in the woods and branches are smacking my face and I hear Bradley cry out once but he doesn't let go of Angharrad–

And it's up a hill to a flat–

And then another uphill–

And through some shrubs–

And then we're sailing into the clearing, hooves thumping into the crowd, scattering screaming people this way and that, taking in the scene in a flash–

Seeing the probe cameras still projected on the sides of tents–

They know what's been happening–

They know what's coming–

"Viola!" I hear shouted in surprise as the horses race through the camp.

"Get people off the drive up the hill, Wilf! The river–!"

"There's an army!" Jane shouts next to him, pointing across the clearing to the entrance–

Where we can see Captain Tate leading what must be nearly the entire army–

Marching up the hill–

Their guns raised, ready to attack–

Cartloads of artillery ready to blow the hilltop to pieces–

(THE SKY)

The Sky hears everything.

I knew that before but I did not really *know* it until now. He hears every secret hidden in every heart of the Land. He hears every detail, important and nonsensical, loving and murderous. He hears every wish of every child, every memory of every old crone, every desire and feeling and opinion of every voice in the Land.

He is the Land.

I am the Land.

And the Land must survive, the Source continues at me as we ride east over the hills, fast on our battlemores.

The Land is surviving, I show back to him. *And will continue to do so under the leadership of the Sky.*

I can see what you're planning and you must not—

I turn round to him sharply. *It is not your place to tell the Sky what he must do.*

The fog and the falling ice combined have damped down some of the fires in the forests that surround the valley as we continue on. Those to the north still rage and I can see in the voices of the Land that they will *continue* to rage despite the river. Numbered among the damage the leader of the Clearing has done will be a blackened and scorched country.

But the south is rockier. There are paths through the hills where the trees are thin and the brush is low, and the fires do not burn so hard.

And so we march in the southern hills.

We march east.

All of us. Every member of the Land that has lived through the blaze, every Pathway, every soldier, every mother, father, and child.

We march east in pursuit of the Clearing.

We march east to the far hilltop.

Our weapons are ready, weapons that drove them back before, weapons that killed them in their hundreds, weapons that will destroy them now—

Then I hear the voice of a soldier riding up next to me—

He is bringing me a weapon of my own—

For the Sky must not enter battle unarmed.

I thank the soldier as I take it from him. It is an acid rifle of the Land, not unlike the rifle the Knife himself carried.

Not unlike the rifle I promised that I would use one day to—

I open my voice to the Land.

I summon them again.

I summon them all.

We are marching east, I show them. *The Land that survives is marching toward the Clearing.*

To what end? the Source demands again.

I do not answer him.

And we march faster—

{VIOLA}

"Viola, stop!" Bradley calls after me–

But I'm already riding forward, almost without having to tell a weary Acorn to do it–

We gallop through the people on the hilltop as they start to scream and run from the approaching army, some of them raising the guns they got from the Answer, the mistresses racing for their own larger weapon stock–

War is coming, right here in insane miniature. The world is falling to pieces and the people here are going to waste their last moments fighting each other–

"VIOLA!" I hear–

It's Lee, at the edge of the crowd, turning his head to read the Noise of the men around him, trying to get a picture of what's happening, trying to stop me–

But I won't be responsible for another single person dying, not if I can help it–

This started with the missile I fired, the decision *I* made to involve us in this war, a decision I've spent all the time since trying to rectify, and what's making me angrier than even the fire or the flood or Todd being flown out of here by the Mayor, is that even when peaceful cooperation is the *obvious* thing, the *only* thing that will keep any of us alive–

There are *still* people who won't make that choice.

I pull up Acorn at the front of the advancing soldiers, *forcing* Captain Tate to stop.

"PUT THAT GUN DOWN!" I find myself screaming. *"RIGHT NOW!"*

But he just raises his rifle.

And points it at my head.

"And then what?" I shout. "There's no more city below and you're going to kill off the only people who can help you rebuild it?"

"Get out of my way, little girl," Captain Tate says, a faint smile on his face.

And my heart sinks as I see how easily he'll kill me.

But I lift my gaze to the army behind him, to the men readying the artillery to fire.

"What happens after this attack, huh?" I shout at them all. "You all march to the ocean to meet your certain death as a million Spackle cut you down? Are those your *orders*?"

"As a matter of fact," Captain Tate says. And he cocks his rifle.

"Did you come to this planet to be soldiers?" I'm still shouting and now I'm also shouting at the hilltop behind me. The Answer and its remnants, the people gathered here, the ones picking up their own weapons. "Did you? Is that what any of you wanted? Or did you come for a better life?"

I look back to Captain Tate.

"Did you come to make paradise?" I say. "Or to die because one man told you to?"

"He's a great man," Captain Tate says, looking down the barrel of his rifle.

"He's a killer," I say. "If he can't control something, he destroys it. He sent Captain O'Hare and his men to their deaths. I saw it with my own eyes."

There's murmuring in the army behind him at this, especially as Bradley rides up, opening his Noise to the sight of Captain O'Hare and his men on the road. I'm close enough to Captain Tate to see a bead of sweat coming down his temple, even in the cold, even in the snow.

"He'll do the same to you," I say. "He'll do the same to all of you."

524

Captain Tate's face looks like he's fighting with himself and I begin to wonder if he *can* disobey the Mayor. If the Mayor hasn't done something to–

"NO!" he shouts. "I have my orders!"

"Viola–" I hear Lee shout from close by–

"Lee, get back!" I yell–

"I HAVE MY ORDERS!" Captain Tate screams–

And there's a gunshot–

(THE SKY)

The fog grows thicker, twining itself with the smoke and steam rising from the valley below us.

But fog does not stop the Land. We simply open our voices wider, passing the small steps in front of us along and along and along, each to each, until a whole picture of the march opens in front of us and our own limited physical sight in the fog becomes a single walking vision.

The Land is not blind. The Land marches.

The Sky at its front.

I can feel the Land gathering behind me, streaming in from north and south, winding their way through the burning forests and the hilltops around the valley, coming together to march in their hundreds, then their thousands and beyond. The voice of the Sky reaches back and back and back, passed along through the Pathways and the Land itself, through forests I have never seen, across lands unknown by any of the Clearing, reaching voices of the Land that sound strangely accented and different—

But the same, too, the same voice of the Land—

The Sky is calling out to all of them, every voice, reaching farther at once than any Sky ever has—

The entire voice of the Land streams itself into the march—

All of us coming together—

To meet the Clearing—

And then? shows the Source, still on his beast, still on my heels, still pestering me—

I think it is time for you to leave us, I show. *I think it is time for the Source to return to his own people.*

And yet you haven't forced me, he shows. *At any time, you could have done so.* His voice rises in intensity. *But you **haven't**. And that means you know, **the Sky** knows that what I say is correct, that you can't attack the Clearing—*

The Clearing that killed the Burden? I show back, anger growing in me. *The Clearing that **killed the Sky**? Does the Sky not answer that attack? Does the Sky turn back and allow the Land to be killed?*

Or does the Sky take one victory that will cost the Land its entire self later? the Source shows.

I turn away. *You wish to save your son.*

*I do. Todd is **my** Land. He represents everything worth saving. Everything the future **can** be.*

And I see the Knife in the Source's voice again, see him alive and real and fragile and human—

I cut him off. I open my voice again to the Land. I tell them to pick up their pace.

And then a strange sound rises from the voice of the Source—

{Viola}

I jump at the sound of the shot, expecting the same burning I felt through my middle when Davy Prentiss shot me–

But I feel nothing–

I open my eyes, which I hadn't even realized I'd closed–

Captain Tate's flat on his back, an arm twisted across his chest, a bullet hole in his forehead–

"Stop!" I shout, whirling round to see who fired, but all I see are confused faces among the women and men with guns–

And Wilf standing over next to Lee.

And Lee with a rifle in his hands.

"Did I get him?" Lee says. "Wilf aimed for me."

I look immediately back at the soldiers, all of them heavily armed, all of them still holding their guns–

All of them blinking strangely, like they're just waking up, some of them looking outright confused–

"I'm not sure they were following him voluntarily," Bradley says.

"But was it Captain Tate?" I ask. "Or the Mayor *through* Captain Tate?"

And you can hear the soldier's Noises getting louder, clearer, as they look at the frightened faces of the people on the hilltop, the faces they were about to fire on–

And you can even hear the worry of the ones at the back as the river rushes perilously close to them.

"We've got food," Mistress Lawson shouts, coming out of the crowd. "And we'll start making tents for any man who's lost his home." She crosses her arms. "Which is all of us now, I reckon."

And I look at the soldiers and I realize she's right.

They're not soldiers anymore.

Somehow, they're just men again.

Lee comes over to me with Wilf, Wilf's Noise showing him the way. "Are you okay?"

"I am," I say, seeing myself in Wilf's Noise and then in Lee's. "Thank you."

"Welcome," Wilf says. "What happens now?"

"The Mayor's gone to the ocean," I say. "We need to get there."

Though with how heavy Acorn is still breathing beneath me, I'm not sure how he's going to be able to–

Bradley makes a sudden, loud gasping sound and drops Angharrad's reins, reaching up both hands to the sides of his head, his eyes bulging open wide–

And a sound, a strange, strange sound echoes through his Noise, unintelligible as language or image, just *sound*–

"Bradley?" I say.

"They're coming," Bradley says, in a voice that's his own but also more, echoing weird and loud across the hilltop, his eyes unfocused and black, not seeing anything before him. *"THEY'RE COMING!"*

(T H E   S K Y)

What was that? I demand of the Source. *What have you done?*

I peer deep into his voice, searching for what the sound was—

And I see it there—

And I am too shocked at first to be rightfully angry.

How? I show. *How can you do that?*

I was speaking the voice, he says, looking dazed. *The voice of this world.*

Echoing through him is a language not of the Land but not quite of the Clearing either, some deeper combination of the Clearing's spoken language and the Land's voice but sent along the Pathways, along *new* Pathways—

Along *Clearing* Pathways—

My voice narrows. *How?*

I think it's been in us all along, he shows, breathing heavy, *but until you opened my voice, we weren't capable. I think Bradley must be a natural Pathway—*

You warned them, I show angrily.

I had to, the Source says. *I had no choice.*

I raise the acid rifle and point it at him.

If killing me will give you vengeance, he shows, *if it'll stop this march that's death to us all, then kill me. I'll gladly make that sacrifice.*

And I see in his voice that he tells the truth. I see him thinking of the Knife, of Todd, with that love again, that feeling that will say good-bye if it means saving the Knife, I hear it echoing through him like the information he sent before—

No, I show and lower my weapon. I feel his voice rise in hope. *No,* I show again, *you will come with us and watch their end.* I turn away and resume a faster march than before. *You will come with us and watch the Knife die.*

"They're coming," Bradley whispers.

"Who?" I say. "The Spackle?"

He nods, still dazed. "All of them," he says. "Every single one."

There's immediate gasping from the people nearest us and the Noise of the men spreads it even faster.

Bradley swallows. "It was Ben. He told me."

"What? How–?"

"No idea." He shakes his head. "Did no one else hear it?"

"No," Lee says. "But who cares? Is it true?"

Bradley nods. "I'm sure it is." He looks at the crowds on the hilltop. "They're coming to attack."

"Then we've got to put up a defense," Lee says, already turning to the soldiers, most of them still standing there aimless. "Get back into line! Get that artillery ready! The Spackle are on their way!"

"Lee!" I shout after him. "We can't even *hope* to beat that many–"

"No," he says, turning back, his Noise aiming right at me. "But we can buy you enough time to get to the ocean."

This stops me.

"Getting the Mayor is the only way this is going to end," he says. "And you gotta figure Todd has a role in it, too."

I look at Bradley, desperate. I look around at all the faces on the hilltop, all the ragged, tired faces of those who have somehow survived this long, through all these trials, waiting to see if this really is their final hour. A thick fog is rapidly spiraling in from the valley below, muffling everything, covering it

530

all in a gauzy white haze, and they stand in it like ghosts.

"Giving them the Mayor could really stop this," Bradley says.

"But," I say, looking down at Acorn, who's still breathing heavy, and I can see the foamy sweat rising up on his flanks. "The horses need rest. They can't possibly–"

Girl colt, Acorn says, head down at the ground. **Go. Go now.**

Spackle, Angharrad says, also heaving. **Save boy colt.**

"Acorn–" I say.

Go NOW, he says again, more strongly.

"Go," Lee says. "Save Todd. You might save all of us, too."

I look down at him. "Can you lead an army, Lee?"

"Why not?" he smiles. "Everyone else has had a shot."

"Lee–" I start to say–

"No need," he says, reaching out to sort of touch my leg but not quite. "I know." And then he turns back to the soldiers. "I said get back into line!"

And what do you know? They start doing it.

"Try for peace if you can," I say to Wilf. "Stall them, tell them we'll bring them the Mayor, keep as many people alive as possible–"

Wilf nods. "Will do. Yoo take care of yourself, ya hear?"

"I will, Wilf," I say and I take one last look at Lee, at Wilf, at the people on the hilltop.

I wonder if I'm ever going to see any of them again.

"The road's underwater," Bradley says. "We're going to have to take the hills and ride through the trees."

I lean down between Acorn's ears. "Are you *sure* about this?"

Girl colt, he coughs. **Ready**.

And that's all there is. That's all that's left.

Bradley and Angharrad and Acorn and I take off through the trees, flat out toward the ocean.

Not knowing what we'll find there.

[TODD]

I blink my eyes open, pain throbbing in my head. I make to sit up from where I'm lying down but I'm tied down tight.

"Nothing to see anyway, Todd," the Mayor says as my surroundings start to come into focus. "We're in an abandoned chapel in an abandoned village on an abandoned coast." I hear him sigh. "Pretty much the story of our time on this planet, eh?"

I try raising my head and this time it comes up. I'm on a long stone table, cracked at one corner by my left foot, and I see the stone pews along the floor, a white New World and its two moons carved in the far wall in front of a podium where a preacher would stand, and another wall that's half-collapsed, letting the snow in.

"So many important things have happened to you in churches," he says, "I thought it only fitting to bring you to one for what is either your last chapter." He steps closer. "Or your first."

"You let me go," I say, concentrating to control him but my head feels so *heavy*. "You let me go and fly us both back there. We can still stop all this."

532

"Oh, it's not going to be that easy, Todd," he smiles, taking out a small metal box. He presses it and it projects an image in the air, one full of white fog and churning smoke.

"I don't see nothing," I say.

"One moment," he says, still smiling. The image shifts and shimmers under the fog–

And then for a second it breaks–

And there's the Spackle, marching along the hilltops–

And there are so many of 'em–

A whole worldful–

"Marching toward the hilltop," the Mayor says. "Where they will find that my army has already dispatched my enemies there before continuing their march here." He turns to me. "Where we will have our last battle."

"Where's Viola?" I say, trying to prime my voice for an attack with her name.

"I'm afraid the probes lost track of her in the fog," he says, pressing buttons to show me the different views of the valley, all hidden by fog and smoke, with fires in the only clear spaces, burning in a huge way to the north.

"Let me go."

"All in good time, Todd. Now–"

He stops and looks into the air, his face momentarily troubled, but not by nothing going on this room. He turns back to the probe projeckshun but it's still all fog and there ain't nothing to see there.

VIOLA! I think right at him, hoping he don't hear it coming.

He barely flinches, just stares up into empty space again, his frown getting deeper and deeper. And then he heads outta the little chapel thru the collapsed wall, leaving me there, tied fast to the table, shivering in the cold, feeling like I weigh a ton.

I just lie there heavy for a long while, longer than I want, trying to think of her out there, trying to think of all the people who're gonna die if I don't move.

And then I slowly start trying to get myself free.

(THE SKY)

The fog is thick as a white night now and the Land marches only according to its voice, tied together, showing us our way as we near the hilltop, coming through the trees—

And I order the battlehorn to be blown—

The sound spills out into the world, and even from a distance we can hear the Clearing's terror at it—

I press my battlemore on, faster through the forest, feeling the pace of the Land pick up behind me. I am at the front of the guard now, the Source still with me, ahead of the first of our soldiers, their fires lit and ready to be shot, and behind them—

Behind them the entire voice of the Land—

Quickening its stride—

Nearly there, I show to the Source, as we pass through a deserted Clearing farm swamped by receding waters and on up through a dense forest—

We march through it, faster, faster still—

The voices of the Clearing hear us coming now, hear our voice, hear our *innumerable* voice bearing down on them, hear the battlehorn blown again—

And we march onto a small flat of land and up through another rise—

And I burst through a wall of foliage, acid rifle raised—

And I am the Sky—

I am the *Sky*—

Leading the Land into its greatest battle with the Clearing—

The fog is thick and I seek out the Clearing in the whiteness, preparing my weapon for its first firing and ordering the soldiers to raise their burning bolts and ready them to fire—

To purge the Clearing from the world once and for all—

And then a single man from the Clearing emerges.

"Wait," he says calmly, unarmed, alone in the sea of fog. "Ah have somethin to say."

{VIOLA}

"Look at the valley," Bradley says, as we race through the forests on the hilltops.

In glimpses down to our left, through the leaves and tendrils of drifting fog, you can see the river in full flood. The first wave of debris is well past us and it's just water now, settling its way above the riverbed, flooding the road that takes you straight to the ocean.

"We're not going to get there in time," I shout to Bradley. "It's too far—"

"We've come a long way," Bradley shouts back. "And we're moving fast."

Too fast, I think. Acorn's lungs have started rasping in an unnerving way. "Are you all right, boy?" I ask between his ears.

He doesn't answer, just keeps on chugging forward, foamy spit flying from his mouth. "Bradley?" I say, worried.

He knows. He's looking down at Angharrad, who seems better than Acorn but not by much. He looks back at me. "It's the only chance we've got, Viola," he says. "I'm sorry."

Girl colt, I hear from Acorn, low and pained.

And that's all he says.

And I think about Lee and Wilf and others on the hilltop we left behind.

And we keep on riding.

(THE SKY)

"My name is Wilf," the man says, standing alone in the fog, though I can hear hundreds behind him, hear their fears and their readiness to fight if they must—

And they must—

But something in the man's voice—

Even as the first rows of soldiers on their battlemores line up next to me, weapons at the ready, burning and blazing and ready to fight—

The man's voice—

It is as open as a bird's, as a pack animal's, as the surface of a lake—

Open and true and incapable of deceit—

And it is a channel, a channel for the voices behind him, those voices of the Clearing hidden in the fog, full of fear, full of dread—

Full of the wish that this would end—

Full of the wish for peace—

You have shown how false that wish is, I show to the man called Wilf.

But he does not answer, merely stands there, his voice open, and again the feeling, the certainty that this man is incapable of an untruth—

He opens his voice further and I see more clearly all the voices behind him, coming through him, as he disregards all their lies, takes them away and gives me—

"Ah'm only lissnen," he says. "Ah'm only lissnen to what's true."

Are you listening? the Source shows, next to me.

Do not speak, I show.

But are you listening? he shows. *Listening as this man is?*

I do not know what you mean—

And then I hear it, hear it through the man called Wilf, his voice calm and open, speaking the voices of all his people.

As if he was their Sky.

And with that thought, I am listening to my own voice—

Listening to the Land massing behind me, streaming toward this place, at the command of the Sky—

But—

But they are also speaking. They are speaking of fear and regret. Of worry for the Clearing and for the Clearing to come from the black world above. They see the man Wilf in front of me, see his wish for peace, see his *innocence—*

They are not all like this, I show to the Land. *They are violent creatures. They kill us, enslave us—*

But here is the man called Wilf with the Clearing behind him (and an army ready, I can see it in his voice, a frightened but willing army led by a blind man) and here is the Sky with the Land behind *him,* willing to do what the Sky wants, willing to march forward and obliterate the Clearing from this planet, should I tell them to do so—

But they fear as well. They saw peace as the same chance that the man called Wilf saw it, as a *chance,* an *opportunity,* a way to live without constant threat—

They will do what I tell them—

Without hesitation, they will do it—

But what I tell them is not what they want—

I see it now. I see it as clearly as anything in the voice of the man called Wilf.

We are here for my revenge. Not even the Sky's revenge, the revenge of *the Return.* I have made this war personal. Personal for the Return.

And I am no longer the Return.

One action is all it takes, shows the Source. *The fate of this world, the fate of the Land, rests on what you do now.*

I turn to him. *But what do I do?* I show, asking it unexpectedly, even to myself. *How do I act?*

You act, he shows, *like the Sky.*

I look back at the man called Wilf, see the Clearing behind him through his voice, feel the weight of the Land behind me in my own voice.

The voice of the Sky.

I am the Sky.
I am the Sky.
And so I act like the Sky.

{ V I O L A }

We're outrunning the fog now, but the snow keeps falling,
thicker here, even through the trees. We keep the flooded river
to our left in the valley below and go as fast as the horses can
carry us.

The horses.

Acorn no longer responds to anything I ask him, his Noise
focused only on running through the pain in his legs and his
chest and I can feel how much this is costing him–

And at the same time I realize he must know it, too–

He won't be making the journey back.

"Acorn," I whisper between his ears. "Acorn, my friend."

Girl colt, he says back, almost tenderly, and he
thunders on, through a thinning forest that opens out onto an
unexpected plateau, sandwiched under the snow clouds, a
thick dusting of white already accumulated across it, and we
race through a surprised herd of animals calling **Here** to
each other in alarm, and just before we plunge back into the
forest–

"There it is!" Bradley calls–

Our first, fleeting view of the ocean.

It's so big I'm almost overwhelmed–

Eating the world all the way to the cloudy horizon,
seeming bigger than the black beyond, just like Mistress
Coyle said, because it hides its hugeness–

And then we're back in the trees.

"It's still a ways," Bradley calls. "But we'll make it by night-fall–"

And Acorn collapses beneath me.

(THE SKY)

There is a long silence as I lower my weapon while the whole world waits to see what I mean by it–

While I wait to see what I mean by it, too.

And again I see the Clearing through the Noise of the man called Wilf, see them rush with a feeling behind him, a feeling I know very little of–

It's hope, the Source shows.

I know what it is, I show back.

And I feel the Land behind me, waiting as well–

And I feel the hope there, too–

And that is the decision the Sky made. The Sky must act in the best interests of the Land. That is who the Sky is.

The Sky *is* the Land.

And the Sky who forgets, that is no kind of Sky at all.

I open my voice to the Land and pass a message back to them, back to all those who have joined the fight, back to all those who united behind me when I called them–

And who now unite behind my decision not to attack–

Because another decision accompanies it. A decision necessary for the Sky, necessary for the safety of the Land.

I must find the man who attacked us, I show to the

Source. *And I must kill him. That is what is best for the Land.*

The Source nods and rides his beast into the fog ahead of us, disappearing past the man called Wilf and I hear him calling out to the Clearing, telling them we will not attack. Their relief is so pure and strong that the wave of it nearly knocks me off my mount.

I look to the soldiers beside me to see if they agree with my decision only through obedience to the Sky, but they are already turning their voices back to their own lives, the lives of the Land, the lives that will now, inevitably, involve the Clearing in ways no one can foresee, ways that will first involve cleaning up the mess the Clearing made.

Perhaps even helping them to survive.

Who can say?

The Source returns. I feel his concern as he approaches. *The Mayor's flown the ship to the ocean,* he shows. *Bradley and Viola have already set out to find him.*

Then so shall the Sky, I show.

I'll go with you, the Source shows and I see why.

The Knife is with him, I show.

The Source nods.

You think I will kill the Knife, I show back. *If I finally have the chance.*

The Source shakes his head, but I see his uncertainty. *I'll come with you,* he shows again.

We stare at each other for a long moment, then I turn to some of the Land soldiers at the front line and show them my intention, telling ten of them to accompany me.

Accompany me and the Source.

I turn back to him. *Then let us be on our way.*

And I tell my battlemore to run toward the ocean, faster than it has ever run before.

{VIOLA}

Acorn's front legs crumple midstride and I go tumbling hard through some undergrowth, jamming my left hip and arm into the ground with a painful grunt, and I hear Bradley yell, "Viola!" but Acorn's still falling forward, still crashing in a heap in the brush–

"ACORN!" I yell and I'm getting up and limping quickly over to where he's lying twisted and broken and I get to his head, his breath coming out of him in great raking sounds, his chest heaving with the effort. "Acorn, please–"

Bradley and Angharrad ride over to us, Bradley leaping down and Angharrad putting her nose down close to Acorn's–

Girl colt, Acorn says, pain wracking through his Noise, not just from his front legs, which I can see are broken, but the tearing in his chest which caused him to collapse in the first place, it's too much, he's run too hard–

Girl colt, he says–

"Shh," I say, "it's okay, it's okay–"

And then he says–

He says–

Viola.

And then he falls silent, his breath and his Noise both stopping in a final sigh–

"*No!*" I say, holding on to him tighter, pushing my face

542

into his mane. I feel Bradley's hands on my shoulders behind me as I cry, and I hear Angharrad quietly say, **Follow,** as she rubs her nose against Acorn's.

"I'm so sorry," Bradley says, gently as ever. "Viola, are you hurt yourself?"

I can't speak, still holding on to Acorn, but I shake my head.

"I'm sorry, sweetheart," Bradley says, "but we have to keep going. There's too much at stake."

"How?" I say, my voice thick.

Bradley pauses. "Angharrad?" he asks. "Can you take Viola the rest of the way to save Todd?"

Boy colt, Angharrad says, her Noise strong at the mention of Todd. **Boy colt yes.**

"We can't kill her, too," I say.

But Angharrad's already putting her nose under my arm, urging me up. **Boy colt,** she says. **Boy colt save.**

"But Acorn–"

"I'll take care of him," Bradley says. "You just get there. You get there and you make it worth it, Viola Eade."

I look up at him, look at his faith in me, his certainty that good is still possible.

And I give Acorn a last, tearful kiss on his unmoving head, and I stand and let Angharrad kneel next to me. I get up on her slowly, my vision still cloudy, my voice still thick. "Bradley," I say.

"It can only be you," he says, giving me a sad smile. "It can only be you who saves him."

I nod slowly and I try to put my mind on Todd, on what's happening to him right now–

On saving him, saving *us,* once and for all–

I find I can't say good-bye to Bradley but I think he understands as I give a yell to Angharrad and we race off on the final stretch to the ocean.

Here I come, Todd, I think. *Here I come–*

[TODD]

I don't know how long it takes me to loosen the strap around one wrist even slightly. Whatever medicine was in that bandage, still stuck to my neck, itching where I can't scratch it, it was enough to slow me way down, in body *and* Noise–

But I work and work and all the while the Mayor's out there somewhere, on what I guess is the beach, a little stretch of snow-covered sand thru the broken wall in the corner. I see a sliver of waves crashing, too, a sound that's constant with another sound beyond it, a roar I reckernize as the river, loud and full of all that water now finally returning to the ocean. The Mayor musta flown us straight down it, landing here to wait for whatever's sposed to happen. The two armies fighting their last war.

All of us dying under a million Spackle.

I strain against the strap on my right wrist again, feeling it give a little.

I wonder what it musta been like to live here, to settle a community by the big, big water for fishing. Viola told me the ocean fish on this planet are more likely to eat you than the other way round, but ways coulda been found, ways to make a life there, a life like we nearly did in the valley.

What a sad thing men are. Can't do nothing good

without being so weak we have to mess it up. Can't build something up without tearing it down.

It ain't the Spackle that drove us to the end.

It was ourselves.

"I couldn't agree more," the Mayor says, coming back inside the chapel. His face is different, way downcast. Like something's wrong. Like something really big is *really* wrong.

"Events transpire out of my hands, Todd," he says, looking nowhere, as if he's hearing something, something that's disappointed him beyond belief. "Events on a far hilltop—"

"What hilltop?" I say. "What's happened to Viola?"

He sighs. "Captain Tate's failed me, Todd," he says. "The Spackle have failed me, too."

"What?" I say. "How can you know *that*?"

"This world, Todd, this *world*," he says, ignoring my asking. "This world that I thought I could control and *did* control." His eyes flash at me. "Until I met you."

I don't say nothing.

Cuz he's looking scarier.

"Maybe you did transform me, Todd," he says. "But not just you."

"You let me go," I say. "I'll show you all about how I'm gonna *transform* you."

"You're not listening," he says and there's a pain in my head, enough to leave me speechless for a second. "You transformed me, yes, and I've had no small effect on you." He walks down the side of the table. "But I've also been transformed by this *world*."

For the first time I notice how weird his voice sounds,

like it ain't entirely his own no more, all echoey and strange.

"This world, because I've noticed it, because I've *studied* it," he continues, "has warped me out of recognition from the proud and strong man I used to be." He stops at my feet. "War makes monsters of men, you once said to me, Todd. Well, so does too much knowledge. Too much knowledge of your fellow man, too much knowledge of his weakness, his pathetic greed and vanity, and how laughably easy it is to control him."

He gives a sour chuckle. "You know, Todd, it's only the stupid who can truly handle Noise. The sensitive, the *smart,* people like you and me, we *suffer* by it. And people like us *have* to control people like them. For their own good and ours."

He drifts off, looking at nothing. I strain harder at the ropes.

"You did transform me, Todd," he says again. "You made me better. But only enough to see how bad I actually was. I never knew until I compared myself to you, Todd. I thought I was doing good." He stops over me. "Until you showed me otherwise."

"You were bad from the beginning," I say. "I didn't do nothing."

"Oh, but you did, Todd," he says. "That was the *hum* you felt in your head, the *hum* that connected us. It was the good in me, the good you made me see. Something I could see only through you." His eyes go blacker. "And then Ben arrived and you were going to take it away. You let me glimpse a goodness I'd never be able to grasp on my own, and for that sin, Todd Hewitt, for that sin of self-knowledge—"

546

He reaches down and starts untying my leg.

"One of us is going to have to die," he says.

{VIOLA}

Angharrad feels different from Acorn, broader, stronger, faster, but still I worry.

"Please be okay," I whisper, not even to her, knowing it won't do any good.

Because she just says **BOy colt** and runs even faster.

We press on through more trees as the hills begin to flatten out and lower down closer to the river, which I see more and more often to my left, wide and rushing over a flooded riverbank.

But I don't see the ocean, just more trees and more trees again. The snow remains thick, coming down in fat flakes, twisting through the air and starting to leave noticeable drifts even in fairly dense forest.

And as the daylight starts to fade, I get a sick feeling in my heart at not knowing what's happened on the hilltop, what's happened to Bradley, what's happened to Todd at the ocean ahead–

And then, all at once, there it is–

Through a break in the trees, close enough to see the waves crashing, close enough to see docks on a small harbor with abandoned buildings and there, sitting among them, the scout ship–

And it disappears behind more trees–

But we're nearly there. We're nearly there.

"Hang on, Todd," I say. "Hang on."

[TODD]

"It's gonna be you," I say, as he unties my other leg. "It's gonna be you who dies."

"You know what, Todd?" he says, his voice low. "A part of me hopes you're right."

I keep still till he unties my right hand and then I take a swing at him but he's already backing away toward the opening out to the beach, watching me free my other hand with an amused look on his face.

"I'll be waiting for you, Todd," he says, stepping outside.

I try to send a **VIOLA** at him but I'm still feeling weak and he don't take any notice before disappearing. I pull at the final knots and I'm free and I leap off the table and have to take a groggy minute to catch my balance but then I'm moving, moving out thru the opening–

Onto the freezing cold beach beyond.

The first thing I see is a row of broken-down houses, some of 'em nothing more than piles of wood and sand, with a few concrete ones like the chapel lasting a bit better. To the north of me, I can see a road heading off into the woods, the road that no doubt goes all the way back to New Prentisstown, tho it's covered in a rushing, overflowing river before it gets any farther than the second tree.

The snow is really coming down fast now and the wind has picked up, too. The cold cuts thru my uniform like a stab with a steely knife and I clutch the jacket closer around me.

And then I turn toward the ocean–

Oh my God–

It's effing *huge*.

Bigger than anything possible, stretching outta sight not just toward the horizon but north and south, too, like an endlessness that's set itself down on yer doorstep, waiting to swallow you up the second you turn yer back. The snow don't have no effect on it neither. The ocean just keeps on churning, like it wants to fight you, like the waves are punches it's throwing to try and knock you down.

And there's *creachers* in it. Even in the frothy and muddy waters churning on the shore, even in the spray and foam from the river crashing into it to the north of me, even then you can see shadows moving in the water–

Big shadows–

"Quite something, isn't it?" I hear.

The Mayor's voice.

I whip round. He ain't nowhere to be seen. I turn round again slowly. I'm noticing there's a bit of sand-covered concrete beneath my feet, like this used to be a little square or walk along the beach or something, something that came outta the front of the chapel a long time ago where people could sit in the sun.

Except I'm here now and I'm effing *freezing*.

"SHOW YERSELF, YOU COWARD!" I shout.

"Oh, cowardice is one thing you could never accuse me of, Todd." His voice again but sounding like it's coming from somewhere else.

"THEN WHY ARE YOU HIDING?" I shout, turning again, crossing my arms hard against the cold. We're both gonna die if we stay out here.

And then I see the scout ship, down the beach, parked by itself, waiting–

"I wouldn't try, Todd," the voice comes again. "You'd be dead before you reached it."

I turn round one more time. "YER ARMY AIN'T COMING, IS IT?" I shout. "THAT'S WHAT YOU MEANT ABOUT MR. TATE FAILING YOU! HE AIN'T COMING!"

"Correct, Todd," the Mayor says and this time the voice sounds different.

It sounds like a real voice spoken across a real area.

I whirl round again—

And there he is, by the corner of one of the wrecked wooden houses.

"How do you know?" I say, flexing my Noise, getting myself ready.

"I heard it, Todd," he says. "I told you I heard everything." He starts walking toward me. "And slowly, slowly, that's become literally true. I opened myself up to the voice of this world. And now—" He stops at the edge of the sand-covered square, snow blowing everywhere. "Now I hear every piece of information in it."

And I see his eyes.

And I finally get it.

He *does* hear everything.

And it's driving him mad.

"Not yet," he says, his eyes black, his voice echoey. "Not before I finish my business with you. Because one day, Todd Hewitt, you'll hear it, too."

I'm pumping my Noise, raising its temperature, circling round the one word, making it as heavy as possible, not caring if he can hear it cuz he'll know it's coming anyway—

"Indeed," the Mayor says.

And sends a blast of Noise right at me—

I jump outta the way, hearing it *whoosh* by me—

I land and roll on the snow and the sand and look back up at him, coming for me—

VIOLA! I fling at him—

And the fight is on—

(THE SKY)

You've done right, the Source shows to me as we ride through the trees toward the ocean.

The Sky needs no confirmation of his choices, I show back.

We make good speed. Battlemores are faster than Clearing animals, more used to trees and running without roads. The river settles deep into the valley below us, maybe even changing its course. The fog is still thick, the snow still falling, some fires still burning in the valley behind. But we are on the move, on the move toward our enemy across a sudden plain through a herd of startled animals—

Wait, the Source calls, and I realize I am leaving him behind, the soldiers, too. *Wait!* he shows again. *I hear something up ahead—*

I do not slow but I open my voice in front of me—

And there it is, heard before we see it, a Clearing man's voice—

Bradley, I hear the Source call, and then we are on him, coming through a section of trees to find him backing quickly away as we pull the battlemores to a stop.

"Ben?" the man called Bradley says, looking at me in alarm.

It's all right, the Source says. *The war's over.*

For now, I show. *Where is the Knife's one in particular?*

The man called Bradley looks puzzled until the Source shows *Viola* to him.

And then we see the body of the animal, covered in leaves and brush, now with a light dusting of snow on him.

"Her horse," the man says. "I covered him and I've been trying to start a fire—"

And Viola? the Source shows.

"Gone to the ocean," Bradley says. "To help Todd."

There is a rush of feeling in the voice of the Source, a rush that fills my own voice, a rush of love and fear for the Knife—

But I am already off, pushing my battlemore to faster and faster speeds, outrunning the Source behind me and the soldiers behind him—

Wait, I hear the Source call again—

But I will reach the ocean first—

I will reach the ocean myself—

And if the Knife is there—

Well, I shall see what I see—

[TODD]

I catch the Mayor with the first **VIOLA** I hurl at him, see him stumble to one side, not quite quick enough to dodge it—

But he's already turning and firing his Noise back at me and tho I duck again I feel like the top of my head's being ripped open and I jump off the little flat of sand and concrete, down the slope toward the waves, rolling in the sand and snow but getting outta the Mayor's eyeline for a brief second—

"Oh, but I don't need to *see* you, Todd," I hear—

And *bam* another blast of white Noise, screaming YER NOTHING YER NOTHING YER NOTHING YER NOTHING—

And I roll back up, gripping the side of my head and I force my eyes open—

And I see the river up the beach in front of me, dumping itself into the ocean and I look out to the water beyond it and see wreckage floating there, getting tossed in the waves, wreckage of trees and houses and no doubt people—

People I know—

Maybe even Viola—

And I feel a rage rise in my Noise—

And I get to my feet—

VIOLA!

I think it at him and I realize I'm doing it without having to find him, that I just feel where he is instinctively, and I send it to him and turn to look and he's falling back hard onto the concrete square, catching himself with his wrist—

Which I hear break with a satisfying *snap*.

He grunts. "Very impressive," he says, his voice husky with pain. "Very impressive indeed, Todd. Your control is better and stronger." He starts pulling himself to his feet with his unbroken arm. "But control comes at a price. Can you hear the voice of the world gathering behind you, Todd?"

VIOLA! I think again at him–

And again he staggers back–

But he don't fall this time–

"Because *I* can hear it," he says. "I can hear it all."

And his eyes flash and I freeze–

And he's inside my head, along with the *hum,* connecting to me–

"Can you hear it?" he says again–

And–

And I *can*–

I *can* hear it–

There, like a *roar* behind the roar of the waves, the roar of the river–

A *roar* of everything on this planet that lives–

Speaking in an impossibly loud single voice–

And for a second I'm overwhelmed by it–

Which is all he needs–

There's a flash of pain in my head so bright that I black out–

Falling to my knees–

But only for an instant–

Cuz in that roar of voices–

Even tho it ain't possible–

Even tho she ain't got Noise–

I swear I heard her–

I swear I heard her coming–

And so without even opening my eyes–

VIOLA!

And I hear another grunt of pain–

And I get back up to my feet–

The ground starts to slope steeply down and we're seeing the ocean constantly now–

"Almost there," I gasp. "Almost there."

Boy colt, Angharrad says–

And with a jump, we clear the last line of trees out onto the beach, Angharrad's hooves kicking up snow and sand as she scrambles to turn left, toward the abandoned town, toward the river–

Toward Todd and the Mayor–

"There they are!" I shout and Angharrad sees them, too, surging forward across the sand–

Boy colt! she shouts–

"TODD!" I yell–

But the waves are crashing too loud and huge–

And I swear I hear something, Noise coming from the ocean, and I get a glimpse through the crashing water of dark shapes moving beneath–

But I keep my eyes ahead, shouting, "TODD!" over and over again–

And I see–

He's battling the Mayor, across some kind of sand-covered square in front of what looks like a chapel–

And I get a sinking feeling of how many terrible things have happened to me and Todd in churches–

"TODD!" I call again–

And I see one of them staggering back from what must be a Noise hit–

And then the other jumping away but grabbing his head–

But I can't tell which is which from this distance–
They're wearing those stupid uniforms–
And I'm seeing again how tall Todd's grown–
So tall it's hard to tell him and the Mayor apart–
And worry clenches my chest even harder–
Angharrad feels it, too–
Boy colt! she calls–
And we race even faster–

[TODD]

Get back, I think at the Mayor and I see him take a step back but just the one and another flash of Noise comes back at me and I grunt with pain and I stumble to one side and I see a broken hunk of concrete in the sand and I grab it and spin round to throw it at him–

"Drop it," he *buzzes.*

And I drop it–

"No weapons, Todd," he says. "You don't see me armed, do you?"

And I realize I don't. He ain't carrying a gun and the scout ship's too far away to be of use. He wants us to just fight with our Noises–

"Exactly," he says, "and may the stronger man win."

And he hits me again–

I grunt and hit him back with a **VIOLA** and take off running cross the little square, slipping on the snow and heading for one of the wrecked wooden houses–

"I don't think so," the Mayor *buzzes*–

And my feet stop running–

But then I pick up one—

And then the other—

And I'm running for it again—

I hear the Mayor laugh behind me. "Well *done*," he says.

I scramble behind a pile of old wood, lying down low so he can't see me, tho I know that don't have no effect, but I need a second to think—

"We're well matched," says the Mayor. I can hear him clearly despite the surf, despite the river, despite everything that should be blocking him out. He's talking right inside my head.

Like he always has.

"You were always my best disciple, Todd," he says.

"You SHUT UP with that talk," I shout back, looking round the wood pile, seeing if there's anything, anything at *all* that'll help—

"You control your Noise better than any man but me," he keeps saying, getting closer. "You control other *men* with it. You use it as a weapon. I've said from the very beginning that your power would outstrip mine."

And he hits me again harder than ever and the world goes white but I keep thinking *Viola* in my head and grip the planks of wood and I pull myself to my feet and I think with the heaviest *buzz* I can muster, *GET BACK!*

And he steps back.

"Whoo, Todd," he says, still acting impressed.

"I ain't taking yer place," I say, stepping out from the wreckage. "No matter what."

And he takes another step back, even tho I didn't tell him to.

"Someone has to," he says. "Someone has to control the Noise, to tell people how to use it, tell them what to do."

"Nobody has to tell nobody nothing," I say, taking another step forward.

"You never were a poet, were you, Todd?" he says. He takes another step back. He's on the edge of the sandy square now, still holding out his broken wrist, a bloody bone poking out thru the skin, but it don't look like he's feeling no pain. The only thing behind him is a long slope down to the waves and the dark shapes lurking beneath–

And I see how black the eyes of the Mayor are, how echoey his voice is becoming–

"This world is eating me alive, Todd," he says. "This world and the information in it. It's too much. Too much to control."

"Then stop *trying*," I say and I hit him with a **VIOLA.**

He flinches but don't fall down. "I can't," he says with a smile. "It's not in my nature. But *you,* Todd. You're stronger than I am. *You* could handle it. You could rule this world."

"This world don't need me," I say. "For the last time, *I ain't you.*"

He looks down at my uniform. "Are you sure about that?"

I feel a rush of anger and hit him hard again with another **VIOLA.**

He flinches again but don't step back and hits me with his own blast. I grit my teeth and ready another one, ready to fling it into his stupid smiling face–

"We could stand here all afternoon blasting each other into gibbering wrecks," he says. "So let me tell you the stakes, Todd."

"Shut up—"

"If *you* win, you take over the world—"

"I don't *want*—"

"But if *I* win—"

And suddenly he's showing me his Noise—

The first time I've seen it, seen *all* of it, in I don't know how long, maybe even old Prentisstown, maybe not ever—

And it's cold, colder even than this freezing beach—

And it's *empty*—

The voice of the world surrounds him like the black beyond coming in to crush him under an impossible weight—

Knowing me made it bearable for him for a while but now—

He wants to destroy it, destroy everything—

And I realize that's what he wants—

That's what he wants more than anything—

To hear *nothing*—

And the *hate* of it, the hate in his Noise, *of* his Noise, is so strong, I don't know if I'm gonna be able to beat it, he's stronger than me, he's always been stronger, and I'm looking straight into the emptiness of him, the emptiness that lets him destroy and destroy and I don't know if—

"Todd!"

I look away and the Mayor calls out as if I've ripped something from him—

"TODD!"

And there, thru the snow, riding *my* horse, riding my ruddy great horse—

Viola—

And the Mayor hits me with all he's got—

{Viola}

"TODD!" I yell and he turns to see me—

And he calls out in pain from an attack by the Mayor and he reels back, blood flying from his nose, and Angharrad screams out  and rides right for him across the sand and I'm still calling his name, calling it with all my voice—

"TODD!"

And he hears me—

He looks up at me—

And I still can't hear his Noise, just what he's using to fight—

But I see the look in his eye—

And I say it again—

"TODD!"

Because this is how you beat the Mayor—

You don't beat him alone—

You beat him together—

"TODD!"

And he's turning to the Mayor and I can see the nervousness on the Mayor's face as I hear my own name roared out as loud as a thunderclap—

[TODD]

VIOLA

Cuz she's here—

She came—

560

She came for *me*—

And she calls *my* name—

And I feel her strength coursing thru my Noise like a fire—

And the Mayor staggers back like he's been punched in the face by a row of houses—

"Ah, yes," he grunts, hand to his head. "Your tower of strength has arrived."

"Todd!" I hear her call again—

And I take it and I use it—

Cuz I can feel her there, riding to the end of the world to find me, to save me if I needed saving—

Which I did—

And—

VIOLA

The Mayor staggers back again, holding onto his broken wrist, and I see some blood trickling outta his ears—

"Todd!" she says again but this time in a way that asks me to look at her and I do and she stops Angharrad at the edge of the square and she's looking at me, looking right into my eyes—

And I read her—

And I know exactly what she's thinking—

And my Noise and my heart and my head fill up fit to burst, fill up like I'm gonna explode—

Cuz she's saying—

She's saying with her eyes and her face and her whole self—

"I know," I say back to her, my voice husky. "Me, too."

And then I turn to the Mayor and I'm filled with her, with her love for me and my love for her–

And it makes me big as an effing mountain–

And I take it and I slam all of it into the Mayor–

{Viola}

The Mayor's flung backward down the slope, tumbling and sliding toward the crashing waves, before stopping in a heap–

Todd looks back at me–

And my heart leaps to my throat–

I still can't hear his Noise, even as I know he's gathering it for another attack on the Mayor–

But "I know," he said. "Me, too."

And he looks at me now, a twinkle in his eye, a grin on his face–

And though I can't hear him–

I know him–

I know what he's thinking–

Right now, at this moment of all moments, I can read Todd Hewitt without hearing his Noise–

And he sees me doing it–

And for an instant–

We know each other again–

And I can just *feel* the strength of us as he turns back to the Mayor–

And he doesn't hit him with Noise–

He sends a low *buzz* through the air–

"Walk backward," Todd says to the Mayor, who's slowly

gotten to his feet, holding his wrist—

And he starts to walk backward—

Backward toward the surf—

"Todd?" I ask. "What are you doing?"

"Can't you hear 'em?" he says. "Can't you hear how hungry they are?"

And I glance into the surf—

See the shadows, the *huge* shadows, big as houses, swimming this way and that, even in the crashing waves—

And **Eat** is what I hear—

Simple as that one word—

Eat—

And they're talking about the Mayor—

Gathering around where he's walking backward toward them—

Where Todd is making him do it—

"Todd?" I say—

And then the Mayor says, "Wait."

[TODD]

"Wait," says the Mayor.

And it's not a controlling thing he's trying, not a *buzz* returning along the one I'm sending to him, the one that's making him walk toward the ocean, to drown himself in it, to be eaten by the creachers that are swimming closer and closer, waiting to get a bite. He just says, "Wait," like he's asking politely.

"I ain't sparing you," I say. "I would if I thought I could

save you, but I can't. I'm sorry bout that, but you can't be saved."

"I know," he says. He smiles again, full of sadness this time, sadness I can feel is real. "You did change me, you know, Todd. In a little way, for the better. Enough to recognize love when I see it." He looks over at Viola and back at me. "Enough for me to save you now."

"Save *me*?" I say and I think *Step back* and he steps back one more step.

"Yes, Todd," he says, sweat forming on his upper lip, trying to resist me. "I want you to stop forcing me into the surf–"

"Fat chance of that–"

"Because I'll go into it myself."

I blink at him. "No more games," I say, forcing him back another step. "This is finished."

"But Todd Hewitt," he says, "you're the boy who couldn't kill."

"I ain't no boy," I say. "And I'll kill *you*."

"I know," he says. "And that would make you just a little bit more like me, wouldn't it?"

I stop, holding him there for a second, the waves crashing in behind him, the creachers starting to fight among themselves, and boy are they *big*–

"I never lied about your power, Todd," he says. "Powerful enough to be the new me, if you wanted–"

"I *don't*–"

"Or powerful enough to be like Ben."

I frown. "What's Ben got to do with it?"

"He hears the voice of the planet, too, Todd, just like

me. Just like you will eventually. But he lives within it, lets himself be part of it, lets himself ride the current of it without losing himself."

The snow's still falling, sticking to the Mayor's hair in white bits. I realize again how cold I am.

"You could be me," the Mayor says. "Or you could be him."

He takes a step back.

A step that I didn't make him take.

"If you kill me, it's one step further away from being him," he says. "And if that's as far as the goodness of you has changed me, goodness enough to stop you *becoming* me, then that'll have to do."

He turns to Viola. "The cure for the bands is real."

Viola glances at me. "What?"

"I put a slow-acting poison in the first batch to kill all the women. The Spackle, too."

"WHAT?" I shout.

"But the cure is real," the Mayor says. "I did it for Todd. I've left the research on the scout ship. Mistress Lawson can easily confirm it. And that," he says, nodding at her, "is my parting gift to *you*, Viola."

He looks back at me, the sad, sad smile on his face. "This world will be shaped by the two of you for years to come, Todd."

He sighs deeply.

"And I, for one," he says, "am glad that I shall never have to see it."

And he spins round and takes one big stride toward the surf, then another and another–

"Wait!" Viola calls after him—

But he don't stop, he keeps striding, almost running, and I feel Viola slip off Angharrad and both of 'em come over next to me and we watch the Mayor's boots splash in the water and he wades in deeper, a wave nearly knocking him over, but he keeps upright—

He twists back to look at us—

His Noise is silent—

His face unreadable—

And with a yawning grunt, one of the shadows in the water breaks the surface, all mouth and black teeth and horrible slime and scales, surging toward the Mayor—

Twisting its head sideways to grab his torso—

And the Mayor makes no sound as the huge creacher slams him into the sand—

And drags him back under the water—

And as quick as that—

He's gone.

{VIOLA}

"He's gone," Todd says, and I share every bit of the disbelief in his voice. "He just walked in." He turns to me. "He just walked right in."

He's breathing heavy, looking startled and exhausted by what's just happened.

And then he sees me, really *sees* me.

"*Viola*," he says—

And I take him in my arms and he takes me in his and we

don't have to say anything, anything at all.

Because we know.

"It's over," I whisper. "I can't believe it. It's *over*."

"I think he really wanted to go," Todd says, still holding me. "I think it was destroying him in the end, trying to control it all."

We look back at the ocean and see the huge creatures still circling, waiting to see if Todd or I will offer ourselves up next. Angharrad sticks her nose right between us, bumping Todd in the face, saying **BOY COLT** with enough feeling to bring tears to my eyes. **BOY COLT.**

"Hey, girl," Todd says, rubbing a hand along her nose but still holding onto me, and then his face looks sad as he reads her Noise. "Acorn," he says.

"I left Bradley behind," I say, tearing up again. "Wilf and Lee, too, but I don't know what happened–"

"The Mayor said Mr. Tate failed him," Todd says. "Said the Spackle failed him, too. That can only be good."

"We need to get back." I twist in his arms and look at the scout ship. "I don't suppose he taught you how to fly that?"

And then Todd says, "Viola," in a way that makes me turn back to him.

"I don't wanna be like the Mayor," he says.

"You won't," I say. "That's impossible."

"No," he says. "That's not what I mean."

And he looks me in the eyes.

And I feel it coming, feel the strength surging through him, finally free of the presence of the Mayor–

He opens up his Noise.

Opens it and opens it and opens it–

And there he is, all of him, open to me, showing me everything that's happened, everything he felt–

Everything he feels–

Everything he feels for me–

"I know," I say. "I can read you, Todd Hewitt."

And he smiles that crooked smile–

And then we hear a sound up the beach, back where the trees meet the sand–

(THE SKY)

My battlemore makes the final leap onto the beach and for a moment I am dazzled by the ocean, the sheer huge fact of it filling my voice–

But my mount races on, turning toward the abandoned Clearing settlement–

And I am too late–

The Knife's one in particular is here with her horse–

But the Knife is nowhere to be seen–

Only the leader of the Clearing, grabbing on to the Knife's one in particular, his uniform a dark blot against the snow and the sand, and he is holding the Knife's one in particular close to him, imprisoning her in his arms–

And so the Knife must be dead–

The Knife must be gone–

And I feel a surprising hollowness because of that, an emptiness–

Because even the one you hate leaves an absence when they go–

But those are the feelings of the Return—

And I am not the Return—

I am the Sky—

The Sky who made peace—

The Sky who must kill the leader of the Clearing in order to secure that peace—

And so I race forward, the figures in the far distance coming closer—

And I raise my weapon—

[TODD]

I squint thru the snow, which is getting thicker by the minute—

"Who's that?" I say.

"That's not a horse," Viola says, stepping away from me. "That's a *battlemore*."

"A battlemore?" I say. "But I thought—"

And the air is torn from my lungs—

(THE SKY)

He pushes the girl away, seeing me coming, and I have an open shot—

I hear a voice behind me, shouting something in the distance—

A voice shouting *Wait*—

But it is hesitation that has hurt me in the past, being at the moment to act and not acting—

And that will not happen now—

The Sky will act—
The leader of the Clearing is turning to me—
And I will act—
(but—)
I fire my weapon.

{VIOLA}

Todd makes a sound like the world collapsing and grabs at his chest—

His bloody, burning, smoking chest—

"TODD!" I shout and leap for him—

And he's falling back onto the sand, his mouth open in pain—

But no air is coming out or in, just raking, choking sounds in his throat—

And I'm throwing myself down on top of him, blocking another shot if it comes, reaching for his burning clothes, which are disintegrating across his chest, just vaporizing away—

"TODD!"

And he's looking into my eyes, terrified, his Noise wheeling wildly out of control, spinning with terror and pain—

"No," I say, "No no no no no—"

And I can barely hear the hoofbeats of the battlemore still racing for us—

Barely hear another set of hoofbeats behind that—

Hear Ben's voice echoing across the sand—

Wait! he's yelling—

"*Todd?*" I say, tearing the melting clothes off his chest,

seeing the terrible, terrible burning beneath, his skin bleeding and bubbling and still that awful choking sound from his throat, like the muscles in his chest have stopped working, like he can't make them move to take in a breath–

Like's he's choking to death–

Like he's dying right now, right here on this cold, snowy beach–

"TODD!"

And the battlemores are closing in behind me–

And I hear the Noise of 1017, hear that he fired the weapon–

Hear as he realizes his mistake–

That he thought he was shooting the Mayor–

But he wasn't, he *wasn't*–

And Ben is riding in behind him–

Ben's Noise ramming forward with fear–

But all I can see is Todd–

All I can see is him looking back at me–

His eyes wide open–

His Noise saying, No, no, not now, not NOW–

And then he says, Viola?

"I'm here, Todd," I say, my voice breaking, shouting with desperation. "I'm *here!*"

And he says, Viola? again–

Asking it–

Asking like he's not sure I'm there–

And then his Noise falls completely silent–

And he stops struggling–

And looking right into my eyes–

He dies.

My Todd dies.

THE FUTURE OF THE WORLD

{VIOLA}

"TODD!" I SHOUT –

No–

No–

No–

He can't be dead–

He *can't* be–

"TODD!"

Like saying his name will make it untrue, will make time go backward–

Make Todd's Noise start again–

Make his eyes *see* me–

"TODD!"

I shout it again but it's like my voice is underwater and all I can hear is my own breath in my ears and my voice rasping his name–

"TODD!"

Another set of arms crosses mine, Ben, falling into the

sand next to me, his voice and Noise tearing to bits, saying Todd's name–

And he starts grabbing handfuls of snow to pack onto Todd's wound, trying to freeze it, stop the bleeding–

But it's already too late–

He's gone–

He's gone–

Todd is *gone*.

And everything is suddenly moving so slowly–

Angharrad calling out BOY COLT–

Ben putting his face close to Todd's, listening for his breath, not finding it–

"Todd, please!" I hear him say–

But it's like it's from a great distance–

Like it's happening out of my reach–

And there are more footsteps behind me, footsteps I can hear as if there were no other sounds in the universe–

1017–

Off his battlemore, his Noise reeling from his mistake–

His Noise wondering if it was a mistake after all–

And I turn to face him–

(THE SKY)

She turns to face me—

And though she has no voice, I see enough to step back—

She rises to her feet—

I step back again, dropping my weapon onto the snowy sand, only now realizing I still held it—

"You!" she spits, coming toward me, the chirping

sounds from her mouth making a terrible sound, a sound of rage, a sound of *grief*—

I did not know, I show, still stepping away from her. *I thought he was the leader of the Clearing*—

(did I?)

"You *liar!*" she shouts. "I can *hear* you! You weren't sure! You weren't sure and you fired *anyway*—"

It is a wound from a weapon of the Land, I show. *The medicine of the Land might save him*—

"It's too late for that!" she shouts. "You've killed him!"

I look beyond her to the Source, who holds the Knife in his arms, packing more ice onto the Knife's chest, knowing it does no good, his voice rending with grief, his human voice wailing from his mouth—

And I see that it is true—

I have killed the Knife—

I have killed the Knife—

"SHUT UP!" she shouts—

I did not mean to, I show, realizing too late that it is true. *I did not* **want** *to.*

"Well, you *did!*" she spits at me again—

And then she sees my weapon lying on the sand where I dropped it—

{Viola}

I see the weapon, the white stick weapon of the Spackle lying on the ground, lying there white against the white snow—

I hear Ben crying behind me, saying Todd's name over and over again and my own heart is painful in my chest, so

575

painful I can barely breathe—

But I see the weapon—

And I reach down and pick it up—

And I point it at 1017—

He doesn't back away any farther, just watches me raise it—

I am sorry, he says, raising his hands slightly in the air, those too-long hands that killed my Todd—

"Sorry won't bring him back," I say through clenched teeth and though my eyes are filled with water, a terrible clarity comes over me. I feel the weight of the weapon in my hands. I feel the intention in my heart that will let me use it.

Though I don't know how.

"Show me!" I shout at him. *"Show me how so I can kill you!"*

Viola, I hear behind me, Ben's voice choked with grief. *Viola, wait*—

"I will *not* wait," I say, my voice hard, my arm still raised with the weapon. "SHOW ME!"

I am sorry, 1017 says again and even in my fury, I can see that he means it, I can see that he really *is* sorry that he did it, that his horror at it just grows and grows, not only for what he did to Todd but for what it will mean for the future, that his mistake will reach far beyond us here, that it's a mistake he would take back for anything in the world—

I can see all this—

And I don't care—

(THE SKY)

"Show me!" she shouts. "Or I swear to God I'll beat you to death with this thing!"

Viola, the Source says behind her, still holding the Knife in his arms, and I look into his voice—

And the Source's heart is broken—

Broken so much it infects everything, reaching out into the world beyond him—

Because when the Land mourns, we mourn together—

And his grief overwhelms me, becomes my own, becomes the Land's—

And I see the full extent of my mistake—

A mistake that may have ruined the Land, a mistake that may have cost us our peace, a mistake that may destroy the Land after all I have done to save it—

A mistake that the Sky should not have made—

I have killed the Knife—

I have finally killed the Knife—

The thing I have wanted for so long—

And it has gained me nothing—

Only knowledge of the loss I have caused—

I can see it written across the face of the voiceless one—

The voiceless one holding out a weapon she does not know how to use—

And so I open my voice and I show her—

{ V I O L A }

His Noise opens up in front of me and it shows me exactly how to use the weapon, where to place my fingers and how to squeeze it to send out the white flash from the end—

He's showing me how to kill him–

Viola, I hear Ben say again behind me. *Viola, you can't.*

"Why can't I?" I say, not looking back, keeping my eyes firmly on 1017. "He killed Todd."

And if you kill him, Ben says, *where will it stop?*

This *does* make me turn around. "How can you say that?!" I shout. "How can you say that with Todd there in your arms?"

Ben's face is clenched and shuttered, his Noise giving off so much pain I can hardly bear to look at him–

But still he's saying it–

If you kill the Sky, Ben says, *the war will begin again. And we'll all die. And then the Land will be killed in huge numbers from orbit. And then the settlers who come down here will be attacked by the Land that remains. And there will be—*

He can't go on for a second but then he makes himself, makes himself say it in his own voice–

"There will be no end of it, Viola," he says, cradling Todd against his chest.

I look back to 1017, who hasn't moved. "He wants me to do it," I say. "He *wants* me to."

"He wants to not have to live with his mistake," Ben says. "He wants the pain to end. But how much better a Sky will he be knowing what this mistake feels like for the rest of his life?"

"How can you talk like this, Ben?" I say.

Because I hear them, he says with his Noise. *All of them. All the Land, all the **men**, I hear every one of them. And we can't just let them die, Viola. We*

can't. That's the very thing Todd stopped here today.
The very thing—

And then he really can't go on. He holds Todd closer to him. *Oh, my son,* he says. *Oh, my son—*

(THE SKY)

She turns back to me, still pointing the weapon, her hands placed exactly on it now to fire it—

"You took him from me," she says, her spoken words breaking. "We came all this way, *all this way* and we *won*! We *WON* and you *took* him!"

And she cannot say anything more—

I am sorry, I show again—

And it is not just the echo of the Source's grief—

It is my own—

Not just for how I have failed as the Sky, for how I have put the entire Land in danger after saving them from it—

But for the life I have taken—

The *first* life I have taken, ever—

And I remember—

I remember the Knife—

And the knife that gave him his name—

The knife he used to kill the Land at the side of a river, a member of the Land who was merely fishing, who was innocent, but who the Knife saw as an enemy—

Who the Knife killed—

And who the Knife regretted killing every moment since—

Regret painted on him every day in that labor camp,

every day as he dealt with the Land, regret that drove him mad with anger when he broke my arm—

Regret that caused him to save me when the Burden were all killed—

Regret that is now my own to carry with me—

Carry with me forever—

And if that forever is only as long as the next breath—

So be it—

The Land deserves better—

{VIOLA}

1017 is remembering Todd–

I can see it in his Noise, see it as the weapon trembles in my hand–

See Todd stabbing the Spackle with the knife when we came upon it on the side of the river–

When Todd killed the Spackle even when I was screaming for him not to–

And 1017 remembers how Todd *suffered* for it–

Suffering I see 1017 start feeling in himself–

Suffering I remember feeling, too, after I stabbed Aaron through the neck underneath the waterfall–

It's a hell of a thing to kill someone–

Even when you think they deserve it–

And now 1017 knows it as well as Todd and I do–

As Todd did–

My heart is broken, broken in a way that will never be healed, broken in a way that feels like it's going to kill me, too, right here on this stupid, freezing beach–

And I know Ben's right. I know if I kill 1017 then there's no way back. We'll have killed a second Spackle leader, and in their greater numbers they would kill every single one of us they could find. And then when the settlers arrived–

Never-ending war, never-ending death–

And here's my decision again–

My choice to send us deeper into war or keep us out of it–

I chose wrong before–

And is this the price I pay for having chosen wrong?

It's too high–

It's too *high*–

But if I make this personal again–

If I make 1017 pay–

Then the world changes–

The world ends–

And I don't care–

I don't *care*–

Todd–

Oh please, Todd–

And, *Todd*? I think–

And then I realize–

My heart aching–

If I kill 1017–

And war starts again–

And we're all killed–

Who will remember Todd?

Who will remember what he did?

Todd–

Todd–

And my heart breaks even more–

Breaks forever–

And I fall to my knees in the snow and sand–

And I yell out, wordless and empty–

And I drop the weapon.

(THE SKY)

She drops the weapon.

It falls to the sand unfired.

And so I am still the Sky.

I am still the voice of the Land.

"I don't want to see you," she says, not looking up, her voice cracking. "I don't want to see you ever again."

No, I show. *No, I understand–*

Viola? the Source shows–

"I didn't do it," she says to him. "But if I see him again, I don't know if I'll be able to stop myself another time." She looks up beside me, not at me, not able to face me. "Get *out* of here," she says. "Get out of here!"

I look to the Source, but he is not seeing me either–

All his pain and sorrow, all his attention fixed on the body of his son–

"GO!" she shouts—

And I turn away and go to my battlemore and look back once more, the Source still huddled over the Knife, the girl called Viola slowly crawling toward him—

Excluding me, forcing themselves not to see me.

And I understand.

I climb back up on my mount. I will return to the valley, return to the Land.

And we will see what the future of this world holds for all of us. The Land and the Clearing both.

Saved first today by the actions of the Sky.

Saved again by the actions of the Knife.

Saved once more by the actions of the Knife's one in particular.

And now we have done all that, we will have to make it a world worth saving.

Viola? I hear the Source show again—

And I notice a puzzlement growing in his grief—

{VIOLA}

Viola? Ben says again.

I find that I can't stand up and so I have to crawl over to him and Todd, crawl next to Angharrad's legs as she paces in sadness, saying **bᴏy cᴏlt, bᴏy cᴏlt,** over and over again.

I force myself to look at Todd's face, at his still-open eyes.

Viola, Ben says again, looking up at me, his face streaked with tears–

But his eyes are open, wide open–

"What?" I say. "What is it?'

He doesn't answer right away, just puts his face down close to Todd's, peering into it, then looking down to where his own hand rests on all the ice he packed on Todd's chest–

Can you–? Ben says, stopping again, concentration crossing his face.

"Can I what?" I say. "Can I *what*, Ben?"

He looks up at me. *Can you hear that?*

I blink at him, hearing my own breathing, the crash of the waves, Angharrad's cries, Ben's Noise–

"Hear *what*?"

I think–he says, stopping again and listening.

I think I can hear him.

He looks up at me. *Viola*, he says. *I can hear Todd.*

And he's already rising to his feet, Todd in his arms–

"I can hear him!" he's shouting from his mouth, lifting his son into the air. *"I can hear his voice!"*

ARRIVAL

"AND THERE'S A CHILL IN THE AIR, SON," I read, *"and I don't mean just the winter coming. I'm beginning to worry a little about the days ahead."*

I look over at Todd. He still lies there, eyes unblinking, unchanged.

But every now and again, every once in a while, his Noise will open and a memory will surface, a memory of me and him when we first met Hildy, or of him and Ben and Cillian, where Todd is younger than I ever knew him and the three of them are going fishing in the swamp outside of old Prentisstown and Todd's Noise just *glows* with happiness–

And my heart beats a little faster with hope–

But then his Noise fades and he's silent again–

I sigh and lean back on the Spackle-made chair, under cover of a large Spackle-made tent, next to a Spackle-made fire, all of it surrounding a Spackle-made stone tablet where Todd rests and has rested since we got him back from the beach.

A pack of Spackle cure is pasted onto where his chest is scarred and burned–

But healing.

And we wait.

I wait.

Wait to see if he'll come back to us.

Outside the tent, a circle of Spackle surround us without moving, their Noises forming some kind of shield. The Pathways' End, Ben says it's called, says it's where he slept all those months while his bullet wound healed, all those months beyond sight of the living, on the very edge of death, the bullet wound that should have killed him but didn't because of Spackle intervention.

Todd was dead. I was sure of it then, I'm sure of it now.

I watched him die, watched him die in my arms, something that makes me upset even now and so I don't want to talk about that anymore–

But Ben put snow on Todd's chest, cooling him down fast, cooling down the terrible burns that were paralyzing him, cooling down an already cold Todd, an already *exhausted* Todd, who'd been fighting the Mayor, and Ben says Todd's Noise must have stopped because Todd had become used to not broadcasting it, that Todd must not have actually died, more *shut down* from the shock and the cold, and then the further cold of the snow kept him there, kept him just enough there that he wasn't quite dead–

But I know otherwise.

I know he left us, I know he didn't want to, I know he held on as tight as he could, but I know he left us.

I watched him go.

But maybe he didn't go far.

Maybe I held him there, maybe me and Ben did, just close enough that maybe he didn't go too far.

Maybe not so far that he couldn't come back.

Tired? Ben says, entering the tent.

"I'm okay," I say, setting down Todd's mother's journal, which I've read to him every day these past few weeks, hoping he'll hear me.

Every day hoping he'll come back from wherever he's gone.

How's he doing? Ben asks, walking over to Todd, putting a hand on his arm.

"The same," I say.

Ben turns back to me. *He'll come back, Viola. He will.*

"We hope."

I came back. And I didn't have you to call for me.

I look away from him. "You came back changed."

It was 1017 who suggested the Pathways' End and Ben agreed with him and since New Prentisstown was nothing but a new lake at the bottom of a new falls and since the alternative was locking Todd in a bed in the scout ship until the new convoy arrived—a method favored quite strongly by Mistress Lawson, who's now head of pretty much everything she doesn't let Wilf or Lee run—I reluctantly agreed with Ben.

Who nods at what I said, looking back down at Todd. *I expect he'll be changed, too.* He smiles back at me. *But I seem to be doing okay.*

I watch Ben these days and I wonder if I'm watching the

future of New World, if every man will eventually give himself over so totally to the voice of the planet, keeping his individuality but allowing in all the individualities of everyone else at the same time and willingly joining the Spackle, joining the rest of the world.

Not all men will, I know that, not with how much they valued the cure.

And what about the women?

Ben is certain women *do* have Noise and that if men can silence theirs, why shouldn't women be able to *un*-silence *theirs*?

He wonders if I might be willing to give it a try.

I don't know.

Why can't we learn to live with how we are? And whatever anybody chooses is okay by the rest of us?

Either way, we're about to have five thousand opportunities to find out.

The convoy just confirmed, Ben says. *The ships entered orbit an hour ago. The landing ceremony will go ahead this afternoon as planned.* He arches an eyebrow at me. *You coming?*

I smile. "Bradley can represent me just fine. Are *you* going?"

He looks back at Todd. *I have to,* he says. *I have to introduce them to the Sky. I'm the conduit between the settlers and the Land, whether I like it or not.* He brushes Todd's hair away from his forehead. *But I'll come back here straight after.*

I haven't left Todd's side since we brought him here and won't until he wakes, not even for new settlers. I even made

Mistress Lawson come to me to confirm what the Mayor said about the cure. She tested it inside and out, and he was telling the truth. Every woman is healthy now.

1017 isn't yet, though.

The infection seems to spread more slowly through him, and he's declining to take the cure, saying he'll suffer the pain of the band until Todd wakes up, as a reminder of all that was, of all that *almost* was, and of what we should all never return to.

I can't help it. I'm a little glad that it still hurts him.

The Sky would like to visit, Ben says lightly, as if he could already read the Noise I don't have.

"No."

He's arranged all this, Viola. If we get Todd back—

"If," I say. "That's the key word, isn't it?"

It'll work, he says. *It **will**.*

"Fine," I say. "When it does, then we can ask Todd if he wants to see the Spackle who put him here in the first place."

Viola—

I smile to stop him from the argument we've already had two dozen times already. An argument about how I can't quite forgive 1017 yet.

And maybe never.

I know he often waits outside the Pathways' End, asking Ben how Todd is. I can hear him sometimes. Right now, though, all I hear is Angharrad, munching on grass, patiently waiting with us for her boy colt.

The Sky will be a better leader for all this, Ben says. *We might actually be able to live with them in peace. Maybe even in the paradise we always wanted.*

"*If* Mistress Lawson and the convoy rework the cure for the Noise," I say. "*If* the men and women who land don't feel threatened by being so outnumbered by the native species. *If* there's always enough food to go around–"

Try to have some hope, Viola, he says.

And there's that word again.

"I do," I say. "But I'm giving it all to Todd right now."

Ben looks back down at his son. *He'll come back to us.*

I nod to agree, but we don't know that he will, not for sure.

But we hope.

And that hope is so delicate, I'm scared to death of letting it out.

So I keep quiet.

And I wait.

And I hope.

What part have you reached? Ben asks, nodding at the journal.

"I'm near the end again," I say.

He comes away from Todd and sits down in the other Spackle-made chair next to me. *Read it through,* he says. *And then we can start all over where his ma was full of optimism.*

There's a smile on his face and so much tender hope in his Noise that I can't help but smile back.

He'll hear you, Viola. He'll hear you and he'll come back to us.

And we look at Todd again, laid out on the stone tablet, warmed by the fire, Spackle healing pastes on the wound in his chest, his Noise ticking in and out of hearing like a barely remembered dream.

"Todd," I whisper. "Todd?"

And then I pick up the journal again.

And I continue reading.

Is this right?

I blink and I'm in one memory, like this one here, back in a classroom in old Prentisstown before Mayor Prentiss closed down the school and we're learning about why the settlers came here in the first place—

And then here I am again, in this one, where she and I are sleeping in an abandoned windmill just after leaving Farbranch and the stars are coming out and she asks me to sleep outside because my Noise is keeping her awake—

Or now here, with Manchee, with my brilliant, brilliant dog, when he takes the burning ember into his mouth and sets off to start a fire, the fire that will let me save—

Let me save—

Are you there?

Are you *there?*

(*Viola?*)

And then sometimes there are memories of things I never saw—

Spackle families in huts in a vast desert I didn't even know existed but that now, right here, as I stand in it, I know it's on the other side of New World, as far away as you can get but I'm inside the Spackle voices and I'm hearing what they say, *seeing* it, *understanding* it even tho the language ain't mine and I can see that they know about the men on the other side of the planet, that they know everything about us that the Spackle near us do, that the voice of this world circles it, reaches into every corner and if we could just—

Or here, here I am on a hilltop next to someone

whose face I just about reckernize (Luke? Les? Lars? His name is there, just there, just outta reach–) but I reckernize the blindness in his eyes and I reckernize the face of the man next to him who I know is *seeing* for him somehow and they're taking the weapons away from an army and they're sealing 'em in a mine and they'd rather just destroy the whole lot of 'em but the voices around 'em all want the weapons there, just in case, just in case things go wrong, but the seeing man is telling the blind man that maybe there's hope anyway–

Or here, too, here I am, looking down from a hilltop as a huge ship, bigger than a whole town, flies overhead and comes in for a landing––

And at the same time I'm having a memory of being next to a creek bed and there's a baby Spackle playing and there are men coming outta the woods and they're dragging the mother off and the baby is crying and the men come back and pick him up and load him on a cart with other babies and I know this is a memory that ain't mine and that the baby is, the baby Spackle is–

And sometimes it's just dark–

–sometimes there's nothing but voices I can't quite hear, voices just beyond reach and I'm alone in the darkness and it feels like I've been here for a long, long time and I–

I can't remember my name sometimes–

Are you there?

Viola?

And I don't remember who Viola is–

Only that I need to find her–

That she's the only one who'll save me–

She's the only one who *can*–

Viola?

Viola?

"*. . . my son, my beautiful son . . .*"

And there!

Like that!

Sometimes there it is in the middle of the darkness, in the middle of the memories, in the middle of wherever I am, doing whatever I'm doing, sometimes even in the middle of the million voices that create the ground I walk on–

Sometimes I hear–

". . . I wish yer pa were here to see you, Todd . . ."

Todd–

Todd–

That's me–

(I think–)

(Yes–)

And that voice, that voice saying those words–

". . . say 'ain't' all you like, Todd, I promise not to correct you . . ."

Is that Viola's voice?

Is it?

(Is it you?)

Because I'm hearing it more often lately, more often as the days pass, as I'm flying thru these memories and spaces and darknesses–

I'm hearing it more often among all the other millions–

". . . Yer calling for me, and I will answer . . ."

I will answer–

                    Todd will answer–

Viola?

          Are you calling for me?

               Keep calling for me–

                    Keep doing it, keep coming to save me–

          Cuz every day yer closer–

I can almost hear you–

I can almost–

Is that you?

Is that *us*?

Is that what we did?

Viola?

Keep calling for me–

And I'll keep searching for you–

And I'll find you–

You bet yer life on it–

I'll find you–

Keep calling for me, Viola–

Cuz here I come.

TODD AND VIOLA'S JOURNEYS BEGIN

CHAOS WALKING

BOOK ONE

★ "A penetrating look at the ways in which we reveal ourselves to one another, and what it takes to be a man in a society gone horribly wrong. . . . As effective as a shot to the gut."
—*Booklist* (starred review)

BOOK TWO

"A stunningly clear depiction of the moral wreckage of civil war: power-lust, shifting loyalties, betrayals, and seductive competing justifications for violence."
—*The Wall Street Journal*

Available in hardcover, paperback, and audio and as e-books

www.candlewick.com

The LOVES of
CHARLES II

ALSO BY JEAN PLAIDY

From Three Rivers Press

THE WIVES OF HENRY VIII
The Rose Without a Thorn • *The Lady in the Tower*
Katharine of Aragon • *The Sixth Wife*

THE TUDOR PRINCESSES
Mary, Queen of France • *The Thistle and the Rose*

THE TUDOR QUEENS
In the Shadow of the Crown • *Queen of This Realm*
The Royal Road to Fotheringhay • *Victoria Victorious*

THE NORMAN TRILOGY
The Bastard King • *The Lion of Justice*
The Passionate Enemies

THE PLANTAGENET SAGA
Plantagenet Prelude • *The Revolt of the Eaglets*
The Heart of the Lion • *The Prince of Darkness*
The Battle of the Queens • *The Queen from Provence*
Edward Longshanks • *The Follies of the King*
The Vow on the Heron • *Passage to Pontefract*
The Star of Lancaster • *Epitaph for Three Women*
Red Rose of Anjou • *The Sun in Splendor*

THE TUDOR NOVELS
Uneasy Lies the Head • *Katharine, the Virgin Widow*
The Shadow of the Pomegranate • *The King's Secret Matter*
Murder Most Royal • *St. Thomas' Eve*
The Sixth Wife • *The Spanish Bridegroom*
Gay Lord Robert

THE STUART SAGA

The Captive Queen of Scots • *The Murder in the Tower*
The Wandering Prince • *The Three Crowns*
The Haunted Sisters • *The Queen's Favorites*

THE GEORGIAN SAGA

The Princess of Celle • *Queen in Waiting*
Caroline the Queen • *The Prince and the Quakeress*
The Third George • *Perdita's Prince*
Sweet Lass of Richmond Hill • *Indiscretions of the Queen*
The Regent's Daughter • *Goddess of the Green Room*
Victoria in the Wings

THE QUEEN VICTORIA SERIES

The Captive of Kensington Palace • *The Queen and Lord M*
The Queen's Husband • *The Widow of Windsor*

THE FERDINAND AND ISABELLA TRILOGY

Castile for Isabella • *Spain for the Sovereigns*
Daughter of Spain

THE LUCREZIA BORGIA SERIES

Madonna of the Seven Hills • *Light on Lucrezia*

THE MEDICI TRILOGY

Madame Serpent • *The Italian Woman*
Queen Jezebel

THE FRENCH REVOLUTION SERIES

Louis the Well-Beloved • *The Road to Compiege*
Flaunting, Extravagant Queen

Evergreen Gallant
Myself, My Enemy • *Beyond the Blue Mountains*
The Goldsmith's Wife • *The Scarlet Cloak*
Defenders of the Faith • *Daughter of Satan*